FOREVER DOESN'T ALWAYS LAST

A COUPLE OF FOREVERS 2

ASHLEY CHANNAE

To my friends, for being constant inspirations for my writing. Y'all bring life to every one of the characters in this story. Thank you for always being an ear when I needed one, a shoulder to cry on, and comedians when I needed a good laugh.

PROLOGUE

With bloodstained hands, Jaz sat shaking as she stared down the long hallway. Luminescent lights flickered above her head while people eyed her skeptically. Tears stained her face, blood covered her clothing, and her unborn daughter was doing backflips in her stomach. Her disheveled appearance caused parents to hold their children closer. Jaz couldn't care any less. The kind of pain she felt at that moment was far beyond the disgruntled looks she received from common strangers. No one knew the kind of hurt she was going through. Just minutes before she was holding the love of her life's hand as he slipped into unconsciousness from a gunshot wound to the chest.

Now Jaz waited impatiently to hear back from the doctors. The nurses told her repeatedly that he was in surgery, and the doctors would let her know a status once they were done. But Jaz was consistent with asking them at least every ten minutes. Her unborn daughter could feel her uneasiness as she fidgeted in her stomach. Jaz pressed down on her stomach to calm her, but baby

Kylee wasn't having it. She did everything to let Jaz know that she, too, wanted answers. She kicked, tossed, turned, and fought back when Jaz tried to settle her. There was no doubt in Jaz's mind that her daughter was going to be a hothead just like her mother. *Kylee, please calm down. Mommy can't take it right now,* she silently begged her. Jaz adjusted herself in her seat, and Kylee finally calmed down just as a doctor approached.

Jaz looked on as a medium-built white man approached the nurse's station. Several times in the past hour, Jaz thought every doctor was the one she wanted to see, but none of them were Kyree's doctor. So this time she waited impatiently for the nurse to point the doctor in her direction. When she did, Jaz immediately rose to her feet.

"Ms. Elliott?" the doctor asked.

Jaz nodded and pursed her shaking lips.

The doctor took a huge sigh, and it was just like all of the movies Jaz had seen. He slowly removed his surgical hat, held it close to his chest, lowered his head, and said, "I'm sorry…"

Jaz didn't wait for him to finish before her eyes rolled into the back of her head and she collapsed, just in time for the doctor to catch her. This was not how things were supposed to go. She and Kyree made a promise to spend forever together. They had a child, they were going to get married, and nothing could keep them apart.

"NOOOOOOO!" Jaz screamed at the top of her lungs. "I love you, Kyree! Why, God? Ahhhhhhh!"

"Ms. Elliott?" the doctor called out to her. "Ms. Elliott? Jazmine?" He held her in his arms and tried to calm her down. "Jazmine, can you hear me?"

Jaz continued to cry uncontrollably. She heard someone calling her name, but it was off in the distance and she couldn't put together her own reality.

The doctor continued to call out to her. "Jazmine...Jaz...Jaz...wake up..."

Jaz popped her head up. She was confused. She wasn't in the hospital lobby where she last remembered. She was in a room now. She looked around and noticed Monica calling her name and staring at her worriedly.

"You were having a dream," Monica assured her, one hand on her shoulder.

Jaz tried to steady her breathing. She wasn't sure which part was a dream and which part was real. She was sure Kyree had indeed been shot, because she was still in the hospital. But what the doctor had said...she needed to know for certain. Jaz looked up at Monica and slowly asked, "Is Kyree...is he...is he dead?"

Monica slowly shook her head no. Jaz took a huge sigh of relief, but the look on Monica's face said that there was more she needed to know.

"He's not dead, Jaz. But he is in a coma."

Jaz dropped her head and cried somberly, and Monica brought her in close to her chest and cried with her. Monica didn't know the whole story because soon after Jaz called her hysterically crying, she rushed over to the hospital expecting answers, but Jaz had passed out and was now a patient herself. Monica felt horrible. Not only was her best friend's fiancé fighting for his life, but that was also her brother. She was almost certain that whatever illegalities her brother was involved in were the cause of all of this. The only person with any answers was Jaz. Just as she was finally starting to calm down, Monica was going to ask her, but in walked Monica and Kyree's mother, Jackie.

She immediately ran to embrace Jaz now that she was awake. Jaz cried on her shoulder as she rocked her back and forth. "I know, baby. It's going to be alright," she assured her. Nothing but muffled cries were heard throughout the room for a while.

But their family time was interrupted by a knock at the door. No one had enough time to invite the visitor in before the door was opened.

In walked two of Virginia's finest. Two white detectives dressed in white shirts with black ties and slacks, with pens and pads in hand. They were ready for questions, and answers as well.

"Hello, Ms. Elliott. I'm Detective Sherman, and this is my partner, Detective Lance. We were wondering if you could answer a few questions for us."

Jackie looked at Jaz and asked, "Are you up to answering questions right now, baby?" Jaz shook her head no, and Jackie threw her hand up. "Say no more." She got up from the bed and walked over to the two men. "Now, I understand y'all want answers, and you'll get them -WHEN she's feeling up to it. And like I told you earlier, NOW is not the time." Jackie had already lit into the detectives about an hour ago.

"But, ma'am, we're just trying to find out who shot your son. Don't you want to know that?" Detective Lance asked.

"And as soon as she's up to telling you something, she will. But right now, she's traumatized. Now I suggest you two leave before I call your supervisor about you harassing my family during our time of grief," Jackie firmly stated.

The detectives wanted to protest. But there were rules to follow, and they knew they weren't following them correctly. "We received enough information from the other gentleman involved, so we'll take that back to the station. But we'll be back tomorrow, Ms. Elliott," Detective Sherman announced before shutting the door behind him.

"What other gentleman involved?" Monica wanted to know.

"Michael," Jaz solemnly spoke.

"Michael?" Monica turned up her lip. "What the fuck was he doing there?"

"Monica, don't get slapped," Jackie warned.

"But, Ma, why was he there?" Monica fumed.

Jaz took a huge sigh. She knew it was either now or never. She propped herself up in the bed and told them everything, as the scene played like a movie in her head. She told them how her ex-fiancé Michael had come over to her house with a gun on some lunatic type shit. But she calmed him down, only for him to confess that he was in cahoots with her enemy, Asia. When Asia stormed in her house trying to kill her, Michael mentioned how unstable she was. Asia eventually knocked him out with the gun and aimed it at Jaz. With nothing left to do, Jaz tried to reason with Asia as she toyed with the voices in her head. Once Jaz had her stable, Kyree walked in. "She shot him!" Jaz cried out.

Monica immediately felt like shit for getting defensive with Jaz. She knew she'd never do anything to intentionally harm her brother, but her anger got the best of her. She held her friend until the doctor walked in, and everyone sat up at attention.

"Doctor, how is he?" Jackie asked.

"Well, after six hours of surgery, we were able to remove the bullet from his chest. Lucky for us, the bullet was a half a centimeter from his heart and didn't touch any vital organs. But there was a lot of internal bleeding, which could cause major problems, and right now that's our biggest concern. During surgery, he did fall into unconsciousness, and he has yet to come to. But we are hopeful that he will regain consciousness."

"When?" Monica wanted to know.

The doctor rubbed his chin. "I can't really say for sure. Could be in an hour, could be next week, or even next month. It's hard to say for sure."

"But he will wake up, right?" Jaz asked.

"We are extremely hopeful, yes. But, like I said, we can't really say for sure. It's truly up to Mr. Wright. The best thing you can do now is just pray."

"Can we see him?" Monica asked.

The doctor looked hesitant at first, but the looks on their solemn faces forced him to give in. "Alright. But only two at a time." Talking to the family was always the hardest part of Dr. Arnold's job, so delivering good news was always a comforting feeling for him.

They all followed the doctor toward Kyree's room, where they saw Fat Boy coming back from the coffee run they'd sent him on. When Fat Boy heard about his best friend being shot, he had rushed right over to the hospital and had been there ever since. They decided that Jaz and Jackie should go first, but upon stepping her foot across the doorway, Jackie couldn't take it. She nearly passed out, but Fat Boy was there to catch her.

"I got her. Go in there with Jaz," Fat Boy instructed Monica.

She nodded her head and walked in. Jaz thought she'd also pass out from the sight before her. Seeing Kyree lying there with all of the needles in his arms, tubes in his mouth, and a beeping machine that monitored his every breath was the worst thing she could ever possibly imagine. She approached his bedside, then tried to turn around and head toward the door. But Monica stopped her. The look Monica gave her said it all, and Jaz knew it. She had to see Kyree and let him know that he was loved and needed to pull through this - not just for her, but for their child.

Jaz lifted his hand while hers shook in fear. "Baby, it's me, Jazzy," she whimpered. She felt her stomach kick. "Oh, and Kylee's here too." She slightly laughed. "We need you to pull through this and come home to us." She looked at him. He was still and unresponsive. With her lips pursed, her mouth began to tremble. She kissed him on the forehead as a small tear fell from her eye and landed on his face. For a second she thought she saw him open his eyes, but he hadn't. She wished that her tear could have woken him up, and that he'd hold her until all of her hurt was nonexistent, but she knew that only happened in movies. She wiped her tear from his face as Kylee began to move.

Monica noticed her uncomfortably rubbing her stomach and placed her hand on her shoulder. "Jaz, are you okay?"

"Yeah," Jaz hissed. "Ow, wait...no." She quickly changed her mind as the kicking turned into a jolting pain.

Beep...Beep
Beeeeeeeeeeeeeeeeeeeeeeeeeeeeeeeeeeeeeeeeeeeeeeeeeeeeeeeeeeeeeeep.

"What's going on?" Jaz looked at the machine that now showed a straight line going across. She didn't even have time to react before nurses and doctors were running inside the room, rushing to Kyree's aide.

"Ma'am, we're going to have to ask you all to leave," one of the nurses said.

"But wait...owwwwwwwwwwww!" Jaz couldn't even finish her sentence before she had doubled over in pain.

Amidst all of the commotion, Monica yelled, "Somebody help her!"

CHAPTER ONE

Beep...Beep...Beep...Beep...

J az awoke ten hours later to more deafening sounds from the EKG - only this time, the machine was hooked up to her. She looked around the room but saw no one in sight. She figured she must have passed out again. The last thing she remembered was being carted off to a room for the excruciating stomach pains she was experiencing. She didn't even know if Kyree was okay. She placed one hand up to her face while the other rested on her stomach, and she cried.

"Kyree, I just need you to be okay for Kylee and me. Please, baby!" she cried aloud. She rubbed her stomach, only to realize that it was a little flatter than usual. She quickly began to panic as she removed the covers from over her stomach.

"No...no...no!" she cried out as she frantically lifted the hospital gown. "Ahhhhhhh!" Jaz screamed at the huge bandage that covered her once eight-month pregnant belly.

Monica rushed in the room upon hearing her. "Jaz, calm down. Please," Monica pleaded with her as she noticed her heart monitor going up.

"Where's my baby, Mo? What happened? Where's Kylee? Where is she?" Jaz yelled.

"Jaz, please calm down." Monica held her hands trying to get Jaz to settle down. Once Jaz had started to compose herself, she looked to Monica for answers. "Listen, you went into early labor after Kyree flat-lined," Monica said.

"After he flat-lined?" Jaz repeated in disbelief. "Oh my God!" Jaz cried out.

Monica embraced Jaz and rubbed her back. "It's going to be okay, Jaz." She rocked her back and forth.

"But I need him, Mo. I love him!" she cried.

"And I love you too," a deep voice said.

Jaz thought she was going crazy. There was no way she heard the voice that she thought she heard. She frantically turned around to see the curtain drawn back on the bed beside hers. And there he was.

She gasped as she saw him. It all felt too real. She just hoped it wasn't a dream this time. "Ky...Kyree? Is it really you?"

"In the flesh, Jazzy." He attempted a smile. Jaz frantically tried to get up from the bed, but she was still in pain. "Don't get up, baby." Kyree stopped her as he pushed the button to raise his bed. He reached across to hold her hand while she just looked at him.

Jaz waited for the part where she'd wake up, but it didn't happen. She let out an exasperated breath as she felt Kyree's strong embrace squeeze her hand. It was real. She squeezed his hand back and cried.

"Don't cry, baby."

"I can't help it. I thought you were gone."

"Didn't I tell you I'd never leave you? Didn't I?" Kyree said sternly.

Jaz simply nodded her head. Kyree never lied to her. He promised to always come back to her, and he always did. "But what happened? I thought you flat-lined."

"I did. But that jolt from when they revived me with the defibrillator helped wake me up."

"But, our baby. She's...she's...gone." Jaz dropped her head and cried.

Having been there through the whole ordeal, Monica decided to speak up and put Jaz's mind at ease. "Jaz, they had to do an emergency C-section. And - "

Before she could finish talking, Jackie was walking in with a nurse, who pushed in an incubator cart with a tiny baby inside.

"Is that - " Jaz began.

"Yeah, that's our Kylee, baby," Kyree chuckled.

Jaz, noticing the tubes in her nose, had to ask, "Is she okay?"

The doctor walked in just in time to answer her question. "Yes, she's perfectly fine. The tubes are just a precaution. She did arrive two months ahead of schedule, so this is pretty much standard procedure. Her birth weight is low, and she will have to stay in the hospital until her weight increases and we see improvement in her eating without a tube, but other than that, she's perfectly fine." The doctor gave Jaz a reassuring smile, and Jaz returned the gesture.

"Can I hold her?" Jaz eagerly asked.

"Sure you can, but not out here in the open. She's still very susceptible to infection in this room. I'll have a nurse come get you in an hour to take you to the nursery. She's not even really supposed to be in here now, but I thought you could use some cheering up after the day you've had."

The doctor wheeled baby Kylee closer to Jaz so that she could say goodbye before he carted her back to the nursery.

"Bye, pretty girl. Mommy is going to give you a thousand hugs and kisses when I get back there." Jaz smiled as she placed her hand against the Plexiglas window separating her from her beautiful daughter. She couldn't stop staring at her. Her face was something she wanted to take in and remember for every second she wasn't around. Jaz couldn't wait to hold her, but knew that she had to get back to the nursery, so she nodded to the doctor to let him know it was okay.

"Baby girl, we're going to let you get some rest, but I'll be right outside the door if you need me for any reason," Calvin assured her, and then gently kissed her on the forehead.

"The whole family is in the hospital. Y'all better stop scaring my mama like this. Y'all know she has high blood pressure," Monica joked, and they all let out an overdue laugh. "But I'll be outside too." Monica bent down to hug Jaz and whispered in her ear, "I'm going to see my niece so I can tell her how fucked up this family is."

Jaz laughed at her foolishness as the rest of the family, too, decided to hug Jaz and Kyree before departing after such an exhausting past two days. Once everyone was gone, Jaz just gazed at Kyree. She was afraid to even blink for fear that he'd be gone in the nanosecond it took to open her eyes again. She couldn't imagine her life without him in it. He was her everything.

"What you staring at?" Kyree smirked.

"You." She smiled. "Everything happened so fast, baby. I'm just so happy to see you." A small tear fell down her cheek. Kyree smiled as well, a slight grimace in his face. Noticing his pain and uncomfortableness, Jaz asked, "Are you okay? Did they give you anything for the pain?"

Kyree nodded. The pain was excruciating, but he didn't want

to press the morphine button because he knew that it would make him tired. He didn't want to go to sleep because he wanted to be wide awake for Jaz. The whole time he was unconscious, her face kept him fighting. No one could keep him away from her.

"Kyree, that medicine is supposed to help you. Press the button."

Kyree chuckled at her forwardness. He pressed the morphine drip, and let out a breath of relief as the drug made its way through his system, numbing any of the pain he felt. Licking his lips, he stared at her with admiration. "You did it, Jazzy. We're parents now."

"I know. It's crazy. I wish I could have been awake to see it all."

"My mama recorded the whole thing, don't worry. I already watched it. Mo's ass passed out too. Shit is hilarious." They both laughed.

"But, baby, I feel like I should explain everything that happened."

Kyree put his hand up to stop her. Monica had already told him everything, and he knew and trusted Jaz enough to know the truth. He was already plotting to dead both Michael and Asia when he found them. But for right now, he didn't want to worry Jaz with that. She didn't need to know that. "I hear we're getting married." He changed the subject as his eyes began to get heavy.

Jaz bit her lip and shook her head. She could still remember saying yes to a marriage proposal as Kyree stood on his knees, bleeding profusely. "What'd you expect me to say? You were dying," she joked.

"Ha ha, real funny."

"But no, in all seriousness..." Jaz reached for his hand again. "I want to spend the rest the rest of my life being with you, and only you. I don't want to lose you. I can't wait to be Mrs. Wright," she smiled. "I love you, Ky."

When he didn't respond, Jaz sat up in the bed, only to realize he'd fallen asleep. She smiled, and pushed the button for the nurse to come into their room. The nurse was there in seconds. She helped Jaz to a wheelchair, and then wheeled her into the nursery. Jaz was instructed to scrub her hands and then sit down as the nurse gave her a crash course in holding the baby. She didn't need the instructions, but she pretended to listen anyway, eager for her to leave her alone and give them some privacy. The nurse finally placed Kylee in Jaz's arms and there was nothing in the world that could break her happiness at that moment.

The nurse was speaking, and Jaz nodded her head. But she couldn't hear a word she, or anyone else around her, said. The nurse could see that the mother and daughter needed some time alone to get acquainted, so she gave Jaz a bottle for feeding and gave them some space.

Jaz smiled from ear to ear as she looked down at Kylee's beautiful sleeping face. It was almost like a piece of her that she never knew was missing was placed right where it needed to be. Jaz placed the bottle up to Kylee's mouth, but she wouldn't take it.

"Open your mouth, mama," Jaz softly spoke. Kylee continued to squirm. She wasn't having it. Jaz laughed at her stubbornness. "Just like your mommy, huh? We're gonna give Daddy hell." Jaz put the bottle down for now. The nurse had already explained to her that it was going to take a while for Kylee to warm up to the bottle. She spent the rest of the time getting to know every inch of her. She counted all of her fingers and toes, noticed a spot directly behind her right ear that she was sure would become a birthmark, changed her diaper, and then sat back down while she rocked back and forth in the rocking chair.

With Kylee's hand grasping Jaz's finger, Jaz looked down at her and vowed that no one was ever going to hurt her again. Asia had not only endangered Jaz's and Kyree's lives, but she'd also put

Kylee in danger as well. Jaz didn't know where Asia was but for Asia's sake, she'd better not find her. Kylee strengthened her grip on Jaz's finger. Even she could sense how serious her mother was. Jaz softly kissed Kylee's forehead. No one was going to break up Jaz's family again. Not if they valued their lives.

CHAPTER TWO

6 WEEKS LATER

With Kyree being in the hospital for two weeks and Kylee there for four weeks, Jaz was relieved to have her whole family home. She was tired of spending every waking minute at the hospital. She never left either one of their sides. She'd just had her six week checkup the day before, and the doctor informed her that her blood pressure was still extremely high. He knew the stress she'd been under lately, and he suggested she needed something to get her mind off of things. So Kyree decided to throw a fight party at their house with a couple of close friends. Jaz wasn't really feeling it, but Kyree wouldn't take no for an answer. He called up his mother to watch the baby, bought a bunch of food and drinks, and all of their friends were down and ready to have some fun.

Jaz had no idea how this was supposed to make her feel better. She'd spent all day cleaning the house she'd been neglecting because of her new mommy duties, Kyree forgot to buy ice so she was now going to buy some, and she missed Kylee and it hadn't even been two hours. Kyree was trying his best to help, but Jaz had to have everything her way. She hadn't even finished getting dressed yet. Everything was a mess.

As she pulled up to her house with the ice, she tried calling Kyree to come help her bring it up the stairs. He didn't answer, but she figured he probably had a lot going on. The parking lot of her complex was already filled with the cars of all of their friends. She did her best to grab all four bags of ice at once. She was not one for making two trips.

Jaz could hear the music and comradery before she even made it all the way up the stairs. When she opened the door, there were at least ten people in the house. She didn't see Kyree, but Fat Boy walked over and greeted her by taking all the bags from her hands.

"Hey, Slim." She hugged him and called him by the name she'd called him since they were kids.

"Hey, Jazzy Jeff." He hugged her back. "Why you didn't call me? I would've helped you with this shit."

"'Cause you know Jaz. Ms. Do Everything Herself," her close friend, Ms. Ray, interjected. She shook her head as he wrapped his arms around her for a hug. "Hey, boo. We miss you at the shop."

"I miss y'all too," she admitted. "I'll be back next week though."

"Please hurry back, girl. Mo charge too damn much." Her homegirl, Jeneisha, laughed. Jaz laughed as she embraced her for a hug.

"I heard that shit," Monica let them all know.

"Oops," Jeneisha laughed.

"Heeeyyyyy, mama!" Her other friend Ahnesty approached her - drink in hand, as always. "You don't even look like you had a baby. All that weight went straight to ya ass, girl." Ahnesty tapped her butt, and Jaz laughed.

"You're crazy as hell. I can't wit'chu. And what the hell is that in your cup?" Jaz looked at the purple concoction in her Styrofoam cup.

"Girl, I don't know. Ya crazy baby daddy and Fat Boy's big ass tried to say I couldn't hang, so I told them to pour up or shut up. And girllllll, this shit is skrong...with a K." They all laughed. Ahnesty could hang with the best on any day.

"I know it's strong if yo' ass can't hang," Monica laughed.

"Ay, Ahnesty," Stacy, Ahnesty's ex-fiancée, called out to her from the spades table. Ahnesty turned in his direction. "Get me a Heineken. I can't get up. I'm too busy whoopin' ass. Bam!" he yelled as he slapped a card on the table. "Give me my books!" he boasted as he dapped up his partner, Toni.

Ahnesty shook her head as the other women laughed. They knew how much she hated when he showed up to social events. She rolled her eyes and ignored him like she always did.

"Mo, let's go beat these niggas' asses like we do every year." Ahnesty took a quick swig from her drink, shook off the chills it gave her, and then headed to the spades table with Mo right behind her.

Jaz made her way to her room. She didn't really want to be around anyone until she'd changed from the sweats she had on while making her runs. On her way down the hallway, she bumped into Kyree. "Hey," she solemnly said.

"Hey? That's how you greet yo' man?" Kyree looked at her like she was crazy. They embraced and she kissed him softly on the lips. "You okay?" he asked, noticing her distance.

"Yeah, I'm fine," she said as she proceeded to her room.

Kyree looked up at the ceiling. He knew what that meant. He knew Jaz too well to know that she wasn't fine. He just had to figure out why. He walked in behind her and locked the door.

"So what's up?" Kyree asked as he watched her rummage through her closet for something to wear.

"Nothing, Kyree. I'm just tired."

"This party is supposed to help you relieve stress. I did this for you."

Jaz tossed a pair of jeans and a denim shirt on the bed. "I know, baby. I just don't feel like being bothered tonight."

Since having the baby, Jaz had been so consumed with taking care of everyone else that she rarely took care of herself. Even right now, her hair was in a bun. She still looked cute, but she'd been rocking the same hairstyle for six weeks. Jaz was a stylist and she usually switched up her hairstyle at least three times a week. When Kyree heard that she needed a stress reliever, he thought a kick-back was the perfect idea. But now, he was strongly questioning his plan.

"Come here." He grabbed her on her way to the bathroom.

"What, Kyree? I have to finish getting dressed," she pouted.

"Hey, I did this for you. If my Jazzy's not happy, all these niggas can go. I'll tell 'em like ol' Marty Mar: get tuh steppin'!"

Jaz laughed and began to lighten up a bit. "Don't worry about all of that. It's fine. I think I just need a drink. I haven't had one in damn near ten months."

"Nah, I know what you need." He gave her a devious grin.

"Boy, stop," she grinned, waving him off. She went to her dresser and began to put on her earrings in the mirror. Kyree approached her from behind and wrapped one arm around her waist.

"You had your six week checkup the other day, right?" He kissed her neck.

"Yeah, but we're not doing that while we have a house full of guests just a few feet away. There will be plenty of time for that later. Now, stop playing, Kyree." She moved her neck, trying to dodge his advances.

"Jaz," he stated seriously as he pressed her ass against his crotch. "Does it feel like I'm playing to you?"

Jaz could feel the growth in his pants, and her eyes lit up as he began to kiss the spot behind her neck. "Ky, please stop. Our friends are right outside that door," she said as she bit her bottom lip.

"What, you scared?" He looked at her through the mirror and she returned his gaze. Kyree knew how to get her attention.

Jaz was never one to back down from a challenge. With one arm still wrapped around her waist, he placed his free hand down her pants. Kyree could feel through her underwear that she was ready. They hadn't had sex in almost two months, so they were both well overdue.

Kyree slid down her sweatpants, turned her around, and placed her on top of the dresser. He bent down to his knees and began to suck on the lips of her pussy. He teased her walls with the tip of his tongue and then dipped it right it the middle, working at a feverish pace.

"Oh, my..." Jaz thought she was going to lose consciousness. She grabbed ahold of the dresser to keep her balance.

Knock...Knock! Jaz's eyes lit up as someone knocked on her bedroom door. "Jaz, open the door. I have to pee, and someone is in your hall bathroom!" Ahnesty yelled over the music. *Knock... Knock!* "Girl, come on! I think that purple shit broke my bladder." Ahnesty squirmed on the other side of the door.

Jaz tried to purse her lips to keep herself from screaming out, but Kyree was still going steady and she was on the verge of her first orgasm in weeks. "Ahhh...shit..." she moaned. She grabbed the dresser and ended up knocking over a few perfume bottles.

Ahnesty pressed her ear to the other side of the door. "Aw, hell naw! Y'all nasty," she said, just above a whisper. She didn't want to let the other party guests in on their business as well, so she walked away.

Kyree looked up at her and grinned. She hit the top of his head. She was so embarrassed. He dropped his pants and she reached down to touch it. She grasped his penis in her hands and slowly licked her lips. He smirked as she released it, and he slowly placed himself inside of her. The warmness was so inviting that Kyree and Jaz both just sat still for a moment. From the outside of the door, they could hear Future & Drake's "Life is Good" playing in the background.

With himself still inside, he carried her over to the bed and worked her nice and slow. His chest was slightly bothering him from the gunshot wound, but he'd worry about that later. Right now felt too good to stop. He worked himself around, hitting all of her sweet spots. Jaz's eyes rolled around her head as she clawed at his back. Kyree and Jaz both found a way to move at a decent rhythm to the rap music playing in the background.

"Shit!" He bit his lip.

Jaz contracted her walls around his penis and Kyree couldn't control it anymore. Jaz came immediately after, but Kyree held on for a few seconds before releasing a month's worth of pent up frustration and stress. He kissed her neck as she lay limp. He smiled at her. There was nothing he wanted more than to lay in that bed with her, but they did have a house full of guests. He smiled at how peaceful she looked. He used up what energy he had left to take a quick shower. Once he was dressed, he woke a sleeping Jaz.

"You gotta get up, bae."

"I'll be out in twenty minutes," she assured him, her eyes still closed.

"Alright. If you're not out in twenty, I'm coming for your ass," he warned as he smacked her butt.

Jaz rolled her eyes. Right before he left out, she called to him,

"Ay!" He turned around. "You go, boy," she laughed as she imitated Gina from *Martin*.

He shook his head, just happy to see her happy for once in a long time. He left the room and Jaz tried her best to work up the energy to do the same. It took her five minutes, but she finally was able to get in the shower. Once out, she spritzed on her favorite Guilty Gucci perfume, put on her clothes, and threw on a pair of red heels. She added a simple red lip to her face for color, some earrings, and a couple trinkets on her neck and finger. She took one last look in the mirror, and noticed her ass had indeed gotten bigger. She smirked and headed outside to her awaiting guests.

Jaz immediately went over to everyone she hadn't spoken to and said hi. The main fight hadn't started yet, so people were either playing cards or talking it up until Mayweather hit the ring. Kyree was now playing cards at the table with Fat Boy as his partner. She went over and wrapped her arms around him.

"You want anything to eat, bae?"

"Nah, I'm good." He slapped the card on the table.

"Get that nigga some Kleenex. He's going to need it after we make him cry. Bam!" Toni slammed a card on the table.

Jaz rolled her eyes and made her way over to her girls. The looks they gave her said it all. They could see a change in her attitude - something they hadn't seen in months.

"What?" She looked at them skeptically.

"Look at her ass. Glowin' and shit," Ms. Ray laughed.

"I'm not going to even say anything. I'm just going to sip my tea," Ahnesty took a sip of her purple concoction and nearly choked it was so strong. "Shit!"

They all laughed. "See, that's what ya ass get," Jaz teased.

Ahnesty waved them all off. She was going to finish that drink, even if Stacy had to carry her out of there over his shoulder.

"I need a drink," Jaz said as she thought about how long it had been since she'd last had one. She strutted over to the kitchen with her friends in tow. Ahnesty knew exactly the drink to make her. She poured two shots of Red Berry Ciroc, a shot of raspberry tea, and a splash of Red Bull. She topped it off by adding two of the vodka-infused strawberries she'd made the night before, gave it a quick stir, and then handed it off to Jaz.

"I call this Nest's Tea," Ahnesty boasted as she waited for Jaz to try it.

Jaz was hesitant to drink it at first. Ahnesty was known to make drinks to put an elephant on its ass. But she took the drink any way. After the first sip, she was hooked. It was so good, she could barely taste the alcohol. That was Ahnesty's secret. The hidden alcohol taste usually got people fucked up before they even knew what hit them.

"Sooo," Jaz directed her attention toward Monica. "I know I've been out of commission for a couple of weeks, but where's bae?"

Monica rolled her eyes. Jaz was so nosy. "For your information, he's on his way. He had to go home to change."

Jaz simply nodded her head, knowing Monica was probably hiding something, but she knew it would come out when Monica was ready. Monica was relieved that no one could see that she was really having doubts about her relationship with Mario. What they had was still very new, but they were already having problems. Together, they were great. It was mainly outsiders testing their relationship, that outsider mainly being Mario's best friend, Shannon.

Monica didn't want to worry her friends with her problems right now. Besides, it was nothing she couldn't handle. This was a joyous occasion. Her brother and niece being okay was more important.

"Enough about Mo-Problems," Ms. Ray interjected.

"Screw you." Monica rolled her eyes.

"Y'all, I think I'm in love." Ms. Ray held his chest as his eyes drifted off.

They all burst out laughing.

"Boy, boo. That's every week. I bet he has some crazy-ass stripper name too." Jaz cracked up laughing.

"Ha...ha." Ms. Ray turned up his lip.

"Okay, what's his name?" Monica got serious for a moment.

"For your info, his name is Quest."

The girls laughed even harder now.

"I hate y'all asses," he snarled.

"Well, hate my ass from afar, because there goes my baby." Monica smiled as Mario walked in and she sashayed over to him.

"I swear dick will change a bitch," Ms. Ray joked. But he, along with everyone else, was actually happy that Monica now had someone in her life. She deserved it after what she'd been through in past relationships.

Jaz enjoyed her time with her girls. It felt good to let loose and not have to worry when the next shoe was going to drop. She lived her life waiting for the worst to happen. She cherished the times where she could just be carefree and enjoy the moment. And Ahnesty's special tea had her enjoying it even more. Before she knew it, she was ready for the fight to be over so that everyone could leave and she could have her house, and Kyree, to herself.

The fight was winding down, and there was no doubt in anyone's mind that Mayweather was going to add another name to his undefeated title. Kyree looked over at the seductive looks Jaz was giving him and he knew what time it was. But out of respect for his guests, he'd wait until the fight was officially over.

She sat with her legs crossed across the room as Ms. Ray went on and on about Quest. Jaz had no idea what he was saying. She couldn't keep her eyes off Kyree's arms in his T-shirt. Kyree's chocolate frame was cut just right. Jaz loved everything about him, from his flawlessly chiseled chin and piercing brown eyes to his perfectly-kissable lips. And the best part of all was that he was all hers.

Before anyone knew it, the fight was over. Mayweather was once again the undisputed champ, Ahnesty was lying on the couch dead drunk, and Ms. Ray was on his way to go see Quest. Stacy lifted Ahnesty off the couch and she leaned on him as they headed for the door. Jaz said goodbye to everyone, letting them each know how much their company was appreciated.

"See you Tuesday, Mo," Jaz said, hugging her.

"Does Kyree know you're going back to work?" Monica looked at her skeptically.

"Nope. But he'll be a'ight."

Monica shook her head and chuckled. "He's going to beat your ass. Keep playin'."

Jaz rolled her eyes. Kyree wanted her to take another month off, but Jaz was eager to go back to the salon.

"Bye, girl. Don't get none on ya," Jaz quoted their favorite movie, *What's Love Got to Do with It.*

Monica laughed and rolled her eyes. "You're so stupid."

Jaz shut the door behind her, only to be startled by Kyree standing right behind her. He eyed her suspiciously. "What?"

"So where are you going Tuesday?"

"Huh?" She pursed her lips, knowing she'd been caught.

"Don't play with me, Jazzy. You said another month. We agreed on it. Yo' ass is not going back to work until then, and that's final."

Jaz gave a slight laugh at his seriousness as she approached him. Standing just inches away from him, she said, "Whatever you say, zaddy." She bit her lip as a delicate finger traced his pec. She was lying for the moment, but the drink, mixed with her horniness, would have made her agree to quit her job if he'd asked her.

Kyree smirked. He knew she was bullshittin'. But she was so

cute when she was drunk, so he'd let it slide - for now. "I'm gon' fuck you up. Keep playin'."

"Please do," she seductively begged.

Kyree laughed as he took her into his arms and carried her into the bedroom.

CHAPTER THREE

Kyree and Jaz made love until neither of them could do nothing but lie in bed, trying to catch their breaths. Kyree embraced her from behind and kissed the nape of her neck. He closed his eyes and almost drifted into a deep sleep, until Jaz spoke.

"Ky?" He didn't respond, so she turned around. "I know you're not asleep that fast. Kyree!" She nudged his chest, and he chuckled.

"What's up?"

Jaz used the light from the street outside to illuminate his face. She needed to see him when she spoke. They hadn't really talked about the seriousness of everything that had transpired, and Jaz wanted to know where his head was.

"Kyree, do you understand the odds we've fought to be together?"

"Of course I do."

"Seriously, baby. We can't let anything come between us. Not anymore."

Kyree scrunched his face. "What're you getting at?"

"I'm telling you to let the Asia and Mike shit die."

He sucked his teeth. "I'm not even thinking about that shit," he lied.

Kyree wasn't sure how she knew, but he was indeed out to get them both. For a few weeks since the incident, he'd had a bounty out on Asia's head. He wanted to handle Michael himself, but not until he found Asia first. He had to be cunning in how he handled the situation. Asia didn't have any family or friends to miss her, but Michael came from wealth and privilege. Kyree had done his research. He was always cautious and patient when it came to handling business. Kyree could never really sleep peacefully until his family was safe. And as long as Asia and Michael were breathing, that was impossible in his eyes.

"Kyree, tell me anything. I know you." Kyree didn't respond. His face was stern. Anyone who didn't know him would've assumed he was telling the truth. But Jaz knew better. "Kyree, I understand; they hurt your family. And I know niggas have died for way less," she stressed, trying to reach him on a hood level. "But we're going to have to take this as an 'L'. As much as I want to drag Asia up and down the street for what she did, I can't let that take over my life. Let the police handle her. And let Michael be."

Kyree licked his lips as if he were considering what she was saying. Jaz understood that she was asking a lot from him, but there was too much on the line now. They were too old to be playing the same games they did when they were younger. "Kyree, I don't want to lose you again. And I'm tired of fighting to be with you. I was fighting for you when you didn't even know it sometimes. I've been doing this shit for fifteen years, and I'm exhausted."

Jaz pleaded to him with her eyes, and Kyree could see her pain. He was tired too. He left the street life alone for Jaz, but there were some parts that always seemed to call him back. But now he had Kylee to think about too. He'd never forgive himself if he risked his life, or his freedom, and could never be with them again. So, for once, he was going to make it easier on everyone.

"Okay," he said.

Jaz was confused. He seemed sincere, but she didn't think it would be that easy. She fixed her mouth to speak, but he kissed her before she could. The kiss was simple and sweet.

"I'm serious. The street life is no longer for me. I'm gonna take a crack at this straight life for once," he chuckled.

"I love you." She kissed him again and wrapped herself in his arms.

He kissed the top of her head. "I love you, too." Kyree sat and thought for a moment while Jaz was drifting off to sleep. "Hold on, what did you mean by fifteen years?"

"Huh?" Jaz groggily answered.

"Huh means you can hear." She rolled her eyes and sucked her teeth. "We didn't start messing around until your sophomore year in college, and you hated my ass back in high school. So what'd you mean about fighting when I didn't know it."

Jaz realized she'd probably said too much. Nothing got past Kyree.

"You remember Kendall?

Kyree's eyes lit up at the sound of his high school girlfriend's name. "What'd you do?" He demanded to know.

"Kyree, grow up. That was over ten years ago."

Kyree couldn't let it go though. So he picked up his phone.

"What are you doing?" She asked.

"I'm calling Mo," he stated.

Jaz shook her head. "You're petty. It's three in the damn morning." He looked at her skeptically and proceeded to put the phone to his ear. "Fine then. I'm going back to sleep." She abruptly turned on her side. She really didn't want to hear this.

"Hello? What's wrong?" Monica immediately asked. She knew there had to be something important for her brother to be calling her this early in the morning.

"Mo, what the fuck did Jaz do to Kendall?"

"What?" Monica was so confused.

"From high school. Remember?"

"Kyree, you and Jaz are fucking crazy. You're calling me about some shit that happened years ago? This shit couldn't wait?"

"Man, just tell me," Kyree demanded.

Monica took a deep breath. She couldn't believe that she was going down memory lane this early in the morning, especially a lane that she and Jaz swore they'd never travel down again.

12 Years Ago

Jaz and Monica were budding freshmen in high school. At fifteen, they'd already started making a name for themselves. Every girl in school went to them to get their hair braided. They were equally street and book smart, and both of their bodies had filled out the summer before. Boys flocked to them from all grades although Kyree, the star running back of their high school football team, wasn't allowing that. He kept a tight leash on the both of them. Jaz was like a little sister to him as well, so he took her under his wing, making sure that, like his sister, she stayed on the right path. The two argued whenever in each other's presence, but it was nothing more than brother-sister bickering.

At the end of the day, no matter how much they hated the way Kyree always interfered in their lives, they still respected him. At eighteen, he had a job mowing lawns around the neighborhood, cutting hair for all of his friends, and he also sold some of the best weed in the city. He was "That Nigga", but still carried himself as though he was just a normal eighteen-year-old trying to get through high school. His humbleness, money, and grown man features made him every teenage girl's dream and every father's nightmare.

Kyree had several girls on his roster, but they were all second to his girlfriend, Kendall. Kendall was every young niggas wet dream. At seventeen she had a body most women would pay for, caramel-colored skin, long curly hair, and piercing gray eyes. She was the most popular girl in school and the captain of the cheer-leading squad that Jaz and Monica were both members of. Most girls their age weren't even allowed the opportunity to join the varsity team, but Kendall thought it would be nice to give her boyfriend's sisters a time to shine. She told everyone she was doing them a favor, but really, she just wanted to keep Jaz close. In Kendall's eyes, Jaz was too close for comfort to Kyree for her not to be blood.

Jaz and Monica hated Kendall. She was the designated mean girl that they saw in every movie growing up. She walked around with her nose in the air, thinking she was better than everyone else. They saw right through her, but Kyree could not. She was the exact opposite when she was around Kyree. For someone so good at reading people, Kyree was blind to the ugly that lay beneath Kendall's pretty face.

"Again!" Kendall drilled the team at their 5:00 a.m. Saturday practice.

"Ugh!" Everyone huffed, tired and drained from practicing for so long.

"Oh, y'all think I'm playing? Do y'all want to come in Sunday morning too? I don't care how much you groan, we're going to get this right. Regionals are in two weeks, and y'all look weak!" Kendall spat.

Monica shook her head. She was pissed and tired.

"Ugh, I can't stand that bitch," Jaz mumbled to Monica when Kendall turned her head.

"Me either. She can't do half the shit she's making us do."

"I wanna see them lift her big ass up on top of that pyramid and watch it come tumbling down. Fat-ass bitch."

Monica covered her mouth and snickered. Talking while Kendall was speaking was a no-go in their practices, but she couldn't keep her laughter in.

"What was that?" Kendall snapped, turning around in their direction.

Monica was the one she heard, but she directed her attention toward Jaz. She was positive that Jaz was responsible for whatever had Monica laughing. When Monica saw that Kendall's raft was directed at Jaz, she stepped up.

"Sorry, that was me," Monica said as she stood in front of Jaz. She was only five feet tall, but she didn't allow anyone to mess with Jaz.

"No, it wasn't you. I'm sure it was Jaz," Kendall said as she made her way to the middle row where Jaz was lined. She stood with her arms folded, ice grilling Jaz. Jaz gently moved Monica to the side, assuring her that she could handle it.

"What?" Jaz grilled her back.

"Do you think you can do better than me? Do you want to stand front and center and show us how to fall flat on our faces?" She laughed and the rest of the team laughed with her. Whenever Kendall laughed, it was as if she had her own studio audience on a ninety's sitcom.

Jaz sighed heavily. "That's not what I said," Jaz lied. She didn't want to take it there with Kendall today. She was tired, her stomach was cramping from receiving her period that morning, and she had to practice all these moves with her hormones on ten.

"Naw. Since you're so big and bad, front and center. I want to see you do the whole routine by yourself."

Jaz bit her bottom lip. She wanted to haul off and slap Kendall for putting her on the spot like that in front of everyone. She really wasn't in the mood, but Kendall had the right one on the wrong day. Jaz nodded her head as she cut through everyone, hearing them mumble under their breaths as she made her way to the front.

Wearing small workout shorts, a halter top, and her favorite purple Nikes, Jaz took her place at center line, pulled her long ponytail tighter, and took a deep breath.

"Here goes nothing," she whispered to herself.

The whole team watched as Jaz did a double back flip, somersaulted from one end of the gym to the next, rocked the weak-ass step routine Kendall had created by throwing a few of her own moves into the mix, and then did a handstand and landed with a split. Everyone cheered her on and rushed over to congratulate her. Jaz had done something none of them, with the exception of Monica, had the courage to do. She'd put Kendall in her place. Hell, even Kendall knew it. But she would never give Jaz the satisfaction of knowing it. Instead, she had to step on whatever high Jaz was on after performing a perfect routine, worthy of a regional title.

"I'm glad y'all like it so much. Because you'll all be here at 5:00 a.m. tomorrow morning learning whatever that was she threw into with *my* routine."

They all groaned and were now pissed with Jaz.

Jaz sucked her teeth. She didn't even want to be on the cheerleading squad. She and Monica had both gone out for the dance team, but the dance captain didn't allow freshmen on the team. So they ended up settling for the cheerleading squad, with hopes of making it to the dance squad the next year. But Jaz wasn't going to let Kendall kill her vibe. She was confident in her skills, and knew she could teach the team the steps better than Kendall ever could.

"If anyone needs extra help with the steps, y'all can meet me at my house around 5:00 today. I want us all to get this right. And I know if I can do it, y'all can do it too," Jaz stressed with an upbeat, perky smile. The team actually liked that idea and several of them took her up on her offer, which only pissed Kendall off even more. Jaz smiled at her. "Thanks for the opportunity, Kendall." Kendall returned her smile with one as equally fake.

Once practice was over, Monica smirked at Jaz. "You know you just made King Kendall's Shit List."

"Oh, I *just* made it?" Jaz played, dumbfounded. "Damn, I thought I always lived at the top of that list." Monica laughed. "And stop laughing at every damn thing, Mo. You're always getting me in trouble."

"Bitch, please. You got me in trouble at the beginning of the year for talking in class. Now my ass has to stay back every Thursday for the whole semester, to tutor the dumbass basketball players."

"But isn't one of those dumbass niggas your boyfriend now?"

"Shut up," Monica stressed, looking around to make sure no one heard her. The last thing she needed was for someone to tell Kyree that she was dating Marcus Davis. He most certainly would not approve. Marcus was a senior, and Kyree would say that he was too old. The only time they got to spend together was on Thursdays when she had to tutor him and in Geometry class, where they sat near each other.

"Uh huh. You know your secret is safe with me," Jaz promised her.

Monica knew Jaz would never squeal. They held secrets

about each other that would never allow them to stop being friends for longer than twenty-four hours. Jaz, too, had a boyfriend. He was a junior and also played on the basketball team. Jared was her boyfriend going on six months now, and Jaz didn't feel like he was her first love. Sure they had fun together, but that was it. They hadn't had sex yet. Although Jared hinted at being the one to take her virginity several times, Jaz just didn't feel like he was the one.

It was also hard for Jaz to spend time with Jared because of their busy schedules. They were always at practice. But after winning regionals with Jaz's routine, she was going to have a lot more time to spend with him. Two weeks later, Kendall happily took credit for that win, and Jaz just let it roll right off her shoulders. As long as she and the rest of the team knew who was responsible, that was all that mattered. She'd worked tirelessly with the girls trying to make sure they got the routine right. They all worked hard, so the win was for the team, not Kendall.

One Thursday, Jaz sat outside in front of the school hugged up with Jared. She was wearing his letterman jacket while he begged her to come over his house to braid his hair, because his mom was out of town for the weekend. No matter how many times she said no, he always came up with an excuse as to why she should.

"We can eat popcorn. Watch movies all night. Whatever you want, baby."

Jaz rolled her eyes. She was starting to see just how weak Jared's game was. "I don't know, Jared. My dad is not going to go for that."

"Just tell him you're staying at Mo's. Plus, I need you to braid my hair. You don't want your man going around with this shit, do you?" Jared tugged one of his long braids and Jaz laughed at how bad they looked. She loved his braids. When his hair was all done up and he was speeding down from one end of the court to the next, he reminded her of Allen Iverson. She lightly pulled on one of his braids and brought him into her face for a kiss.

Beeeeeeeeep

Jaz looked off into the distance and could see that Kyree was there to take her home in his black 1998 Honda Accord. She sucked her teeth and grabbed her purse. Jared picked up her book bag and walked her to the car.

"So, what do you say?" He asked again, once they were at the car.

"We'll see," Jaz said.

Beeeeeeeeep

"Alright, boy! Damn!" Jaz barked, annoyed.

She rolled her eyes at Kyree, and Jared pulled her in for a hug. He reached down to grab a feel of her ass, and Kyree blared on the horn again.

"That's enough, playboy," Kyree stressed. Jared put his hands up in surrender. He didn't want any beef with Kyree. He wasn't stupid. Kyree carried the clout of an OG, even in high school.

"Call me when you get home." He smiled, shutting her door. Jaz returned his smile as Kyree pulled away.

"Why are you so rude?"

Kyree ignored her, and just shook his head. "You're too good for that nigga, Jazzy."

"I told you to stop calling me that shit," she stressed, her gaze directed out the window.

Kyree didn't care how much she hated the name. He called her that because he liked how much it got under her skin. He playfully nudged her, and she smirked.

"Naw. But for real. Just be careful with him. And you know I'm just a jump, hop, and a skip away if ever you need me."

Jaz didn't say anything, she just nodded her head in agreement. She loved Thursdays because those were days that Monica stayed after school, and she and Kyree usually chilled until it was time for her to get out. Jaz loved talking to him sometimes. When he wasn't being a meddling pest, he actually gave her good advice.

He was the first person she'd told when her mother died three years ago. It wasn't intentional. She actually went to their house in search of Monica. She needed a friend, and Monica was always her go-to. But she wasn't home and Kyree answered the door. Jaz wasn't even crying, but upon looking at her, he could see a sadness in her eyes. And instead of pushing her, or throwing his usual insult, he instantly pulled her in for a long hard hug. Jaz didn't realize how much she needed it until it was actually happening. She cried for the first time since finding out the breast cancer her mother was suffering from for two years had taken her life. Kyree knew how sick she was and knew how hard it was for Jaz. In that moment, he became everything she needed.

They joked and bickered a lot, disagreed more than they should have, and often drove each other crazy, but they loved each other like family - at least, that's what they thought. Neither knew the love they felt deep down, which they often hid behind their jokes, was actually strong feelings for the other. In their eyes, no one would ever be good enough to date the other.

Kyree pulled away from the school and a girl's voice called out to him. He stopped and pulled the car over to the shoulder of the road.

"Hey, Sherry." Kyree looked her up and down, liking what he saw. Sherry was exactly his type: Round ass, skin the color of chocolate, and she was cool as hell. She sometimes let him cheat off her paper when he dozed off in class.

"You think you can give me a ride to my house? It's just up the street."

"Sure." He motioned with his head for her to get in the backseat. She hopped in and Kyree introduced them. "Sherry, this my big head sister, Jazzy."

Jaz rolled her eyes and turned to speak. "Nice to meet you. But the name is *Jaz*," she stressed in annoyance.

"Oh, nice to meet you. I think you did my homegirl Nikki's braids."

"Oh yeah, I did."

"I might have to get you to hook me up soon."

"Well, just let me know. Ky has my number."

Sherry nodded. She and Kyree talked about a few things that happened in class while Jaz laughed at their antics. Jaz noticed instantly that Sherry was more of Kyree's type, but he couldn't see that. "Okay, it's the brick house on the left. Just pull behind that blue truck," she instructed. "Thanks, Ky."

"You're welcome. But if you ever need a ride again, just give me a call."

"I don't have your number," she said, knowing where this was going.

She pulled out her flip phone and Kyree programmed his number. She called him and instructed him to save hers. He smirked and licked his lips as he watched her walk away.

He looked over at Jaz who was shaking her head. "What?"

"You're such a hoe," she laughed.

"Don't hate the player. Hate the game," he laughed as he drove away.

Kyree then received a call from Kendall, demanding that he come pick her up from school and take her home. He huffed, but headed back to the school. When Kendall came outside, she saw Jaz in the car and that just made her blood boil inside. She didn't show it, but it really irked her. Jaz didn't feel like getting into it with her today, so she just hopped in the backseat. No questions asked.

"I told you Jaz and I were on our way to McDonald's, so why couldn't you wait another thirty minutes until I picked up Mo?" Kyree questioned her as she situated herself in the seat.

"Because I didn't want to," she simply said. She reached over to kiss him, and Jaz rolled her eyes from the backseat. "Oh, hey, Jaz. I forgot you were back there."

"Hey," Jaz dryly responded.

Jaz pretended to busy herself as Kyree drove, and Kendall talked his ear off about whatever she wanted to whine and complain about. Before going to McDonald's, Kyree made a stop at the gas station. He asked them both if they wanted anything, and they both shook their heads. Jaz didn't want to be left alone with Kendall, but she didn't think it would be too bad, seeing as though he was only going to pay and come right back. But she had underestimated the time it would take him to come out of the busy gas station. The minutes ticked by as Kendall played with the radio a bit, finally realizing there was nothing she wanted to listen to more than herself. She turned toward Jaz in the back, who was busying herself with her phone.

"Hey, you still talk to Jared?" Kendall pried.

Jaz didn't even bother looking up from what she was doing. "Yeah."

"Oh," Kendall snickered, then turned around in her seat.

This immediately got Jaz's attention. "What was that supposed to mean?"

"Oh, nothing. I just thought he was single now. That's all," Kendall said as she cleaned her fingernails with her famous file. Jaz envisioned herself on many occasions stuffing that file down her throat.

"And why would you think that?" Jaz defensively asked.

"Because I saw him and Avery together the other day. I just thought y'all had finally called it quits."

"Him and who?" Jaz's eyes grew big.

Kendall sympathetically shook her head as she reached into her purse and pulled out her Sidekick phone. She scrolled through her photos, found the one she was looking for, and passed it back to Jaz. Jaz was skeptical at first, but she grabbed the phone anyway. Upon looking at the phone's screen, Jaz's heart dropped to the pit of her stomach and her mouth began to water. She thought she was going to throw up from seeing the photo of her cheerleading teammate, Avery, lying on her naked boyfriend, Jared.

"I'm sorry you had to find out like this, Jaz." Kendall placed her hand on Jaz's knee and Jaz quickly jerked her knee away. Kendall smiled to herself, knowing she'd done what she set out to do: hurt Jaz like it hurt her to see her with Kyree every time.

Jaz wanted to cry. There were so many questions she wanted to ask about the photo, but she refused to give Kendall the satisfaction of knowing that she was partially responsible for her pain. So she closed the phone, handed it back to Kendall, and gave a sly laugh. "It's fine. Thanks for letting me know."

"I had to. Avery's my girl, but I couldn't let you get played like that. You're like a sister to Ky, so you're like a sister to me too," she lied. "Are you going to be alright?"

"Yeah, I'll be fine. He wasn't the only one," Jaz lied. In actuality, she'd turned down plenty of guys just to be with Jared. She grew fond of the time they spent together and loved talking to him. He wasn't the only one who wanted her, but he was the only one she wanted.

Kyree finally returned to the car and pumped the gas. Once he was inside the car, he threw Jaz a pack of her favorite bag of Skittles. She only ate the purple bag, and he knew it. Kendall was so pissed. He hadn't bothered to bring her anything, even though they'd both said they didn't want anything.

"You a'ight?" Kyree questioned Jaz, noticing a distant look in her eyes. She nodded her head and he pulled away from the gas station. Jaz didn't want to let him know that he was right about Jared all along. But the thought of Jared doing this to her made her want to go out for blood. And she knew the first place she'd start. She gazed out of the window, pondering how she would go about it.

That night, Jaz cried on the phone to Monica. Monica didn't even wait for an invitation before she was at Jaz's house, giving her a shoulder to wipe her tears. The pain hurt so bad, that it made Jaz realize how much she did love Jared. Monica wasn't going to have her best friend crying over a no-good nigga. So she devised her own little devious plan, and Jaz was down for it.

Although Jaz was hurt, before giving Kendall her phone back, she quickly sent the photo to her own phone. Not only was Avery Jaz's teammate, she was also the girlfriend of Jared's teammate, O.J.

Jaz called O.J. and told him everything. O.J. was a starting center at 6"6, 260 pounds with the body build of Shaquille O'Neal. He was crazy about Avery, and everyone knew it. After Jaz told him what happened, he didn't believe it. So she sent him the picture and he went ballistic. He broke up with Avery in front of the whole school. He called her all kinds of bitches and hoes, and just before he was suspended for a week, he beat Jared's ass before getting on the school bus and was suspended for an extra week. It was the fight to see that school year. The whole school cheered as Jared's small frame was tossed around like a rag doll.

Jared called Jaz crying later that day. He professed his love and devotion to her, but she wasn't trying to hear it. Jaz and Monica shared a huge laugh, but Jaz still didn't feel the vindication she thought she should. She had another plan to help heal the pain she still felt in her heart.

It took a few days of planning, but it all started to come together the next week. Kyree was sitting on his front porch with his friends drinking a red fruit punch, when out of nowhere...

Whack!

"Damnnnnnnn!" everyone yelled when Kendall smacked Kyree in the back of his head.

"What the fuck?" Kyree yelled as he spilled juice all over his plain white T-shirt. He had no idea who was behind him as he turned around, pissed. "What is wrong with you, Kendall?" he seethed.

"You're fucking Aisha now, nigga?" She punched him in his chest, and he took a deep breath. He had no idea how she knew about Aisha. He was really good at keeping the other girls he fucked with in line. They knew their place and usually didn't give him much lip about the situation.

"Don't do this shit right now," he calmly, but firmly, stated.

His calmness made Kendall even angrier. She hauled off and smacked him again. Kyree grabbed both of her arms to try to stop her from swinging again. But Kendall seemed to have super strength today. Kyree would never hit a girl. His mother had raised him better than that. But Kendall wasn't letting up. He tried to block her as she wildly kicked and punched him with a crowd of onlookers to amp her up. Fat Boy was finally able to break through the crowd and lift Kendall up into the air. She was still kicking and screaming as he tried to subdue her.

Mrs. Johnson, the nosy neighbor from across the street, rushed over to help out. "Girl, calm down. That's no way for a lady to act," Mrs. Johnson chastised her.

She seemed to be getting through to her as Kendall snapped out of her trance and composed herself. Her nostrils were still flaring though as Kyree examined the scratches on his arms and neck. His lip was bleeding and the crowd was still laughing. Kyree was usually such a calm person, and he didn't like a lot of chaos in his life. So instead of going off on Kendall and feeding into her drama, he took a deep breath and walked into the house.

"Fuck you, Kyree!" she yelled after him.

Mrs. Johnson shook her head as she ushered Kendall away to her car. Once Kendall was gone, Fat Boy and Mrs. Johnson cleared the crowd. With Mrs. Johnson as a witness, it didn't take long for the news to get back to Kyree's mother. Jackie was so embarrassed. She smacked Kyree upside his head for bringing that drama to her home. He was also grounded for a month. Jackie didn't play when it came to her children. She was especially harder on Kyree because she knew that he was into more than just cutting heads and mowing lawns. She couldn't prove it, but she did her best to keep him safe. Her biggest fear was burying her son. They didn't live in the greatest neighborhood, but it wasn't the worst either. Jackie raised her children on her own on a CNA's salary. Her ex-husband left before Monica was even born, and Kyree was her rock. He'd become the man of the house early, and he took on the responsibilities of helping raise his sister. Kyree was extremely overprotective of Monica, and she was as equally overprotective of her brother.

So when Monica heard about the altercation, she went to school out for blood. She waited impatiently for the lunch bell to ring. Once it finally did, she nearly raced out of class, headed for the lunch room.

"Mo, slow down!" Jaz demanded, as she tried to keep up. Monica ignored her, hell bent on getting to the cafeteria. "Mo, please! I have something to tell you." Jaz grabbed her arm and stopped her from walking.

"What, Jaz?" Monica barked.

"I may have done something. Please, don't be mad."

Monica skeptically looked at Jaz. She knew that look. Jaz was into some shit, and she needed a way out. She sucked her teeth. "What you do?"

Jaz took a deep breath. "I put pictures of Kyree hugged up with Aisha in Kendall's locker." She lowered her head.

"Say wha nah?" Monica squinted at her.

"I was so mad, Mo. She's been doing shit to me on purpose all year. I just wanted payback."

"Shit, Jaz! Why'd you have to get Ky involved?"

"I'm sorry. I didn't think it would go this far."

Monica could see Jaz's sincerity, but she was still disappointed. "You could have at least told me."

"You would have tried to stop me. But now, I wish I had told you."

Monica sucked her teeth. This time, they slowly walked to the cafeteria. Monica had suddenly lost the energy to pounce on Kendall. She and Jaz went to their usual table and sat down.

Monica stood up from her seat. "I'm going to get a cookie. You want anything?"

Jaz shook her head and Monica proceeded to the lunch line. Jaz sat and contemplated the consequences of her actions. She usually wasn't this quick to react, but Kendall brought out the worst in her. She never thought Kendall had the guts to go on the attack the way she had. If Kyree found out Jaz was responsible, she knew he'd be pissed with her. So much shit was wrong, and it was all her fault. She stretched her arm across the lunch table and rested her face on her arm. Just as she closed her eyes, there was a loud smack on the table, causing her to jump.

Jaz looked up to see Kendall standing in front of her with her sidekick, Avery, right behind her. Jaz rolled her eyes. She didn't need this shit today.

"Since I'm not with Kyree anymore, you're not on the team anymore."

Jaz nodded her head. "Okay, Kendall. Is that all?" Jaz's face pretty much said she didn't care.

"Bitch, no. I never liked your ass anyway. I should fuck you up right now," Kendall threatened.

"I wish the fuck you would!" Monica came from out of nowhere, stepping in front of Jaz.

"Mo, let's go. We're not going to do this today," Jaz reasoned as she pulled Monica away.

Monica shook her head as she began to walk away.

"That's right. Walk away! Because Monica knows I will fuck her up just like I did her brother!"

Before anyone knew what happened, Monica jumped on Kendall like a wild animal. Kendall was 5'8" and Monica trampled over her like a linebacker. Once Avery realized what was happening, she tried to jump in, but Jaz had her by the hair before she could even raise her hand. Both girls had a point to prove and they proved it with every blow they threw. Monica hated Kendall, and the fact that she'd put her hands on her brother really made her furious. She knew her brother would never raise a hand to a girl, so in her mind, she was doing it for him. Jaz wanted a few licks off Kendall, but Avery would suffice. She still couldn't believe that she'd slept with Jared. It was a low blow, especially since Jaz had been nothing but kind to her, even going as far as working overtime to make sure she mastered the routine for regionals.

Jaz and Monica both knew that Kendall was all talk. She ran her mouth a lot, but she wasn't about that life. People feared her because she was intimidating and powerful. But her popularity had finally landed her in hot water. Their classmates looked on, hooting and hollering, making it impossible for security to make their way through to the brawl. By the time security broke through the barricade of people, Kendall's face was lumping up and

Avery's once beautiful brown skin was now starting to turn black and blue.

Everyone's hair looked a mess when they were done. Kendall and Avery didn't stand a chance. They blocked as many punches as they could, but Jaz and Monica were both faster and more skilled. They'd never been in such a situation, but Kyree had trained them well over the years. He'd be pissed if he saw them now though.

"I'm pressing charges!" Kendall cried aloud as the security escorted them all to the principal's office.

Monica rolled her eyes at Kendall's dramatics. She looked over at Jaz, and she was starting to cry too. Monica scrunched her face. She had no idea why Jaz was crying. Avery looked a mess, and Jaz only looked like she'd gone to sleep without her head scarf.

"Wait right here!" The security guard, Mr. Burley, ordered. He sat them all in separate rooms and then headed to get the principal.

Once he was out of sight, Monica poked her head around to where Jaz was and asked, "What the fuck are you crying for?"

"Because, Mo. My daddy is going to kill me," she sniffled. Monica started laughing. "It's not funny, Mo!"

"Girl, stop crying. You won. And your dad is easy. He'll give you a slap on the wrist for this. But Jackie? Oh, Lawd! Jackie is going to beat both of our asses."

Jaz let out a slight laugh, she knew Ms. Jackie didn't play games. She was serious when she made a promise to Jaz's mom to treat her as if she were her own daughter.

"I'm sorry, Mo," Jaz admitted. "This is all my fault."

"Nah, it's Kendall's fault!" Monica spoke loud enough so that Kendall could hear her. She was daring her to say something, but she didn't. She'd learned her lesson for one day. "Ay, Jaz," Monica called out.

"Yeah?"

"We can't tell Ky about this. He'll kill us." Monica shook her head.

"Take it to the grave," Jaz said.

"To hell and back," Monica agreed. They both shared a laugh as they were each called to the principal's office to receive their suspensions. Since none of them had ever been in much trouble, they each received a week. Kendall would have received less if Avery hadn't unknowingly admitted that they were the ones who instigated the fight.

After that incident, Kendall never spoke to the girls again and Jaz and Monica happily left the cheerleading team. The head captain of the dance team was thoroughly impressed with how they handled themselves. She couldn't stand Kendall either and was glad to offer the first freshmen in twenty years a position on the team. She was also fascinated to learn that Jaz had created the routine that helped them to win regionals. The ass whoopin' they received from Jackie was well worth it.

Present

"What the fuck?" Kyree shook his head. He'd never heard this part of the story before. Sure, he knew about the fight, but never about the pictures.

"Yes, Kyree. In case you didn't know already, your baby mama is bat shit crazy. Now, if you and Jaz are done bringing up old shit, my ass is going back to bed. Bye! Crazy mother..." Monica's voice trailed off as she hung up the phone.

Kyree didn't say anything. He was still floored. He nudged a sleeping Jaz, but she didn't move. He pushed her harder, nearly knocking her out of the bed.

"Boy, what?" she barked.

"Why didn't you ever tell me about that shit?"

"Because Mo made me promise not to."

"Your ass is crazy," Kyree let out a slight chuckle.

"Don't flatter yourself. That bitch had it coming. She's lucky it was Mo, and not me."

"How'd you get the pictures?" Kyree just had to know.

"I waited for you to bring Aisha over the house, and I snapped a picture of the two of you together. I don't even think y'all were doing much but watching TV, but I knew Kendall would think more of it." Jaz laughed to herself, thinking of how devious she'd been. "And to think, that hoe tried to get back with you after a week, apologizing and shit. Ugh!" Jaz rolled her eyes.

"What can I say? Dick too bomb." Kyree gave a sly smirk, and Jaz hit him in his bare chest.

"Don't play with me, Kyree!" Jaz warned. Kyree laughed as he embraced her. When Kyree was with Kendall, he always had thoughts of Jaz, but he would never allow those feelings to manifest for fear of breaking their friendship. They were equally happy when they were finally able to admit and realize that they both shared the same feelings. Jaz was the only girl for him - always had been. He just hoped she'd grown over her hatred for Kendall, or else he didn't know how he was going to tell her that Kendall's publishing company was working closely with his studio company. He kissed her lightly on the head and wondered how he'd tell her.

CHAPTER FOUR

The phone call from Kyree and Jaz had Monica strolling down memory lane herself. She remembered those days, and every guy who had come into her life and tried to screw it up. Her first boyfriend, Marcus, went off to college and forgot about her. Her next boyfriend took her virginity senior year and cheated on her a few months later. And her college sweetheart, Latrell, got her pregnant and then bounced. Sure, he'd shown up recently, but that wasn't until her son was two years old. He'd missed all of the important things in Kayden's life, and his excuse was inexcusable. But for the sake of her son having his father in his life, she put aside her ill feelings toward Latrell. She'd do anything for her son's happiness.

In the past, Kayden's happiness meant risking her own. But with Mario, she felt so at ease. He treated her like she felt every man should treat a woman. And her having a son didn't run him away. Mario didn't have kids of his own, which meant he was baby-mama-drama free. But he had other drama that did worry Monica. His best friend, Shannon, was always popping up at the most inopportune times, claiming to need Mario. The other night her boyfriend kicked her out of the house so Mario went to pick her up. Before that, she needed money to help on her rent. Monica's relationship with Mario was still so new, and she didn't want to ruin it by mentioning how much it bothered her.

When she met Shannon, they were both very cordial. Shannon actually seemed like a sweet girl on the surface. Monica didn't necessarily have a problem with her, but she knew it was only a matter of time before Shannon and Mario's relationship got to be too much for her to handle. She could only hope that it never came to that.

Monica tried to go back to sleep, but she never really made it into a deep sleep like before they called. She turned on the TV and watched a few shows. Finally forcing herself out of bed around 6:00, she got up to brush her teeth and then grabbed a bowl from the kitchen and filled it with Kayden's Frosted Flakes and almond milk. She sat and ate at the kitchen table while scrolling through her Instagram timeline. She came across a picture posted a few hours ago from Latrell. She cooed at the sight of her son smiling with a mouthful of pancakes. She quickly rolled her eyes when she read Latrell's caption:

Any ladies want to come meet me and my lil man at IHOP? His treat. LOL. #WePoppinAppleJuiceBottles #HeGetsMorePlayThanMe LOL.

Monica instantly regretted the other day when she approved his follower request. It took everything in her to follow him back. But she finally decided that they were both adults and didn't have to be so trivial. She couldn't believe how many women fell for his thirst-trap. They left heart-eyed emojis under his picture, offered to meet them, and a few even offered to babysit. Monica had to stop herself from responding under the picture. One girl even said she'd be "Mommy #2". Monica had just hit the comment bubble when her phone started to ring.

"Hello?" she answered.

"Why'd you tell Kyree that shit? Now his petty ass won't let it go!" Jaz started in.

Monica laughed. "I don't have time for you and Kyree's mess. We were supposed to take that shit to the grave, Jaz. I should kill you."

Jaz chuckled as she busied herself on her laptop. "Your brother irks my nerves. Now he wants to know what other shit he never knew about."

"And you better not tell him shit," Monica warned.

"Oh, I'd never tell him about that time he came home early from football practice when you made Marcus hide in the closet for three hours," Jaz whispered into the phone.

Monica laughed and Jaz followed after her. Growing up, they were close. Their closeness hadn't faltered in the almost twenty years they'd been friends. Which was why Jaz knew something was up with Monica.

"So, what's been up with you? Everything good?" Jaz pried.

Monica turned up her face. "Yes."

"Mo, I know you. What's going on with Mario?"

Monica rolled her eyes to the ceiling. Jaz didn't miss a beat. "We're good. But his homegirl is another story. When we're together, she's always calling him for something."

"Mo, I hate to say it, but you're going to have to trust Mario. He hasn't given you a reason not to, right?"

"Nah, he's a good guy," Monica admitted.

"Well then, let it go. And if the bitch gets out of line, kick her ass back in place."

Monica laughed and stuffed a spoonful of cereal in her mouth. "So what're you up doing anyway?"

"I'm at the computer going over a few last minute things for the hair show theme. Watch, when I'm finished, y'all are going to want to go with my idea this year," Jaz exclaimed.

"So what'd Kyree say about you going back to work?"

"Huh?"

Monica laughed. She knew what that meant.

"Shut up. He'll get over it. I can't stand being in this house, Mo. I'm going to go crazy."

Monica laughed, but Jaz was serious. She spent most of her day taking care of Kylee while Kyree went to work. When Kylee finally went to sleep, Jaz was tired, but too afraid to go to sleep because she knew she'd have to be up in a few minutes because Kylee didn't sleep long. It was a job that never ended. She loved spending time with Kylee more than anything, but she didn't want that to be her whole life. She wondered how housewives did it. Her number one priority was being a mother, but that wasn't her only priority. Doing hair gave her purpose. It was her true passion. She couldn't wait to get back to the salon.

"Hey, do you want to go to IHOP or Egg Bistro? I'm hungry," Jaz said.

"You're always hungry. And besides, I'm eating cereal now anyway."

"So? You'll be hungry again in five minutes."

Monica rolled her eyes. "Hold on, I have a beep." She clicked over and the caller instantly put a smile on her face.

"What you doin'?" Mario asked.

"Nothing. On the phone with Jaz."

"Oh, word? J-Money," he laughed. "But look, you want to go get breakfast right quick?"

"Kayden's on his way home in about an hour."

"That's cool. Bring 'em."

Monica smiled. She loved how attentive Mario was to Kayden.

He didn't see him as a burden or huff his breath when she couldn't find a sitter, or even put up a fuss when she had to cancel their plans to tend to him. He would make a day of it by bringing whatever they'd planned on doing for the day to Monica's house.

"Okay, I'll call you when we're ready." Monica ended the call and clicked back over to her other line. "I'm surprised you haven't hung up yet," she said to Jaz.

"I'm waiting on you to give me an answer."

"Oh, shit. I almost forgot you asked me too. Mario wants Kayden and me to go with him."

"Ugh! You ain't shit, Mo," Jaz playfully snapped.

Monica giggled. "Go with your fiancé."

"I will. And while we're eating, I'll be sure to tell him about the weed you dropped in the kitchen, and Ms. Jackie beat his ass because she thought it was his."

"Wait, what – " Monica couldn't even finish her sentence before Jaz had hung up the phone.

Monica tossed her bowl in the sink and went to get dressed. By the time she was zipping up her jeans, there was a knock at the door. She approached the door and stood on her tip toes to see through the peephole. She smiled and quickly opened the door.

"Hey, baby, I missed you," she admitted with open arms.

"Mommy!" Kayden screamed and clung to her leg. She reached down to pick him up. His little legs swung lightly in the wind as she hugged him tightly.

"Well hey to you too, Mo," Latrell snickered. He rubbed his hands together, trying to warm his body from the brisk February chill.

"Oh, hey, Latrell." Monica moved to the side to allow him entrance and then closed the door. "I just missed my baby, that's all." Monica smiled as she kissed Kayden all over his face.

"Mommy, put me down," Kayden giggled. Monica kissed him

one last time before putting him down. He hugged Latrell before taking off running into the house.

Latrell shook his head. "That boy is a handful."

"I am well aware. Trust me."

Latrell rolled his eyes. He knew he should have been around more while his son was growing up. But he was making up for it now.

"So, how've you been?" Latrell asked.

"I've been good." Monica nodded her head. She hated this part of their encounters. Latrell still wasn't one of her favorite people and their small talk was usually very awkward. "What about you?"

"I'm chillin'. You know me." He threw his hands in the air and clasped them together. He was sporting his Navy fatigues, on his way to work. "You look good."

Monica gave him the side eye. "Thanks."

Latrell couldn't control himself around Monica sometimes. Even in her jeans and plaid button up, she was the picture of perfection to him. He'd messed up his chances long ago with her, but that didn't stop him from shooting his shot. He was trying his hardest to flirt, but Monica wasn't biting his bait. So he decided to change the subject. "Ay, I meant to ask you if Kayden can go with me to my family reunion in Texas next month."

"For how long?"

"A week."

Monica's eyes grew big. That was a long time. She was just starting to get used to him leaving for the weekends. And even then she called constantly to make sure Kayden was okay. She gave a long sigh, "That's a long time, Latrell. I'll have to think about it."

Latrell licked his lips and nodded his head in understanding. "A'ight. Just let me know." He handed her Kayden's book bag before turning around to leave.

Monica closed the door behind him and shook her head. There was a time when she'd worshipped the ground Latrell walked on. Now, she couldn't get past the hurt. She'd forgiven him for the sake of their child, but she could never forget. He'd caused her so much hurt with the marriage he'd hidden from her and then he disappeared without so much as a phone call or any concern at all for the well-being of his child. Sure he was trying his best now, but the past was still very present and too close for Monica to completely let it go.

Monica finished getting dressed before Mario arrived. Since they weren't going anywhere special, she opted for minimal nude makeup and a red lip. She pulled the Peruvian bundles she'd sewn into her hair, in a ponytail. She accentuated her hair with purple highlights she'd decided to try the other day. As a stylist, she had to be on her a-game, so she was always trying something new.

An hour later, Mario was at her door to walk her to the car. She loved that about him. He didn't honk the horn or call her and tell her he was outside. No. Mario was a gentleman. He practiced chivalry like it was the latest fad.

Mario decided to go to Dave & Buster's instead of breakfast since they had Kayden and it was already after noon. Kayden was having so much fun. Monica loved seeing the look of excitement on his face. But she was worn out. So she sat down at the table, sipping on her mimosa while the boys played. The buzzing from Mario's phone instinctively caused her to glance over. She wasn't trying to be nosy, but she did see the message that came across.

>>>> **Shannon 1:15 PM: Thanks for everything last night, Booby.**

Monica rolled her eyes so hard that they seemed to disappear into her head for a moment. *Here she go with this Booby shit,* Monica said to herself. Sure, it was his nickname, and when Mario's mom called him that, Monica laughed because she thought it was cute. But whenever Shannon said it, Monica couldn't get past how close it was to "boo". She took a deep breath to calm herself. There were times when she had to remind herself to chill because she had a good man that actually cared for her and her son. It was a rarity, and Monica didn't want to do anything irrational to push him away.

Mario's phone screen had gone back to black when Monica looked up to see him approaching holding Kayden in the air like an airplane. Kayden was laughing so hard he was drooling. Monica laughed as Mario put him in the booster seat. Kayden sat down and finished the rest of his French fries while Monica secretly waited for Mario's reaction to the text message. She smirked when she saw him roll his eyes too.

"Man, this girl is crazy," he laughed. "Her nigga kicked her out in the middle of the night with nowhere to go, and she's back with the dude." Mario shook his head. "I can't with her ass, man."

"Let me ask you something," Monica spoke. Mario turned to face her. "Have any of the women you've dated in the past had a problem with Shannon?"

Mario was pretty sure this conversation would come eventually. And no, it definitely wasn't the first time so he was well prepared in what to say. The only difference being, this time, he actually gave a damn how Monica responded to the situation. "Listen, Mo, Shannon is like my hot-mess sister," he chuckled. "I don't, nor have I ever, seen her in that way. But I do look out for her, because she cool peoples."

Monica nodded her head and took another sip from her drink. She really regretted asking him. Although she didn't put anything past a man, Mario had yet to give her a reason not to trust him. She felt like an idiot, and didn't know what else to say.

"Just remember," Mario began. "You're my girlfriend, and she's my girl-friend. Most times I just tell women that have asked me, 'it is, what it is'. But you deserve more than that. I'm not here to hurt you, Mo," he assured her.

Mario's words were right on time, but Monica hadn't heard anything past girlfriend. They'd been dating for almost three months now, but they hadn't yet decided on a title. "Since when am I your girlfriend?" She perked up.

Mario shook his head. "Girl, you know you been bae since my mama gave you the last slice of pecan pie. The fact that I didn't go postal on my whole family should tell you that."

Monica cracked up laughing, remembering how he reacted when he saw her eating the pie a few Sundays ago when she went to meet his family. Mario gave her a quick peck on the cheek and Monica's heart melted.

Monica didn't know it, but Mario was really falling for her. He hoped she could get over Shannon. It hindered progress in a lot of his other relationships, but he was never as invested in those as he was with Monica. To Mario, Monica was like a breath of fresh air. Together they'd laugh, talk about current events, music, and even their goals. When he told her about his dream to open up his own service and repair shop, she didn't just tell him to "go for it" just because it sounded like the right thing to say. She encouraged him to pursue it. She helped him talk to the right people, and he was now in the process of one day working for himself.

Monica tugged on a loose dread, a habit she'd acquired since they'd been dating, and ushered him toward her. She kissed him sweetly on the lips and Kayden covered his eyes and giggled.

"You're a hater, Kay," Mario laughed.

After lunch, Kayden was exhausted and long overdue for a nap. He fell asleep as soon as they pulled away from Dave & Busters. Mario carried him in the house and put him in his bed and then he joined Monica on the couch to watch Netflix. Monica had recently gotten him hooked on the show *Ozark*. He was skeptical at first, but after two episodes, he was hooked. As Monica rested her head on his chest, she cherished the current calmness in her life. She wished it could be like this forever. As soon as she started feeling comfortable, Mario's phone started to ring in his pocket. When she saw Shannon's name, her jaw tightened.

Mario looked at the message and put his phone away. "She'll be a'ight," he nonchalantly mentioned. He looked down at Monica to pick up on her mood. She didn't look at him and he knew she'd seen the message that read: **Booby, let's go get something to eat. I'm hungry! LOL**

"You a'ight though?" he asked.

Monica nodded her head, but on the inside, she was losing it. She wasn't sure how much of this would be too much for her to stand. She just hoped she figured it out before she got too invested and someone got hurt.

CHAPTER FIVE

J az gleefully strutted around the kitchen preparing breakfast. It was Tuesday and she was finally going back to work after being out for nearly two months. She started singing and dancing to Rod Wave's "Heart on Ice" as Kylee looked on in her swing.

Kyree walked in to see what the commotion was all about. He laughed at the sight before him. Jaz was flipping pancakes, wearing only a T-shirt while trying to rap the words she barely knew to Kylee.

"You gotta chill," he laughed, breaking her out of her song and dance. She had no idea he was standing there.

"Shut up," she blushed. After knowing him for nearly twenty years, he still managed to make her nervous. It was the kind of nervous that gave her goosebumps, as if she were meeting him for the first time and falling in love instantly. He sat down at the table as she fixed him a plate. "Okay, here's your food. I have to go get ready." She kissed him and Kylee and made her way to the shower.

Kyree had stopped hassling Jaz about going back to work.

They'd worked out a set schedule so that they could both be home at a decent hour each day. Kyree would drop the baby off during the weekday with Ms. Johnson, who still lived across the street from Jackie, Friday was date night, Saturday was their day to spend separately with their friends, and they promised that Sunday would always be family day. Kyree agreed to the schedule, partially because it made her happy, and also because he felt guilty. If Jaz knew about Kendall, she was sure to fuck up everybody's world. But Kendall did PR for one of the biggest record labels in the area, so when she approached him about business, Kyree was down without hesitation. He just hoped Jaz saw things the same way. He knew he had to tell her; he just wasn't sure how.

Thirty minutes later, Jaz was dressed and ready to head out. "How do I look?" She did a full spin so that Kyree could take in her whole outfit.

With Kylee in his arms, Kyree nodded his head in approval. Jaz wore a white shirt with a black blazer, black form-fitting pants, and a pair of black knee-high flat boots. Her hair was curled and pinned up into a Mohawk and she'd accessorized with nothing but a deep lipstick and her beaming engagement ring.

"Mommy leaving us, Lee." Kyree pretended to sob.

"Awwww." Jaz hugged him from behind. "Kyree, don't be mad. I promise every day I'll do like we agreed: no appointments after 5:00 so that I can be home by seven to make your dinner, burp your baby, and suck your dick," she smirked.

Kyree sucked his teeth. "Real funny, man."

Jaz laughed and kissed him on the cheek. She placed her bag on the counter and rummaged through it so that she could make sure she didn't leave anything behind.

Kyree licked his lips and sighed. "Can I tell you something?"

Jaz didn't even look up from her bag. The tone had changed in his voice and she already wasn't feeling where this conversation was going. "Is it going to make me mad before work?"

"It shouldn't."

Jaz sucked her teeth. She knew that answer usually meant that it would. "What is it, Kyree?" She still hadn't looked at him as she rolled up her curling wand and put it in her bag.

"Well, the big deal I've been working on was set up by someone you know." Jaz looked up at him, now intrigued by what he had to say. "Kendall, from high school, does PR for Solo Entertainment. She set everything up to allow the artist's studio time at The Shop whenever they're in town."

Jaz's lips were pursed. She thought she'd heard the last from Kendall over ten years ago. The business was the furthest thing from Jaz's mind. Her main concern was what Kendall had up her sleeve. She doubted time had changed that much about her. But time had, in some way, changed Jaz. She no longer concerned herself with petty matters such as the next chick stealing what was hers. If it was that easy, she could have him. Besides, she trusted Kyree. They'd come so far in their relationship that she knew he respected her and wouldn't do anything to jeopardize their family.

Jaz zipped up her bag, threw it over her shoulder, and approached him. "It's cool, babe." She reached up to kiss him on the lips.

Kyree was utterly surprised. "You sure?"

Jaz kissed Kylee too. "Yeah. That shit happened years ago. I'm over it. So go make that money. I want a big-ass reality TV type wedding." She beamed. Kyree laughed as she headed out the door. She stuck her head back inside the house to speak. "And make sure you don't have my baby going to daycare looking a mess." Kyree waved her off. "I'm serious, Kyree. She's already been dressed, fed, burped, and changed. Just do a double check of her face before you drop her off."

"Okay. Bye, Jaz." Kyree got up to shut the door – but not before Jaz opened it again.

"Oh, and double check with Ms. Johnson to make sure she has my cell number and the number to the salon."

"Okay. Bye."

She pushed through the door again. "And please make sure she has on her hat. It's cold outside."

"Bye, Jaz!" Kyree yelled, annoyed.

Jaz poked out her lip and kissed Kylee one last time. She didn't realize leaving her would be this hard. She was eager to get out of the house at first, but now she felt like she wanted to stay with Kylee and never let her out of her sight until she turned eighteen. She somberly turned around to walk down the stairs. When she got to her car, she looked up to see Kyree and Kylee at the window, waving goodbye. It made her smile from ear to ear seeing their faces. She blew them an air kiss, and instantly felt better about her day.

When Jaz arrived at the salon, she was greeted with open arms. She wasn't even fully in the door when everyone approached to hug and congratulate her. A few of them had stopped by to see her since her absence, but some hadn't seen her in months. When Jaz finally approached the small platform stage that housed her station, she was in total awe. It was covered in pink. Different baby items surrounded her station, making it impossible for her to work without moving it. She held her mouth as she perused the playpens, clothes, toys, and tray filled with pink cookies. She grabbed a cookie before opening anything.

Ms. Ray laughed, "Girl, sit your fat ass down so we can watch you open up these gifts." Everyone laughed and Jaz rolled her eyes. Ms. Ray moved a box out of her chair so that she could sit down and open her gifts. Jaz had Kylee before she could have her baby shower, so the whole staff was at the salon early to watch and celebrate with her. When Jaz was done, she had to call Kyree to tell him to come pick up everything before he went home for the day.

Jaz's first client was due in any minute so she called Ms. Johnson to check on Kylee - the first call of what she knew would be many.

"Hello?" Ms. Johnson answered.

"Hi, Ms. Johnson. It's Jaz."

"Girl, I know who you are. I gots the caller ID."

Jaz rolled her eyes. Ms. Johnson was always putting "the" in front of nouns. "How's she doing?"

"Well, she hasn't been here long enough to be doing much of anything. Hell, I ain't even got the girl's coat off and you're calling already. And why y'all don't have no snowsuit on the baby? She like to caught the pneumonia outside in this chill."

Jaz instantly regretted calling. Ms. Johnson got on Jaz's nerves growing up, but she was the only one she trusted with her child. She also watched Kayden, and Monica swore by her. Jaz remembered how Ms. Johnson kept the whole neighborhood in check back in the day and at sixty years old, she hadn't lost a step. She was also the only one Jaz knew with nothing else to do but sit in the house and never work. They often joked that she was paid to be the neighborhood detective.

"Okay, Ms. Johnson. I'll call back around lunchtime. Talk to you later."

"I don't know why? Hell, the girl will be fine then too -" Ms. Johnson continued to ramble on to herself about absolutely nothing before finally hanging up.

Jaz laughed to herself and took a deep breath. She could tell dealing with Ms. Johnson was going to be like deja vu. As she was putting on her smock Tori, one of the stylists, approached her.

"Hey, mama," Tori greeted her with a hug.

"Hey, girl." Jaz smiled.

"Did you like all your stuff?" Tori asked.

"Did I?" Jaz beamed. "I had to put it in the back until Kyree could come take it home. Thanks for the outfits. She's going to look so cute."

"It's nothing. You better take some pics of her in them."

Jaz laughed as Tori stood in front of her with an awkward look on her face. Jaz hoped Tori said something quick, because out of everyone in the salon, Jaz rarely spoke to Tori.

"Um, I wanted to talk to you about Asia."

Jaz's nostrils flared at the mention of Asia's name. Tori wasn't close with anyone at the salon except Asia when she was there. They weren't that similar. Tori was actually laid back, in her own world. But Tori was more like Asia's flunky. Her head was usually so far up Asia's ass that Jaz wondered if she ever had a thought of her own.

"What about her?" Jaz dryly asked.

"She was my girl, but I didn't think she'd ever do something like that. I knew she was sick, but I didn't know it was *that* extreme." Tori could tell that Jaz was waiting for her to get to the point. "I just wanted you to know that I thought what she did was really fucked up and if I knew where she was, I'd tell you. But I haven't seen her since it happened."

Jaz nodded her head, but she didn't know if Tori was completely being honest with her. "It's cool, Tori. That shit is so far behind me now. The police will find her soon enough. But thanks for having my back," Jaz said as she gave her a warm hug. Jaz didn't need Tori anyhow. She knew Asia would come out of hiding soon enough. She was too attention-hungry not to.

The rest of the day went by smoothly. Jaz had her last client at 5:00 and by 6:30, she was heading out to pick up Kylee. She was dead tired, but when she saw Kylee's face, she perked right up. She picked up Kayden too and dropped him off to his mother at the salon. This arrangement worked out perfectly for Monica.

By 7:15, Jaz had finally made it home. She prepared dinner, gave Kylee a bath, fed her, and by the time she was done, Kyree was coming in the house and she was taking the garlic bread to go with the spaghetti out of the oven. Jaz was no Stepford wife, but by the time she got off work, she came pretty close.

"How was your day?" she asked as they sat down to dinner.

"It was a'ight. Missed y'all though," he admitted as he gave a now-sleeping Kylee a kiss on the cheek. "I cut heads until about 5:00, headed over to see what they were doing in the studio, met with a few producers who want permanent slots too. It's turning out to be very lucrative. One of the producers wants to meet with me to discuss some investment opportunities with a new restaurant he's thinking about opening up."

Jaz listened intently. She was happy hear that the path Kyree was taking was leading him into enough money for a legal hustle. Worrying about him all day was not something she could handle at this point in her life.

"What about you?" he questioned.

"I did six heads and Mo made me do a few nail appointments." Jaz rolled her eyes. "She knows I hate doing nails. But until we find someone to fill Asia's spot, she and I have to rotate." Jaz was good at doing nails. Hell, she and Mo could do them just as well as Asia. But they lacked the drive to do so. Hair was their thing; always had been. "Oh, and I talked to a wedding planner. We just have to set a date."

Kyree nodded his head as he took a sip from his drink. They hadn't really discussed the wedding, but Kyree didn't care. He'd marry Jaz at the courthouse tomorrow if he thought she'd be down for it. But he knew it was her dream to have a big wedding filled with family and friends. Whatever made her happy made him happy.

"How about June?" he offered.

Jaz looked at him crazy. "The hair show is in June. And besides, that's a little too soon. And July won't work because it'll be too much stress after the show. What about the end of August?"

Kyree agreed. He knew he had no real say-so anyhow. "That'll work."

Jaz was elated. "You sure you wanna marry me?" She beamed.

"Nah, not really," he joked.

"Shut up." She laughed as she kicked him under the table.

"Nah, for real. I've been ready for a long time now." Kyree watched her smile light up as he thought back to the time he went to New York to make a run, and was sent to jail for three years. On his way home to Virginia, he was going to purchase an engagement ring from a jeweler up there. When he got locked up, he ended up breaking it off with Jaz because he thought he was looking at way more time. His own stupidity had caused him to lose her for three years back then and he wanted to cherish every second he had with her now. Even times like this, where they could sit and talk, he cherished them like each conversation was the last he'd ever have with her.

For about a month, Jaz and Kyree stuck to a pretty good schedule. But, gradually, Kyree started to come home later. By the time he did make it in, his dinner was cold and Jaz was already in bed for the night. Their family Sundays were even spent less and less together. Jaz had finally had enough, and when Kyree got home at 11:00 that night, she was up waiting for him in the living room.

"Damn, Jazzy. What are you doing up?" Kyree asked, surprised.

"We need to talk."

Kyree rolled his eyes to the ceiling and instantly started

thinking of what he could have done wrong. "What's on ya mind?" He plopped down on the couch next to her.

"We haven't been spending any time together lately," she somberly spoke.

"What are talking about? We just went to Chick-fil-a last night," he joked.

Jaz pushed him in the arm. "I'm serious, Kyree!"

He laughed. "A'ight, I hear you."

"I just feel so overwhelmed. I'm starting to think the wedding planner thinks I'm actually marrying my damn self."

Kyree laughed, but quickly changed his attitude when he saw the seriousness on her face. "I've just been busy. I'm trying to stack this money so that you can have the wedding you want."

"Now you know we're good with the money for the wedding. Don't try to blame you not being here on that."

Kyree huffed. This was one of those arguments he knew he wasn't going to win so to appease her, he gave in. "A'ight, how about this? We get Mo to watch Kylee and we spend the whole day together tomorrow. We can play hooky." When Jaz wrapped her arms around Kyree's neck and kissed him, he knew he had to find a way to make this work. His whole week was crazy busy, but tomorrow wasn't so bad. After moving a few things around, he was able to make it happen.

The next day, Jaz and Kyree spent the whole day together. They went shopping, to the movies, and Kyree even met the wedding planner. They ate breakfast, lunch, and finally dinner together at The Cheesecake Factory. Kyree knew cheesecake was her weakness and it was the perfect place to tell her that he had to cut their evening short. There were some important people at The Barbershop who wanted to meet him about possibly opening up another location. It fucked him up because he really was having a good day with Jaz and he was expecting some ass later. This was definitely going to fuck that up for him.

"Bae, this shit is fuckin' clutch," she boasted as she ate the chocolate cheesecake, slowly taking the fork out of her mouth. "You must want some ass tonight, huh?" She smirked at him.

He gave an uncomfortable laugh. *Fuck! She's gonna kill my ass when I tell her this shit,* he thought to himself.

Once they were in the car, Kyree asked, "You want to go pick up Kylee?"

Jaz looked at him skeptically. "For what? Mo said she could stay the night."

"Oh, yeah. That's right."

When they pulled up to the house, Jaz got out of the car, but Kyree didn't. She looked at him, and his ashamed expression said it all. She shook her head and slammed the door. She marched away from the car. Kyree could tell by the switch of her hips that she was pissed. He thought about going in after her, but he knew she needed time to cool off. His being there wasn't going to help. So, he pulled away from the house and headed to his shop.

It was only 8:00 and Jaz was seeing red. She couldn't believe that Kyree had cut their day short to go to work. His businesses always seemed to take over his life. Before it was the streets, and now it was everything else. Kyree wanted to get his hands into everything. He was a silent partner in a club, he owned a barbershop and a music studio, and he was in talks about a restaurant.

"I wish he'd sit his ass down somewhere," Jaz said aloud to herself as she sipped her third glass of red wine. An hour and two more glasses of wine later, Jaz had taken a shower and was resting in her bed. Kyree strolled in around 11:30 and Jaz hadn't even noticed. He showered and climbed in the bed with her, surprised to see that all she had on was a T-shirt with nothing underneath. He slid his hand between her legs and played with the lips of her clit. Jaz's eyes opened as she realized what was happening. The feeling was stimulating, but she couldn't let him have it that easy after the stunt he pulled.

"Move," she protested, moving his hand.

"Come on, Jazzy. I'm sorry." He kissed the nape of her neck and she jerked away. "Look, I know you didn't go to bed with no clothes on for nothing."

"Hmph." Truth was, she was horny after all of that wine, but she wanted him to work for it. Kyree was already hip to her game. He continued to kiss and suck every inch of her body until his face was planted right between her legs. Jaz could no longer protest. She spread her legs and allowed him to feast on her kitty until her body went limp. "Shiiiiiiit," she moaned when he was done.

"You still mad?" he questioned as he positioned himself on top. Jaz didn't speak. She was too weak to go through this with him right now. He placed one of her legs across his shoulder and worked her insides. "You still mad, huh?" he asked as he sped up the pace.

"Noooooo," Jaz whimpered. He smiled because he had her right where he wanted her.

He hit her with one last stroke, forcing her stomach to convulse and him to grunt. "Uhnnnn!" He kissed her behind the ear, causing her to let out one last sweet sigh. Kyree lay on his side and pulled her in closely.

"Kyree, I'm still mad. We have to do better, baby." Kyree rolled his eyes as she spoke. "Sex can't fix everything." She turned over on her side to face him. "Home by 9:00 every day."

"But, what if - "

"Nope. No later than 9:00," she stressed.

Kyree nodded his head and rested her on his chest. He really hated their after-fuck talks, as he secretly referred to them in his head. Jaz could make him agree to sell his soul to the devil if she promised to throw some ass his way. He laughed to himself at the thought as he drifted off to sleep.

One Monday, Jaz dressed Kylee and put her in her car seat. "Daddy's been such a good boy lately. I think he deserves a surprise," Jaz said to Kylee as she cooed in her seat. For a few weeks now, Kyree had been coming home at a decent hour every weekday like they had agreed on. Jaz was happy. She knew it was hard for him to pull away from business, so she and Kylee were headed to the shop to surprise him with lunch and company.

Dressed comfortably in jeans with the matching denim jacket, a pair of wheat Timbs, and her hair pulled into a cute messy bun, Jaz was headed to see her man. When she arrived, the guys in the barbershop said he was next door in his office. Jaz walked over, pushing Kylee in her stroller. She wasted no time and went straight to Kyree's office. The door was shut, so she knocked first.

"Come in," she heard him say.

Jaz opened the door with her elbow, her back facing Kyree as she pulled the stroller in. "We came to surprise you," she beamed. She turned around to see that Kyree wasn't alone. In his office was Fat Boy, and someone she hadn't seen in ages.

"Hey, Jazmine!" Kendall jumped up from her seat to hug her.

Jaz reluctantly hugged her in return, still taken aback by her presence. "Hey, Kendall."

"Oh my gosh, you haven't changed a bit, girl," Kendall boasted.

"Neither have you," Jaz returned her enthusiasm. But as she sized her up she noticed that Kendall had, in fact, changed a lot. Her ass and breasts were out of this world in her red pencil skirt and white halter, her lips were plump, her nose was slightly pointier, and in Jaz's expert opinion, she wore at least thirty-two inches of Malaysian straight in her hair. Plastic surgery had turned her into the perfect reality star.

"OMG, is this little Kyree?" Kendall bent down to get a better view.

"Hey, baby." Kyree got up from behind his desk to greet her with a hug and a kiss. He could see that Kendall was the last person in the world she expected to see. "Kendall, Fat Boy, and I were just talking about the rapper K.O. He's in town and might come through."

Kendall spoke up. "Yeah, he's an old friend."

Jaz rolled her eyes in her mind. "That's what's up! I'm happy for you, babe."

"Ay, thanks for lunch. You didn't have to do that." Kyree grabbed the bag. He couldn't wait to dig into the Thai food from his favorite restaurant. Jaz never came by his place of business, so he couldn't wait to show off his family. "Come on, Lee," he picked her up from her car seat.

"Y'all go ahead. Jaz and I have to catch up." Kendall dismissed them.

Kyree was reluctant at first, but Jaz nodded her head, so he and Fat Boy left.

"So, I hear you and Mo are still doing hair. I heard y'all can slay," Kendall boasted.

Jaz snickered. "Yeah we're still doing hair. Full salon and spa downtown. You should stop by some time," Jaz lied. "Ky told me you're into public relations now. That's fantastic, girl."

"Yeah. You know I got tired of modeling. Wanted to do my own thing."

I'd hardly call that one Target ad you had modeling. But, okay, Jaz thought to herself. She'd heard about Kendall's stint on *The Bad Girl's Club*. She was kicked off for fighting after only three episodes. And now she just got her rocks off by dating rappers and being InstaFamous.

"Oh yeah, I heard you were doing big shit in New York," Jaz said.

"Yeah, girl. I can't believe you and Ky are still together. I'm happy for you guys. You're all he talked about when he was locked up."

"Um, excuse me?" Jaz's ears perked up. She was sure she'd misunderstood her.

"You know. You were all he talked about when I used to visit him while I was staying in New York."

Jaz instantly started feeling lightheaded. She couldn't believe what she was hearing. Kendall was still going on and on, but Jaz had temporarily gone deaf. It was like she had an out of body experience where she momentarily left her body to go kill Kyree. Her face was straight, but her mind was going over the many ways she could murder him without getting caught.

"Ay, baby, them niggas say my baby look Asian. You got something to tell me?" He laughed.

"No. But do you have anything you want to tell me?" She stood with a slight scowl on her face and Kyree instantly got a lump in his throat. He had no idea what was bothering her, but the look she gave him pretty much said he'd done something wrong. Jaz started to laugh. "Kendall was just telling me about the time the lady snapped off on her baby's father and one of the CO's had to subdue her." Jaz and Kendall were laughing hysterically at the parts of Kendall's story that Jaz had managed to hear. Kyree, on the other hand, was sweating bullets. He didn't know why Kendall would bring up such a thing.

"Oh, yeah." He gave a nervous laugh.

Jaz took Kylee from Kyree's arms and placed her in her stroller. "Sorry to cut this reunion short, Kendall, but Kylee has to go down for her nap. Say bye to Daddy, Kylee." Kyree bent down to kiss

Kylee and then Jaz turned her cheek and motioned for him to kiss her as well. He reluctantly did as she turned to leave.

"Hold up a sec," he called out to her down the hall. Jaz kept walking, not bothering to turn around. He caught up to her and grabbed her arm. She quickly cut her eyes at him.

"Don't you fuckin' touch me!" she seethed through her teeth. Her nostrils were flaring and Kyree could see her heart beating through her shirt. He released her arm and let her go. He rubbed his chin as he watched her get in the car. He had no idea how he was going to come back from this one.

"Fuck!" he barked under his breath. Jaz was too calm. He knew it was going to be hell when he got home.

CHAPTER SIX

Kyree took the long way home. He needed time to think of how he was going to explain this to Jaz. In his defense, he hadn't technically lied to her; he just neglected mentioning a few things. Jaz and Kendall had never quite gotten along so he didn't want to bring up any bad memories. The fact that he'd kept this from Jaz would only make things worse than what they actually were. In reality, he was just locked up and lonely in a city far away from his home, and Kendall just happened to be close by. She reached out to Fat Boy, who got word to Kyree to put her on his visitor's list. He had planned on telling Jaz...eventually. But Jaz heard it from Kendall, not him, which only made matters worse. Kyree had tried calling her several times since lunch, but each time he was met with one ring and then her voicemail. It was evident that she was intentionally ignoring his calls.

Kyree looked up to their apartment window and he could see the light on. He took a long breath before walking up the stairs. Once inside, he wasn't met with his usual feeling. Usually, Jaz and

Kylee would be on the couch waiting for him and the smell of dinner would hit him before he entered the house. But not this time. He could hear the TV on in the bedroom and Jaz talking on the phone. He walked in the kitchen to see empty McDonald's bags and uncooked food on the stove. It looked like she had started to cook, but then changed her mind. Chicken was unthawed in the sink and green beans were in a pot that had never been turned on.

"Shit!" Kyree slowly tugged at his beard. He made his way toward the bedroom. Jaz was lying down, Kylee was fast asleep in her swing, and he was surprised to see Kayden there as well.

"Uncle Ky!" Kayden yelled, running into his arms.

"Wassup, Kay!" Kyree pretended to box with him and Kayden laughed as he held up his fist like Kyree had taught him. Kyree tickled him and tossed him on the bed and Kayden broke out into hysterics. Kyree laughed, then looked over at Jaz. She was still on the phone, and hadn't bothered looking at him since he'd walked in the room. He nudged her foot and she gave him an evil glare. He sucked his teeth, grabbed a few things to shower and a blanket, and headed to the couch.

"Was that Kyree?" Monica asked Jaz on the phone.

"Yep," Jaz nonchalantly said.

"Sooooo, are y'all going to talk about the shit that happened?"

"Nope."

"Ooooookay," Monica said, instantly regretting she asked. She hated getting involved in their relationship because she always felt conflicted. Kyree was her brother and Jaz was her best friend. There was no winning.

"So," Jaz changed the subject. "What are you and Mario about to get into?"

"Um, Mario has tickets to the Kevin Hart show, and then we're going to dinner. Thanks again for taking Kay for the night."

"Girl, you know there's always a spot at Aunt Joss house for my Kay-Man. Besides, he'll be the only man in this bed for a while."

Monica laughed. "You don't mean that. What're you going to say to him anyway?"

Jaz sighed heavily. "I don't know, Mo. I'm just so hurt, I don't know what to do. I just need some time to think before I snap off."

"Well, don't go creating your own theories until you've talked to him."

Jaz nodded her head. "I hear ya."

"Oh, that's my door. Gotta go. Kiss my baby for me."

Monica hung up the phone and gave herself one last glance in the mirror. She wore a pair of cut up blue jeans, a long white fitted shirt, and tan fringe heels. Her now jet-black hair was flat-ironed bone straight and her makeup consisted of a slightly-dramatic eye and a nude lip. The weather was pretty nice, but she grabbed her navy blue blazer just in case. Mario was laying on her doorbell as she took her time getting ready. She rolled her eyes, grabbed her purse, and headed down the stairs.

When she opened the door Mario looked her up and down, and then licked his lips. He brought her in for a hug and then whispered in her ear, "You look good, ma."

"Thank you, baby. You do too," she admitted, admiring his fresh edge-up, neatly locked dreads pulled into a ponytail, dark blue jeans, black button up shirt, and all black Jordan 11s. His hug was strong and his scent was invigorating. Monica never wanted to let go.

"Yo, we can skip the show and sit in the house and watch Netflix," he suggested with a wink.

Monica laughed. She knew they would never get through a movie at home without having sex before the opening credits. Monica looked good tonight and she wanted to go out.

"Ha! Real funny. But let's go." She pushed him out of the house.

He watched her lock the door and his eyes roamed to her ass. "Damn. Can't blame a man for trying."

Monica hopped into Mario's black Infiniti truck and Mario shut her door. She started flicking with his radio and when he got inside, he playfully smacked her hand.

"Don't you know not to touch a black man's radio?" Monica threw her hands up in surrender. "I got this," he said as he roamed through his phone for the perfect playlist. "What you think about this?"

Monica burst out laughing as Mario started to sing. "Making my way downtown, walking fast, faces pass, and I'm homebound."

Mario always found a way to make Monica laugh. Whenever they were together, they always had a good time, and tonight was no different. They laughed their asses off at Kevin Hart, had dinner at Texas de Brazil, and walked along the waterfront. Neither of them wanted the night to end.

"A'ight, you got a nigga walking and doing shit like it's senior prom 2005," Mario joked as they approached the car.

Monica laughed. "And what's wrong with that?" She stood at the car door as he held it open.

"Nothing," Mario admitted. "I actually like this. You're really changing me. Makes me feel like I want to settle down."

Monica blushed. It always made her feel good when Mario revealed his feelings to her. In past relationships, she often felt like she was the one putting in all of the effort and seeing no results. But with Mario, things just fell into place.

Monica kissed him passionately, gently biting his bottom lip as she pulled away. "Let's go to your house," Monica suggested.

Mario nervously rubbed his hand on the back of his neck. "Nah, I was thinking we could go to yours."

"Why? Yours is closer." She looked at him skeptically.

He sighed heavily. "Shan asked if she could stay at my place tonight. Her new spot won't be ready until next week, and her mom was getting on her nerves."

"Mario, are you kidding me right now?" Monica snapped.

Mario had never heard her so vocal, but Monica was tired of holding it in. She wouldn't be herself if she let it slide.

"What's wrong? She like family."

"Mario, what kind of woman would I be if I let my man have slumber parties with other women?"

"But it's not even like that," he promised.

"I understand. And I trust you. But I don't know her, and it makes me uncomfortable."

Mario nodded his head. He understood where she was coming from. He liked how strong-willed Monica could be. She was accepting of his friendship with Shannon, for the most part, so he felt obliged to honor her request.

"Well, I can't kick her out."

"And I'm not asking you to. When will her place be ready?"

"Five days from now."

"Okay. Well, you can stay at my place until then."

Mario reluctantly agreed. He'd stayed at Monica's before, but never longer than a day or two. He liked living on his own. But as the thought of in-house ass rolled across his mind, it suddenly didn't sound so bad playing house for a while.

The decision wasn't an easy one for Monica. She too liked living on her own. But the thought of Mario being that close to Shannon made her skin crawl. She knew they said they were just friends, but something still didn't sit right with her about it.

Monica needed to vent and she was happy that Jaz was at the salon early the next morning. Jaz's suggestion was that Monica and Shannon really didn't know each other. She and Shannon were going to have to have a long talk and set some ground rules if there was ever going to be any trust between them. Monica always appreciated Jaz's advice, but she could see in her eyes that she was going through it too. Jaz still hadn't talked to Kyree, and Monica could tell that she was distracted.

"Talk to him, J," Monica stressed.

Jaz knew Monica was right, but she wasn't sure she was ready to hear what he had to say. She'd left so early, he didn't even know she was gone. While he was still sleeping, Jaz took Kylee and Kayden and left before he tried to talk to her. Being at work always helped her to put things into prospective. When she was styling, her mind was focused. By 1:00, she'd done four heads and was finally taking a break in the back office.

"Ay!" She called out, when she saw Ms. Ray walk past her. "Are you going to get lunch?"

"Nope. I went last time."

Jaz sucked her teeth. "I hate you."

"Ask your baby daddy. He's walking in now." Ms. Ray smirked at Jaz. "Ooooh, he got treats!" Ms. Ray dashed up to the front while Jaz frantically thought of how she could escape without him seeing her.

Kyree set down two dozen donuts from Happy Day Donuts on the receptionist desk. They had some of the best cake donuts around and the whole shop loved them - especially Jaz.

"Thank you, Ky!" they all said in unison.

Kyree coolly nodded his head and then walked over to Monica. By the look on her face, he knew Jaz had already told her what happened. "Hey, Mo." He hugged her and gave her a kiss on the cheek.

"You think you're slick, huh?" She smirked, hinting at his bribe.

He chuckled. "Where is she?"

Monica motioned toward the back and Kyree headed that way. When he walked in the office, Jaz was styling a mannequin head. He placed the half dozen box he'd brought just for her on the table. He knew her favorites: Oreo & cream cheese, cinnamon apple, and chocolate with sprinkles. She had yet to acknowledge his presence, and Kyree wanted to see how long she'd last. He closed the door, and posted up on the wall with his arms folded, staring her down.

When he had woken up to see her gone, he was shocked. Every morning he took Kylee to daycare on his way to work. Jaz usually woke him up, but not this time. She was out of the house before 9:00. He walked over to her and her heart stopped. His presence still made her weak, but she was too pissed off with him to give him the satisfaction of letting him know he existed.

"So this is one of the styles y'all been working on for the hair show, huh?" Jaz nodded. Kyree circled around her as he admired the big spiked blonde hair. "This definitely looks like something from the movie *BAPS*." Jaz had been studying the movie for weeks, trying to incorporate todays fashion and style from that of when the movie came out. They were sure to take home the grand prize this year.

"Kyree, what do you want?" Jaz finally spoke, not bothering to look at him.

"To talk."

"You've been home for a year now. You've had plenty of time to *talk* to me."

"Cut it out," he warned.

"Pish!" Jaz rolled her eyes.

Kyree shook his head. He knew this wasn't the place. "Look, I'll pick up Lee from daycare, and when you get home, I'll explain everything. A'ight?" She wouldn't look at him, so he turned her chin toward him. "A'ight?" He stated more firmly.

Jaz sucked her teeth. "A'ight. Just go."

He pulled her chin toward his and kissed her. When she didn't return his affection, he looked at her sideways. Jaz knew he wouldn't leave easily. She exhaled deeply, and kissed him back. He turned to leave and picked up the box of donuts.

"Kyree! Leave the damn donuts!" she barked.

He smirked and dropped the donuts back on the desk. "Don't spoil your appetite. Lunch just arrived."

Jaz looked at him suspiciously, and then she heard the commotion in the front. She made her way through all of the staff and clients, to see Fat Boy bringing in an array of different goody trays from Chick-Fil-A: chicken strips, salad, wraps, fries, and fruit.

"Kyree!" Ms. Ray called out to him with food in hand. "We love when you fuck up." He saluted him with a chicken strip and everyone fell out laughing. Kyree just shook his head and he and Fat Boy made their exit.

Once he was gone, Jaz didn't hesitate to grab a plate and fill it with everything in sight. Ms. Ray whispered in her ear, "So what, you sucked a nigga dick for a chicken strip, or nah?" She elbowed him in the chest, almost causing him to drop his food. "You play too much."

Lunch was great, but that didn't mean Jaz and Kyree were good. The food fixed the pang in her stomach, but it did little for the pain in her heart. Jaz was still heated. The thought of him and Kendall kept popping up in her head. The more she thought about it, the more upset she became.

Around 7:00, she came in the house to the smell of Chinese food. Kyree wasn't a great cook, but he knew her better than anyone. Chinese was her favorite. She grabbed a shrimp egg roll, and sat at the kitchen table. Kyree walked out of the bedroom comfortably dressed in a pair of gray Nike sweats and a black T-shirt.

"Kylee sleep?" she asked.

"Nah. I dropped her at my mom's house. We needed some time alone."

He grabbed two plates and filled them with rice and General Tso's chicken. Just as he dropped the last piece of meat on her plate, Jaz broke down.

"Why, Kyree? Huh?" She was on the verge of tears.

"Jaz, I didn't mean for you to find out that way. Kendall was out of line for telling you the way she did."

"In her mind, I'm sure she was justified." Jaz blinked back a tear before it could fall from her face. "Besides, you should have told me a long time ago. You don't know how that shit made me feel. I would've been there for you through it all, but you pushed me away and welcomed her in."

It really hurt Jaz to find out Kendall was on Kyree's visitor's list and she wasn't. Kyree took Jaz's name off his list after he broke up with her through a letter. He said he didn't want to hurt her and hold her back from a better life by making her wait for him. Jaz cried for a whole year over him. She wrote him every day, but he never responded. Finally, she intercepted one of his calls to Monica while she was in the bathroom. Although he was surprised to hear her on the line, his heart had been pounding inside just from the sound of her voice. She made him promise to put her on the visitor's list, and she told him she would be there that weekend. Jaz racked up $600 on a flight and when she got there, she wasn't on the list. She demanded to see him until the CO's escorted her out of the building. Jaz had been so embarrassed.

Now she was finding out that Kendall got HER time. It was crushing to her soul. She longed to talk to him when she was having a bad day. She missed his laugh, his smile, the way he always made her feel safe, and most importantly, his presence. Jaz didn't understand how he could leave her stuck without him.

It was the hardest thing Kyree ever had to do. He kept all of her letters, although he never wrote her back. She had his heart way in Virginia, but with the time he was looking at, he didn't want her waiting around for him. A lot of men in prison felt like they were the shit because they had a Trap Queen, a ride-or-die, a down-ass chick. But not Kyree. That shit wasn't cool to him. As a man, his woman was supposed to be his queen, and he her king. In his eyes, he couldn't be the man that she deserved if he couldn't provide for her. Eventually, Jaz would have started to hate him for keeping her trapped, so he had to let her go.

She'd been to visit him a few times in the beginning but the last time, he swore it would be the last. The look of pain and hurt in her eyes when he saw her, confirmed that he couldn't continue to hold her back. She deserved someone who could give her the world, something he couldn't offer her in prison. But, after his lawyer found a loophole in the search warrant and Kyree's sentence was reduced to three years, he vowed to get Jaz back. Now that he had, he never wanted to do anything to jeopardize it.

"Jazzy, if I gave a fuck about Kendall, she would have never been allowed to visit me either. But I was bored. Everyone I knew was miles away. When Kendall found out we were both in the same city, she reached out, and I added her to my list." He wouldn't dare tell her that Fat Boy was responsible for the linkup. She cared about him like a brother, and that would most surely put a damper on their relationship. Jaz just shook her head, trying to process the information she'd been given. "And we haven't fucked around like that since high school, if that's what you're thinking."

Jaz's eyes shot up and she glared at him. "Kyree, if I even thought for a second that was what's going on, then your shit would be outside in the community pool." He slightly chuckled, but quickly gathered his bearings when he saw the seriousness on her face. "But I should NEVER have to walk into a room where another woman knows information about you that I don't even know." Kyree dropped his head in defeat. He knew he'd crossed the line by not telling her sooner. "That shit made me feel like I was the butt of y'all's jokes or some shit."

"I'm sorry. I should have told you. I know. I fucked up. But I knew you hated her. I wasn't sure how to approach it."

"I am a grown-ass woman. That petty high school shit is a thing of the past. All I ask of you, Kyree, is to not have me out here looking stupid. I'm fighting for you, for us, for our family. Don't make me regret it," Jaz said, tears now falling freely from her face.

Kyree approached her and wiped her face with his thumb. "I promise you don't have shit to worry about," he stressed. "But I need you to promise me something too." She looked up at him, waiting for him to speak. "We never go to bed mad at each other again. It's not healthy to sleep on our issues. It only makes us angrier."

Jaz nodded her head. She knew she was being childish by running from her problems. "I promise."

He grabbed her face and gently kissed her lips, and this time she kissed him back without hesitation.

"Oh, and, Kyree?" She pulled away to look him in the eye. "I was calmer than I expected. But if this shit happens again, I won't hesitate to fuck you up."

Kyree laughed, but he knew she was being dead honest, so for the next couple of weeks, he rarely even saw Kendall. That was fine with him. He mainly wanted the presence of the artists she knew at his studio. And now, with the restaurant almost done, Kyree rarely had time for the studio. He had solid contracts with a lot of the big names in the area, and a few national artists as well, so there was nothing that worried him about the studio. The restaurant and club businesses would make sure he retired very young, and legal.

"Come on, Jaz! We're going to be late!" Kyree yelled from the front room.

Jaz huffed, "I don't know why you want us to spend our Sunday with your business partners anyway. I'd much rather go shopping," she whined as she put on her earrings.

"I told you already. Lex is having a cookout, and he wanted me to invite my family. I can't let the man down. Now, bring ya ass!" he yelled with Kylee's car seat in hand.

Jaz rolled her eyes. She was not up for playing nice with the wives today. She smoothed out her navy blue striped maxi skirt, adjusted her breasts in her white halter, threw on her oversized Chloe shades, and met Kyree at the car.

Kyree looked at the scowl on her face and shook his head. "At least act like you love me." Jaz gave a fake smile and he nodded. "See, was that so hard?" He chuckled and she hit him in the arm.

The ride to Kyree's partner Lex's house in Chesapeake was actually relaxing. While Kyree drove, Jaz made him lip sync to Jay-Z & Beyoncé's "(Part II) On the Run" and Jaz posted the video to her Snapchat and Instagram. Kyree was against it at first, but he couldn't help acting silly around Jaz. The smile on her face was enough to make him commit to anything. After a while of being foolish with Kyree in the car, Jaz started to loosen up about going to the cookout. She'd only met Lex once, but he seemed like a cool guy. She just wasn't in the mood for entertaining today.

The ride through the upper class neighborhood was starting to make Jaz feel uneasy about the party. Every house was at least two stories high with perfectly manicured lawns and luxury cars in the driveway. The neighborhood was perfect. It was obvious that Lex was doing well for himself.

Kyree pulled into a huge wraparound driveway and Jaz looked up at the house in awe. The brick and vinyl two-story home was gorgeous. She loved the dark blue shutters, huge porch, and double garage. As she stepped out of the car, she began to notice there was only one car in the driveway.

"Kyree, you tricked me! I thought you said this shit started at 4:00. It's 5:30 and there's no one here," Jaz complained. She hated being the first to arrive at a party. Kyree was usually the total opposite, always prompt and organized.

"Jazzy, you're late for everything. Would it kill you to be on time for once?" Kyree said as he got the baby from the backseat.

They walked up to the door and Jaz rang the doorbell. When a white woman answered, Jaz was shocked. *Damn, I would've never thought she was Lex's type.* She laughed to herself. Jaz couldn't blame Lex though. She was beautiful: tall with long blonde hair and blue eyes, and she filled out her blue blouse and black skirt perfectly. She looked like a movie star.

"Hey, Sandy. This is my fiancée, Jaz. Jaz, this is Sandy," Kyree introduced them.

"Hello, nice to meet you." Sandy extended her hand.

"Nice to meet you as well."

"And who do we have here? I am in love with those dimples." Sandy poked Kylee's cheek, and she giggled. "Where are my manners? Come in, won't you?" She moved to the side and allowed them entrance.

"You have a beautiful home," Jaz admitted, admiring how the inside was just as lovely as the outside.

"Thank you. So do you." Sandy smiled.

Jaz looked at her skeptically. "You and Lex have been to my house?"

Kyree and Sandy both laughed. Jaz didn't, and the look on her face said she wanted to be let in on the joke, and fast.

"Jazzy, I haven't been completely honest with you. This isn't Lex's house. It's yours, baby!" A mile-wide smile stretched across Kyree's face as he watched the expression on Jaz's face change from confusion to pure exhilaration.

"You fuckin' with me?" she quizzed.

"Nope." He shook his head.

When Jaz saw that he was serious, she started jumping up and down, running from one end of the house to the next. One might have thought she'd been told to "Come on down" on *The Price is Right*. Kyree and Sandy laughed as they watched her act a fool. But Jaz could care less what they thought. This was one of the happiest days of her life. She stopped running and nearly trampled over Kyree while he was holding the baby. She hugged him tightly around his neck and Kylee started crying. Sandy took her from his arms so that Kyree could hold Jaz. She was so excited, she was shaking as he held her.

"Thank you, baby," she cried as tears of joy fell from her face.

"You deserve it," he admitted, hugging and rocking her. Kyree had been planning this for months. He wasn't hard to please, but Jaz was very particular. He'd known her almost all of his life, so he knew her style and taste. He was able to give the realtor, Sandy, specific instructions, and she was diligent about following them to the tee. Getting away from all of his different ventures made the time he put into finding a house very difficult, especially when he was trying to keep Jaz happy in the process. Sometimes he wasn't able to meet with Sandy until late in the evening, and Jaz wanted him home at a certain hour. He spread himself so thin that he often wished there were two of him to go around. Kyree wanted a place that he and his family could call home. Although it had taken longer than he expected, it was well worth it to see the look on Jaz's face at that moment.

Jaz released Kyree and gave him a quick peck on the lips.

Sandy smiled at the happy couple. "I'm so happy to finally meet you. Kyree has told me so much about you during this process. You should know he put a lot of energy and time into finding the perfect house for you. I wish my husband was as attentive."

Jaz smiled at Kyree. "Thank you, too, Sandy. I'm sure he couldn't have done any of this without you."

Sandy smiled and handed Kyree the baby. "Well, I better get going. Jaz, you can stop by the settlement company tomorrow to add your name to the contract. But, other than that...the house is all yours. I can't wait for the wedding," Sandy beamed as she hugged them both.

"Bye, Sandy! Thanks again," Jaz said as she watched her walk to the car. She shut the door and turned toward Kyree. She held her hand out and he pulled her by his side to take her on a tour. The house had four bedrooms, three bathrooms, a huge kitchen, beautiful backyard, and what Kyree dubbed his man cave. It was the deal maker that had helped him to close on the property. The previous owners had installed a full media room equipped with a black leather theater style couch, surround sound stereo, and a projector screen.

Jaz instantly fell in love with the kitchen and its stainless steel appliances, white cabinets, granite countertops, and beautiful island that sat in the middle. She couldn't wait to decorate. When Kyree took her upstairs, she was pleased with the size of Kylee's room, and even more pleased with the size of her own. Kyree had the room furnished with a new cherry wood California king bed, matching dresser, nightstand, and armoire. The room was so big that she could practically put her old room in her new walk-in closet.

"Kyree, this bathroom!" Jaz squealed at the sight of her huge vanity, double sink, standup shower, and jetted tub. "I love it, baby!" She kissed him all over his face. "Thank you...thank you... thank you," she proclaimed.

"You're welcome, bae. Now we just have to fill these rooms with a few playmates for Lee."

Jaz squinted her eyes at him. "Uh-uh, Kyree. I know what you've been trying to do." Lately Kyree had been trying to have sex every time she walked into a room. She was serious when she told him she didn't want more kids until Kylee was at least in kindergarten, but Kyree thought he could change her mind. Jaz wasn't the most responsible person when it came to remembering to take her birth control pill. "I have a trick for your ass though. I have an appointment with Rena coming up real soon."

"Who?" Kyree looked confused.

"Mirena, nigga. The five year plan."

He positioned himself behind her and whispered in her ear, "What, you don't trust me?" She shook her head no. "I promise to pull out?" He kissed her on the neck.

"Tuh ha," she laughed.

He laughed too, not even taking himself seriously. "But ay." He gave her a side eye. "You see the size of that tub though?" He winked at her.

She looked at him skeptically, and then it hit her. "Oh, hell no, Kyree! I told you I'm not doing that shit anymore. Last time I almost drowned." She dropped her head in shame as Kyree laughed, remembering last Valentine's Day when she had tried giving him head underwater in the hot tub of their hotel suite. It started off alright, until Kyree forgot where he was and pushed her head down and Jaz started to choke. Kyree laughed hysterically at the thought and Jaz punched him in the arm. She was trying to be romantic, but only ended up messing up her hair, coughing for five minutes straight, and feeling completely embarrassed. "That shit's not funny. I could've died!" Kyree only laughed harder, and even Kylee joined him. "Ugh! I hate you." She pushed him and walked out.

"I told you not to breathe through your nose!" he yelled out to her while still laughing.

"Fuck you, Kyree!" She yelled from the other room.

CHAPTER SEVEN

J az was in love with her house. She took no time getting straight to the decorating. She didn't even own enough furniture and supplies to fill all of the rooms, so she shopped until Kyree told her to stop. They were in no way going to go broke from her expenses, but Kyree knew he had to set limits with Jaz. She was indeed spoiled and sometimes she could go overboard. Jaz obliged his request. She wanted to keep the peace in their house, so she'd allow him to think he'd won a few rounds.

Within two weeks, they were all moved in and unpacked. Now they could enjoy a gathering of all of their friends and family with a nice cookout. The weather was a gorgeous seventy degrees, all of their friends and family were in attendance, and Calvin was throwing it down on the grill. Jaz couldn't have asked for a better time as everyone sat outside and kicked back with good food and laughs.

Jaz loved her backyard. The deck that led from the patio was beautifully stained to match the brick color of the house and there was plenty of yard space, a built-in grill, and relaxing sun-room. They also had an in-ground pool, but it wasn't quite warm enough for them to open it just yet.

Jaz was happy that everyone was able to attend. Monica had even made it a point to invite Mario's family. She thought it might be a good time to get to know Shannon as well. Mario's mother and sisters loved Monica. His mother, Gale, wanted them to get married the moment she met her, his older sister Rhonda thought she was perfect, and his baby sister Shay practically wanted to be Monica. Shay raved about following Monica and Jaz on Instagram and wanting them to do her hair. She was only sixteen and Jaz instantly wanted to adopt her. Everyone was happy, and Monica couldn't be at a greater place in her life.

Monica handed Gale a bottled water and sat down beside Rhonda, ready to dig into her food. Her plate was filled with barbeque ribs, baked beans, macaroni, deviled eggs, green beans, and a yeast roll. She had just brought a fork filled with Jackie's famous baked beans up to her mouth when Rhonda said, "Ugh, I can't stand that bitch."

"Huh?" Monica looked at her to make sure she'd heard her right.

"You know who. I know you don't like her either."

"I'm lost. Who are we talking about?" Monica quizzed.

"Shannon, girl. I know you don't like her. Who does?" Rhonda turned up her nose as she watched Shannon fixing her plate.

"Oh, she's cool. I don't have a problem with her, for real," Monica lied. She didn't know Rhonda that well to be expressing her true feelings toward Shannon with her.

"I know you don't know me like that, but I like you for my brother so I'm going to keep it one hunnid wit'chu. That bitch is a pain in my side. I don't know how Booby can't see right through her bullshit. She uses him because she knows he's loyal and some-times, he's loyal to the wrong ones."

Monica had more questions, but she still didn't feel comfort-able enough around Rhonda to ask. But if she was volunteering the information, Monica sure as hell wasn't going to stop her.

"My momma hates her ass too, but we won't get her started on that today. Just watch your back around her. Booby doesn't like her in that way, but I don't think she understands that. I've seen her run too many women in his life away because she selfishly wants him to herself."

Monica nodded her head in understanding as she, too, now focused her attention on Shannon. She was such a pretty girl, but there was no doubt that she was slightly insecure. She was about 5'6" with glowing butterscotch skin, long auburn hair, and a waist that looked like she worked out at least four times a week. She wore a tank top, short shorts, and five inch heels. Monica wanted so badly to ask who she was trying to impress. It wasn't that hot outside and the food was free. Monica noticed her looking around for somewhere to sit. She didn't know anyone there and Mario was in the garage with the guys so she waved her over and made a space for her to sit at the picnic table. Shannon gestured a thank you, but pointed to an empty seat beside a few of the guys in attendance.

"See, that's the kind of sneaky shit I'm talking about." Rhonda shook her head.

Monica made a mental note to watch her as she noticed Shannon laughing a little too hard at a boyfriend of one of her close friends, but she wouldn't let that mess up her day. She had a great time talking with Rhonda and had even managed to hook her up with Fat Boy. Rhonda had a four-year-old daughter and just wanted someone who was going to keep it real with her, so Monica didn't hesitate to set the two up. Fat Boy was actually a good guy and even though he was 6'3" and 300 pounds, that didn't stop the women who flocked to him. His smooth brown skin, hazel eyes, full beard, and bodacious smile made him hard not to love. It also didn't hurt that he, too, was now legally making long money with his different business ventures, and he was kid free. That was all of the information Rhonda needed for her to give Monica the go ahead to play matchmaker. The two seemed to be hitting it off, so Monica left them to get better acquainted.

"Ay, Mo," Jaz called out to her, and Monica turned in her direction. "I'm about to beat these li'l kids' asses in a dance battle," she bragged.

"Oh, I gotta see this," Monica laughed. She hurriedly went to rally up everyone from the salon so that they could watch Jaz make a fool of herself. It was hilarious as Jaz tried to do the whip and all of the kids were clearly out-whipping her. By the end of the song, everyone was in tears with laughter and Jaz was sweating from her roots.

"A'ight, I'll give that one to the kids. Y'all win. But that's only because that's the new school dancing. Y'all don't know nothin' about when Juvenile was takin' over for the '99 and the 2000's." The kids looked at her like she was crazy, but all of the adults laughed. "Heartbeats, front and center." Jaz put her hand out while she stood in the middle of the deck. Everyone laughed at her foolishness, but Jaz was dead serious as she ice-grilled her friends. "Mo, Jeneisha, and Ahnesty...if y'all don't get up here..."

"Uh uh, Jaz. I am not going to sweat out my hair so you can relive your glory days," Ahnesty protested.

"I'll do your hair for free."

"Free? Oh, that's all you had to say." Ahnesty put her hair in a ponytail, hopped on the deck, and smacked Jaz's hand. She looked at Jeneisha and she huffed, but made her way on the deck anyway.

Everyone looked at Monica, and she shook her head no.

"Come on, Mo, we all know you don't have no rhythm anyway." Ahnesty laughed.

Monica gave the three of them a sideways glare as they all nodded in agreement. She took that as a challenge as she hopped on the deck too and slapped her hand in as well. "And I wasn't the one with no rhythm. That was Ahnesty." Everyone laughed, but Ahnesty's mouth dropped.

Growing up, the four women danced for rival high schools back in the day. Even though they competed in numerous competitions and the score was always close between them, they still respected each other and would always speak when they came in contact. They didn't really become close friends until college, but deep down, the old high school rivalry was still there.

Jaz gave the DJ instructions to play all of the greatest dance songs from the early 2000's. She also reminded him to keep it classy, because there were elders present. Thankfully, everyone was comfortably dressed: Jeneisha in a cute white one piece capri set with sandals, Ahnesty in jean shorts with a Yankees jersey and white Nike Huaraches, Mo in a navy blue one piece with silver sandals, and Jaz in pants and a crop top. The girls all put their hair into ponytails and effortlessly got into formation like they'd just performed in front of their high school days before.

Jaz and Monica stood in front of Jeneisha and Ahnesty as they prepared to battle it out on the patio deck. Jeneisha and Ahnesty won the coin toss, and Jaz and Monica went first. The DJ dropped Missy Elliott's "Work It", and it was on from there. They switched between combinations, did facial expressions like they were going to win a trophy, and danced like no one was watching. When Jaz and Monica ended their dance, the ball was in Jeneisha and Ahnesty's court, and they hadn't lost one step. When Jeneisha looked at Ahnesty, she knew exactly which stance they were going to do. The DJ switched to Sean Paul's

"Gimme da Light", and then ended it with Timbaland's hit "Drop".

When it was all over, Toni hopped on the deck to crown the winner. "A'ight, y'all. Over here we have The Dancing Waist Trainers." He positioned his hand over Jaz and Monica, and Monica smacked his hand away. "And over here we have The Dirty 30's," he joked, and Ahnesty elbowed him in the stomach. The whole crowd laughed at his antics. "So, who do y'all have to win this battle for Lil Saint? The Waist Trainers or the Dirty 30's?" He held his hand over each one, and the crowd cheered the loudest for Ahnesty and Jeneisha. "There you have it, folks. Bundles and edge control will be given out in the lobby. Thanks for coming out."

After the crowd cleared, the women were still out of breath. Even though they'd only danced for five minutes, it was nothing like when they were young. The kicks weren't as high, the steps weren't as coordinated, and the counts were a tad off. They were tired as hell. They'd put on a good show for everyone and no one could tell that it wasn't up to par, but they knew they'd pay for it in the morning. Their bodies were no longer used to the conditioning, and Jaz looked as if she was going to pass out.

"I think I need my inhaler," she wheezed.

"Can y'all hear my heartbeat?" Jeneisha asked.

"No, but I can see mine." Monica looked down as if her heart were going to come out of her chest.

"I worked hard for that hairdo. Shit, I need a drink." Ahnesty fanned herself as she walked away.

"I'm about to go find Toni. That nigga tried to call us old," Jeneisha said.

Monica laughed as she watched while Ahnesty limped off, Jeneisha went to find Toni, and Jaz retreated to the house to retrieve her inhaler. She took a rest on the steps and her friend Tameka took a seat beside her.

"Hey, Mo. Y'all got down." Tameka laughed.

"Girl, I'm paying for it now," she admitted.

Tameka smirked, and then squinted off into the distance. Monica followed her eyes and knew exactly what had her attention. Tameka was a stylist at the salon and she was one of the women everyone envied. She was in her early thirty's with a loving husband, a beautiful daughter and one son, and her finances were in order. Tameka was also not one to be stepped on in the looks department either. She had ombre black and gold locs that touched the middle of her back, smooth caramel skin, and a naturally thick figure. She was like a mother to them all. The girl was on her shit. She was also the most level-headed person Monica knew and anyone could see the uneasiness on her face as she looked at her husband chatting it up with Shannon. Monica had noticed the two talking earlier and she let it slide, but it was clear to her that Tameka was obviously getting a different vibe.

"How well do you know her?"

"Who?" Monica played dumb.

"The one talking to Marquell."

"Oh, she's really good friends with Mario. Why?"

"Because I have known Marquell for ten years, and I have NEVER known him to be THAT damn funny."

Oh Lord, Monica thought to herself. "I'm sure they're just having a friendly conversation," Monica reasoned, although she wasn't too sure herself. With every laugh, Shannon tossed her head back, and placed one hand on Marquell's thigh.

"Okay, we'll see." Tameka rubbed her tongue across her teeth, took a swig from her drink, and made her way over to the table where they were seated. Monica wasn't too far behind her, ready to break up any altercation that may ensue.

"You good?" Tameka looked directly at Marquell.

He did an uncomfortable shift in his seat. "Yeah, we were just talking about you."

"Yep. Quell was just telling me how you specialize in locs. I was telling him that I might send some business your way," Shannon interjected.

Tameka almost lost all sense of courteousness she had when she heard Shannon shorten her husband's name. "That's fine. Get my info from Mo. Quell, let's go."

He sucked his teeth and shook his head. "It was nice meeting you." He stuck out his hand for a handshake.

"Same to you." Shannon laughed once they were out of earshot. "Hell, we were just talking," she said to Monica. "I can't deal with females and their insecurities."

Monica turned to Shannon and shook her head.

"What?" Shannon turned up her face.

Monica wasn't going to say anything at first, but, since she asked... "You don't get it, do you? It's one thing to have a conversation with a man, but to be blatantly flirting with him when you know he's married, that's borderline disrespectful."

"Really, Monica, it's not that deep. I seriously didn't mean any harm," Shannon reiterated.

Monica couldn't tell if she was sincere or not. She was seconds from asking the bitch if she was dumb, but Kyree interrupted them before she could.

"Mo, Jaz needs your help in the kitchen." He wrapped his arm around her shoulder and ushered her in the opposite direction. He just happened to be close enough to ear-hustle on their conversation, and knew his sister well enough to know when she was about to pop off.

"You good?" He questioned as they walked toward the house. She shrugged her shoulders. "Look, ignore that girl. I hear you and Jaz's conversations. You know she's loud when she's on the damn phone." They both laughed. They sat down at the kitchen island once they were inside. "I just want to tell you that I think Mario is a good guy, and if he says she's just a friend, then that's probably who she is."

Monica nodded her head and gave Kyree a reassured smile. She was so happy he was home. The three years he was away felt like an eternity to her. Growing up, he was always able to talk her off the ledge. He was only three years older, but still the only father figure she'd ever known. When it came to the men in her life, Kyree was always cautious. So for him to say such good things about Mario, meant a lot to her. Kyree taught her how to protect herself over the years, but he failed to mention how to protect her heart. It could often be so easily broken.

"So you're good now?" He looked at her to be sure.

"Yeah, I'm good, Ky-Ky." She playfully nudged him.

"Ay, you know better," he warned, and they laughed. She hadn't been allowed to call him that since they were little.

"Thanks, Ky. I needed that."

"Needed what?" Jaz interrupted.

"Nothing. Nosy ass." Kyree playfully pushed Jaz as he retreated back outside.

"I almost cussed Shannon out." Monica let Jaz in on what happened. Jaz couldn't believe it.

"Damn. She better leave Tameka alone. That girl will sweat out her Shea Moisture going to war for Marquell."

Monica laughed at Jaz's silliness.

"Mo, you're going to have to talk to Mario about her. Immediately," Jaz stressed.

"I am. I'm so over this shit, Jaz. I probably would've flung her ass in the pool. Luckily, Ky showed up when he did."

Jaz rolled her eyes. "Da fuck does Ky know anyway? He's probably just defending Mario because he understands him." Monica looked at Jaz with a raised brow. She was talking crazy. She didn't know what was in the cup she was holding, but she was sure it was something potent. Jaz was quickly going from 0 to 100. "What? Don't look at me like that. Look who that dummy let in my damn house."

Monica looked on, squinting her eyes, trying to see afar. "I don't see...ooooooh." She shook her head when she saw Kendall walk in with a few of the rappers from the studio.

"He'd be mad as fuck if I invited Michael." She caught herself, hoping Monica hadn't heard. She didn't mean to say that out loud.

Monica didn't take her seriously though. She actually laughed. "Don't get fucked up." Jaz took a silent sigh of relief. She knew that she was out of line for what she'd said, but sometimes Kyree disregarded her feelings.

Monica placed a hand on Jaz's shoulder. "For real though, are you good?"

"Tuh ha! Do I look worried?" Jaz did a full spin in her army green joggers, white crop, and fringed sandals. Her hair weave was laid with two bundles of black Malaysian strait that she'd done in loose curls and her face was beat to the African Gods.

Monica nodded her head in approval, but she still had to ask, "How many drinks have you had?"

"Ummm..." She thought for a moment. "Two shots of peach Ciroc, and now I have some of Nest's Tea. I'm feeling lovely." Jaz danced, popping her ass in front of Monica. "Go best friend, that's my best friend. She finna...she finna..."

Monica doubled over in laughter. "Move, Jaz!" She pushed her off of her.

Monica was going to make it her business to stay close to Jaz. She didn't want her going off the rails tonight. If Jaz went to the bathroom, Monica was going to be right there. So while Jaz wasn't looking, she dumped Ahnesty's special tea down the drain and replaced it with pure raspberry lemonade. Jaz didn't even notice the difference. On occasion, Jaz had to do the same to her when she was in her feelings and drinking too. She had no idea why Kendall was there, but she didn't want to see her there either.

Kyree didn't know why K.O. showed up with Kendall either. He wished he hadn't. When he told people at his work about the cookout, he made it his business not to invite Kendall. But since everyone knew that she was dating K.O., he felt that would be slightly easier for Jaz to digest. She seemed to be doing fine as he looked over at her talking with her friends. Mario's little sister was trying to show her how to do the Whoa dance. She was laughing and having a good time. He wasn't sure if it was just for show or not, so he made his way over to her and planted a kiss on her cheek. She blushed like a giddy school girl.

"Watch me, Kyree. I think I got it." She excitedly turned around and started dancing in front of him. He laughed, relieved that she was in a good mood. She tripped into him and buried her face into his chest in embarrassment. Everyone laughed. Jaz saw it as the perfect opportunity to whisper in his ear. "I'm not mad. I'm good," she assured him. She knew he'd come over there to check on her. "I love you," she sincerely said. Kyree took a silent sigh of relief and kissed her gently on the lips.

Kendall was cordial with Jaz and Monica. They were even able to laugh and make small talk about old times. The rest of the evening went by beautifully - until it was time to go.

"Bye, best fraaaan." Jaz hugged Monica on her way out of the door. "Bye, Rhonda. It was nice meeting you, and thanks for coming." She hugged her as well.

"Thanks for having me, girl." Rhonda beamed.

"Thanks for coming, Shannon!" Jaz waved goodbye. Jaz didn't know her, but she gave her a bad vibe. She didn't want to alarm

Monica with her worries just yet. She knew she was already on the edge about Shannon anyway.

"Call me when you make it home."

"Like always. I know the drill." Monica waved goodbye as they walked to Rhonda's car. Mario had left an hour earlier so that he could take his mother and younger sister home. He also had to stop by his job to find a set of keys that no one could find.

"Uh uh." Rhonda shook her head.

"What?" Monica asked.

"Why is that bitch in the front seat?" Rhonda pointed to Shannon relaxing in the front seat.

Monica didn't really care. Kayden was in the backseat anyway, so she wasn't about to stress it. "It's cool," Monica assured.

"Nah, fuck that. She knows I don't even like her ass. Ay, Thot!" Rhonda knocked on the window. "Get'cho ass in the backseat with the kids!"

"Excuse me?" Shannon quipped. She pretended not to hear what Rhonda had said. She was always throwing snide comments her way. She and Rhonda were always going at it. Rhonda couldn't stand her. If Mario hadn't stepped in, they would have gone to blows on more than a few occasions. Shannon was going to keep her cool for now though. She needed the ride home.

"It's cool, Rhonda." Monica had to stop herself from laughing at the "thot" comment. "I'll be fine back there with my baby."

Rhonda looked at Monica to make sure, and she nodded her head. "Okay, girl. But just remember what I said earlier."

Monica nodded her head and before they knew it, they were pulling off. When Monica arrived home, she sent Jaz a text letting her know that she and Kayden were safely in the house. She dressed Kayden for bed, took a hot shower, and then helped herself to some of the to-go items she'd managed to take from the cookout. She'd just sat down to eat when her cell phone rang.

She looked at the caller ID to find that it was Latrell. It was ten o'clock at night. She had no idea why he'd be calling this late. "Hello," she answered.

"Hey, Mo. You think I can come get my sunglasses tonight?"

Monica rolled her eyes. She'd told him to take the sunglasses when he dropped Kayden off last week. He'd let Kayden wear them, and once he dropped him off at home, Kayden cried to keep them. Neither one of them wanted to see him have a tantrum, so Monica told Latrell to ride up the street and come back in ten minutes after she distracted him. But Latrell said he'd just get them the next time he saw her.

"Ugh, where are you?"

"Outside."

She sucked her teeth and hung up the phone. When she opened the door, she was greeted with the scent of his cologne. Even though he worked her nerves 90% of the time, she couldn't deny how good he looked tonight. His goatee was trimmed perfectly around his mouth while his bald head was shiny enough to see herself in. Given his fitted white jeans, white boat shoes, and white button up shirt, Monica figured he must have been on his way to the all-white yacht party tonight.

"So, how a nigga look?" he asked as he posed with his hand under his chin.

"Like a marshmallow with a Milk Dud center." She tried to keep a straight face, but when he scrunched his face in shock, she couldn't help herself. She doubled over in laughter.

He shook his head. "You're a hater."

"I'm just playin' wit'cha sensitive ass." She playfully pushed him. "You look really nice tonight, Latrell."

He bashfully flashed her his megawatt smile. Monica knew that smile all too well. It had gotten her to forgive so many of his indiscretions in the past that she used to consider it dangerous. It did little for her now though. "Hold on, let me go get your glasses." She let him in and closed the door.

He watched her walk away, her ass jiggling in her pajama shorts and tank top. *My Gawd, dat ass doe?* he thought to himself. Latrell had spent many nights thinking about having his way with Monica again. To him, she was the one who got away. Being young and stupid back in the day had caused him to lose his family, and he was determined to get it back.

"Ay, whose food is this?" His mouth watered at the sight of her leftovers on the kitchen table.

"Mine! Don't touch my shit!" she yelled from the back.

Latrell ignored her rant and grabbed a paper towel. He picked up a hot dog and a yeast roll. He wrapped the roll in a paper towel and took a water bottle from out of the fridge.

"Ay, where's the king?"

"In his room asleep!" she yelled. She couldn't recall where she'd put the sunglasses, and then she remembered wanting to put them some place high so that Kayden couldn't get to them. They were Gucci frames and she didn't want to be responsible if they broke. Why Latrell let him play with them in the first place was beyond her. He could be so careless at times. She finally found them in her shoebox on the top shelf of her closet.

As she headed back to the front, her doorbell rang. When she got there, Latrell was nowhere to be found. She figured he must have gone to see Kayden. She shrugged it off and opened the door. It was Mario.

"Hey," she looked surprised. She figured he'd head home after leaving his job since it was so close by. But she was still extremely happy to see him, no matter when it was. She let him inside and closed the door behind him.

"Dang, don't act so excited to see me," he chuckled as she went in for a hug.

"I just wasn't expecting you. Thought you'd just head home after finding the keys."

"I did. I went home to shower and change, and then I headed here."

"Ay, Mo, you find my glasses?" Latrell came from the back.

Mario looked up when he heard Latrell's voice. He was slightly shocked, but he didn't show it.

"Oh, what's up, man?"

"What up, La."

Latrell and Mario dapped hands. Monica had already introduced the two. She felt it was necessary that they meet seeing as though Mario would also be a part of Kayden's life. Although Monica couldn't stand Latrell for what he'd done to her in the past, she still respected him as a father. She felt she owed him that much, and could only hope that he'd extend her the same courtesy if the roles were reversed.

The two men's first conversation was brief and cordial, but they seemed to be okay with one another - or so Monica thought. In actuality, Latrell saw Mario as just someone in his way as he tried to get Monica's heart back. And Mario didn't trust Latrell. Something inside told him that Latrell was a fuck boy up to no good. But for the sake of his relationship with Monica, he'd remained pleasant.

"You 'bout to head to the all-white?" Mario asked.

"Hell yeah, just came to get my glasses I left around here." Latrell gave a sly smirk as Monica handed him his sunglasses.

"Well, shit, have fun for the both of us. We're probably not about to do nothing but watch Netflix and chill." Mario also smirked.

Monica looked between them both. She didn't know if they were trying to be slick or not, so she dismissed it from her mind.

"A'ight, well you two enjoy the rest of your night. Kiss our son for me, Mo." He licked his lips, and then bent down slightly to hug Monica. No one could see it, but her eyes grew bug. They never gave each other more than a wave hello and goodbye. *What the fuck is he doing?* she wondered. Before she had enough time to react and pull away, he'd already released her. Mario clenched his jaw. It took everything inside of him not to snap the fuck off. It was clear to both men the sign of disrespect just shown.

Latrell and Mario dapped each other up one last time, and then Latrell left. Monica went back to the kitchen table to finish her food. "He ate my hot dog and my fuckin' yeast roll!" she snapped. She had another hot dog, but that was the last of her mother's homemade yeast rolls. "I'm going to kill his ass next time I see him!" Monica was so furious, that she barely noticed the unsettled look on Mario's face. "What?" She looked at him quizzically.

"Nothing, man." He walked away into the den.

Monica had no idea what the hell was causing his sudden change in attitude. This wasn't like him at all. She threw her head back in frustration. She was never going to finish her food at this rate. She got up to find him in the den flicking through channels on the couch.

"Do you have something you want to say to me?" She asked with her arms folded.

He put the TV on mute and looked at her. "That's the kind of shit you wear when your ex is around?"

Monica looked down at her shorts and tank top. It's true, they barely covered her ass, but it wasn't hanging out. And her cleavage was definitely showing, but she couldn't help that either. She wore that kind of stuff around the house all the time. Besides, she didn't know Latrell was coming over. She had no idea why Mario was acting so strangely. He couldn't call himself being jealous, not after all of the shit she had to deal with on a regular.

"I know you're not jealous," she quipped.

"Man, whatever." He waved her off and unmuted the TV.

Monica tossed her head back and laughed. "You are jealous, huh? And of Latrell? Please, I have no desire to travel down that fucked up road ever again. But the shit doesn't feel so good now that the shoe is on the other foot, does it?" she challenged him.

"You can g'on ahead with all of that jealous shit. But what do you mean by 'now that the shoe is on the other foot'?"

"It means that on a daily, I have to deal with you and your *best friend,* and I'm supposed to be cool with it. But when my son's father comes over – unannounced, by the way - to pick up something, you're about to lose your mind."

"You're still trippin' off that?"

"Hell yeah, I am!" Monica had to catch herself. She wasn't trying to get loud. "I'm still trippin' off of it, because I don't like the bitch. There. I said it. You happy now?"

Mario had never heard her say those words. He knew that she had her doubts about his and Shannon's relationship, but he didn't know she didn't like her. "I thought you were cool with all of this."

Monica took a deep breath before speaking. "Mario, I've tried to be as cool as I can with this shit. Something about her attitude just puts me in a different place. She's not a very nice person, and everyone knows it. But I deal with it and don't throw a fit because I trust you, and I respect how you're there for the people you love. This shit with you and Latrell doesn't even come close to my feelings about Shannon." She shook her head.

"You're right, because the shit with him is different. The nigga has ulterior motives, Mo."

"And how is this different?" Monica folded her arms tight and ice grilled him.

"Nothing. Just forget it."

She quickly walked up on him. "Nah, tell me!" she dared him as she stared him down on the couch.

Mario matched her gaze and said, "Because I've never fucked Shannon!"

Monica disgustedly looked down at him. She was beyond hurt by what he'd said. "Fuck you!" She smacked the remote control out of his hand, causing the batteries to scatter across the floor. "Get the fuck out of my house!" She quickly walked away before the urge to slap him in the face got to be too strong for her to control.

"Fuck!" Mario mumbled to himself. He rubbed his hands down his face. He had no idea how things had gotten to this point. He never meant for his jealousy to get the best of him. He'd never admit it to Monica, but the fear of her getting back with Latrell ate at him whenever he came around. She'd never shown an inkling of interest in getting back with Latrell, but it didn't stop him from wondering.

Mario knew that Monica was beautiful, but she had more than just her looks going for her and that's what he loved most about her. Women he'd dated in the past lacked Monica's ambition and drive. She was in a class all her own. She made him nervous at times. He hadn't been in a real relationship with anyone since high school. He'd never even had a desire to be. But when he was around Monica, everything naturally fell into place. He thought about her all the time, he felt the happiest when she was happy, and her presence gave him a calmness that he never knew existed until she walked out of a room.

He took a deep breath and went to find her. She was seated at the kitchen table, finally eating her food. She saw him walk in the dining room through the corner of her eye, but she wouldn't dare give him the satisfaction to look at him. Mario had hurt her in ways he didn't even know. She was sensitive about her past relationship with Latrell. Even being around Latrell without wanting to kill him was still new to her. And Mario knew more than anyone how hard that transition was. She'd spent many nights on the phone with him talking about her insecurities with allowing him to be a part of Kayden's life. She felt like it was selfish of him to ask her to deal with everything in his life, when he was not willing to do the same for her.

Mario saw that she wasn't trying to pay him much attention, so he stood on the opposite side of the table, so that she'd have no choice. "I'm sorry," he sincerely said.

She still refused to look his way, only focusing on the food in front of her.

"Ay, look at me!" he demanded.

"Why are you still here? Didn't I tell you to leave?" Her voice slightly quivered. She was trying her hardest not to cry, but the tears were so strong she could feel them in her throat.

"Mo, please, look at me, baby," he begged.

Monica took a long sigh and looked up at him as a single tear cascaded down her face. She quickly wiped it away. Mario instantly felt worse. This was their first fight, and he'd managed to make her cry. Sure, they'd had their disagreements in the past, but they never talked to each other like this. Mario had never seen her so upset. He didn't want to bring that kind of pain to her heart.

Mario reached across the table to wipe her face and she turned her head. She was so angry with herself for allowing a man to bring her to that level. After Latrell broke her heart years ago, she vowed to never let another man do that to her again.

"I really am sorry. You were right. I was jealous as fuck. I think what sealed the deal was when he hugged you and you were wearing those little-ass shorts, maybe because I know any man would have to be a fool not to look twice at you with those shorts on," he admitted. "Hell, when you first opened the door, my mans was about to poke a hole through my damn draws."

Monica slightly smirked.

"I hate that you feel that way about Shannon, but I can only respect it. I won't ask you to associate with her again. That wasn't fair of me, I know. The shit with her really is different than you know though."

"How?" She still wanted to know.

He rolled his eyes and started fiddling with his phone. Monica sucked her teeth. "Mario, I didn't even know Latrell was coming over here, but he does have a right to come see his son. So if it's not a bad time, sure, I'll allow him. The difference here being I *have* to be around that man, and you *choose* to be around her. So why shouldn't I feel some type of way about her?"

He nodded his head. She waited for him to respond, but he was still toying around with his damn phone and it was clear that he wasn't paying her any attention. "Mario! You're not even listening to me!" she fumed. "Ugh! You know what? I don't know why I'm even wasting my time with this shit. Just go!" She was pissed that he was still sitting there so unfazed.

Monica's phone beeped, alerting her that she had an Instagram update. She wanted to ignore it, but since Mario was so into his phone, she figured she'd play his game too. She opened up her notifications to see the picture she'd been tagged in. It wasn't unusual for her to be tagged in a picture. It was the life of a stylist. Either she'd done someone's hair and they were giving her credit, or someone wanted her to do their hair so they were seeking information. She had three pages to manage on Instagram alone: One for the salon, her stylist page, and her personal. The incoming message was from her personal page. She proceeded to open the photo. It was a picture she'd taken the other day after Jaz styled her hair with ombre hues of brown. Her lips were popping matte red, her eyebrows were on fleek, and the slightly opened mouth pose she gave was celebrity worthy. She looked past the pic and her hands began to tremble as she read the caption.

@Super_Mario757 #WCE She has no worries. I LOVE @TheOtherMonicaWright. #BaeDay #NetflixAndChill #ImTrynaWatchAMovie #SheTrynaTakeAdvantage

Mario could see the shock on her face as she read it. He waited for her to finish reading it and then he stood up. Monica wasn't sure what to make of it all. She was almost certain she was just reading too much into an Instagram caption. But then Mario pulled his chair beside her, and turned hers so that she was facing him.

"Look, Monica, I've never been jealous of another nigga in my life. But you bring out all of these different emotions and insecurities in me that I never even knew I had. Believe me when I say, I've NEVER felt this way about anyone. And the shit scares the fuck out of me. And I don't care if you don't feel the same way right now, but I lo --"

"I love you too," she quickly cut him off.

He chuckled in relief. "Can you let me finish, please?" She held her hands up in surrender. He was glad that he wasn't in this alone, but he needed to hear himself say it. "I love you, Monica. I think I've known it for a while now. I mean, I probably lost like fifty followers just for posting that picture." They both laughed.

"I think I've known it too. And I'm sorry too. I realize how disrespectful that was of me to be dressed like this in front of another man that wasn't you. But, honestly, babe, I didn't know he was coming over."

Mario nodded his head. He believed her when she first told him, but he was so in his feelings before that he wasn't trying to hear it. "I know you're not on no crazy shit like that. My bad for trippin'. I was being a mitch, huh?" He chuckled.

"Nah, it's understandable. Besides, I thought it was kinda cute seeing you all riled up." She tugged on a loose dread and pulled him closer to her face.

"I love you." He kissed her. He pulled back but she grabbed his face, inserting her tongue into his mouth. She stood up from her chair and straddled him with her thighs. She could feel his tool getting harder through his shorts. She devilishly glared at him and inserted her tongue back in his mouth with one hand on the back of his neck while the other massaged his penis through his shorts.

Monica was playing with his emotions, and she wasn't playing fair. He gripped her thighs and stood up with her legs tightly wrapped around his waist. He carried her up the stairs and stopped when they walked past Kayden's room. He was fast asleep.

"That boy can sleep through an earthquake," she said, out of breath.

He smirked and carried her into her bedroom, kicking the door shut with his foot. He stood her up and turned her around so that her back was against the wall and quickly removed her shirt, allowing her breasts to spill out in front of him. He hungrily sucked her erect nipples and then led a trail of kisses down to her stomach, sliding her panties and shorts down with his teeth. Placing one leg across his shoulders, he found her sweet center, and feverishly worked his tongue around her insides. Monica's eyes rolled wildly around her head as he licked and sucked the life out of her kitty.

"Mmmmmmm," she moaned.

Grabbing ahold of his head, Monica felt her knees go weak as she slowly slid down to the floor. With her head on the floor, he lifted her ass and legs in the air. As the blood rushed to her head from being on the floor, he continued to lick and suck until he felt her warm juices grace his tongue. "Ahhhhh!" she screamed, cumming all over his face. He lapped up every morsel until she was all cleaned up. He smiled at how helpless she looked just lying there. Monica was always playing tough and he liked to see her in this state.

He rose to his feet and removed his shirt. He bent down to help her up as she lay breathless on the floor. She stretched her arms out and he lifted her on to her feet. "What are you doing to me?" She rested her head on his chest as she breathed heavily.

"What, you can't hang?"

She seductively looked at him. She knew the game Mario was playing. He loved to play, and she loved to call his bluff. She placed a trail of kisses all over his lower abdomen. Monica loved his body. It was the smooth color of Jiffy peanut butter and ripped to perfection. His mother's name was on his forearm and angel wings with his dad's name were on his back. He was an Adonis in her eyes.

Monica had the hardest time removing his shorts, as his dick was already at attention and rock hard. She pulled them over his tool and slid them down to the floor. He kicked them off to the side and admired her as she began to massage his balls while placing sweet kisses around his dick. She licked the tip and he jumped.

"Ah, shit," he moaned in anticipation of what was to come next. Monica's head game was on point. After the first time he had a dose of what she was working with, he knew he never wanted anyone else to have it. He never had to tell her how he liked it; she just knew.

While still massaging his balls, Monica greedily took about six inches of his tool inside of her mouth. She sucked, bobbed, slurped, and moaned while Mario guided her along the way by gently tugging on her hair. He felt the blood rush to the tip of his dick and he couldn't take anymore. He pulled her mouth away and picked her up off the floor. He tossed her on the bed and slowly inserted himself inside of her wet slit.

"Shiiiiiit!" she screamed out in pleasurable agony. He worked her insides with a beautiful rhythm as she moved her hips to match his motion. He loved the way her walls clamped perfectly around his dick like a warm blanket. He kissed her neck as she clawed at his back. Monica couldn't take it. She was so weak she couldn't move anymore so she clamped her Kegel muscles around him and they both lost it, cumming at the same time.

"Gotdamn, girl," he huffed.

They both lay there panting, unable to move. Monica was exhausted, but she got up to turn on her ceiling fan and then headed to the bathroom. She returned with a glass of water and a warm rag. She handed them both to Mario.

"That's why I fucks with you," he smirked, pleased with her for being so attentive.

She crawled under the covers and after drinking all of the water and giving his penis a quick wash, Mario joined her. Together the two were so in sync with each other. Mario felt like nothing or no one could break the bond they had.

Little did Mario know, but his best friend was at home selfishly pining over him. For years she'd been his shoulder to cry on when women did him wrong. When he had a question about a girl, he asked Shannon what to do. She was always available when he needed her. But he still saw her as nothing more than a friend.

Shannon didn't know what it was. She knew she was bad as fuck. Her body was out of this world. Most men went crazy if she even glanced at them. Not Mario. They'd been buddies for five years, and Shannon was tired of being in the friend zone. She'd invented the friend zone with all of the guys she curved on the regular. No matter who she spent her time with, told her secrets to, or shared her bed with, none could ever compare to Mario. Although the two had never been involved sexually, that didn't stop the many sleepless nights she spent thinking about it. She compared every man she'd ever dated to him, which was why her ex-boyfriend had kicked her out a few weeks ago. He couldn't stand how much she talked about Mario. But she couldn't help it. No man had ever treated her like Mario had. He listened to her, wanted her time and not her body, and he made her feel like she was the only girl in the world.

Although lately, Monica was taking up most of his time. Shannon would never tell Mario, but she hated Monica. She wanted to be in her shoes so badly that it pained her to see her with the man she thought should be hers. Mario had never put any woman before her, and if he did, it was probably just for some ass. Shannon could see that Monica was different than any other female to Mario. When Shannon would mention Monica's name, he'd nonchalantly say that they were still cool and he liked her, no complaints like he usually did with women. He kept Monica private and their problems were unknown to Shannon.

Shannon didn't know how she was going to break up this relationship. The others were easy. The women before usually lacked depth, so it didn't take much of a seed to plant in Mario's head to get him to drop them. "I think she's clingy," she'd say. Or, "She talks to a lot of guys. I've heard a few things about her being a hoe." Monica was going to be a lot harder to get rid of. Breaking the perfect image Mario had of her was going to be difficult, but Shannon was up for the challenge. She was tired of wanting something she couldn't have. Shannon always got what she wanted. This time wouldn't be any different. She was going to make sure of it.

CHAPTER EIGHT

J az sat up in bed catching up on episodes of *Power* while Kyree and Kylee slept peacefully beside her. She smiled at the sight of Kyree's shirt, covered in Kylee's drool as she slept on his chest. Kyree's light snore was like a peaceful medley to Kylee, as she always found comfort in resting when her daddy did. Jaz often had the hardest time getting her to sleep unless Kyree was there. She loved being in her daddy's presence. Kylee could be crying for no reason at all, but as soon as Kyree walked in the door, she perked right up.

On one particular occasion, Jaz had spent an hour trying to find Kylee's pacifier. Kylee would throw a fit if she didn't have it. Jaz tried everything to get her to calm down. She rocked her, changed her, fed her, burped her, but nothing worked. Kylee cried for an entire hour, until Kyree walked in the house. He looked at a crazed Jaz as she searched high and low, explaining to him her dilemma. He simply sucked his teeth and said, "She don't need that shit." He'd picked Kylee up, kissed her on the cheek, rocked her for five seconds, and she'd instantly calmed down. Jaz joked that it was a setup, and they were both out to make her life hell, but she thought it was cute. She wondered if she'd given her mother the same problems when she was a baby. There was no doubt that she used to be, and still was, a daddy's girl.

Jaz paused the TV to get her phone. Kylee was smiling in her sleep and she had to take a picture. She snapped the picture and received a text immediately after. The ding from the notification caused her to jump and Kyree to stir in his sleep. She was nervous that she'd wake him, so she got up from the bed to respond to the message. After sending the text, she went to the fridge to grab something to drink. When she closed the fridge door, Kyree was standing behind it.

"Ah!" she screamed, nearly dropping her orange juice.

"Damn," he slightly laughed. "My bad."

"You scared the shit out of me." She held her chest to calm her beating heart. "What are you doing up?"

He pointed to his drenched shirt and Jaz giggled as he shook his head. He grabbed her juice from her hands and took a huge gulp.

"Kyree! Give me my juice!" She snatched it back. "I don't know where your mouth has been," she joked.

"Oh, it's been on yo' juice." He winked at her.

"You are so nasty." She playfully hit his chest.

"You like it though." He brought her in close and kissed her neck. Her phone dinged again, causing her to jump. Kyree threw his head back. "Tell Mo ass to go to sleep."

Jaz rolled her eyes, and Kyree took her cup and retreated back to the bedroom. Jaz read the message, sent a return text, and powered her phone off. She knew she wasn't going to get any sleep if she didn't. She was too worried that Kyree might see her text messages to her ex, Michael. There would be no coming back from such a revelation, no matter what the explanation was. She didn't like keeping things from Kyree, but he'd never understand her reasoning.

For a few weeks now she'd been in contact with Michael trying to get information into Asia's whereabouts. The police were not working fast enough and Jaz didn't want to let Kyree know that she still had nightmares about everything that transpired. Sometimes she woke up, in the middle of the night, and could see Asia standing over her with a gun. Every time she was aiming her gun at someone Jaz loved. The thoughts were so vivid that Jaz was in fear for her life and the lives of the ones she cared about.

Michael was the only one she trusted to get her the information she needed. Kyree would only seek street justice and she didn't want him to put himself in that kind of danger. It was too risky for him to be caught up in anything illegal, especially with everything positive he was doing with his life lately. She was so proud of him. His studio and barbershop were booming, the restaurant was opening in a couple of days, and the clubs were the spot to be among the 757's partygoers.

Life was good and she wanted to do her best to keep it that way. She was doing a good job of it, and she and Kyree were in engagement bliss. Jaz was driving Monica crazy with maid of honor duties, Kyree crazy with fiancé duties, and herself crazy because none of them were paying her enough attention. She was like a mini bridezilla. Kyree was just happy the restaurant opening gave them a reason to leave the house. There were only so many color patterns he could tolerate before he lost his mind.

"Okay, I'm ready. How do I look?" Jaz asked Kyree. He didn't respond. When Jaz approached him, she noticed he was asleep on the couch. Jaz hit his thigh and he popped up.

"What?"

"I asked how I looked," she said, matter-of-factly.

Kyree blinked his eyes several times and rubbed his hand

down his face to gather his thoughts. Jaz was supposed to have been ready over an hour ago. But once his eyes adjusted to the light and he looked at her, it couldn't have been more worth it. He smiled as he admired her. She wore an all-white jumper with a deeply plunged neck, showing just the right amount of classy cleavage on her C-cups and clinging to her ass like it was especially made for her frame. Her hair hung down her back with loose flowing curls. She completed her look with a pair of red crocodile pumps and gold accessories.

Kyree stood up and lightly kissed her on the lips. He knew better than to mess up her lipstick after waiting hours for her to apply it. "You look fuckin' amazing," he admitted.

She smiled and wiped the lipstick from his lips. "You look good too." She inhaled his scent. He smelled amazing and looked even better. His beard was perfectly tapered to his face and freshly lined with his low cut. He donned a navy blue blazer with a black collar, a white button-up, dark denim jeans, and a pair of black suede tassel loafers. Jaz straightened his collar and they headed out the door.

When they arrived, everyone was trying to get inside The Soul Bistro. The restaurant stood on the historical streets of Old Towne Portsmouth. The spot was featured in the local paper, as it was set to draw up competition among a lot of the local businesses. Kyree loved the ambiance of the place as soon as he walked inside. He thought it was a great investment, but also a cool place he could chill and enjoy some of his favorite foods with his favorite lady. As he and Jaz walked inside, bypassing the crowd, her face lit up in amazement. He smirked upon seeing the admiration in her eyes.

Jaz thought the restaurant was breathtaking. It had come a long way since she'd seen it months before when it was still in talks. The rustic brick walls and dim lighting gave it a calming feel as soon as they walked inside. It had beautiful hardwood flooring and burgundy and warm colors displayed throughout. Smooth R&B played from a live band while waiters maneuvered back and forth through the heavy crowd. The hostess recognized her boss immediately and escorted him to his reserved booth in the back. Kyree picked that spot specifically so that he could watch all of the comings and goings of his investment. Jaz slid into the round booth first and Kyree followed after. She didn't hesitate to quickly pick up the menu. Her mouth watered just from the pictures and descriptions of the some of the foods. All types of soul food adorned the menu, from shrimp and grits to chicken and waffles. Kyree had hired one of the best soul food cooks in the whole area to cook food that made everyone who tasted it feel like they were at home having Sunday dinner at their grandma's house.

The waiter came by immediately to take their drink orders. Kyree had his usual Hennessey straight while Jaz wanted to try the house special: strawberry mojito. Upon seeing Monica and Mario walk in, Jaz waved them over.

"Oh shit! If it isn't Bey and Jay!" Jaz joked, standing to greet them with a hug. Monica rolled her eyes, but she had to admit that she and Mario did look great tonight. She wore an olive-colored blouse, white form-fitting pants, and tan suede tie-up booties. Mario looked fresh in an army green button up, black jeans, and army and black Nike Huaraches. Monica slid into the booth beside Jaz and Mario slid in beside her.

The waiter returned to take the order of the new guests and Jaz was ready to order her food. She ordered the chicken and waffles, Kyree and Mario ordered the BBQ ribs with collard greens, yams, and a side of cornbread, and Monica got the turkey legs with macaroni and cheese, cabbage, and cornbread. The waiter said their food was due out shortly, so Monica excused herself to the bathroom while the rest of them sat and chatted over drinks.

Kyree and Mario were deep into an NBA playoff discussion

while Jaz texted on her phone. She couldn't be less there for the intense conversation. Their food had finally arrived and it looked amazing. Jaz couldn't wait to dig in. Monica returned and Mario moved so that she could sit down, but she stopped him.

"J, guess who's here?" Monica beamed. She just knew Jaz was going to lose her shit when she found out.

"Who?"

"Girlllllll, Trey Songz!"

"Oh my gosh! Shut the front door!" Jaz shot up from her seat, nearly knocking Mario down. Mario moved out of her way before she trampled him. She kissed Kyree and said, "If I don't come back, tell Kylee I love her. Y'all will see me on the red carpet at the BET Awards."

Kyree turned up his lip. "Don't get fucked up."

Jaz waved him off and she and Monica headed to see where the R&B star was seated.

"Can you believe that shit, man?" Mario chuckled, shaking his head.

"Their asses will be back as soon as that nigga get a glimpse of their damn attitudes." Kyree and Mario both laughed.

He and Mario discussed the food and turnout while enjoying their meal.

Bing!

Kyree looked over at Jaz's phone she'd left on the table. It was the fifth time since she'd stepped away that he'd heard it. It started to ring like she had a phone call, so he picked it up to silence the call. His brow furrowed as he stared at the phone intensely. He was also able to read a few of the text messages that were on the front screen.

"Boy! This cornbread though?" Mario boasted as he shook his head, snapping Kyree out of his trance.

"Oh yeah, shit hits the spot," Kyree agreed.

Monica and Jaz returned, smiling from ear to ear. Trey had asked both of them to join him on his tour bus later. They were each flattered, but declined the offer. No matter how fine he was, Jaz only had eyes for one man. He stood for her to sit down, and she kissed him on the cheek before sliding into her seat.

"Mo, send me the pics." Monica nodded in agreement. "OMG," Jaz moaned as she tasted her food. "Baby, you gotta taste this." She brought her fork up to Kyree's mouth, but he turned his head.

"I'm good."

Jaz shrugged it off. "Well at least let me try yours," she said, placing her fork over his food.

"G'on 'head, Jaz." He moved her fork out of the way.

Jaz sat back, slightly appalled and embarrassed. She looked over at Monica and Mario and they hadn't seemed to notice, too wrapped up in their own conversation. She had no idea what had caused his sudden change in attitude. She knew he didn't take the whole Trey Songz thing seriously. He wasn't the type to be insecure.

Bing!

Jaz picked up her phone to see Monica had sent her the photos they'd taken with Trey. She opened up her messages and noticed she had a missed call and couple of missed text messages from Michael. Her heart stopped when it hit her what had changed Kyree's attitude so suddenly.

>>>>> **9:43 PM, Mike: I have that info you wanted. I'm only giving this to you because I will always love you, and I want you to be happy.**

>>>>> **9:45 PM, Mike: It's time sensitive Jaz. Call me ASAP.**

Jaz looked over at Kyree. She could see from his clenched jaw that he was pissed off with her. But she knew he wasn't one to make a scene. Kyree was always calm and didn't get out of character in public unless he truly had to.

Kyree felt like Jaz was really trying to take him to that level. He was sure if she said another word to him, he'd fuck her up in front of everyone. He didn't know what the messages were about, but he truly didn't care. It was obvious she was hiding it from him, or else she would have told him from the beginning.

Kyree finished his food and took the last swig of his drink without saying one word to Jaz. He'd even managed to make casual conversation with Monica and Mario, but it was almost as if Jaz wasn't there. She thought long and hard about how she'd explain herself to him. She knew he was hurt. Although he didn't say one word to her, his demeanor spoke volumes.

"A'ight, y'all. I think I'm about to get up out of here."

"Already?" Monica whined. They were having such a good time; she hated to see them go.

"Yeah, sis. I have a busy day tomorrow. But y'all enjoy yourselves. It's on the house tonight." He hugged his sister and dapped Mario up.

Kyree didn't even wait for Jaz before he started leaving. She exhaled deeply and got up to give Mario and Monica a hug.

"Y'all okay?" Monica quizzed, suddenly noticing the change in their moods.

Jaz simply shrugged and told her she'd call her later. When she got to the car, Kyree was waiting right in front, leaned against the passenger side, looking at his phone. He noticed her trying to use her arms for warmth, so he removed his blazer and draped it around her shoulders.

"Thanks." She smiled.

He opened her door and shut it behind her. For a split second, Jaz thought that Kyree had calmed down. But that thought was quickly nipped in the bud the second he got in the car. He didn't speak to her, but instead turned up Roddy Rich's "The Box" and pulled off. Jaz swallowed hard. She didn't know how to talk to him, but she had to let him know what was going on before he started creating his own theories.

"Ky," she called out to him. He ignored her and kept his eyes on the road. "Kyree, answer me, baby." Jaz knew he was mad, but this silent treatment was killing her. She turned off the music and he quickly cut his eyes from the road to her. His glare made her nervous. She turned her head and focused on the floor.

"I'm sorry. It's not what you think. I swear."

"Well, then what the fuck is it, Jaz! Because it looks to me like you're talking to your ex and keeping the shit from me."

"I am, but –"

"But what, Jaz!" He cut her off. "But ya ass got caught? Huh? Since when did you get on this sneaky shit? Here you are getting mad at me every day for dumb shit when you're the one out here fuckin' around!" he fumed.

"Kyree, I'm not fuckin' with him like that!" she yelled, tears falling from her face. "I just wanted to get information from him. That's it." She sniffled, and used her wrist to wipe her face.

Kyree shook his head. He knew she was keeping something from him. She preached about them being honest with each other every day, but she was keeping a big secret from him.

"I thought we were taking that shit as an 'L'," he reiterated their previous conversation. Jaz didn't have any words to say after that and neither did Kyree. It was hard for him to let everything that happened the night of the shooting go, but he had managed to do so because it was what Jaz wanted. He turned the music back on and they drove the rest of the way in silence.

Jaz had never meant for this to happen. It killed her to see him so hurt. Knowing she'd caused it made her feel like shit. She had a great man by her side who would go to the ends of the world and back for her and the only thing she wanted to do was protect him from ever having to do so. She made up in her mind that she was going to explain all of that to him once they were in the house. She was tired of hurting him and she wanted to clear the air completely. He had no idea about her fears and her nightmares. *I'm just going to tell him everything. Nobody is worth me losing him,* she thought to herself.

Kyree pulled into their driveway and put the car in park. He got out, opened her door, and then opened the front door to the house. He allowed her to walk in first and then he shut the door behind her.

"What the hell?" Jaz swung the door back open and followed him back to the car. "Where are you going, Kyree?"

"I can't be around you right now. I'm going out," he stated firmly as he opened his driver door.

Jaz slammed his car door closed. "No, you're not. We need to talk!" She stood in front of the door with her arms folded.

"Jaz, move," he calmly stated. She shook her head no. "I'm not going to tell you again. Move!" The anger in his voice caused her to jump. She moved out of his way and he hopped in the car.

She stopped the door from closing. "What time will you be home?" she asked, her eyes watering.

"I don't know. Go in the house."

"No. Not until you tell me where you're going."

Kyree hopped out of the car and grabbed her by the arm. He walked her like a child being scolded by a parent into the house.

"Stay yo' ass in the fuckin' house!" he yelled, locking the door from the inside and slamming it.

Jaz stood on the other side of the door and listened as the car started up and he drove off. She wouldn't dare go after him again after seeing the seriousness on his face. She slid down to the door. "I fucked up!" she cried aloud. She held her knees up to her chest and prayed to God that she could fix things before it was too late.

Kyree didn't know where he was headed. He just knew he had

to get away from Jaz because he saw himself physically hurting her. He had to clear his head before he did something truly out of his character. He drove around the city for an hour before finally deciding to go to his studio. K.O. was celebrating the wrap of his album so there were a few people there celebrating. Kyree wasn't really down for being bothered with a lot of people, but he popped his head in to see what was up with everyone.

"All of this shit couldn't be possible without my man, Kyree!" K.O. boasted with a bottle of Rosé in his hand. Everyone raised their cups to Kyree. Kyree modestly nodded his head. "Help yourself to anything here," K.O. offered.

Kyree declined, only asking K.O. if he had any extra rolling K.O. went into his pocket and gave him a fresh pack of Honey Bourbon Backwoods. They offered him weed, but Kyree declined. He had his own stash in his office. He didn't like smoking weed when he didn't know where it came from. These days, niggas were known to base their weed with all kinds of things. Kyree didn't get down like that. He rarely smoked anyway, only using the herb to relieve stress when he could no longer deal.

He said goodbye to everyone and congratulated K.O. one last time. As he was walking down the hallway, he ran into Kendall.

"Wassup, Ky?" She smiled.

"Ain't shit." He gave her a head nod. "I'm just headed to my office. You?"

"Oh, I was getting tired of all the partying in there. Shit was getting too wild for me."

Kyree nodded his head in understanding. "Well, a'ight. I'll catch you later."

"You okay?" Kendall asked, noticing his solemn mood.

"I'm good."

"You sure don't look good. You wanna talk about it?"

"Nah, I'm good."

"Are those papers? What you holding?" she asked, wanting to partake.

Kyree smirked. "You don't miss a beat, do you? K.O. and them got weed in there."

"Boy, I don't know what that shit is laced with. I don't fuck around." She quickly dismissed that option.

"True," Kyree stated, recalling his reasons as well. "A'ight. But don't be smoking up all my shit."

Kendall threw her hands up in mock surrender and waited as he opened the door to his office. Kyree's phone started to ring and he sent the caller to voicemail. He powered his phone off and tossed it on the couch.

"Trouble in paradise?"

"Nah, not at all. Just needed a break from all of these damn wedding plans," Kyree chuckled. He'd never discuss his relationship problems with anyone before he actually discussed them with Jaz - especially not someone who Jaz had her own qualms about.

Kendall nodded her head as Kyree retrieved his stash of weed from his desk drawer. He sat down and rolled up, heavy in thought about his current situation.

"Mind if I have a drink?" Kendall asked as she browsed his minibar.

"Help yourself."

Kendall took two glasses and filled one with Hennessey and Coke and the other with Ciroc and cranberry juice. She placed the Hennessey on the desk for Kyree, and sat down to finish hers. She watched intently as he added the weed contents to the cigar. Kyree was never much for words and Kendall didn't mind. She loved being in his calming presence. He was a relief from her often chaotic life. They always had a nice time kickin' it.

"Ya man album is gonna blow up," Kyree said, taking a pull from the now-rolled blunt.

Kendall rolled her eyes. K.O. was already yesterday's news to her. "I guess."

"What?" Kyree asked, passing her the blunt.

She brought it up to her mouth and instantly loved the euphoric sensation. "There's no future there."

"Oh, shit. Let me find out Kendall tryna settle down," Kyree laughed.

"Shut up." She smiled. "But on some real shit, this life gets old real quick. Every time I look up, my business is on the internet for the world to see. Bitches commenting dumb hateful shit under everything I post. The other day I posted a picture of my puppy, and some basic-ass hoe had the nerve to say, 'Damn, that's an ugly-ass dog'." Kyree couldn't help but laugh and Kendall could also find the humor in it now. "I guess I'm just tired."

Kyree took a swig of his drink. "Nah, you gotta do what makes you feel good at the end of the day."

"Truuuuuue," she agreed. She looked at him and noticed the faraway look in his eyes so she asked, "Is that what you're doing? Are you happy?"

Kyree smirked. He didn't even have to think about his answer as he looked at a photo of Jaz and Kylee on his desk. "Happier than I've ever been in my life." No matter what he and Jaz had going on at the moment, there still was no doubting that she was the reason for every moment of happiness he'd experienced in his life.

Kyree and Kendall chilled out the rest of the night, laughing and drinking. Kyree felt kind of guilty because he knew Jaz wouldn't be too happy about it if she knew. His need to clear his head was clouding his judgment. He knew he should probably head home, but his head was pounding. He couldn't remember the last time he'd felt so fucked up. It was nothing out of the usual to drink as much as he had, but now he felt like he was going to collapse. There was no way he could drive in this condition so he and Kendall decided to poke their heads into the party in K.O.'s studio to join in on the festivities.

The next morning, Kyree cautiously returned home. Several calls and texts from Jaz went unanswered, and even though she had been in the wrong the night before, he knew it was out of line for him to not come home. When he entered the house, he expected to see her sitting on the steps waiting for him. But he was surprised to see her nowhere in sight. He breathed a sigh of relief. He really wasn't for any drama this early in the morning. His head was still hurting too much from last night to be bothered with the theatrics. He took to the stairs and heard the shower in their bedroom so he grabbed a few items and headed to the hall bathroom to shower and change.

While Jaz was in the shower, she thought she'd heard Kyree come in. She finished her shower, eager to speak with him. She'd stayed up all night, but he never showed. It wasn't like him to not call or come home so she knew that he was still pissed with her. She'd never meant for things to go as far as they had.

Jaz dried off and put on her bathrobe. When she opened the door, she expected to see Kyree sitting in the room. She went to the window to see if his car was in the driveway. When she confirmed he was there, she knew that he probably was still avoiding her, but hearing the shower in the hallway put her mind at ease. It also gave her time to think. Even though she'd spent most of the night going over what to say to him in her head, the feeling of nervousness consumed her. Finding out where the hell he'd been all night was at the top of her list of things to ask him, but seeing as though she was already treading on thin ice, she decided against it.

Jaz grabbed her favorite lotion and sat on her bed to moisturize her body while making sure to listen for Kyree's shower to end. He'd been in there for at least fifteen minutes and Jaz was getting anxious. When she finally heard the water stop, she prepared herself. She repositioned herself on the bed several times. She sat up straight, crossed her legs, uncrossed her legs, leaned back, and then sat up straight again with her legs crossed and hands placed studiously on her knees.

Jaz heard the door open, but Kyree never came in the room. She shook her head and took a deep breath. This was going to be more challenging than she thought because now she was getting pissed. He was really trying her now. She decided to suck it up and headed downstairs to find him. He was in his man cave watching TV. When he saw her walk in, he glanced at her and then back at the screen.

Aw, hell nah, she said to herself. She stood in front of him, blocking his view of the TV. "I know you see me standing here, Kyree!"

Kyree sighed heavily. There was no more putting it off. "Wassup, Jazzy?"

She softened up and sat in the La-Z-Boy beside him. "Ky, I've been contemplating how to talk to you about this shit all night." She rubbed her sweaty hands down her bathrobe.

Kyree's anger had subsided and he could now see the worry in her eyes. He sat up in his chair to give her his undivided attention.

"Kyree, the only reason I was contacting Mike was to get information about Asia. Ever since the shooting, I've been having nightmares. I can't sleep without waking up in a cold sweat."

Kyree thought for a moment to see if he could recollect, and it hit him. She was good at covering it up. When she woke up in a panic, she told him that she could sense Kylee was awake and she'd leave to go check on her. Kyree sensed something was off, but when he questioned her about it, she always had a plausible excuse. She couldn't even look at him as she spoke. He used his finger and lifted her head so that she was facing him.

"I don't feel safe not knowing where she is and the police aren't doing shit about it, so I called Mike because he's known her for a long time. He knows how her mind works, and more importantly, he knows all of her doctors. If she contacted them to re-up on her meds, they were on strict orders to notify him."

"Baby, I didn't know you were feeling like this. Why wouldn't you come to me?"

"And say what? That I can't sleep knowing that bitch could be at my door? Kyree, you would find her and have her neck for that. I don't want you getting involved in business like that again," she admitted.

"See, that's the thing, you and Kylee are my business. I always handle my business." Kyree licked his lips. He never wanted to tell her this because he didn't want her getting involved, but he really didn't have a choice at this point. "Jazzy, you don't have anything to worry about. It's handled."

Jaz looked him in the eye and could see the fire inside. She put her hands up to her face, shocked by his revelation. "Kyree, you promised me you wouldn't."

"And I kept my promise. *I* didn't do shit. But it's been done since a month after the shooting. The less you know, the better."

Jaz wrapped her arms around his neck and he embraced her deeply. He knew as soon as he made the promise to Jaz back at the hospital that he had to have Asia handled. It didn't take long for the streets to find her, especially with the $10K price tag Fat Boy put on her head. He was supposed to take that secret to his grave. But Jaz needed to know so that she could live her life in peace.

He pulled her away to look at her. "Don't ever keep no shit like this from me again. You hear me?" She looked down and he brought her head up. She nodded. "I'm your king. If you can't feel safe with me, then I'm not doing my job."

"I know. I'm sorry." She kissed him on the lips. She wasn't happy with what he'd done, but couldn't help feeling a huge sense of relief. She didn't have to keep secrets from him about Michael, Asia was gone, and she could finally rest peacefully. Things weren't perfect, but then again, they never were.

CHAPTER NINE

With an infant to care for, a relationship that needed attention, and a very important hair show in less than two weeks, Jaz thought she was going to lose her mind. It seemed like her attention was needed everywhere and there wasn't enough of her to go around. Kyree was extremely supportive of everything she had going on so he was always helping out as best he could. When Jaz had to work late to stay for the hair show practice, Kyree would pick Kylee up from daycare and have her dressed and ready for bed by the time Jaz got home. On days when he couldn't work it out in his schedule, Calvin or Jackie were just as willing to help out.

The entire staff at the salon was putting in overtime to make sure the show was a success. The $10,000 prize money was sure to add some great upgrades to the shop. Jaz's idea to incorporate hers and Monica's favorite movie, *BAPS,* into the show was going to put them a step ahead of the competition. The hair designs that they'd created were like nothing anyone had ever seen before.

Ms. Ray was in charge of choreography, Jaz was in charge of

style and design, and Monica was in charge of everything, and everyone, else. Together, they had a great team system. When Jaz and Ms. Ray would get off track, Monica was sure to put them back in line - when she could, of course. Today she was having the hardest time getting everyone to calm down after Jaz and Ms. Ray got the whole practice squad in an uproar trying to imitate each other. She couldn't help but join in on the laughter too.

Tameka hopped in front of everyone and asked, "Okay, y'all, who am I?" She stood up extra straight, stuck her chest out, sucked her cheeks in, and walked with her nose in the air. "Y'all, I think I'm in love." She batted her eyelashes and popped her tongue.

Everyone burst into laughter - all except Ms. Ray.

"Oh, you's a funny bitch." He rolled his eyes.

"You know we love you, boo." Tameka hugged him.

"But I do be in love, y'all."

"No, nigga. You be in love with the dick," Monica called him out, and everyone laughed. "Like that time you were messin' with that one dude with the unibrow. What was his name? Um..." Monica tried to remember.

"Johnquaveus!" Jaz helped her out.

Monica snapped her finger. "Yep, that's it. And that nigga cut you off after two weeks, so you broke into his house - "

"Correction," Ms. Ray stopped her, "I had a key!"

"Okay, my bad. You entered his house, with the key that you copied after he told you to give him back the original, and replaced his moisturizer with Nair." Everyone in the shop was in shock. Very few knew that story, besides Jaz and Monica.

"You did what?" Tameka asked, just to be sure.

Ms. Ray refused to speak, so Jaz jumped in to clarify. "Girl, that boy went from having one brow, to NO brow." There wasn't a dry eye in the shop as everyone broke down and laughed until they couldn't breathe.

Ms. Ray dropped his head, and then quickly raised it as he strutted down their practice runway. He began to sing to the tune of Deborah Cox's hit "Nobody's Supposed to Be Here", "No, no, no, no, no, no, no, no, no...dick will make you do, some crazy things."

Ms. Ray joined in on their laughter. His life was an open book. There was nothing he didn't mind sharing with anyone, especially if he got a good laugh out of it. He enjoyed every moment of life, which was why he was quick to keep it real when he saw fit. The women admired his honesty, even though sometimes it came without warning or a filter.

"Don't forget how much I know about you bitches too. So ya better act right," he warned. That was all it took for everyone to straighten up.

"And on that note, it's time for me to roll out," Tameka laughed. Everyone followed Tameka out the door and the only ones left were Jaz, Monica, and Ms. Ray.

"We have such a good team this year. If we don't win, that shit is rigged," Monica said while cleaning up.

"We are guaranteed not to lose this year because I'm going to sleep with one of the judges. You know the tall chocolate one? Yeah, that's bae."

"Oh lawd, please don't. Because we'll lose automatically as soon as you fall in *love*." Monica laughed and Ms. Ray stuck up his middle finger.

"Hell you doin', J?"

"Shhh," she quieted him. "I'm trying to catch up on my tea."

"Let me know if anything good happened," Ms. Ray said on his way to take the trash out.

Monica shook her head. Jaz loved the celebrity blog sites. Whenever she had time to unwind, she was catching up on the latest gossip in the industry. She got a kick out of other people's drama. Her own was often too much for her to deal with, so if she could see a comment Chris Brown left under one of his ex's photos professing his love and apologizing, then she was there for it.

"Y'all wanna go to the bar or something?" Ms. Ray asked as he swept under Jaz's feet.

"Yeah, I could do that. I need a drink. What about you, Jaz?" When she didn't respond, Monica looked up from counting her drawer. "Jaz!"

"Huh?" She looked up. She was so caught up in her phone screen that she barely realized they were talking to her.

"We asked if you wanted to go out for drinks," Monica reiterated.

"Nah, I'm good. I'm just going to head home. I'll see y'all tomorrow morning." She got up and threw her purse over her shoulder.

"Okay. And my mama said don't worry about us getting the kids. They're both asleep anyway." Jaz nodded her head in agreement. "What time is your first appointment?" Monica asked.

"It's at 10:00. I'll see y'all then. Bye."

They both waved goodbye and continued their tasks at hand.

"Oh, hell nah!" Ms. Ray said.

"What?" Monica quizzed.

"That heffa left without helping clean up!"

Monica shook her head and laughed. That was so like Jaz. She was good at easing her way out of doing things.

Jaz walked in her house with a lot on her mind, and all she wanted to do was relax. Kyree wasn't home when she arrived, and she was relieved. She needed that time to herself to think and unwind. As soon as she slid down in her hot bubble bath, the stress that so heavily consumed her seemed to melt away for the time being. With the sounds of Tink playing from her Alexa speaker, Jaz laid her head back and relaxed as she sipped on a glass of red wine.

Within a year, she'd gone from being engaged to one man, and then pregnant and engaged to another. Kyree was her protector, her lover, her best friend, and her peace. Whenever in his presence, time seemed to stand still. Over the years she'd put up with a lot just for them to be together and there was nothing she wouldn't do for him. There was no one she trusted more to keep it real with her and never tell her only what she wanted to hear. Jaz felt assurance in knowing that Kyree was there for her - no one else.

The bath pushed all of her worries aside. As she was stepping out, she heard Kyree's keys at the door. She dried her body and put on a pair of pajama pants and a tank top. She could hear him coming up the steps as she removed her shower cap. The pin curls she'd put in while at the shop would hold up just nicely in the morning. As she was putting her satin scarf on her head, Kyree entered the bathroom. He wrapped his arms around her from behind while kissing her on the cheek and she smiled.

"Fat Boy is downstairs. We're about to head out. You wanna roll with us? Kick it like old times?"

"Nah, I think I'll sit this one out."

Kyree nodded his head. "So what'd you do today?" he asked.

"I had a few heads until about 5:00, and then we practiced for the show until about 9."

"Oh, word?" He released her and removed his shirt in one quick motion. "How's it coming along?"

"Really good," she said as he made his way to the bedroom. "I think we're going to take home the grand prize this year."

"I know y'all are. I'm so proud of you too."

"Speaking of being proud, I heard K.O.'s album today. Shit is tight!" she boasted as she sat down on the bed.

"I know, right? Shit's gonna have the streets goin' crazy."

"Yeah, you know Tori fucks with his right hand man, Jermaine. She kept trying to get me to go to the release party with her, but that was the same night of the restaurant opening. She said it was lit though," Jaz said as she began to moisturize for the night.

"You don't need to be around that crowd anyway." Kyree kissed her on the cheek and threw his towel over his shoulder.

"Yeah, that's what I told her. Did you happen to check it out though?"

Kyree furrowed his brow in confusion as he searched for a pair of socks in his drawer. He had no idea where Jaz was going with all of the questions out of left field. "Yeah, I stopped by. It was a'ight. You know them niggas be poppin' them pills and shit. I don't have time for all of that."

"So, was Tori there? That girl always says she's going to be somewhere, and don't do shit but stay in the house," Jaz laughed at her own joke.

"Nah, I didn't see her."

"Oh, anyone else there I might know?" she nonchalantly asked.

"Yo, what's with all the twenty questions?" Kyree wanted to know.

"Was Kendall there?" Jaz folded her arms.

"Of course she was. She is dating the nigga. Damn, Jaz. I know you're not on no insecure shit right now."

Jaz took a deep breath. She was going against her better judgement by asking him, but she just had to know.

"Did y'all hang out?"

Kyree thought for a split second. There was no way he could tell her that he and Kendall chilled. Jaz would flip. They were at a good place right now, and he didn't want to fuck that up with something that truly meant nothing.

"Nah, man. We spoke. But she was chillin' with her nigga most of the night." He was positive she had some information from somewhere, or else she would have never questioned him.

Jaz stood up in front of his bare chest. She slowly shook her head and pulled out her phone. "Then what the fuck is this?"

Kyree looked at her crazy. "What the fuck are you talking about?" She pushed the phone into his chest and he grabbed it from her. He examined the photo on her phone screen intently, and he couldn't for the life of him figure out how the fuck she had a picture of Kendall's hand down his crotch.

"What, nigga? Cat got ya tongue?" Jaz seethed, waiting on him to respond.

Kyree didn't really have an answer for her. He was more fucked up that night than he'd been his entire life. Most of that evening's events were a blur to him. From the look on her face, she wanted answers immediately and he couldn't give her the answers she wanted. But that didn't stop him from trying his hand.

"Jaz, you fuckin' buggin'. This dark-ass picture. You can't even tell who the fuck that is."

Jaz snatched her phone back. She closed her eyes and bit her bottom lip trying to gather her thoughts before she said or did something truly out of her character. But Kyree was doing the unthinkable, something she thought she'd never have to experience in their relationship. He was lying to her.

Jaz had spent the last two hours examining the photo after seeing it at the salon on a blog site. In the photo a man, that appeared to be Kyree, was lying on a couch while Kendall was on top of him with her hand down his pants. The top of the man's face wasn't visible, but there was a clear shot from the mouth down. The headline read: **Looks like reality star Kendall has herself a new boo. #WeAintMad**

Jaz wanted to breakdown in the salon upon seeing it, but she didn't want her friends to know. Besides, she trusted Kyree and wanted to give him the benefit of the doubt. As much as she tried to deny to herself that the photo couldn't be him, she couldn't get past it. Yes, the photo was dark, but there was no doubt in her mind that it was Kyree. She'd screenshot the photo and zoomed in several times to clarify that it was him before she jumped to conclusions. And even though she knew it was him, she still wanted him to say something, anything, to assure her that it wasn't. But instead, he was lying to her face as if they hadn't known each other almost their whole lives.

"Kyree, please don't try to play me for stupid," she spoke through clenched teeth.

"I'm not!" he countered. "I don't remember that shit!"

"Sooooo, which one is it? It's not you? Or you don't remember?"

"I don't know who the fuck that is. I just know it's not me!"

Jaz laughed neurotically. She didn't even mean to laugh; it just happened on instinct. It was almost like a reflex to keep from crying.

"Kyree, this is the same shit you had on the night of the restaurant opening so don't fuckin' try to tell me otherwise. I'm not fuckin' stupid! I didn't say shit about you not coming home because I knew I fucked up and you needed time to clear your head. But I can't believe this is the shit you're on!" She pushed him in the chest.

"Chill out, yo!" Kyree tried to gather his thoughts. He had no idea how they'd gotten to this point. Shit was happening too fast and he couldn't wrap his head around everything.

"Call her. Put all of this shit to bed."

"You buggin'." He shook his head.

"Do I look like I'm fuckin' playin'?" She glared at him with her arms crossed.

Kyree started to question her seriousness again, but from the look in her eyes, he knew better. So he picked up his phone and dialed Kendall's number and put the phone on speaker.

"Wassup?" she gleefully answered. "I've been meaning to call you to thank you for the other night. It really meant a lot to me."

Kyree looked at Jaz and he swore he could see visible steam coming from out of her ears. "No problem. Anytime you need to talk about your *man*," Kyree stressed so that Jaz could know, "I don't mind giving my opinion." He could tell Jaz wasn't buying it, but he continued anyway. He hoped Kendall could sense where he was going with his phone call. "Look, there's this photo online of what looks like you and some nigga on the couch."

"Oh, yeah, the paps love to follow me."

"Nah, I mean, it looks like y'all were kind of intimate, and Jaz seems to think it's me."

"Um…Jaz isn't around, is she?" Kendall stammered.

Kyree was confident that Kendall would have his back in this. Besides, he knew better than to say Jaz was standing right in front of him. "Nah, she's not here."

Kendall thought for a moment. She knew what she'd agreed to after her conversation with Kyree the night before. If asked, she was supposed to say, "nothing happened." And if he ever called her about it, Jaz knew and was probably standing right next to him. Kyree couldn't stress that enough. But she hated the way he made her feel afterward. They'd had an incredible night, and he was treating her like a mistake. She felt cheap. So she did what would make her feel good: she told the truth.

"Wellllllll…We did have a lot to drink, so you probably don't remember." Kyree's brow furrowed in confusion. This was not how they planned what they were going to say. His jaw tightened as she continued. "We were in your office fooling around, and one thing led to another, and we ended up fucking on the couch."

BOP! Kyree never even saw Jaz's fist before it connected with his jaw, causing the phone to fly out of his hands and him to grab his face.

"Ah, shit! What the fuck is wrong with you?" he fumed, trying to grab her.

Jaz dodged him and sprang for the phone.

"Hello? Kyree? Are you okay?" Kendall asked.

"Naw, bitch! And he won't be okay when I'm finished with him! And don't let me catch yo' hoe ass either. I swear on everything I love I'm going to beat yo' ass right back into that high school cafeteria. Fuck wit' it if you want to, bitch!"

Jaz didn't have to finish talking. Kendall had hung up the phone right after she mentioned the cafeteria. She tried to throw the phone at Kyree's head, but he caught it just in time.

"Ahhhh!" she screamed. She charged him and tried throwing punches at his chest. He grabbed her before she could land one and held her tightly in his arms. She jumped and kicked wildly while he held her, finally subduing her to the floor.

Hearing the ruckus from downstairs, Fat Boy ran upstairs to see what the commotion was about. "Yo, what the fuck is going on?"

They'd both completely forgotten he was there. But that didn't stop Jaz from trying to break free. She continued to kick and scream.

"Hold her legs down," Kyree instructed.

Fat Boy didn't want to get involved, but Jaz seriously did need to calm down.

"Let me go!" She yelled.

With Fat Boy holding her legs, Jaz eventually wore herself out. She couldn't move if she wanted to. So she just broke down and cried, causing Kyree's tight hold to turn into a strong, comforting hug. Fat Boy released her legs. He stood up and scratched his head. He never thought he'd see the day that this would happen to his favorite couple. It was obvious they needed to sort some things out, so he left the room to wait downstairs. He didn't venture too far, just in case things got out of hand again.

"Why, Kyree? Whyyyyyyy?" Jaz screamed through her tears. "How could you do this to me?"

Kyree really didn't have an answer as to why. He could barely remember how it even happened. So instead of speaking, he just rocked her back and forth. Drunk or not, he couldn't believe he'd fucked up so majorly. One night could have possibly cost him everything.

"I know baby, I know," he uttered, holding her. Jaz began to shake, and Kyree only held her closer. "We're going to get through this, Jazzy. This shit is forever, baby."

As soon as she heard him utter their favorite line to say to each other, Jaz lost it all over again. "Get the fuck out of my house!" she yelled.

"What?" he looked at her.

Jaz bit his arm.

"Ah, shit!" he yelled, grabbing his stinging arm and unintentionally letting her go.

She quickly rose to her feet. "You heard me, nigga! Get the fuck out!"

"Hold the fuck on. This is my house too! I ain't going no damn where!"

"Fine then. I'll go!" she challenged him. She briskly walked toward her closet, pulled out her suitcase, and frantically started throwing all of the garments from her closet inside.

Kyree flung the suitcase off the bed. "You're not leaving either!"

"Fuck you, Kyree!" Jaz started putting the things back in the suitcase.

"Calm down!" He grabbed her arm and she almost punched him again, but he caught her hand. "You're gonna stop putting your fuckin' hands on me!" he warned. "Look, it's obvious you need a day to cool the fuck off, so I'll go to Fat Boy's crib for the night."

"You can go to hell for all the fuck I care. I just want you out of my fucking life!" She snatched her wrist free from his grasp.

Kyree shook his head and grabbed the shirt he'd taken off and put it on. He took one last look at Jaz and didn't know what to say to her. The hateful glare in her eyes was something he'd never seen in anyone before, especially not his sweet Jaz. In a matter of moments his world had come crashing down, all for a quick fuck. In his right state of mind, he would have never done anything like this to Jaz.

"I love you, Jazzy," he said just before shutting their bedroom door.

Jaz snarled and waited by the window for him and Fat Boy to pull off. As soon as his headlights had disappeared, she broke down. She fell onto her bed, grabbed her pillow, and cried. She cried so hard that it hurt her to breathe.

She couldn't believe what had just happened. It was like a bad dream that she couldn't wake up from. Never in a million years did she think this would be her life. This was the kind of shit she laughed or shook her head at when she heard about it during salon gossip. This wasn't supposed to be her life. Her man was one of the good guys - or so she thought.

Jaz felt as though a blindfold had finally been removed from over her eyes and she hated the surprise behind it. There was a pain in her heart that she'd never felt before. She held her pillow tighter and cried herself to sleep.

The next morning the sun made its way through the blinds, only confirming that last night really did, in fact, happen. Jaz raised her head and could see that her pillow was soaked with tears. She wiped her face with her hand and got up to go to the bathroom. After relieving her bladder, she washed her hands. She added a dab of toothpaste to her toothbrush and looked in the mirror. It was the first time she'd looked at herself. During her struggle to break free from Kyree's grasp, her scarf had fallen off her head so her hair was a mess. But that was the least of her worries. Her face was dry and stained with tears, her eyes were red and weary, and her beautiful brown skin had lost all of its glow. If anyone were to see her in this state, there'd be no doubt in their mind that she was going through something.

There was no hiding her current emotional state behind foundation and concealer. Putting on a fake smile to cover up the pain in her heart was just not something she was up for today. So she grabbed her phone, after bypassing a bunch of texts and calls from Kyree, and sent Monica a text saying that she wasn't feeling well and asking if she and Ms. Ray could take her appointments for the day. Jaz didn't trust anyone else to take care of her clients but the two of them. Monica wished her well and said they'd gladly do it. Jaz let all of her clients know she wouldn't be in and only two out of the six said they'd reschedule.

Her next call was to Jackie to check on Kylee. Jackie placed the phone to Kylee's mouth so that Jaz could hear her coo. It was the first time Jaz had genuinely smiled in hours. Jackie assured Jaz that she'd watch Kylee while she recuperated. With her affairs momentarily in order, Jaz had nothing to do but sit and think.

Knowing that the happy home she and Kyree once shared was falling apart was heart-wrenching. They both wanted to give Kylee a home with both parents. Now, that was impossible. Jaz could forgive a lot of things, but she could never forgive him for sleeping with another woman. The fact that he tried to lie about it to her face were all the signs that she needed to confirm that getting caught was what he was most sorry about.

On the other side of town, Kyree was also going through hell.

He stared at the ceiling as he lay in the guest bed at Fat Boy's condo. He would've much rather been at his own house, lying in his own bed, fucking the shit out of his fiancée. But he'd committed the ultimate no-no in any relationship. He racked his brain from the night until the morning trying to figure out how he'd slipped up. That night he'd been hitting the Hennessey hard because he was angry with Jaz. Soon after that, he headed over to K.O.'s party and they were popping bottles of Ace and Rosé. He was also very high off the purp he smoked.

At the time, Kyree knew he was taking things to the extreme, but he needed the release. Drunk or not, any man would be a fool not to notice how sexy Kendall looked. He just never thought he'd be the fool to fuck up his life because of it. He couldn't believe he was so weak. He could vaguely remember her riding his dick. He wanted to stop her, but he couldn't. It was already too late, and there was no going back once they'd started. Once he realized what he'd done, he made Kendall promise never to tell anyone. He thought they'd had an understanding, but he was obviously wrong. He was pissed off with her and had managed to ignore several of her calls since last night. He swore if he saw her, he'd kill her. But he knew it wasn't 100% her fault. He blamed himself for ever being in the situation in the first place.

Now his main focus was to figure out how he could fix things - or if it was even possible to fix. Jaz was a headstrong woman and she didn't play those kinds of games.

He grabbed his phone for the umpteenth time and dialed her number. But just like all of the other times, he was met with her voicemail.

"Fuck!"

Kyree exhaled deeply. Jaz couldn't avoid him forever. He'd give her a day, but that was it. He got up from bed and ran into Fat Boy in the hallway.

"I left a toothbrush and towel on the counter," Fat Boy mentioned.

"A'ight, good lookin' out."

"So, uh...you gon' make breakfast, or nah?"

Kyree looked at him like he was crazy. "Fuck you, bruh."

Fat Boy laughed and Kyree retreated to the bathroom. He washed his face and brushed his teeth, and then he rode up the street to the mall and purchased a few clothes to last him the weekend. It was Saturday, and he was sure that they would have worked out their problems by then. He had a few appointments at the barbershop and figured Jaz would be working out her issues at the salon like she usually did.

He would have never guessed she'd be at home wallowing in self-pity. Jaz felt as though she was drowning in her own tears. She sat in bed, only getting up to relieve her bladder every so often. Her blinds were shut so tight that she wasn't even sure of what time of day it was. She thought constantly about Kyree. She couldn't eat, sleep, or even think straight. The only thing she'd managed to do was cry.

"How could he do this to me? And with her?" Jaz asked herself aloud.

Nothing could get her out of the bed with her restless thoughts. She rummaged through her bathroom cabinet, trying to find something to help with the aches in her body from fighting with Kyree. Her fist had landed on his teeth and her hand was killing her. Kyree's Percocet bottle from his gunshot wound glowed in the cabinet like an award. She happily grabbed it and took one. The drug did little for her emotional pain, but it did help her to fall asleep.

The next morning was just as hard as the first. Jaz's phone had been off for a whole day and she refused to turn it on, which was why Monica and Ms. Ray made it their business to see how she was doing. Monica had been calling Jaz to check on her and Jaz hadn't answered the phone. She thought it was strange, but she dismissed it, figuring she was just sick in bed. But then Jackie called asking about her too, and that just didn't sit well with Monica. Jackie was watching Kylee, and Jaz would've answered that call in a heartbeat. Monica tried getting answers from Kyree, but he was vague when she spoke with him. Monica needed answers, so she went to the source.

Ms. Ray rang the doorbell repeatedly, causing Jaz to wake up. She dragged her heavy body from the bed to look out the window. She rolled her eyes when she saw Ms. Ray's car. There was no doubt in her mind that Monica was with him. Although she hoped they'd leave, she knew better. Besides, Monica had a key. It wouldn't take them long before they decided to use it.

Monica had just placed the key in the lock when Jaz flung the door open. They both jumped back, more so from Jaz's appearance than anything. She looked a mess. They knew she was sick, but she looked as though she hadn't seen the light of day in ages.

"Wassup?" she asked with the door cracked.

"We were just checking up on you. You haven't been answering your phone," Monica said.

"Oh, I'm fine. Just trying to beat this cold." Jaz faked a cough.

"Oh, well let us in. We brought soup," Ms. Ray said, holding up a Panera Bread bag.

"Nah, I don't want y'all getting it too."

"Girl, please. I have Purell and Lysol wipes in my purse." Monica pushed past her anyway.

Jaz sighed heavily and shut the door behind them. They made their way toward the kitchen and Jaz instantly regretted opening the door. She took a seat at her island while Monica and Ms. Ray prepared her a meal of what they thought would help cure her cold.

"Girl, you missed all of the drama at the shop," Ms. Ray began, getting a glass from out of the cabinet and filling it with orange juice. He didn't even wait for Jaz to say anything before he started telling her. "Girl, you know how Tori is always claiming to be dating this nigga, that nigga, and the third?" Jaz smirked and nodded. "Yeah, well, Ms. Tori came into the salon with a black eye."

Monica placed a bowl of chicken noodle soup and a spoon in front of Jaz.

"Why?" Jaz furrowed her brow.

"Turns out my client, Tika, with that cheap ass Yaki weave, caught her fuckin' around with her husband, Andre. Girl, Tika caught the bitch coming out of WaWa and snuck her with a two piece while she was putting $2 on pump two. Tika stopped the pump on $1.58, beat her ass, and then literally finished pumping the other .42 cents."

Monica laughed even though she'd heard the story yesterday.

"Turns out, Dre has been taking this bitch out of town, giving her money, and flaunting her around like he ain't tied down. And yet Tori's hair costs more than everything Tika owns, and Tika still manages to come to me with that $5 un-curllable-ass stiff weave. I just don't understand, Lawd." Ms. Ray placed his hand across his head in confusion.

Monica and Ms. Ray burst out laughing. Jaz was crying laughing - or so they thought. The crackle in her voice went from tears of laughter to tears of pain.

"Jaz, are you okay?" Monica rushed to her side.

"Nooooo," Jaz whimpered.

Ms. Ray rushed to her aide too, and rubbed her back while Monica rocked her. They had no idea what could be bothering her.

Little did they know, but hearing Tika's story of how her man was cheating on her and flaunting another woman around town made Jaz sick to her stomach. She couldn't help but feel like maybe Kyree was out doing the same things with Kendall.

"What's wrong, mama?" Ms. Ray asked.

Jaz contemplated telling them. They were her best friends. They shared everything with each other. Jaz knew all of their secrets and they knew all of hers. She just didn't think she could handle the embarrassment of them knowing this. She was ashamed of being like the women they usually laughed and joked about. She felt stupid, and she didn't want them to pity her. She pitied herself enough.

"You can tell us, J."

Usually, the things that happened in her relationship didn't leave the walls of their home. Jaz didn't think it was necessary that everyone in the world was involved in something that should have been strictly shared between two people. If she saw that it could be worked out amongst her and Kyree, she kept it to herself. But this was an all-time low, and Jaz couldn't yet see them coming back from this. As embarrassed as she was, it was killing her keeping it all bottled inside. She was tired of having conversations with herself and getting no response. Another second alone with her thoughts and she was sure to be committed to an insane asylum. Jaz exhaled slowly.

"Ky...Ky...and...Kendall," she said through her tears. "He... they...he...he cheated!" she blurted out.

Monica and Ms. Ray's eyes both bugged in shock. They couldn't believe their ears. There was no way Kyree would have done something like that. He loved her, and he wasn't afraid to let the world know about it. Jaz had to be mistaken.

"Are you sure?" Monica asked.

Jaz sucked her teeth. She knew it would be hard to convince

anyone that Kyree was anything less than a saint, especially his little sister. "Give me your phone."

Monica handed her the phone and Jaz went online to find the article with the photo that had killed her world. She showed it to them, and neither could believe their eyes. They couldn't see his full face, so Monica asked, "Are you sure that's him?"

"Monica! It's him! I'm not fuckin' stupid!" Jaz barked, annoyed.

Monica threw her hands up in mock surrender and Jaz went on to tell them about the events that took place that horrible night.

"Oh, my...hmm," Ms. Ray, stammered. He fanned himself with his hand. "This calls for something stronger than this orange juice." He went to Jaz's wine cooler and found a bottle of champagne. He retrieved two more glasses and mixed the champagne with the orange juice.

"Well, what'd he have to say?" Monica quizzed.

"He didn't have shit to say." Jaz downed her drink and passed it to Ms. Ray for a refill.

Monica was pissed. She couldn't believe her brother would do something like this. He wasn't that kind of man. In her eyes, he could do no wrong. But Monica didn't take too lightly to cheating. She knew how it felt, and she hated for Jaz to have to feel this way. As much as she wanted to call her brother and hear his side of things, she had to be there for her girl right now.

"Don't worry, Jaz. Y'all are going to work through this." Ms. Ray instantly regretted saying anything after he saw the contorted look forming on Jaz's face.

"I don't want to work shit out! It's over!" she fumed. She drank her second glass and snatched the bottle of champagne from his hands. She didn't need a glass. She took the drink back from the bottle.

"Ooookay, slow down there, Lindsey Lohan." Ms. Ray took the

bottle from her. "What I meant to say was, *you're* going to get through this."

Jaz nodded her head but in actuality, she just didn't believe she could. Her world was crashing down and she just didn't see a way to fix it.

It took a couple hours of convincing, but Monica and Ms. Ray eventually left Jaz to sort through her emotions on her own. Monica agreed not to tell her mother and even offered to go pick up Kylee, which was a relief for Jaz. She didn't want Jackie to know until she told her face to face. Jackie was like a mother to Jaz, after she'd lost her own to cancer when she was little. She respected and valued her opinions and felt she owed her that much.

Jaz was once again left alone with her thoughts - and a shitload of alcohol. Before he left, Ms. Ray had taken the champagne in an attempt to get her to calm down, but he didn't take the good stuff. Jaz went to the theater room and searched through the mini bar Kyree had recently added. She poured herself a shot of Ciroc and quickly downed the drink in one gulp.

"Shit!" She coughed, her chest instantly burning from the sensation.

She took another glass and poured herself a glass of Crown Royal Apple. She didn't usually drink brown liquor but she actually liked the taste of this one, and if she was going to be drinking, she wanted something that didn't make her insides feel like they were on fire. She took a sip and relished the taste.

She turned on the stereo surround sound and began to blast *The Best of Aretha Franklin*. It was her mother's favorite album growing up. The sound of her mother's voice always remained with her throughout her years. Her mother, Simone, had the voice of a Motown headliner. She would sing while cooking and Jaz always remembered how warm her beautiful voice made her feel.

Whenever Jaz needed that comforting feeling, Aretha always made her feel closer to home.

With her drink in hand, Jaz roamed the halls of her home, and she couldn't help but realize how empty it felt. She'd been in the house alone many times before, but never to this extent. Though there were many fixtures and furniture throughout, every space was barer than the next. It was like the house could sense her mood.

She lazily traced her finger along the wall, thinking of how alone she felt. It wasn't long before the urge to cry took over again. "How could he hurt me like this?" she asked herself. "How come I'm the one over here hurting?" When the tears started to fall again, Jaz grew angry. "Ugh!"

As Aretha's voice spoke of a no-good man, she took to the stairs and headed for their bedroom in a fit of rage. She felt like Angela Bassett in *Waiting to Exhale* as she tore through their bedroom closet. She grabbed a pair of scissors off her shelf and picked up Kyree's favorite Jordan's.

She cut the tongue of the shoe and a feeling of euphoria came over her. Still not satisfied, she began to cut the laces down the middle. "Ah hahaha...see how this nigga like this shit." She cut through four more pairs of shoes until she got tired and fell to the floor.

"My best friend...how could he do this to me?" If she knew where her phone was, she would've called him and cussed him out. But she hadn't turned it on since the day before, and she was too tired and drunk to go looking for it. So she wallowed on the floor and cried herself to sleep.

CHAPTER TEN

Kyree never knew it would feel so awkward pulling up in front of his own house. It had been three days since he and Jaz had their argument, but it felt like an eternity. He sat in the driveway and didn't see her car. It was Monday morning and the salon was usually closed. He knew today would be the perfect time to catch her. She wasn't there now, but she had to come back.

Kyree walked up the porch. He couldn't wait to see Kylee. He'd never gone longer than a day without seeing her. He placed his key in the lock, eager to take a shower in his own home.

"What the fuck?" he said aloud as he tried to force turn his key in the lock. "Mannnnn!" he barked as he realized the locks had been changed. He walked to his car and pressed the garage door opener, only it wouldn't open. He jogged over to the key pad on the garage and put in his code. It didn't work the first time, so he tried it three more times. It suddenly became clear that his code had been changed as well. He was pissed as he peeked through the windows like a stranger in his own home.

Kyree couldn't believe that Jaz had gone through such extremes to keep him out of the house. He knew she was mad, but this was lower than low. He was just about to go through the back gate and try the back door, when he heard:

Whoop Whoop!

"Aw fuck!" Kyree cursed, looking up to the sky. The police were the last thing he needed to deal with right now.

He slowly turned around to see the black and white car now blocking him in the driveway. A white officer stepped out, his hand resting on the gun in his holster.

"Sir, please keep your hands where I can see them. Do you live around here?" The officer asked as he approached him.

"Yeah. I live here." Kyree kept a stern face, bypassing the notion to tell the officer to fuck off. "Let me get my I.D. out of the car to show you my address." Kyree started to head to the car, but the officer put his hand on Kyree's chest to stop him.

"Well then, can I ask why you were peeking through the windows just now?"

"I left my key. I was just trying to see if I could pry a window open. That's all."

"Then may I ask why we received a call from the security company, saying that the wrong code was entered into the key pad multiple times?"

Kyree dropped his head. He knew he was fucked.

"Sir, I'm going to have to ask you the put your hands on your head."

Kyree furrowed his brow. "Excuse me?"

"You heard me, son!" The officer reiterated.

"Nah, we're going to clear this shit up real quick. Just let me go get my license to show you I do live here."

"I said to put your hands on your head!" The officer yanked

Kyree's wrist and pushed him against the police car, forcing his hands behind his back.

"This is some bullshit!" Kyree yelled as he yanked his arms, only making the officer tighten the cuffs more. Kyree bit his bottom lip and shook his head as the officer read him his rights.

"You should've thought about that before you decided to bring your ghetto ass to this nice neighborhood. Now come on!" The officer pushed Kyree inside his squad car and then got into the front seat to fill out the paperwork.

Kyree began to laugh. He couldn't believe the morning he was having.

"What the hell is so funny?" the officer asked.

"Nothing, man. I'm just going to have your badge when this shit's over, that's all." Kyree continued to laugh. He hated cops that took their power to the extreme just because they had a badge. Kyree wasn't worried. He had a great lawyer on retainer who would handle this in no time. When Conner Ferguson was done with the officer, he'd be flipping burgers somewhere.

Kyree turned his head and could see Jaz pulling up in the driveway. The officer barely noticed as he was giving the rundown to the dispatcher about the intruder he found on the premises.

Jaz was confused as to why the police were in front of her house. She saw Kyree's car, but she couldn't yet see him because the windows were tinted. She grabbed Kylee from the backseat, and hesitantly approached the car. That's when she saw Kyree. The death glare that he was giving her was burning through the dark tint on the patrol car. Jaz couldn't even look at him. She knew he was pissed.

She knocked on the officer's window and he looked up. He rolled his window down.

"Do you live here?"

"Yes, sir, I do. Now may I ask why you have my fiancé in the back of this car?" Jaz stared the officer down and watched as his eyes grew as large as saucers.

"This man lives here?"

"Yes, he does. Didn't you ask for his I.D.?" Jaz asked.

"Well, he wasn't cooperating when I asked for it so I had no choice but to arrest him."

"Well, now you know. So get him the fuck out of this car!" Jaz fumed.

The officer dropped the pen in his hand and hurriedly went around to open the door for Kyree, who couldn't stop shaking his head. The officer removed the cuffs and Kyree rubbed his wrists.

"I do apologize for the confusion. Please have your key on you next time."

"What's your name?" Kyree squinted at his badge. "Officer Berry, it won't happen again." Kyree held out his hand for them to shake on it, and Officer Berry obliged. "No hard feelings. I will be seeing yo' punk ass in court though. Conner Ferguson will be in touch." Kyree gave a devilish smirk.

The officer released Kyree's hand when he heard Kyree's lawyer's name. Conner Ferguson was hated by all of the cops in the state of Virginia, as well as a few other states where he was licensed to practice law. He was known for destroying the careers of police officers who had been on the force for years. Connor was the reason Kyree only did three years in the penitentiary instead of life. Officer Berry didn't utter another word as he got into his car and drove away.

Jaz and Kyree waited for the officer's car to be out of view. Although she couldn't stand Kyree at the moment, she couldn't bear to see him go to jail. There was so much going on in the world today and the police were focused on locking up the people that were the least threat to society. Overzealous cops killing black people and getting away with it was something she'd seen too many times. She could tell by the look in the officer's eyes that he had no valid reason for arresting Kyree. Jaz could only shake her head. It had to stop somewhere.

Jaz turned to Kyree and rolled her eyes. The sight of him still made her sick to her stomach. She vigorously walked toward the house with Kyree hot on her tail.

"I know you're not still pissed off with me when you're the reason my ass almost went to jail!" he barked.

"Kyree, please. *You're* the reason *you* almost went to jail." She placed her key in the door and it turned smoothly. "Had you not been fucking around, I wouldn't have had to change the locks and the codes."

"Whatever, man." Kyree walked in the house and closed the door behind him. "What the fuck is this?" Kyree barked, seeing two suitcases by the door.

"That's some of your stuff. I'll have the rest ready later," Jaz nonchalantly said.

"Hell, nah! Fuck this!" Kyree picked up his suitcase and headed toward the stairs.

"Kyree!" He turned toward her. "Either you leave, or I leave. Either way, we can't be here together."

"So what're you saying?"

"I'm saying that it's only been three months and my condo hasn't sold yet, so I can take it off the market if I have to."

Kyree dropped his head. He knew that he'd brought this on himself. He walked up close to her and she turned her head. He tickled Kylee under her chin and she giggled like she always did. He reached for her and she nearly leaped from Jaz's arms to him.

"So this is it, huh?"

Jaz shrugged. "I mean, what do you want me to say?" She didn't want it to end, but it had to. There was nothing that could fix their relationship from the infidelity and lies. In the blink of an eye she had been betrayed, her family had been torn apart, and her heart had suffered irreparable damage. This was the beginning of their omega. It wasn't easy, but it was necessary.

"So how are we going to do this with Kylee?"

"I don't know, but we'll figure something out. I'd never do anything to keep you away from Kylee. You're an amazing father, and we're great parents. We're just better off apart."

"That's not true, man. We were put on this earth to be together. I'm sorry for the shit that went down. It didn't mean shit to me. We can work through this."

Jaz shook her head. "Nah, that can't happen. We've tried and tried everything to make this work. It's just too much. Our relationship has run its course."

"So it's that easy for you to just give up on us like that?" He glared at her.

"Easy? Who said this shit was easy? This is the hardest thing I've ever had to do. The only reason I can even stand to be in a room with you right now without punching you in your face is because I don't want Kylee to see us acting like we don't have any damn sense." She swallowed and titled her head toward the ceiling, trying to stop herself before she cried again. "Believe me, this shit is hard, but it has to be done. I'm tired, Kyree. I just...can't anymore." She dropped her head in exhaustion.

Kyree licked his lips and nodded. He refused to believe what she was saying. "A'ight. You can keep the house. I bought it for you anyway." Kyree didn't mind Jaz having the house. He knew it was only a matter of time before he worked his way back in. He was unsure of how he was going to do it, but he wasn't giving up without a fight. There was too much riding on it. He kissed Kylee on the cheek and handed her to Jaz.

Jaz watched as he wheeled his suitcase out the door. She smirked to herself when she thought of how he'd react when he saw half of his shoes in pieces. She opened the door and he turned to her before leaving.

"I love you. I won't give up on us. Remember that."

Jaz could feel herself about to break down again. "Just go, Kyree," she pleaded.

He took a deep breath and headed to his car. Jaz closed the door and a tear fell from her face. Kylee must have sensed something wrong in her home because she, too, started crying. Jaz quickly wiped away her tears, knowing she had to stay strong for her daughter. It took everything in her to wake up that morning, but she did it for Kylee.

Before going to pick her up, Jaz awoke to a killer headache. Still unable to face the world but knowing it must go on, she got up and cleaned her house like she did every Monday morning. In the midst of tossing Kyree's clothes and shoes in a suitcase, she called the security company to have the locks changed. She thought Kyree would give her time to let him know, but it was what it was. There was no way she'd allow her daughter to see her weak. She may have been too young to understand, but Jaz wanted to show her what being a woman and making sacrifices was all about. Sure, it hurt like hell, but she'd pull through it.

Every day was a struggle getting out of bed, but Jaz managed to do it. She went to work and put on a smile like it was any other day. She would slay a few heads, have the whole salon cracking up laughing with her usual antics, and then come home to make Kylee laugh and smile until she fell asleep. No one knew that when she went home, she was all alone, and she cried herself to sleep every night.

Monica and Ms. Ray could sense that Jaz probably wasn't dealing with the break-up well. When they asked her about it, she simply said, "It is what it is." But they also knew how Jaz liked to deal with her issues. She usually kept things bottled inside and was liable to snap at any moment, so they made sure to watch her before she lost it completely.

The other day, after mostly everyone at the salon had gone home, Jaz went into the bathroom and chopped off most of her hair. Ms. Ray was under the wash bowl allowing Monica to add silver and blue to the Johnny Bravo inspired updo he'd been rocking lately when she dropped the dye bottle on his head.

"Oh...see, bitch, you tried it!" He shot up and wiped his forehead with the towel around his neck. "What the hell is your problem?"

Monica didn't say anything. She just tapped his shoulder to direct his attention towards Jaz. They both looked on in shock. In just a matter of moments, Jaz's hair had gone from past her shoulders to mid-neck. They waited for her to explain as they watched her toy around with it in the mirror.

"Ay, Ms. Ray, you think you can touch up my neck and layer the back into a bob? I tried to get it as best I could," she nonchalantly mentioned.

"No problem, love," he hesitantly said.

"Um, Jaz," Monica uttered as Jaz eyed her through the mirror. "You sure that's what you wanted to do? You've been growing your hair out since last year. Just the other day you were saying you were happy your length was finally catching up to what it used to be."

"Well, that was then; this is now. It is what it is." Jaz shrugged her shoulders and headed in the opposite direction. Monica and Ms. Ray looked at each other and simply shook their heads.

Jaz could feel their eyes, so she laughed it off. "It's just hair, Mo," her voice trailed from the back room. She was getting tired of them treating her like she was a baby. She didn't feel like she was on the brink of losing it. She was too numb to emotionally snap.

The hair chop was the first sign that things probably weren't aligning well for Jaz, but it wouldn't be the last. Jaz had been carrying on strangely all week. Monica couldn't watch her 24/7. When she needed to talk, she'd come to her.

Monica had her own drama to deal with so, while she sat at her chair waiting for her next client, she continued with the text message she was sending to Mario. He'd just sent her a picture of the new trampoline place called Cloud 9. He was always sending her adventurous things to do. Most things would be random email alerts he'd get from Groupon, but she usually had a blast whenever they did anything out of the norm. Lots of times, he'd even insist that they bring Kayden. He was always including her son, and Monica loved that about him.

They'd been to wine and paint night, wall climbing, and paintballing. Mario introduced her to a whole new world. There was never a dull moment with him. He took her out of her shell and helped tear down the walls she'd built up around her heart. Shannon was still in the picture, but he didn't force their friendship anymore. Mario had other friends that Monica got along with just fine. A few were even females, none of whom gave her the uneasy feelings Shannon did.

Mario's birthday was coming up this weekend and she knew she'd have to deal with Shannon, but she could handle it. Her girls were coming, so she was sure they could keep her calm if things got out of hand for any reason.

"Y'all still coming to Mario's birthday at The Lounge this weekend, right?" Monica asked Jaz and Ms. Ray. He was coloring her bob. For the past couple days, she'd been wearing it her natural black, but she wanted another change.

"You know I'll be there to keep your firecracker ass off Ms. Shannon." Ms. Ray laughed.

"I don't know, y'all. I'll have to find a sitter," Jaz said.

Monica turned up her face. She knew Jaz was stalling. "You are trippin'. You know you could easily ask my mama, your dad, hell...even Kyree. Yo' ass just wants to sit in the house another weekend. You gotta get out, J," Monica pressed.

Jaz sighed, but deep down, she knew Monica was right. Since breaking up with Kyree, all she did was go to work and home. She even hated going to the grocery store for fear of seeing anyone else and explaining to them that there would be no wedding. The wedding planner blew Jaz's phone up, but she refused to answer. After a week with no response, Jaz figured she'd given up and just decided to keep their deposit.

Their wedding was supposed to be five months from now. She was just relieved she'd procrastinated on sending the invitations out. Jaz hated to admit it, but she felt like a failure. She'd had two failed attempts at marriage in less than a year. She was at the point now where she thought maybe she was just meant to be alone. But there was no reason she couldn't have a little fun in the process so she took Monica up on her offer to go out. Kyree was supposed to watch Kylee this weekend anyway.

They'd been broken up for nearly a month, and Jaz had yet to see him since. Seeing Kyree was too painful. She was always afraid that he'd say something to make her take him back. She couldn't risk it. So to avoid being in his presence, their contact was limited to just a few text messages regarding Kylee. Kyree would always try and revert the subject to something personal, whether it was an apology or just to see how she was doing, but by then Jaz would just stop answering his messages. If he said he wanted to see Kylee, she'd agree, but wouldn't let him know where she was dropping her off until Kylee was already there.

Last time the drop off was at Monica's, but since she was getting ready for the party, Jackie had agreed. She, along with Calvin, thought it was ridiculous how the two were carrying on, but they could only voice their opinion on the issue. Jaz was too set in her ways to listen.

"Mmmmm, what is that smell?" Jaz moaned as she walked into Jackie's house with Kylee resting on her shoulder.

"Just some red velvet cupcakes for the church bake sale tomorrow." She gave Jaz a hug and a kiss on the cheek and then retrieved Kylee from her arms. She was almost ten months old now and growing by the day. "She's getting so big. Give yo' GJ a kiss."

Jaz smiled to herself. She loved Jackie's nickname. Kayden could never pronounce grandma, so she'd shortened it from Grandma Jackie to just GJ. She never liked grandma anyway. Jackie was forty-seven years old and the opposite of your everyday grandmother. Her vibrant brown skin and silky black hair gave her the appearance of a woman in her late twenties to early thirties. The pixie cut she rocked was courtesy of Jaz and Monica. Whenever one could fit her in when she popped up without an appointment, she allowed them to work their magic. They'd been doing her hair since they were twelve years old.

Jaz followed Jackie to the kitchen and admired how stunning she looked in only a pair of jeans and camisole. She wished she would look as half as good as Jackie when she was her age. Jaz reached for a cupcake and Jackie smacked her hand with a spoon.

"Ouch!" She rubbed her hand.

"I told yo' hardheaded ass this was for the church," Jackie chastised.

"Ooooh, you cussed," Jaz teased.

"Lawd, the girl got me cussin' in the same sentence I mention yo' house." She looked up at the ceiling. "If she wasn't so hardheaded, Jesus, this wouldn't have happened." Jaz laughed. "Speaking of which, I need to talk to you." Jaz rolled her eyes. "Did you just -"

"No, ma'am." Jaz quickly cut her off. "I just had something in my eye."

Jackie eyed her suspiciously. "Okay. 'Cause you know I'll still beat yo' butt, li'l girl," Jackie reminded her. Jaz nodded, knowing she was being dead-ass serious. "Well, let me put her down in my bed. She's knocked out."

Jaz breathed a sigh of relief. She didn't mean to be disrespectful. She loved Jackie like she was her own mother. Growing up, she was the only mother Jaz knew. Jaz's mother died well before she could explain things to her that a mother should explain to their daughter. Some stuff dads just couldn't do. When it came time to discuss the birds and the bees, periods, and boys, Calvin allowed Jackie to step in. Jackie and Jaz's mother, Simone, were close when she was alive. They'd grown up together as kids, moved apart, and come right back to their old neighborhood once they were older with their own kids. When Simone died, Jackie took on her role with no problem. If Monica got a whoppin', Jaz usually wasn't too far behind her, and Jaz was probably the reason they were in trouble in the first place.

Once Jaz saw that the coast was clear, she grabbed a cupcake, wrapped it in a napkin, and slid it in her purse. Her heart beat fast the whole time. She looked over at the fridge and laughed to herself at the picture that was stuck to an old refrigerator magnet. It was a picture of her, Monica, Kyree, and Fat Boy back when they were little and above it was one from present day with all four of them at Monica's birthday party last year. It was crazy how they'd all grown up so close to each other. She took the older photo down to examine it more.

"I remember that day," Jackie said, walking back in the kitchen.

Jaz smiled. "That was the day you won big at bingo and took us all to Disney World."

Jackie nodded. "Yep. Y'all were so close then. Still are."

Jaz looked away. She knew where Jackie was headed.

"Look, I've stayed out of this and allowed you and Kyree to handle this on your own, but I have a right to speak my mind too. I'll only say it once because I know it isn't my place, but y'all were about to get married. You've been acting married since you were fourteen." Jackie and Jaz both let out a slight chuckle. "But I have to ask: is there any hope for you two?"

Jaz thought for a moment. She felt so hurt and betrayed by Kyree that she didn't see such a thing happening. "Ms. Jackie, I love you as though you were my own mother. You practically are. But, Kyree and I just weren't meant to be like I thought we were. I love him, but I can't." Jaz shook her head as a single tear strolled down her face.

Jackie knew all too well how Jaz felt. She knew what it was like to love a man so much, and then have him break your heart into tiny pieces.

"Baby, if you don't have anything left to give, then don't try to give it. But be the bigger person for your baby. You have to at least be cordial with the man. You can't have her out here thinking you hate him."

"I hear ya." Jaz nodded her head in agreement. She knew Jackie was right, but she needed more time. Jaz took a deep breath and reached in to hug Jackie.

"I love you like you were my own, Jaz. I just want what's best for you both."

Jaz gave her a reassuring smile and then kissed her cheek. "I know. I love you too." She grabbed her purse and headed for the door.

"And don't think I don't know you stole a cupcake!" Jaz heard her yell just as the door shut.

She laughed, just lucky to make it out of there alive.

Just before she could reach her car, Kyree's truck pulled up.

She hadn't seen him in weeks and her breathing had ceased since seeing his headlights. She quickly started toward her car, but before she could push the start button, he was already at the door. She took a deep breath and rolled the window down.

"So, you ain't gon' say shit?" he affirmed.

She sighed heavily. "What do you want, Kyree?"

His brow furrowed it. He'd been trying to give her space for weeks, but it was killing him. She had him feeling like a fuck boy, and that was far from who he was. Whenever he tried to talk to her on anything other than Kylee, she'd stop responding. There were days where he wanted to wait outside of the house on some crazy-nigga shit, but he was respecting her space. He thought she was being irrational by not telling him Kylee's location immediately. For the past few weeks he'd been waiting at different drop off locations, hoping he could catch Jaz before she was gone, but he was always at the wrong house. Today, he knew Monica was going out, so her only choice was to drop Kylee off at either Calvin or Jackie's house. They lived directly across the street from one another so Kyree waited at Calvin's, only to see Jaz in Jackie's driveway. He'd lucked up, and he was going to get as much off his chest as he could while he had her attention.

"You look good," he admitted, admiring her new bob with honey blonde ombre. Jaz simply nodded. "Can we talk?"

Jaz shook her head. "Nah, I'm running late."

"Where you going?" Kyree looked at his watch. It was a little past 7:00. As far as he knew, Jaz hadn't left the house, besides to go to work, in weeks.

"That's no longer your business," she stated firmly.

He shook his head. "Look, the way we've been going about shit isn't healthy for our daughter. I think we should talk to work out a better way of doing this."

Jaz shamefully dropped her head. She knew she was being

immature. "I agree. We're going to have to work out a better system."

"So, can we talk?"

"Sure. But I really am running late. We'll talk some time tomorrow."

"Cool." He nodded his head.

Jaz watched through her rearview mirror as he waited for her to pull away before going into his mother's house. Once she was off the block, she said a silent prayer to God to help her get through this. Every day she tried to convince herself that she didn't need or want Kyree, that he wasn't good for her. But every time she was in his presence, the rhythm of her heart changed. It wasn't normal. She knew that time healed all wounds, but this one was going to take far longer to heal than anything she'd ever sustained.

CHAPTER ELEVEN

Jaz didn't have much time to get ready, but she couldn't find anything worth wearing in her wardrobe. There wasn't enough time to search through racks at the mall so she made a quick stop at her favorite local boutique. She'd already called ahead and spoken with her girl, Jeneisha, about setting aside a few things for her. Jaz loved Jeneisha's boutique. Her customer service ethic was what all businesses should have. By the time Jaz arrived, there were five outfits there for her choosing, along with a glass of champagne. It took her about twenty minutes of trying on different outfits before she finally settled on a white bandage dress with a gold zipper that zipped up the front. She had the perfect pair of clear pumps to go with it.

She went home to shower and finish getting dressed and Ms. Ray arrived to beat her face around 9:00. Jaz always loved how Ms. Ray could go from a beautiful queen to a handsome king. Whenever they went out to a club where they didn't know anyone, Ms. Ray toned down his glamorous look. He was far from masculine, but when he put on a pair of jeans, it was hard to tell at first glance. His ass was big from surgery, but it wasn't enormous so he usually got away with it by wearing a pair of jeans. Jaz loved his look. Tonight, he wore a pair of light-colored jeans cuffed at the ankle, white boat shoes, a white T-shirt, and a white floral blazer. He'd shaved his hair, but the silver and blue were still uniquely present.

The two rode together in Ms. Ray's C-Class. When they arrived at the packed club in Virginia Beach, it was almost 10:00. Monica wanted to kick both of their asses when she saw them walk in late.

"Can y'all show up to anything on time?" Monica crossed her arms.

"You cute, girl. Ain't she cute, Ms. Ray?" Jaz changed the subject, admiring the green bodycon dress, and Ms. Ray nodded and toyed with her hair.

Monica smacked his hand away. "Don't play with me."

"Who playin'? You're wearin' the fuck outta that dress. If I didn't like bones in my fish, I'd let you ride the sausage, girl."

Monica and Jaz both dropped their mouths in shock, and then burst into laughter. "You're so damn foolish. Come on, y'all, we're over here." Monica ushered them to the three sections in the VIP lounge that they'd acquired for the night. Monica introduced them to everyone they didn't know and gave them each a glass of champagne to unwind.

Mario had gone all out for his 30th birthday party. He was dressed in a pair of white denim jeans, a white button up shirt with black sleeves, and white Nikes. He had bottles poppin', everyone he knew was in attendance, and he had his woman by his side. Nothing could ruin his night - or so he thought. He was drunk as fuck, but he could see that he was definitely going to have to keep Monica and Shannon away from each other. Shannon was constantly in his face and every time he turned around, he could feel Monica's eyes burning into his head. He hoped they could keep it civil now that Monica's friends were there to keep her calm.

The evening was lit and everyone was enjoying themselves, but when Monica left to dance with her man and Ms. Ray went off to talk to someone he knew, Jaz was left to roam alone. The music was live, so she really didn't mind. Every nigga within a ten foot radius had approached her, but Jaz wanted no parts. She was there to have a good time with her girls, and that was it.

The waitress assigned to their section was too busy flirting with the guests in attendance to go get the drink Jaz really wanted, so she got up and retreated to one of the bars. It was crowded and took her some time to squeeze her way through, but she finally managed.

"Don't even try getting this nigga's attention. I've been tryna get me a Henny and Coke for about twenty minutes now."

"I see," Jaz noticed, not bothering to acknowledge the voice behind her.

"If you can get that nigga to come this way, I'll give you $100. This motherfucka is slow as shit!" The guy shook his head.

"Bet," Jaz simply said. She gazed in the bartender's direction and waved a delicate hand in the air and the bartender instantly winked at her. He handed a man his beer and quickly came all the way down to the opposite end to tend to Jaz.

"What can I get for you, gorgeous?"

"Um, let me get a Ciroc and pineapple, and a Henny and Coke for my friend." She pointed behind her.

"You got it."

"How the fuck you do that?" the guy asked in amazement.

Jaz smirked and turned to him, the first time they'd actually seen each other. He was about 6' tall with skin the color of butterscotch. He had the most hypnotizing gray eyes. His eyes made her feel like they knew each other.

"A woman's touch will do it every time," she simply said.

"Hell nah. Half these basic women been tryna get this nigga's attention since I've been up here. But here you come and get a response in just twenty seconds."

Jaz laughed and shrugged her shoulders.

"Here ya go, pretty lady." The bartender winked again and Jaz reached in her clutch for her bank card.

"Nah, I got this." The guy pulled out his wallet and gave the bartender his card instead.

"You sure?" Jaz double-checked.

"Of course."

"Well, thanks..." she paused, realizing she hadn't caught his name.

"Shaun. And yours?"

"Jaz."

The bartender gave Shaun back his card and his tab. Shaun signed it, put his card back in his wallet, and pulled out a $100 bill. "As promised," he said, handing it to Jaz.

Jaz chuckled. "Nah, I'm not going to take your money."

"Nope, a deal is a deal." He tried to force the money in her hand, but she dodged him. "Damn, Jaz. You're hurting my feelings."

"Nah, the drink is enough. Trust me."

"Can you at least come dance with me?" he asked.

Jaz looked him up and down. He was cute, but she wasn't interested in dancing. "Sorry, Shaun. I'm here with my girls tonight. I'd better be getting back to them. Thanks for the drink."

Jaz walked away and Shaun's eyes followed her the whole way. She was breathtaking in his eyes. From the moment she turned around to face him, he just knew he had to have her. He could tell that she came with a lot of baggage. But that didn't bother him.

Back in their reserved section, Jaz sat beside one of Mario's friends, chatting it up. The girl loved Jaz's hair and was interested in making an appointment.

"My seat is always open to a new client," Jaz mentioned.

"What about this seat? Is it open?"

Jaz looked up to see Shaun standing over her. Jaz didn't know what to say. He didn't wait for her to reply; he just sat down beside her. Jaz looked around at her surroundings. She didn't want anyone seeing him. Mario's friend had taken the hint and was now focused elsewhere. But she was the least of Jaz's worries. Monica and Ms. Ray were her main concerns.

"So, Ms. Jaz, you do hair, huh?" Shaun asked.

"Hold on a sec." She stopped him, turning around to check on the status of her girls. Monica was hugged up with Mario and Ms. Ray was still talking to the same gossiping client he'd been talking to since they walked in. Neither was close enough to see Jaz. She sighed and sat back down.

"You good?" Shaun quizzed, noticing her discomfort.

"Yeah, I'm fine. But you shouldn't be here right now."

"Why? You got a man?"

Jaz thought for a moment. Technically, she was single. It was still such a new feeling that sometimes she had a hard time believing it. She didn't know why she was so nervous.

"No, I don't have a man. But..."

"Then there's nothing else we need to discuss. Hell, ain't no ring on ya finger," he chuckled.

Jaz gave an uneasy laugh as she glanced down at her left hand, which had once housed her engagement ring. She had worn it proudly before, but it was a constant reminder of what could have been and what would never be. It was now lying in her jewelry box with a bunch of other trinkets that didn't hold the same monetary, nor emotional, value as her beautiful ring. She needed to move on. Shaun might be just what she needed.

"You know what? You're right." Jaz smiled. "So you know what I do. What do you do?"

While Jaz was meeting a new friend, Monica was trying her hardest to at least be in the same room with Shannon without pulling her weave out piece by piece. So far, Shannon had managed to keep her distance. Monica excused herself to the bathroom and grabbed Ms. Ray on her way.

"Have you seen Jaz?" she asked Ms. Ray.

"Nope. I thought she was with you."

"Well, call her. I have to pee." Monica gave him her purse to hold while she was in the stall.

"She didn't answer," he informed Monica when she came out of the bathroom.

"I hope she's alright. You don't think we brought her out the house before she was ready, do you?"

"I'm sure she's fine," he assured.

Monica nodded her head. When they got back to their section, they couldn't believe their eyes. Jaz was sitting with her legs crossed, laughing it up with some guy.

"Oooooh, looks like J found someone to keep her company."

The feeling was bittersweet for Monica. She was happy to see her girl smiling again; she just hated that it wasn't her brother that was doing it for her.

"Let's go say hi," Ms. Ray suggested.

He practically had to drag Monica. She really didn't want to meet the guy.

"Hey, Jaz. You gonna introduce us to your new friend?"

Jaz nearly choked on her drink when she saw them in front of her. "Shaun, these are my friends, Monica and Ray."

"Nice meeting you." He extended his hand to them both.

Monica rolled her eyes, but shook his hand anyway.

"Well, we won't keep you two. Enjoy your evening." Ms. Ray wrapped his arm around Monica, pulling her away. "He was cute."

"I guess." Monica brushed it off. Ms. Ray handed her a glass of Rosé.

"Chill, girl. She's having a good time. Just be thankful."

Monica sighed heavily. She knew he was right, but she couldn't help feeling like she was betraying her brother by allowing it to happen. "I guess you're right." She took a sip from her glass as she looked over at Mario slumped on the couch. She laughed because she'd never seen him like this. He wasn't much of a drinker and he was clearly fucked up. His boys were snapping pictures of him and making jokes about how he was a lightweight. "What the fuck?" Monica's face turned up.

"Lawd, what is it now, Ms. Drama?" Ms. Ray groaned.

"Do you see that shit, or are my eyes playing tricks on me?"

Ms. Ray followed her gaze to see Shannon grinding on Mario while Nicki Minaj's "Anaconda" played in the background. Monica didn't even wait for Ms. Ray to respond. She swallowed her drink in one huge gulp and beelined it to where they were. Ms. Ray got lost in the crowd trying to catch up with her.

Monica didn't even say anything. She just grabbed Mario's arm, yoking him away.

"Yo, what the fuck?" She ice-grilled him.

Mario couldn't even see straight he was so fucked up. He blinked a few times to focus, but couldn't. "Wassup?"

"Wassup? Nigga, wassup is you dancing with this chick like you don't have a whole fuckin' girlfriend just a few feet away."

"What?" Mario rubbed his face, trying to grasp what she was saying.

"You heard me, nigga!" Monica snapped.

"Monica, it's really not that deep. We were just dancing," Shannon chimed in.

Monica turned her neck swiftly in her direction. "Bitch, who was talking to you?"

"Bitch?" Shannon asked in disbelief.

"Did I stu-stu-stutter? You heard me."

"Whoa!" Mario stepped in between them.

"You better check her," Shannon said.

Ms. Ray had managed to grab Jaz and they were both behind Monica just in case she popped off.

"Come on, Monica. Let's go cool off," Jaz tried to calm her.

"Mo, I don't know what's going on, man. I thought I was dancing with you," Mario admitted.

"You know what?" Monica chuckled. "It's cool. I'm sick of this shit."

Monica turned to leave and he grabbed her arm. She snatched it away. Jaz put her hands up to his chest.

"Just give her some time to calm down. She'll be a'ight," Jaz assured him.

Mario nodded and flopped down on the couch. He didn't want her to leave. Things had gone from bad to worse and he was too fucked up to think straight. He knew he needed to sober up fast if he was ever going to fix this.

They all hopped into Ms. Ray's car and drove around in silence. Monica sat in the backseat fuming and no one knew what to say to her. Even though she was hurt, she didn't want to be the one to ruin the mood.

"I'm good, y'all. I just need a drink," she assured them.

"Well, the night is still young. We can go to one of my spots." Ms. Ray eyed her through the rearview mirror.

Jaz looked back at Monica and they both smiled devilishly.

They always had fun at the gay clubs. They were guaranteed a few laughs whenever they went out with Ms. Ray.

"Let's do it!" Monica yelled.

They all laughed, happy to see Monica in a better mood.

"And, Jaz?" Ms. Ray gave her a glance and quickly turned back to the road. "Don't think we're gonna let that little encounter you had with that caramel dream slide."

Jaz rolled her eyes.

"Yep, spill it," Monica declared.

"Nothing to spill. He was cool."

Ms. Ray laughed. "Okay, let Kyree find out you out here playin' and yo' ass gon' come up missing."

"Whatever. I'm not thinking 'bout Kyree's ass." She focused her gaze out the window.

"You know Fat Boy was there with Mario's sister, right?" Monica informed her.

All of the color drained from Jaz's face. Her heart fell to the pit of her stomach and her throat became dry. For a split second, she considered that maybe since she didn't see Fat Boy, then he didn't see her either. That glimmer of hope she had was quickly put to rest with one text message.

>>>> **Kyree, 12:45 AM: Where the fuck you at?!**

Jaz took a huge gulp.

Ms. Ray shook his head. "Uh huh, I can tell by the look on your face that nigga gon' fuck you up when he see you." Ms. Ray and Monica both laughed.

"Whatever." Jaz waved them both off as her phone vibrated again. She didn't bother looking at the message. She just powered it off.

Ms. Ray laughed. Whenever they hung out, they were guaranteed to have drama of some sort. Tonight, he was going to help them forget all of their troubles. They hit up two bars in Virginia

Beach that Ms. Ray loved to frequent. The last stop was The Shade Club. It was his favorite spot and the drag show they put on usually never disappointed when anyone needed to have a good time. Ms. Ray knew everyone there and easily got them their own section near the stage. It was Beyoncé night at the club and all of the entertainers performed their favorite songs.

When Ms. Sandra O'Neal came to the stage, the crowd went berserk. She was gorgeous. Sandra could fool the average man when she was in costume. She was about 5'9" with mocha skin. Her gleaming body suit got everyone's attention as she worked the crowd. She turned to Jaz, Monica, and Ms. Ray and made them stand up and dance with her on stage. She lip synced for her life and then held the mic to the ladies so that they could join in to Beyonce's hit, "Schoolin' Life."

"This is for them twenty-somethin's. Time really moves fast, you was just sixteen," Monica and Jaz sang their favorite part.

"And this is for them thirty-somethin's...who didn't turn out exactly how your mom and dad wanted you to be," Ms. Ray sang and danced around.

By the end of the night, the girls had forgotten all of the men troubles that awaited them in the real world and enjoyed themselves. But reality set in as soon as they pulled in front of Monica's house.

Monica rolled her eyes as hard as she could when she saw Mario sitting on her lawn chair in front of her door. The way her townhouse was set up it was hard for anyone else to see him, but Monica could.

"A'ight, y'all. Text me to let me know you made it home safe." She hugged both of their necks before retreating down her walkway. When she got closer, she could see that Mario was asleep. She kicked his leg, causing his head to fall from its resting place on his hand.

Monica didn't even want to speak to him. She had no idea what to say. She shook her head as she placed her key in the door. Mario took a deep breath as he stood up. Spending almost two hours outside had given him time to think. His boys had dropped him off because he was so fucked up and he refused to let them take him home. He didn't drink a lot for a reason. He really couldn't handle it. But it was his 30th birthday and he wanted to enjoy it carefree. He walked into the house behind Monica. He was ready to grovel if he had to.

"Mo!" he called out to her. She ignored him and started up the stairs. "Monica!"

"What?" she yelled.

"Look, I'm sorry. That shit was way out of line."

Monica sucked her teeth. She really wasn't here for his apologies tonight.

He met her at the halfway point of the steps.

"After you left, Shannon and I got into it. I really didn't appreciate the disrespect. Intoxicated or not, the shit was foul and I'm sorry you had to witness that." He looked at her and could see her softening up. "I think Shannon and I need to fall all the way back. She's been trippin'," he admitted.

Monica was jumping for joy inside, but she didn't want to show it.

"You know, you really can't hold your liquor," she said. He smirked and pulled her into him for a kiss.

"Can I get my birthday gift now?" he asked.

Monica smirked as she waved her wrist in front of his face. She'd been wearing his gift all night and when he noticed it, he brought her wrist closer to examine it. The Apple Watch was just what he wanted. He tried to unsnap it, but she pulled her wrist away. She kissed him again and seductively beckoned him with her finger.

"Come get it."

Mario grinned and happily followed her up the stairs. The sex was too good for him to ever do anything to risk losing her. Which was why he neglected telling Monica that after she left, Shannon tried to kiss him. Monica would flip. Besides, he was done with Shannon. He often felt like she tried to put bad thoughts in his head about Monica, and he didn't like it. Mario preferred to surround himself with positive people and lately, Shannon had been nothing short of negative. She wasn't good for him. Turning thirty was an eye opener. Monica was his future now and the birthday gift she gave him that night in the bedroom further confirmed his decision to let go of Shannon. He was content, and so was Monica.

Monica's night had ended better than she expected. Jaz could only hope hers was as peaceful. All she wanted to do was get home and go to sleep. She was exhausted. She was sure Kyree was going to come with some bullshit in the morning.

"You want to spend the night with me, Ms. Ray? We can watch *Waiting to Exhale* until we fall asleep," Jaz slurred as she rested on the window while he drove.

"Nah, boo. I have dick waiting on me," he confirmed.

"With who?" she quizzed.

"None ya damn business."

"Please, Ray? I get lonely in that big house by myself," she whined.

"Don't use me," he chuckled.

"Use you? How?"

"Cut the shit, J. I know what you're really saying. You don't wanna go in that house and fuck yo' baby daddy, huh?"

She sucked her teeth. "Nigga, you trippin'."

"Well, if that's not the problem, I guess you won't mind that his car is in your drive."

"What?" Jaz turned toward her house and Kyree's truck became more visible. "Oh, shit!"

Ms. Ray started laughing immediately at the panic on Jaz's face. Jaz's heart was beating rapidly and beads of sweat were forming on her forehead. She was unsure of what he'd heard, but it couldn't have been good if he actually showed up at her house. He hadn't been there in weeks. Jaz quickly turned to Ms. Ray.

"Let's go to your house," she suggested.

"Nope. I told you what I'm about to go do."

"Well, take me back to Monica's."

"Why? So you can mess up her dick tonight too? I think not," he protested. Jaz sucked her teeth. "You'd better go face the music now."

With her hand on the door handle, Jaz took a deep breath. She opened the door and straightened her dress when she stepped out. Standing up straight, she walked with confidence and poise toward her door. Ms. Ray laughed as he watched her with a different strut in her stride. Jaz was slightly tipsy, but she walked as though she was about to go rip the runway and not face her crazy ex.

"Don't get none on ya," Ms. Ray called out as he pulled off.

Jaz ignored him as she continued toward her front door. She saw Kyree sitting in the car, but she pretended as though his car wasn't just a few feet away from her. When she walked past him without saying anything, Kyree was hot. He quickly got out of the car and beat her to the door before she could close it on him.

"Leave me alone, Kyree. I don't have time for your shit tonight!" Jaz tried closing the door on him, but his foot was blocking it. She really didn't have the energy, so she just let him in.

Kyree closed the door behind him as she turned toward the kitchen. "Where the fuck you been all night?" he barked.

Jaz rolled her eyes and grabbed a bottle of water out of the refrigerator. "Out," she stated, unbothered.

"With that little-ass dress on?"

"Kyree, you're not my father, so stop trying to act like it," she huffed.

Kyree nodded his head, almost amused. When Fat Boy called and said she was out, he was okay with it. He thought she could use the night out because he'd been hearing from people how down she'd been lately. But when he found out she was with some nigga all night, he went crazy. He'd been calling and texting her, but Jaz had powered off her phone after the first message. Jaz was trying his patience.

"So who the fuck was this nigga you were entertaining tonight?"

Jaz popped her tongue. "You mad, or nah?"

Kyree ran up on her, practically ready to choke her. Jaz flinched, almost fearful that he might. She knew that last line would set him off. He was so close on her that Jaz could feel his breath against her face.

"Is that how you act now? You leave your daughter and go partying around like some li'l thot?"

Jaz almost smacked him. "Really, Kyree?" She looked at him with disgust. "Get the fuck out of my face." She pushed him out of her way and headed toward her bedroom. "Don't call me out for leaving my daughter because I went out to have a little fun for one night. I'm with her all the time. You have her for two to three days out of the week and all of a sudden you're fuckin' king. Nigga, please." She kicked off her shoes across the room. "And where is Kylee now? Huh?"

Kyree had left her with his mother when Jaz didn't answer her phone. He'd never meant to bring his daughter into this. He knew that Jaz would never do anything neglectful. But that was beside the point. He knew what Jaz was doing. "Jazzy, don't try to flip this shit! I asked who the fuck you were with?"

Jaz shook her head. She could care less about Shaun. Hell, they never even had time to exchange numbers. But Kyree was trying her with his accusations. She wanted him to hurt like he'd hurt her. It was time he knew what it felt like to see the one he loved with someone else, and she knew exactly how to do it.

"Kyree, we are not together. Don't ask questions you don't want to know the answers to."

And just like that, it was as if a switch had been flipped in Kyree's head. Jaz gasped as she saw him coming for her. She flung her water at him, but to no avail. He quickly wiped his wet face and cornered her in the room. With his body blocking her and his hands pressed against the wall, he stared her down, but she couldn't look him in the eye. She turned her face and he whispered in her ear, "This shit is forever."

With her nostrils flaring, she turned to look him square in the eye. "No! This shit is over!" she fumed as a single tear fell from her face. He gently wiped it with his thumb. Jaz shuddered from his touch. He searched her eyes for some sort of want, a glimmer of hope that they still stood a chance. She dropped her head and he raised it back up. He gently kissed her, and when she didn't protest, he inserted his tongue into her mouth. Jaz hungrily kissed him back as she felt his free hand grip her ass.

Her mind argued with her body for her to stop him. "We shouldn't be doing this," she breathlessly said.

"And why not?" he asked as he licked the spot behind her neck.

"Ahhhh," Jaz whined as her body won the battle.

Kyree unzipped her dress in the front. She wore nothing underneath and it bothered him to know she was talking to some nigga dressed like that, but he didn't want to ruin the moment. She removed his shirt and trailed her hands down his chest. It'd been too long since either of them had sex and when he dropped his sweats, her mouth watered. She wanted to suck it, but she decided against it. In her mind, he didn't deserve such pleasure. This was all about Jaz. He placed her legs behind his back and carried her over to the bed.

With each lick of his tongue, thrust of his pelvis, and every drop of juice that poured from her honey pot, Jaz tried desperately to convince herself that she didn't need him. She repeated a mantra to herself in between audible moans of pleasure: *Y'all just fuckin. It's just dick. You don't need him.*

As she came for the second time, Kyree felt his nut rising. This was where he wanted to be. He fell on the opposite side of her, panting and smirking. He could tell by the helpless look on Jaz's face that she was spent.

Just as his eyes were about to close, Jaz asked, "Soooo, what you 'bout to do?"

He scrunched his face. "What?"

"I mean, that was fun. But you can't stay here."

Kyree looked at her in amazement. He couldn't believe what he was hearing. "Wooooow," he laughed. He shot up from the bed and grabbed his clothes. "I can't believe this shit." He shook his head. "Gon' kick me out like I'm the fuckin' female and my Uber outside, huh?"

Jaz wanted to burst into laughter from the Uber comment, but she had to keep her poker face.

"Jazzy, I'm not gon' keep doin' this shit with you. I'm dropping my daughter off at home tomorrow. I don't give a fuck what you gotta say about it either."

Jaz could only listen as he ranted and she lay naked under the covers.

"Oh, and you're going to have a conversation with me face to face sooner rather than later." He stepped into his last shoe. "I'll see you tomorrow. Bye!" He slammed her bedroom door shut.

When Jaz heard the front door shut, she sighed heavily. She placed her hands on her head. She was so ashamed that she allowed herself to be so weak. If sex could fix everything, then they wouldn't have half the problems they had now. But sex was what caused their demise in the first place.

Jaz grabbed the pillow from Kyree's side of the bed, now covered in mascara. It still smelled like him, and even though she'd changed her sheets several times, she refused to change that pillowcase. She held it close to her chest like she did every night since he'd been gone. She felt like a crazy person trying to get along without him. She closed her eyes tight and prayed to God that she could stop the wanting in her heart for him. Life without him was harder than she thought.

CHAPTER TWELVE

Since their night of passion a few weeks ago, Kyree and Jaz were finally on speaking terms. They weren't even close to what they used to be, but they were at least able to stand in the same room with each other without cussing. Jaz even allowed him to pick Kylee up from the house. She really didn't have a choice in the matter. When Kyree said he was done playing games, he meant it. He was tired of carrying on immaturely. They were two grown adults and needed to handle their business as such.

It was Sunday, and Kyree was just happy that he could spend some time with his daughter. He loved every minute with Kylee. Many people said she looked like him, but he saw every bit of Jaz in her: Jaz's slanted eyes, golden-brown skin, and jet-black curly hair. The only feature Kyree noticed of his was the signature Wright dimple on the right side of her cheek. Everyone in his family had it. He loved making her laugh just so that it would show.

There was nothing Kyree wanted more than to give Kylee a

stable home. But even when he and Jaz were cordial, he could still see the hate and distaste for him in her eyes. It was stressful and becoming harder for him to live with than he ever thought imaginable. Instead of the usual family outings they did on Sundays, now it was just him and Kylee. He brought her with him everywhere he went.

"Daddy just has to fill out some paperwork, Lee. I'll only be a minute," Kyree assured her as he placed her in the walker he kept in his office. Kyree watched as she played with the trinkets on her walker. She seemed content so he proceeded with the work he had in front of him. He was just about done when there was a knock at the door.

"Come in." Kyree looked up to see K.O. walk in.

"Sorry to come by unannounced. Just needed to pick your brain about something."

"No problem. Have a seat." Kyree stood and dapped him up.

"Damn, man. You can't deny that one if you wanted to." K.O. laughed.

"Nah, that's all her mama there." Kyree chuckled.

K.O. nodded. "Yeah, that's definitely li'l Jaz."

"What brings you by?" Kyree asked. He was surprised to see K.O. He hadn't seen him in town since the wrap party. He hoped he wasn't on no bullshit about the Kendall drama. Kyree really wasn't in the mood to hear shit else about Kendall.

"I came to give you heads up on a few things."

Kyree's brows furrowed inward.

"I saw the shit with you and Kendall on the internet."

Kyree sat up straight. He already had to defend himself to Jaz on a daily. He didn't want to have to do the same with K.O. Kyree was ready to kick him out if he said something he didn't like.

"I just wanted to let you know that she and I were never an item - I mean, not officially. We fucked around, but that's only because it was there. Hell, I got wifey at home and shit. Kendall was just a good time, so I ain't really trippin' off that shit."

Kyree nodded his head, taking in everything K.O. had to say.

"But I did want to let you know that she's a messy-ass person. I got a girl at home that I try to keep away from this life, and Kendall knew that, but she threatened to tell my girl about us. She claimed she was pregnant at one point, hit me for money so that she could get an abortion. I gave it to her, and like an idiot, I kept fuckin' around with her. Pussy was too damn good, know what I'm sayin'?" K.O. and Kyree both laughed.

Kyree had to shake his head at the thought.

"Well, look, I'm just telling you this because I respect you. You looked out for me when no one else did and I'm never going to forget the shit you've done for me over the years."

Kyree had known K.O. back when he was going by his government name, Alfred. K.O. only came from his ability to knock out his opponent in a freestyle battle. K.O. used to be a corner boy working for Kyree when he was younger. Kyree took him under his wing and schooled him to the game. Kyree had even gotten K.O. a lawyer after he got in trouble on some trumped-up charges. When Kyree got out of jail and heard that K.O. was trying to go legit, he allowed him to use the studio for free. K.O. had always looked up to Kyree and he didn't want any bad blood between them.

"Why are you telling me this now though?" Kyree wanted to know.

"I heard you and Jaz were going through it, and y'all are like the damn Jay and Bey of the 757," K.O. chuckled. "I don't want the bullshit Kendall's on to interfere with what y'all have. It's real, and that's rare these days."

"Good lookin' out, bro." Kyree got up to dap him up once again.

"No problem, man. You taught me well. I'm just tryin' to be a better you at the end of the day," K.O. admitted. "Go get ya lady back, man."

Kyree smirked and walked him to the door. He appreciated K.O. telling him everything. Not many people had the same mentality for a better life like he did.

Kyree picked up Kylee from her walker. She was such a good girl when she was with her dad. She rarely ever cried when he was around. Kyree kissed her cheek and thought long and hard about what K.O. said. He wondered if Kendall was up to something by posting that picture. She'd been trying to get in contact with him lately, but Kyree ignored her calls. He was angry with her at first for not keeping her end of the deal and keeping their trice a secret, but in the end, he knew he could only blame himself. He didn't want any more drama. K.O.'s words rested heavy on his mind: *"Get ya lady back."* He had to get her back before it was too late and she moved on.

Little did Kyree know, but Jaz couldn't be further from thinking about anyone else. She had a hard enough time trying to get one man off her mind. She didn't want to add another one to the list. While Kylee was out with Kyree for the day, she was relaxing in bed. She'd had a long week of doing hair. The hair show was a huge success and the salon had won first place. Jaz and Monica were both so proud of themselves. It was something they'd dreamed about their entire lives. To see it come to fruition was surreal. After celebrating through the wee hours of the morning the night before, everyone needed the day to relax. The only thing on Jaz's mind was watching a little TV and chillin' for the rest of the day. She grabbed her Firestick remote to prep herself for a night of watching movies until she fell asleep.

"What is wrong with this shit?" Jaz asked aloud as she tried to enter the Netflix password for the fifth time.

She was just about to try again when her phone rang. She didn't recognize the number so she let it go to voicemail. It was usually a new client, and Jaz didn't like to answer her phone on her off days. If it was important, they'd leave a voicemail or text her.

>>>> 757-555-9670 8:45 PM: Hey...This Shaun. I'm about to call you back in a sec.

Jaz's eyes lit up. She had no idea how he got her number. They'd never had a chance to exchange information. "This nigga must be a serial killer or somethin'," she said aloud to herself.

The phone rang again, and it was him. She took a huge gulp before answering.

"How did you get this number?" she immediately asked.

"Damn," he chuckled. "I can't get a 'hey, how ya doin'?"

"Nah, you could be a crazy First-48-Ass-Nigga."

Shaun laughed. "Okay, I deserve that. I know me hitting you up is kind of crazy. You wouldn't believe the investigative shit I had to do to find you." He laughed at the thought, but Jaz didn't. She was still on edge about talking to a possible killer. "Well, I remembered you were talking about your salon so I Googled all of the salons in the Portsmouth Old Towne area. Your name was in one of the many listed, so I went to the website. Then I went to the stylist's page where it had all of your numbers listed."

"Wowwww," Jaz said, astonished.

"I know, man. It's crazy. I've never done no shit like that. But I've been thinking about you since the night you left the club. You left before I could get your number." Shaun sighed heavily. He knew it sounded crazy, and he knew it was, but she intrigued him on a different level. He thought about her constantly for a week and after he found her website a few days ago, he played with the number before finally deciding to call it. "I tried calling yesterday," he said.

"Oh, we had a hair show yesterday," she affirmed.

"Oh, word? How'd it go?"

Jaz was skeptical at first, but after a while, she began to talk to him freely. She was actually flattered, after hearing the story of how he'd come to acquire her number, that he'd go through so much trouble just to find her. They talked for an hour and Jaz found out a lot about him. He worked as a UPS delivery driver during the week and had his own side hustle as a graphic designer, and he had a four-year-old son that lived in Florida with his ex.

Shaun asked her to go out to dinner with him, but Jaz quickly shut him down. She told him about the serious relationship she was just in and he said he understood her apprehension.

"I understand, Jaz. But it's dinner. If anything, you can think of it as a free meal."

Jaz laughed and a call started to come through on her phone. "Um, I'll get back to you on that. I have a call coming in."

"A'ight. Think about it though. I'll talk to you later," Shaun said.

"Okay, bye." Jaz hung up with him and clicked over to Monica on her other line. "What's up?"

"You want to go get some froyo?"

Jaz pulled the phone away to look at the time. "It's almost 10:00. What place is open this late?"

"There's a new all-night spot in Virginia Beach," Monica explained.

"Oh. Well, I don't know, Mo. I'm already in the bed," she whined.

Monica rolled her eyes and sighed heavily. "I'm driving and paying."

"Okay." Jaz perked up. Monica knew just the words to get her to change her mind.

"Ms. Ray and I will be there in ten minutes."

Jaz hung up the phone and threw on a black PINK hoodie with the matching sweats and a pair of black Nike Air Max. When Monica pulled up, she was ready to go.

"Why do we all look like we're about to go rob a bank?" She snickered from the backseat as she noticed they were all comfortably dressed in black. Monica and Ms. Ray both gave an uncomfortable laugh, but Jaz didn't notice. "Wake me when we get there." Jaz pulled her hood over her head and stretched across the backseat. Monica hit a pothole fifteen minutes later, causing Jaz to wake from her sleep.

"Damn, Mo, where is this place? I've never gone this far for no damn frozen yogurt."

"I told you, it's deep in Virginia Beach. Go back to sleep."

Ms. Ray sucked his teeth. "Mo, if you don't tell this girl before she goes crazy when she doesn't get her damn ice cream."

Monica cut her eyes at him.

"Tell me what?" Jaz looked between the two of them.

"Ugh! Ray, you and your big-ass mouth."

"Tell me what, dammit!" Jaz fumed.

"Fine then, I'll tell her." Ms. Ray turned toward Jaz. "Monica here is going on a late night old fashioned ride-out."

"Come again?"

"Well, she saw a text that Shannon sent saying she and Mario needed to have a talk at the bachelor party for his homeboy's wedding."

"Hell nah! Take me home!" Jaz demanded.

Monica eyed Jaz through her rearview mirror and shook her head. "This is why I didn't want to tell you. You're still trippin' off that shit from years ago? Really, Jaz?"

Jaz didn't say anything. She just bounced her leg in frustration. Years ago, she'd asked Monica to ride-out with her when she suspected Kyree was seeing someone else. Jaz and Kyree were broken up at the time, and that was Monica's reason for not going with her. Jaz ended up going alone and almost getting arrested for beating the girl's, Shayna's, ass. The fight happened right in front of Monica's house so Monica was able to break it up in time. Jaz always said that if Monica was there from the beginning, like she should have been, then things never would have gotten so out of hand.

Ms. Ray had to laugh at their petty banter. "Jaz, you really need to let that shit go. The famous 'Shayna-Gate 2008' was so long ago."

"Nope. I rode-out with Monica plenty of times over La's mess and the ONE time I ask her to return the favor, her ass bails on me."

"I told you I was sorry about that. Damn, J," Monica sincerely said.

"Maybe if ya ass wasn't fuckin' the girl's brother, she wouldn't have such a problem with riding-out with ya dumb ass," Ms. Ray interjected.

Monica couldn't hold it in; she had to laugh. Jaz was pissed, but she had to laugh too. Ms. Ray had a point. Jaz had a tendency to hold a grudge for a long time but when her girl needed her, she was going to be there for her regardless.

"So I think I have a li'l saved up for your canteen after you beat her ass. What you got, Ms. Ray?"

Everyone laughed. "I swear I'm not trying to go there with her - or anybody else, for that matter. I just...I need to know if he's being honest with me. I'm too grown to be fighting and carrying on like we did when we were in college. I'm also too old to be dealing with a man who I can't trust. I just...need to know, y'all," Monica sincerely said.

Everyone nodded in agreement. They could hear the worry

and fear in her voice. Monica didn't give herself often, so when she did, she took it seriously. As she drove, Monica could only hope that she didn't see what she thought she would. She hoped that maybe Shannon only wrote the message to get a rise out of her. Since Mario broke off their friendship, Shannon blamed Monica, and she didn't mind letting him know it. Monica saw a text message on Mario's phone a couple of days ago from Shannon. Shannon said all kinds of bad things about Monica. She'd called her all kinds of conniving names, said she was using Mario, and even accused her of still messing with Latrell. Shannon had even gone on to say that she was in love with him and she wanted to be more than just his friend.

Monica wanted so badly to confront Mario about everything she'd seen, but then she'd have to admit that she went through his phone. The only reason she even knew his password was because he'd sent her to the bank and given her his pin number one day. When Monica saw a message from Shannon pop up on his phone, she tried the number, which was his mother's birthday, and it worked. Since she'd gotten the password right on the first try, she felt it was only right that she finish her search to see what the messages were about. If the two weren't still friends, like Mario assured her, then they shouldn't have been in contact in the first place.

After reading Shannon's texts to him, Monica didn't know if she was more hurt or angry. Mario responded to her messages by simply saying she was "buggin'" and "crazy". He also told her to fall back because they didn't need to be friends anymore. Monica was pleased with his response. But her last message to him spoke of a meet-up at the party Mario was headed to - a meet-up that Mario had agreed to, but failed to mention to Monica, thus sending her on a quest to spy on him. She hated that she had to resort to such sneaky and childish measures, but she really didn't have time to waste with a relationship that was built on lies and distrust.

Monica pulled alongside the curb a few houses down from the house Mario and his friends had rented for his best friend, Percy's, bachelor party. The house was breathtaking. Cars filled the lot with patrons in attendance. Percy was a beloved person, so there was a huge turnout. Monica adored his and Mario's relationship. They were like brothers. They reminded her so much of her and Jaz. She hated that she had to burst into Percy's party. But if Mario played his cards right, then there wouldn't be a problem.

"So, Mo, what's the plan?" Ms. Ray asked as they watched the house from afar.

"We wait," Monica simply said. "Hand me my binoculars on the floor, Jaz."

"Your what?" Jaz looked at her crazy.

"Just look down there in the bag on the floor," Monica instructed.

Jaz felt around on the floor and pulled up a black bookbag. She reached in it and pulled out a pair of binoculars. "Oh, hell nah!" Jaz turned on the light in the backseat to examine the contents more closely. "Ray, this hoe is crazy. Look at this damn spy gear she has in this bag."

Jaz and Ms. Ray both burst into hysterical tears when they saw the Minions themed binoculars, flashlight, and walkie talkies in Monica's bag. Monica grew frustrated and snatched her bag from them.

"Girl, does Kayden know you stole his toys to go creep on your man?" Ms. Ray laughed and Monica pushed him in the arm. She ignored them as she used the binoculars to look at the house.

They sat in the car for an hour, just waiting for something to happen. But there was never any sign that Shannon was there.

There were too many cars for Monica to see her pull up, plus it was extremely dark outside.

"How much longer is this going to be? I'm getting hungry," Jaz whined.

Monica rolled her eyes and tossed Jaz and Ms. Ray a Snickers bar. Jaz perked up then. Being with those two was a headache Monica couldn't handle sometimes. The whole hour in the car they complained, argued about meaningless stuff, and both had to pee after only thirty minutes. If something had gone down at the party, they'd probably missed it when Monica drove to 7-Eleven for them to relieve their bladders. While there, Monica grabbed a few snacks because she knew that would be the next thing they'd complain about. She knew them like the back of her hand and wouldn't trade them for the world, no matter how much she wanted to strangle them right now.

"Let's just wait five more minutes, and then we can leave," Monica assured them.

Jaz picked up the binoculars and looked through them. "Mo, what color is he wearing tonight?"

"Blue, why?"

"Oh, never mind. I thought that was him, but that looks like black."

Monica snatched the binoculars from Jaz. "He's wearing dark blue." She squinted off into the distance as a dread head figure walked out of the house with a woman leaned up against him. It did look like black from afar, but upon further examination, there was no doubt in her mind that it was Mario, and the woman leaned against him was definitely Shannon. "Ugh!" she huffed. "I can't believe this mothafucka lied to me!"

"You're probably trippin'. Let me see." Monica passed the binoculars to Ms. Ray and dropped her head. She felt like she'd been played. Ms. Ray too dropped his head and passed the binoculars to Jaz. Jaz watched as he started toward the parking lot with Shannon still propped up against him.

"Damn, Mario." Jaz shook her head in disappointment. She didn't want to believe it. Mario was actually a cool guy, and Jaz loved him and Monica together. He was just what her friend needed.

Monica wanted to cry, but she wouldn't allow herself. She quickly opened her door and stormed in their direction. Jaz and Ms. Ray were right on her heels.

"So you tried to play me for stupid, huh?"

"What the fuck?" Mario looked up in shock.

"Nah, you fuckin' lied to me. Y'all just one big happy couple and my ass is sitting at home waiting on yo' ass like Boo-Boo the Gotdamn Fool!"

"Yo, Mo, what the fuck are you talking about?" Mario fumed. He still had Shannon's arm around his shoulder. He released her to approach Monica.

"Don't fuckin' touch me!" She put her hands up in front of her.

Shannon started laughing and it was pissing Monica off. Jaz and Ms. Ray were also getting heated. "What the fuck are you laughing at?" Monica barked.

"You." Shannon staggered in her direction, and Mario caught her before she fell. "You think Mario wants you? You were just a li'l fun because I didn't want him, but now I do, so you and your li'l Hood Mafia better go before you get your feelings hurt."

Jaz and Ms. Ray both looked at each other in disbelief. "Hood Mafia?" they reiterated in unison.

"Yo, Shannon, shut the fuck up!" Mario yelled.

"So the truth finally comes out, huh?" Monica licked her bottom lip and shook her head. She couldn't believe this was happening.

"Mo, don't listen to her. She's drunk!" Mario reasoned.

"Oh, so now I'm lying?" Shannon started to laugh again. She grabbed ahold of his face and sloppily kissed him while rubbing her hand down the crotch of his pants.

Mario smacked her hands away and forcefully pushed her against the car by her wrists. "What the fuck is wrong with you?" he screamed.

"Ya know what?" Monica chuckled. "I'm too old for this. Y'all can have this shit." She turned to walk away.

"Mo, wait!" Mario tried to grab her arm, but she snatched it away.

Shannon jogged up to them in her five inch heels. "Let her go, Mario. I don't know what you want with her anyway. She already has a kid. Let her swallow yours." Shannon laughed.

Monica quickly turned toward them. She looked at Shannon with her nostrils flaring. *Whop!* She knocked her with a strong right hook to her left eye. Shannon's head almost did a 360 around her neck.

"Oh, shit!" Jaz and Ms. Ray dropped their mouths. They never even saw the punch coming.

Mario caught Shannon before she could fall completely. He left her on the ground and then ran after Monica, who was already headed toward her car. She slammed her door shut and Jaz and Ms. Ray hopped in as well.

"Mo, let me explain. Please!" Mario begged. Monica ignored him with her windows up and started her car. "Monica, open this damn door!" he ordered. She continued to ignore him and put the car in reverse. Jaz and Ms. Ray were worried he was going to break the window or worse, that Monica was going to run him over. It was like she had tunnel vision and was blind to her surroundings. Mario tried to open the back door, but it was locked. Monica put the car in drive and he backed away just in time for him to move his foot from her back tire.

"Fuck!" he cursed as he watched her headlights take off down the street.

He looked at Shannon lying on the ground in disgust. He hated her. She'd ruined his life. Oftentimes she'd managed to get him involved in her bullshit and he'd be her sidekick. But not this time. His family and friends hated her, Monica hated her, and now he was starting to see why. The only reason he was even carrying her drunk ass was because Percy didn't want her anywhere near his party. Percy and Shannon used to fuck with each other back in the day and his fiancée wasn't playing when she said she never wanted to see the two in the same room. Monica had asked the same of Mario, and he'd agreed. But he fucked up. He was only meeting up with her to get the $700 he'd loaned her a few months ago. He had no idea that she would act so foolish tonight.

Percy's brother, Ronny, came running over to Mario. "You a'ight, man?" he asked, noticing the darkness that had taken over him. He didn't even care that Shannon was on the ground. He, like everyone else, knew she was a wild card.

"Yeah, I'm good. I just need you to take Shannon home for me. I can't be around her crazy ass right now." Mario didn't even wait for Ronny to respond. He just went back into the party. He had to find Percy to tell him why he had to leave one of the happiest occasions of his life. Monica was his main concern at the moment.

But Monica didn't want anything to do with him. She had enough drama in her life to last a lifetime. She was almost thirty years old. Her patience had run out with people giving her the runaround. If Mario wanted to play games, he could do it without her - at least, that's what she told her girls as she drove them home. But when they were gone and she was in the solace of her own home, she cried. It hurt like hell to finally know the truth.

The pretty lie she tried to convince herself with was much more comforting. But there was always something inside that told her Shannon was just too close for comfort. Every chance he could, Mario would remind Monica that she was the only one for him. Monica tried to not be so insecure, but Shannon's presence was always a reminder of doubt. Knowing she was right about them all along was much less rewarding than she thought.

Mario called her over a dozen times after she left, but Monica didn't want to hear any more excuses. She'd seen the truth with her own two eyes. She sent all of his calls to voicemail and blocked all of his texts.

She was just about to cry herself to sleep when the doorbell rang. She panicked, knowing it was Mario.

"Go away!" she yelled with the door closed.

"What? It's me, Mo."

Monica took a huge breath and used her robe to dry her eyes. She opened the door and Latrell was on the other side holding a sleeping Kayden. A smile crept across her face upon seeing him.

"Hey, Mo," Latrell said. "Li'l dude is worn out. That plane ride was no joke," he chuckled.

"I see," Monica agreed, noticing the drool coming from her baby's mouth. She kissed him on the cheek. She had to resist the urge to wake him because she hadn't seen him all week. Allowing him to go to Texas with Latrell for the whole week was a huge step for her, but she felt like Kayden could benefit from knowing both sides of his family. Monica grabbed the suitcase from his hand and stepped to the side to allow him entry. Latrell headed upstairs to put Kayden in his bed. While he was gone, Monica did a quick check in the mirror to make sure Latrell didn't notice that she'd been crying. She looked a mess. She licked the sleeve of her robe and tried to quickly wipe the dried tears from her face. Once she thought she'd done a good enough job, she sat on her couch and waited for him to come downstairs.

He jogged down the stairs and sat next to her on the couch. "We had a good time. Thanks for letting him go."

"It was nothing. I'm glad you guys had fun."

Latrell nodded. "So, why're you in here crying?"

"What? I'm not crying," she lied.

He sucked his teeth. He'd seen her red eyes the moment she opened the door. "Come on, Mo. Tell me anything."

"I'm serious." She really didn't want Latrell in her business.

"Okay then. If you say so." Latrell decided to drop the subject. "Look, I have something important I need to talk to you about though." Monica turned to face him. "I'm getting stationed in Japan for two years."

"You're what?" Monica asked in disbelief. "When?"

"I leave next month."

"Oh," she somberly said. "Kayden is really going to miss you. You were just getting to know one another."

"Yeah, that's what I wanted to talk to you about. Why don't y'all come with me?"

"To Japan? Are you crazy?" Monica searched his eyes, but he appeared to be very serious.

"Please, Mo. It's obvious you're not happy here. Dude has you up in this house crying your eyes out."

"Like you did? So many times before?" she reminded him.

"That was different. I've changed since then. It's obvious you don't love this guy. Don't you love me?"

Monica took a deep breath. She knew that Latrell was speaking from his heart, but she couldn't return his affections. "Look, La, I love you, yes, but only as Kayden's father. I don't love you like I love him." Monica spoke so calmly. She didn't want to hurt his feelings.

Latrell dropped his head. "Then why are you crying?"

"Because..." Monica paused. "I think I love him more than he loves me." Monica's voice started to crack. Latrell moved in to rest her head on his shoulder.

"Mo, if that man wants to be an idiot like I was in the past, then let him. He'll realize what a great woman you are when it's too late and he's regretting it." He wanted Monica, but not like this. Her happiness meant more to him than anything. They were more than the two foolish college kids from back in the day. They were adults searching for happiness. "Mo, you've done an amazing job raising our son and for that, I am forever grateful. I wasn't there then, but I'm here now. And even though I'm going to be miles away in Japan, I'm going to come home every chance I get to see my boy. I also want him to FaceTime me whenever possible. I'll get him a phone before I leave."

"A cell phone? He's only three." She laughed.

"Hey, he's smarter than me when it comes to phones." They both laughed and Monica nodded. "I never want to miss another minute. After these two years, I'll be an officer and I'll be able to be stationed in Virginia for good."

"Well, Kayden knows you love him. No one will ever take your place in his life."

Those words meant everything to Latrell. He didn't want his son to grow up not knowing who his father was. He trusted that Monica would do what she could to remind him of it, but he was going to go above and beyond to do his part too.

They sat for a few minutes before Latrell got up and Monica walked him to the door. He hugged her and kissed her on the top of her head before turning to leave, but not before they saw Mario coming up the walkway. Latrell looked between the two of them, unsure if he should leave. He wasn't sure what the severities were in their relationship. Monica could see the uncertainty on his face, so she assured him that she was okay.

Latrell and Mario gave each other the head nod in passing.

Mario could see the disdain for him on Monica's face from yards away. He felt as though he were walking down the green mile. She sat down on her patio chair and stared off into the distance.

"So Kayden's back?" Mario tried to make small talk. She nodded her head. "Can we go inside and talk?" She shook her head no. "Really, Mo? The silent treatment? That's the childish game you want to play?" She responded by twisting her lips as if she was in deep thought.

Mario was starting to see that she wasn't going to say anything, but he had to get a few things off his chest. He'd been practicing the right words to say the whole way over and he was going to say what he had to say, whether she liked it or not.

"Listen, I know you're mad, but you have to know that I didn't know she was going to act like that. I just met her there so that she could pay me back the money she owed me. That's it." That still didn't get a rise out her. "Monica, you can't trip about this shit. I'm getting tired of telling you I'm not fuckin' with that girl!" She cut her eyes at him. "You don't see me accusing you of shit."

"That's because I don't give you a reason to!" Monica stormed past him into the house.

"Hold up!" He followed her inside. "You and your ex just came out of the house, and you're in a damn bathrobe!" he pointed out.

"What the hell is that supposed to mean?"

"You know what it means, Mo. Every time you two are together, it always looks like I walked in on an intimate exchange. But do I accuse you? No!" he barked. "Because I trust you!"

"I've never given you a reason not to trust me. Latrell's not sending me text messages claiming he's in love with me."

Mario's brow furrowed. "You went through my phone?" he asked in disbelief.

Monica realized she'd probably said too much, but it was too late now.

"Wow." He really couldn't believe that she'd invade his privacy like that.

"That's all beside the point. Mario, that girl is in love with you and you felt it necessary to keep it from me. Why?"

"Because, Mo, I knew you were going to trip. But you don't have anything to worry about. I don't feel the same about her. Never have. I love you, man. You're the only woman I have eyes for," he confidently stated.

He moved closer, trying to embrace her. Monica held her hands out to stop him. She wished she could believe him, but there were just too many secrets and lies between them for her to get past.

"Look, I think we need a break."

"A break? For how long?"

"I don't know. I just don't think we're good together. We shouldn't be acting the way we have."

Mario couldn't believe this. He felt like his world was being torn apart. There was no way she could've meant the things she was saying.

"You can go upstairs to pack what clothes you have here, and I'll be needing my key back."

Mario shook his head. "Nah. Keep my shit here. And I'm not giving you shit back. Mo, I'll give you your space, but it won't be for long. Believe that."

"Mario, please don't make this harder than it has to be. I'll just Fed/Ex your clothes and change my locks then."

He chuckled. "A'ight. We'll see." He approached her and kissed her forehead and then headed toward the door. He turned back to look at her before leaving. "This is exactly what Shannon wanted. I refuse to give her the satisfaction of dictating my life. This shit ain't over."

When the door shut behind him, Monica wanted to cry. She

didn't want to lose him, but this was best for the both of them. Relationships were built on trust, and she knew that as soon as she felt it necessary to check his phone, their trust was broken. She forced herself to choke back her tears and brush her shoulders off. This was just God's way of saying that Mario was seasonal. If Monica wanted a permanent relationship, then she was going to have to move on now.

CHAPTER THIRTEEN

Dating again was a fear of Jaz's. She still held onto the inkling of hope that she and Kyree would get back together. But since no one could invent a time machine soon enough to change him cheating, she knew that she had to move on with her life.

It had been two months since their breakup and she wasn't looking for anything serious, just someone she could kill some time with. She liked Shaun. They hadn't seen each other since Mario's birthday, but they texted often and found time to talk on the phone when they could. She couldn't blame the man for wanting to actually see her. So after asking her twenty times, Jaz finally agreed to go out with him.

They had plans to go have an early dinner at the Hibachi grill. His first suggestion was the Soul Bistro. She quickly nipped that idea in the bud. They were set to leave at 5:00. Jaz figured that if the date was early enough, she wouldn't see anyone she knew and wouldn't have to answer any questions about why she was out with another man. Many people knew she and Kyree were no longer together, but for the ones who didn't, Jaz didn't have the energy to explain it.

Kyree was supposed to pick Kylee up at 4:30 for their usual daddy-daughter Sunday. Jaz didn't bother asking what they did all day. Whenever he brought her home, she was always worn out and exhausted. That usually made a pretty easy Sunday evening for Jaz. Today was going to be a hard one for Kyree though. She'd made sure to not allow Kylee to take a nap until an hour before it was time for her to leave. That way, she'd be up the entire time she was with him. Kyree always played it cool, like Kylee wasn't a problem. He'd sure lose his mind today.

Jaz smiled to herself at her plan as she rummaged through her clothes for something cute to wear. She finally decided on a long dark green shirt with a pair of black shorts. She wasn't sure which shoes to wear, so she pulled out her stepstool and rummaged through the shoes on her shelf. She reached for a box in the far back, her foot slipped, and she fell flat on her ass, taking a few boxes down with her in the process.

"Ah, shit!" she hissed, rubbing her butt. She had to laugh since no one else was around to witness her make a fool of herself. She looked from her closet to her bed to make sure the noise she'd made hadn't woken Kylee. When she confirmed that she was still sleeping, she started to clean up the mess she'd made. One of the shoeboxes that had fallen was filled with important documents that were now sprawled all over the floor of her closet. She picked them up, stacking them neatly in the shoebox as they were before she dropped them. She stopped when she came across a letter addressed to Jazzy Elliott.

Jaz held her hand across her face as she as she admired the white envelope. She put the box down and slid to the floor, her back propped against the wall. Fanning herself with the envelope, she contemplated going back down that road again. She'd read it so many times that she could recite most of that letter in her sleep. Taking a deep breath, she removed the letter from the envelope that had housed it for the last couple of years.

Dear Jazzy,

I know I've been kind of distant when we talk lately, but that's only because I don't know what to say. I want to comfort you and tell you that everything is going to be okay, but I can't. I don't know for certain what's going to come of my case. Since we were kids you've been trying to steer me away from the fast life, but it's the only life I know. I probably should have listened to you, but it's too late for that now. I fucked up. I'll be the first to say it. Jazzy, I love you with every ounce of my being.

But...I have to let you go. It's selfish of me to allow you to wait around and not live the life you were meant to live. You're one of the smartest women I know. You and Mo are going to dominate the hair industry, and I couldn't be more proud of y'all.

I can't keep a level head in HERE, knowing you're out THERE. Probably worried, crying endlessly, and hoping for a miracle. How can I, as a man, ask you to wait for me? I can't do SHIT for you inside of here. Behind these bars, I am nothing but a caged animal. You deserve someone who is going to give you the world, protect you to no end, and love you without boundaries.

I know this isn't going to be easy. Hell, this is the hardest shit I've ever had to do. But it has to happen. I can never be happy if you're not 100% happy. You may think that your happiness is with me, but trust me, this is what's best for the both of us. You'll hate me momentarily for doing this, but you'll hate me FOREVER if I allow you to live like this.

Please don't try and talk me out of this. My mind is made up. I took you off my visitor's list, so please don't try to contact me after this. Find someone who is going to love the amazing person that you are.

Someone with a legit career. Who doesn't worry you. Who looks into your eyes and sees an endless future. Those were all of the things I wanted to give you, but since I can't, find someone BETTER than me.

Love,

Kyree

P.S.

Find someone worth spending forever with.

By the time Jaz had finished reading the letter, it was filled with new tears to stain it for another couple of years. She remembered reading that letter fifty times in an hour, trying to find a different interpretation, because it being over just wasn't enough for her. She needed an explanation. The letter wasn't enough. She waited weeks for his call, but it never came. She jumped in on one of Monica's calls from him because she needed clarity, and she was driving Monica crazy asking about him. The last straw for her was the trip to New York where he refused to see her. It hurt her to no end. And now, here they were again - different scenario, but hurting each other nonetheless.

She wiped her face and began putting everything back in the box again. Sticking out of the corner of the shelf were the peep toe black booties she'd been searching for. In her mind she tried to convince herself that today would be the day she'd put Kyree out of her head. If only for a moment, it'd all be worth it. She showered and got dressed while Kylee slept. As she was putting on her shorts, Kylee started to wake up. She picked her up and got her ready to go out with her dad.

Kylee was growing so fast that Jaz often found it scary. She feared if she blinked too long, she'd miss something important. At daycare recently, she'd started popping her lips together while making a weird noise. She was disappointed that she wasn't there to see her do it for the first time. But now Kylee was ten months and trying to start walking. She'd find something to prop herself up, like a chair or toy, and her little legs would start to move, but she always fell on her butt. Jaz was determined to be the first eyewitness to see her take her first steps.

They sat on the floor in the den while Jaz cheered her on.

"Come on, Lee-Lee. Walk to Mommy, baby." Jaz smiled as she watched Kylee prop herself on the couch and move her tiny legs while not letting go. It was the first time she'd seen her in that position. Jaz's eyes lit up in amazement. She just knew this would be the defining moment she'd been waiting for. "That's it, mama. Come on." Jaz clapped.

Ding dong!

The doorbell chimed, Kylee started to wobble, her little knees gave out, and she fell flat on her butt. Jaz would've been pissed off had Kylee not started giggling hysterically.

"We'll give it a go next time." Jaz picked her up and they headed to the door. When she opened the door, Kyree was standing on the other side wearing light denim jeans, a white V-neck T-shirt, white Nikes, and black Tom Ford sunglasses.

"Wassup?" he spoke.

"Nothing much. She's all ready for you too." Jaz handed Kylee to him.

"Can I come in? It's hot as shit out here!" He wiped his brow with a napkin he pulled from his pocket.

Kyree was sweating profusely in the 98 degree heat, so Jaz obliged his request.

"I have to use the bathroom right quick." He passed Kylee to Jaz and headed for the downstairs bathroom. Jaz huffed as she looked at her phone. It was 4:45 and she was supposed to be at the restaurant in fifteen minutes. Kyree came out of the bathroom five minutes later.

"A'ight. Well, I have to get going." Jaz handed Kylee back to him. For some reason, she felt like he was trying to stall.

"Where are you going?"

"What?" Jaz's heart dropped. She hadn't told him, but she felt like he could read right through her. Kyree only looked at her. Jaz knew she couldn't tell him the truth. She'd never leave the house. "I'm just going shopping."

Kyree nodded. He felt like she was keeping something from him, but he didn't want to start an argument today.

"Well, Kylee and I will just stay here until you get back." Jaz was just about to ask him if he'd lost his mind when he stopped her. "I just don't want her outside in this heat. You know I'm back and forth. If I'm not at my mom's house, I'm at a hotel."

Jaz pursed her lips and thought for a moment. It was dangerously hot and humid outside, so he had a point there, but she didn't know how she felt about Kyree being there when she wasn't. It could send mixed signals.

She sighed heavily. "Alright, then, but I want you gone when I get home."

He hated feeling like a guest in his own house, especially when he still paid the mortgage every month. It wasn't like Jaz didn't try to pay the bills, but whenever she'd go online to pay them, Kyree always beat her to the punch. She told him it wasn't necessary, but he insisted. He wanted to tell her that he didn't need her permission to stay there. He was legally obligated. But he simply nodded in agreement. He really didn't have the energy to argue.

Jaz grabbed her purse and kissed Kylee.

"Where's my kiss?" Kyree smirked.

"Tuh ha!" Jaz threw her head back and laughed as she headed out the door.

Jaz arrived at the restaurant ten minutes late. As soon as she pulled up, she sent Shaun a text informing him that she'd arrived. She pulled down her sun visor to give herself a quick glance before stepping out of the car. Not a strand of hair was out of place, her makeup was a flawless nude face and purple lip, and she was dressed to kill...but she still felt like she was betraying the only man she'd ever loved.

On her way over she'd had a call with Ms. Ray, who reminded her to go out and have fun. Taking a deep breath, she flipped her sun visor back down. With it closed, she could see Shaun approaching her car wearing denim jeans, a blue and white Supreme shirt, and white and blue Jordans. She smiled at him and he smiled back. As soon as she put her hand on the door handle, she received a text. She quickly looked at it.

>>>> **Kyree, 5:12 PM: What time will u be home?**

Jaz rolled her eyes. She was now more anxious than ever to go on this date. She dropped her phone in her purse and stepped out of the car. Shaun closed her door.

"Long time no see," he said as he reached in for a hug.

Jaz smiled and returned the embrace. She was relieved the club lights hadn't altered his appearance. He was still very attractive. His smooth skin and gorgeous eyes made him look like a model.

"Sorry I was late."

"Oh, it was well worth the wait." He nodded, admiring how good she looked.

As they walked toward the restaurant, Jaz could hear her phone vibrating in her purse. At first it was just a text message, but soon after, there was continuous vibration and she knew it was a phone call.

"Do you need to get that?" Shaun asked.

"Yeah," Jaz pulled the phone out to see that Kyree was calling. "It's just the sitter."

"Well, you answer that. I'll be inside giving our names."

Jaz nodded. As soon as he was out of view, Jaz answered the phone. "What?" she barked.

"Cut it out," Kyree waved her off.

"Kyree, I just left the house. What could you possibly want?" Jaz looked inside the restaurant to make sure Shaun wasn't coming.

"When will you be home?"

She sucked her teeth. "I don't know. Probably in a few hours. Why?"

"Do you think you could stop by the store on your way home?"

Jaz pulled the phone away to make sure she wasn't losing her mind. Once she'd confirmed that she hadn't and he was actually serious, she laughed. "Kyree, I'll see you later when I get home." She ended the call just as Shaun was walking outside.

"Everything alright?"

"Yeah. The sitter was just asking where I left the pacifier."

"Boy, I remember when my li'l man used to lose that shit. It was like World War III trying to find it."

They both laughed.

"Exactly." She silenced her phone and dropped it back in her purse. "How long did they say the wait would be?"

"Thirty minutes. Basically, too damn long," he chuckled.

"Well, do you want to pop into some of the shops around here while we wait?" Jaz offered.

"Bet."

There was a local clothing store right next door. When they were inside, they browsed while making small talk. Jaz saw a yellow pair of caged heels that she just had to have. The store clerk went to the back to retrieve her size while Shaun did some browsing as well. Jaz tried on the shoes and they fit perfectly. She saw a few other items that she didn't mind having, but she figured she'd wait. She, Mo, and Ms. Ray would act a fool in the store later. She didn't want her date to know how high maintenance she was just yet. Besides, she had to make it look good for Kyree when she came home with something that showed she'd actually been shopping.

The store clerk rang her up. She sat and watched as Shaun paid for a shirt.

"You ready?" he asked her. "Where are the shoes you were eyeing?" She raised the bag in her hand so that he could see. "Why'd you go and spend your money? I would've bought them for you."

Jaz chuckled. "I'm fine. Yo' mama never told you not to buy a girl shoes?"

Even the store clerk laughed.

"Nah, you're not walking out of my life that easy." He gave a sly grin and Jaz blushed.

When Shaun was done, they went to put their bags in their cars. By the time they arrived inside the restaurant, their table was ready. The waiter took their drink orders. Shaun ordered a Long Island iced tea and Jaz opted for a strawberry daiquiri.

"So when you're not making me wait like a stalker for my online orders, what do you do?" Jaz and Shaun both laughed.

"Well, I do my graphic design gig in my free time. I went to school for marketing, but when I finished my degree, it was harder finding a job than I thought. So I got a job working for UPS during the day and went into business for myself at night."

Jaz nodded her head. Shaun was pretty cool. He made her laugh and briefly kept her mind off of Kyree for a while. She'd managed to glance at her phone and saw he'd called five times already. She didn't even bother looking at the text messages.

"Dang, I spent all of this time talking about myself, we barely had any time to talk about you." He grinned. "Well, I'm going to the restroom right quick. When I get back, we can have dessert and talk more about Princess Jazmine."

Jaz only gave a weak smile in return. Talking about herself was not something she was looking forward to. The story of her life in the past two years would scare any man away. No one could deal with her drama. She pulled her phone from her purse to read Kyree's texts.

>>>> Kyree, 6:01 PM: Your damn baby is sick and you can't answer the phone? Okay. I see you. That's fucked up.

Jaz's mind went into overdrive as soon as she finished reading the text. She tried calling Kyree, but he sent her straight to voicemail. Kylee had been fine when she left her. For Kyree to blow her phone up the way he had, it had to be serious. Her date was officially over. She left $40 on the table to cover her dinner, told the waiter to tell Shaun she had an emergency, and she jetted out of the restaurant before she had to explain.

Jaz couldn't get home fast enough. She was concerned about her child and Kyree was purposely sending her to voicemail. There was no doubt in her mind that he was doing it out of spite for her not answering when he tried calling. She vowed the whole way there that she was going to fuck him up when she saw him. He knew how she worried when Kylee got sick. The slightest cough sent Jaz searching through articles on WebMD until she came up with something rational enough to take her to the doctor. Being a new mom, she overreacted about everything.

When she arrived at home she searched the whole downstairs, but they were nowhere in sight. She knew Kyree was there because she saw his car when she pulled up. When she was halfway up the stairs, she saw Kyree at the top.

"How is she doing?" she asked.

He only shook his head. Jaz huffed and brushed past him into Kylee's room.

"It's okay, baby. Mommy's here now." She tossed her purse on the dresser as she approached her empty crib. "Kyree, is she in my room?"

"Nah, Mo came to pick her up."

"Wait, what? Why?"

"Because I'm sick, Jazzy. I didn't want the baby to catch whatever it is I have."

Jaz's eyes nearly popped out of her head. He had to be joking.

"So, let me get this straight." She put one hand on her hip while the other waved freely in his face. "You blew my phone up because *YOU* were sick? Not my baby?"

"I am your baby. I didn't say which baby," he gave a slight laugh.

"You have lost your mind completely, I see." She stared at him in disbelief. "I know what this really is all about." She nodded. "You found out I was on a date and you wanted to sabotage my night, huh?"

His brow furrowed inward and he moved within inches of her face. It was then that Jaz knew she'd said too much. "You what?"

"Nothing." She backed away from him and folded her arms.

"If I had known that shit, yo' ass would have never left this house in the first place!"

Jaz stepped up to him and started waving her finger again. Kyree had to stop himself from breaking it in half. "You can't make me do shit! Kyree, we are over. You're just going to have to deal with it."

He shook his head. He needed to get away from her before he snapped her neck. He didn't have the energy to deal with this. Shaking his head, he turned to leave. Jaz wasn't going to let him get away that easily though. She stepped in front of him, blocking his path.

"Move, Jaz. For real," he ordered.

"Nah, I'm here now. Fucked up my whole night because you were sick? Please. Nigga, you knew!"

"Move, Jaz!" he barked.

"No!"

Kyree massaged his weary eyes and hung his head low. Jaz was trying him. Hearing about her with another man put a bad taste in his mouth. Literally. Before either of them knew it, he was covering his mouth to stop the vomit from hitting the floor.

Jaz quickly moved out of his way as he made a mad dash for the nearest bathroom.

Jaz would lose her mind if he threw up on her carpet, so she was right on his tail, making sure he made it to the toilet in time. The small bathroom trash bin was the first thing he saw. He picked it up, and threw up chunks of everything he had inside of him. Jaz looked on in amazement. She didn't believe he was sick at first, but now she was definitely convinced. She grabbed a washcloth and placed it under the warm water. Once he'd stopped throwing up, she handed it to him.

"What's wrong with you?"

"I told yo' ass I was sick," he griped, wiping his mouth.

Jaz rolled her eyes. She felt his forehead. He was burning up. "Do you want to go to the emergency room?" The look he gave her pretty much said he wasn't going that route. Jaz knew better. Kyree hated hospitals. "Forget I asked." She threw her hands up in surrender.

"I'm good now," he assured her. "I think I just needed to get that out of me."

"You don't look good," Jaz eyed him skeptically.

"I told you I was –" The words weren't clear out of his mouth before he was hurling his stomach contents again. This time he was able to make it to the toilet. Jaz shook her head. He could be so stubborn sometimes. She grabbed the thermometer from the drawer and put it toward his mouth. Kyree pushed her hand away.

"This is going into one end or the other. You choose," she threatened, eyeing his butt. He sucked his teeth and she laughed at her own joke. "But for real, Ky. Let me help you," she sincerely said.

"Go help that nigga you was with tonight."

"Wowwww, really, Kyree?" She turned to leave. She didn't have to put up with his bullshit. She still hated him and was just trying to be nice.

"A'ight, man. I'm sorry. I didn't mean that shit."

Jaz slowly turned around. She said a silent prayer to God that she could get through this without killing him first. When she looked at how pathetic he looked propped up against the toilet, she sighed heavily and picked up the thermometer again. This time, he allowed her to check his temperature. The thermometer beeped and Jaz removed it to examine the results.

"How are you still conscious? Your temperature is 102!" He simply shrugged. "Well, clean yourself up. You can stay here tonight."

"Nah, I don't need your pity." He tried to stand but he felt weak, so he sat on the edge of the tub.

"That wasn't a request," she firmly stated. "I'll be back to check on you in a minute."

Jaz retreated to the bathroom in her bedroom and rummaged through the medicine cabinet. Kyree didn't get sick often. She'd known him almost her whole life and she could count on one hand how many times she'd seen him sick. He didn't get so much as a sore throat. But when he did get sick, it was always enough to leave him on his ass. Kyree's character was strong and humble. He saw the common cold as a weakness and didn't like anyone's help. He was the worst patient for anyone to deal with. But Jaz was up for the challenge. She knew him well.

She started by making sure he showered and changed into the shirt and shorts she'd brought for him to put on. She still had a few of his clothes lying around the house. He didn't want to, but Jaz made him take two aspirin to reduce his fever. Since her bedroom had the closest bathroom, she went against her better judgment and let him sleep there. The guest bedroom would suit her just fine. Once he was under the covers, she placed a cool rag on his forehead.

Kyree looked on as she took care of him. No one could care for him the way she did. The best part of his life was slowly slipping away. Every moment he was in her presence, he just wanted her to hold him and tell him that everything was going to be okay like she always did. Nowadays, she didn't even look at him when she spoke. He was starting to lose hope.

"I'll be downstairs if you need me," she informed him as she placed a trash can on the floor beside him. "It's probably just a stomach virus. Maybe something you ate."

Kyree thought back to the new Mexican restaurant he'd tried the other day. Since being away from home he ate out every night. He wasn't used to not having a home cooked meal. That had to be what it was. Jaz cracked the door on her way out. She hadn't reached the bottom of the steps when she received a text from Kyree asking for ice. Exhaling deeply, she prepared herself for the long hours she'd endure taking care of a sick Kyree. It was never pleasant. Kyree never asked anyone for anything...except when he was sick. He'd turn from a confident grown man, to a needy toddler within seconds. She used to cherish those moments, no matter how much she usually wanted to kill him afterwards. But it was hard being in his presence after what he'd done. She hoped that since they were at odds that he wouldn't be as bad. She couldn't have been more wrong.

The amount of calories she'd lost running up and down the stairs was enough to burn off what she'd eaten in the last thirty days. Him falling asleep couldn't have come at a better time. By midnight, Jaz was worn out. The next morning she woke to make him breakfast in hopes that he'd be able to keep it down. She brought him up a bowl of white rice, toast, and a Gatorade. She brought the thermometer to his mouth and he turned his head. The look she gave him said that she was not up for his mess so he opened his mouth.

"100, not bad. But you still need to rest. Eat this to get your energy up. Hopefully you'll be able to keep it down."

She picked up the trash can to empty the vomit he'd accumulated during the night. He found it amazing how well she knew him, like knowing the only flavor Gatorade he liked and giving him rice because she knew how much he hated soup. It took a few hours and a lot of nagging from Jaz, but Kyree eventually finished the food. She even knew the information to get into his appointment book. So when Kyree got out of bed complaining that he had to get to the shop to cut hair, Jaz informed him that she'd already rescheduled his appointments for the day.

Jaz was beat. She plopped down on the couch in the theater room and returned a call to Monica.

"'Bout time you called me back," Monica answered.

"Well hello to you too." Jaz turned the screen on.

"So how's the patient?" Monica snickered.

"Shit is not funny, Mo. He's getting on my last nerve," she groaned.

"I don't know why you're so surprised. You know how he is." Monica could only laugh. She remembered what a pain her brother was when he was sick. Her mother would make them both stay home from school just so that she could ensure someone would be there to make sure he'd stay in bed.

"I know, Mo. I know. It's just so hard being around him when I'm still so angry. I'm trying to be nice, but I don't know how much longer I can last."

Monica sighed. She hoped that this time together could bring them closer and they could repair their relationship. Jaz could hear the disappointment in her voice, so she decided to change the subject.

"So how have you been?"

"You mean running after two kids for the past twenty-four hours? Oh, I've been great," she chuckled. "My son drew all over Kylee's hands and had the nerve to say they were finger painting. Yeah, I've been fantastic."

Jaz snickered. "I mean, how have you been dealing with the other thing?" Jaz really didn't want to say it, but she didn't have to. Monica knew what she meant the moment she asked. It had been two weeks since she'd last seen Mario. She missed him terribly, but she couldn't bring herself to contact him. She buried herself in work as a distraction, and blocked all of his calls and texts so that she wouldn't even be tempted. When Jaz asked, she wanted to express how miserable she was, but Jaz wasn't doing too well herself. She'd spare her the details.

"I'm good, Jaz. You don't have to worry about me. I'll admit it wasn't what I wanted, at first, but it was for the best. I'm happier now because of it."

Monica could tell her whatever she wanted to, but Jaz knew better. "Well, if it ever gets to be too hard, you know I'm here."

"I know. You remember that too," Monica reminded her.

"So where's my baby now?" Jaz asked as Kyree appeared in the doorway, a blanket draped over his entire body. She didn't speak; she just glanced at him and then back at the TV.

"Well, I'm feeding her now. You should have seen Kayden trying to help her walk. It was so cute." They both laughed, as Kyree came to sit down beside her.

"You need something?" Jaz asked. He shook his head no. Jaz focused back on her conversation and Kyree wrapped his arms around her torso. She sucked her teeth. "Boy, move." She pushed his head trying to force him up, only he didn't budge.

"What the hell are y'all doing?" Monica could hear them on the other end.

"Kyree is just being worrisome. Move!" She squirmed.

Monica laughed at their foolishness. "Oooookay. I'm going to let y'all go."

"Wait, Mo!" Jaz tried stopping her but she'd already hung up. "Ugh!" She lightly smacked Kyree on the top of the head. "You play too much. Move!"

"Nah, man. I'm sick," he protested.

Jaz sucked her teeth and shook her head. She really didn't feel like putting up a fight with him. Once she stopped pushing him off, Kyree was able to rest his head comfortably on her stomach. He loved lying on her stomach. It always made him feel at home when he was lying under her. Jaz used to love it too. But now nothing they used to do felt right.

Jaz rolled her eyes and picked up the remote. They were now in a position where she could finally ask him something she'd been wondering for weeks.

"Kyree?" She looked down at him lovingly.

He smirked as he looked up at her. "What's up, Jazzy?"

Her face then quickly turned to a scowl. "Did you change the Netflix password?"

He could only laugh at her seriousness. He knew how much she loved to binge watch shows and watch movies on Netflix on her off days, and after he heard about her talking to niggas in the club, he changed it. He'd be damned if she didn't talk to him and used his shit to watch it with another nigga. His plan was to have her eventually have to reach out to him, but it never happened.

"Ugh! You're so damn petty. What's the password?"

"It's Kylee's birthday."

Jaz hit him on the head again as she tried the new password and it worked. It didn't take her long to find the movie she'd been wanting to see. Kyree's eyes were closing and she just hoped he was going to sleep.

They were cuddled up on the couch and about an hour into the movie when he asked, "So who's this nigga you've been seeing?"

"Huh?" She looked down at him. His eyes were still closed. He wouldn't dare look at her face when she told him, too afraid that he'd see a happiness there that he wasn't responsible for. But he didn't have to see her face. He could feel her heart beating rapidly as he held her.

Jaz was nervous. She didn't want to have this conversation with him. It was sure to take up too much of her energy, her time, and her sanity. "Kyree, don't start. It was a date. I have to start putting myself back out there. We're not together anymore."

Jaz had no problem reminding him of that, but it still hurt more and more each time she did.

"Did you have a good time?"

He was surprisingly calm and Jaz wasn't sure how she should respond. "Yeah, it was okay," she stammered.

Kyree could hear in her voice that she wasn't being completely honest with him. Shaun had been blowing her phone up since the restaurant, even after she'd told him that they were probably not going to work out. Jaz was embarrassed for the abrupt way she'd left their date. She couldn't get the thought of his face out of her head as she imagined his reaction when the waiter told him she'd left. He said he understood, but Jaz couldn't get past it.

Kyree remained quiet, so Jaz focused her attention back on the screen. He eventually fell asleep again, still resting on her stomach. A part of her wanted to tell him to move, mostly due to her leg falling asleep and also because it made her vulnerable to the hold he'd had on her for years. But another part of her wanted him to stay there forever. This was when they were alone and at peace. No one could disrupt their bond when they were alone together - no one except themselves.

Jaz laughed at scene from the movie she was watching and she thought she heard him speak. "Huh?"

"I said I want to come back home," he calmly stated, his arms still wrapped around her torso.

Jaz moved him off her so that she could look at him. "Kyree, what do you want from me?" She sighed heavily.

"I want you to forgive me." He looked up at her.

"Forgive you for what?" Jaz squinted. She wanted him to admit what he'd done for once.

"For fuckin' up," he said.

"No, Kyree. You don't get to tiptoe around this shit anymore. Just admit what the fuck you did!"

He sat up and looked her square in the eye. "I fucked up. I'll admit to that. I was thinking with my dick and not my mind. I disgraced myself and my family."

Jaz thought hearing him admit it would make her feel better, but it didn't. She'd already known what he was admitting to. The damage was already done.

"Kyree, I thought it would help, but it still hurts."

Kyree turned away from her. That was not what he wanted to hear.

"Ky." She placed her hand on his knee. "I don't want us to keep being angry. I want us to be friends." Kyree sucked his teeth. He didn't want Jaz as a friend. He couldn't be *just* her friend. "Listen to me though. It hurts me to see you hurting. I'm hurt too, but I'm trying to move on. I just need for you to let me go." She desperately pleaded with her eyes. There was no way that she could do this on her own. If Kyree kept trying, she eventually would give in. And she knew that she could never live with herself if she did.

Kyree could feel his heart breaking every time she turned him down. It was the worst feeling he'd ever felt. He was an impatient man when it came to things not going the way he thought they should. He'd wipe his hands completely if something didn't make him happy, but when it came to Jaz, he'd find the time to wait forever if he had to. He nodded his head and kissed her cheek. And then, like a dog with its tail in between its knees, he wrapped himself back in the blanket and retreated upstairs.

Jaz choked back tears as she watched him disappear – not just from the room, but from her life. The betrayal outweighed her love for him. They'd made promises of forever, but forever wasn't enough to keep them together.

CHAPTER FOURTEEN

Kylee and Kyree were out on another daddy-daughter day, and it made Jaz realize how much she'd been neglecting her own father. She hated to admit to herself that she'd been avoiding him. She knew how disappointed he was that she and Kyree were, once again, not together. Her dad was one of few people in the world that she admired and looked up to. She searched for him in every guy she dated. Kyree was the only man who'd ever come close.

Calvin had no idea she was coming, so when she walked in with a six pack of Heineken, his eyes lit up like he was seeing her for the first time. He threw a couple of steaks on the grill and they sat and talked over a game of Tonk. They were having such a good time that Jaz almost forgot why she was dodging her father in the first place.

"So, what are you girls going to do with the prize money from the hair show?"

"Mo and I are putting it back into the business. The renovations are already underway." Jaz eagerly pulled out her phone to show her father the pictures of the new wash bowls and other cool ideas they had for the salon.

"Oh, that's going to be dope, baby girl."

Jaz smiled. She could always hear her father's adoration for her whenever he spoke.

"Make sure you ask Kyree who he got to do the shop. He got a good deal on the barber shop when he was doing renovations."

Jaz rolled her eyes. "Here we go," she huffed, pulling her phone back.

"What's that supposed to mean?"

"It means that you're never going to let the thought of Kyree and me go. Daddy, we're no longer together, and we never will be. We've talked about this already."

"I know, but I've talked to the man and y'all were months away from getting married. It's that easy for you to give up on your family?"

Jaz scrunched her face. She never disrespected her father. She never even cursed so much as "damn" around him. But she was starting to feel like Kyree had Calvin on his payroll.

"Daddy, I love you and I don't want to disrespect you, but I'm so tired of you defending Kyree like he's some kind of saint. Dang, I'm your daughter. He's not your son."

"Listen now, I never said he was a saint. No man is perfect. But I can tell he's trying."

Jaz rolled her eyes again and she caught the look of discontent for her attitude that Calvin gave her, so she quickly fixed her face. Calvin allowed it to slide because he knew that Jaz was spoiled and he had no one to blame but himself. Over the years, he'd made excuses for her because her mother wasn't around. To Jaz, her father was the epitome of what a man should be. He was perfect, and nothing could change her view of him. Calvin was from the streets. It ran through his veins through and through. It took the love of a woman to change that for him. He related to Kyree's situation in more ways than one. Most of Jaz's life, he shielded her from a lot. But, for her happiness, he was willing to taint the seamless image she had of him.

"Ya know, your old man made mistakes too." Jaz looked up. He suddenly had her attention. "Don't get me wrong, I loved your mother more than anything in this world. But I was young. I made mistakes. I'm not proud of what I did, but it happened."

"What did you do?" Jaz needed answers and she wasn't going to let her father dance around the issue.

"Well, when you were about two years old, I was out in the streets doing my thing." Jaz knew about her father's past dealings in the streets. They were very similar to Kyree's. "And with that street money came flocks of women who threw themselves at me. I was able to keep my distance from many of them, but when your mother and I got into it, it became harder to resist."

Jaz was disappointed. She never wanted to believe her parents were anything short of flawless. "So you cheated on my mom?" Calvin shamefully nodded his head as Jaz turned up her face at him. "How did she react?"

Calvin grinned as the memory resurfaced. "Well, your mom was a strong woman. I mean that figuratively and physically. After she beat my ass, she got her homegirl Jackie and they slashed my tires and busted my windshield." Jaz couldn't help but laugh at the thought of her mom and Jackie doing something she and Monica would do in a heartbeat. "Then, she beat the girl's ass too. Jaz, ya mama was a feisty li'l something. I knew better than to fuck around on her."

Jaz tried to control her laughter as she asked, "So why did she take you back?"

"It wasn't easy, and it took a lot of months of groveling, but she eventually forgave me. I think she saw that my love for her was stronger than anything." He could see the uncertainty on his daughter's face. "The point of me telling you all of this was because we got through it. Our love was stronger than anything or anyone who could try to break it."

Jaz felt tears luring in the back of her throat, but she refused to let them surface.

"All I'm saying is, if you feel like it's worth you keeping your family, then think long and hard about your decision."

Jaz nodded her head and Calvin stood up to hug her. No matter what he'd done in the past, Jaz could never stay mad at her father. She just wished it was as easy to feel the same about Kyree.

Jaz and her dad finished up their game before Jaz had to head out to spend the rest of the evening with her girls. Jaz thought long and hard about her parents' relationship. She applauded her mother's ability to forgive her father, but she reasoned with herself that the times were different. In the day and age of the internet and social media, looking past one's infidelity was easier said than done.

Jaz needed this night with her girls to relax without the constant thoughts that plagued her on a daily. She was so relieved that she didn't have to spend another night in her home alone. The house was too big. She'd already talked with Kyree about moving back into her condo, but he was against it. The house was for his family and even if he wasn't staying there, he wanted them to. Jaz obliged his request, for now. But she knew she couldn't live there by herself forever. She loved the house; she just didn't love the bad memories it held in only a few short months.

Her friends thought she was crazy for wanting to leave, but they didn't mind coming over to keep her company in the mean-time. Jaz's entertainment room, formally known as the Man Cave, was so much fun. They especially loved the fully-stocked bar. Jackie had Kylee and Kayden for the night, so Jaz and Monica were free to have a good time with Ms. Ray. They opted to spend a night inside in their pajamas drinking wine, playing karaoke, watching movies, and laughing until they cried.

They had just finished watching *Acrimony* and were engulfed with the ending.

"I don't know why y'all are so surprised." Ms. Ray stood up to pour himself another glass of wine. The girls shook their heads at him. They still were having a hard time wrapping their minds around the black teddy he was wearing.

"Could you put on some shorts, please?" Jaz turned up her nose.

Ms. Ray rolled his eyes and put on his robe. Jaz knew it was her fault for not being specific when she told them she wanted to have a pajama party. He never ceased to amaze them.

"See, that's y'all's problem. Damn prudes." He took a sip from his wine glass. "That's why y'all are single now."

"Say wha, nah?" Monica quipped.

"You heard me. Y'all hoes are never gonna keep a man with those attitudes."

"Aw, hell nah. I'm 'bout ta kick his ass out!" Jaz threatened.

"I'll help you." Monica rolled her eyes while Ms. Ray couldn't help but laugh.

"I'm going to do you hopeless hoes a favor and school you right quick." He downed his drink and refilled his glass. "You see, the problem with that movie was that it was too damn true. Y'all are quick to find a man and think you can change him."

"Please shut up." Jaz placed a hand on her forehead. He was killing her buzz.

"Nope. I got something to say. And y'all may hate me for this, but in the end, know that I'm doing this because I love y'all like the females I should have been born as." He pointed his finger at Monica first. She looked behind her. "Yes, you, hoe. You had a good man in your corner. He put up with a lot of shit from you getting over a no-good-ass nigga. You finally had someone to show you a love worth fighting for, and what do you do? You found every reason to run. You let another bitch, who probably meant nothing to him, destroy your happiness."

Monica didn't respond. She turned her head so that she wouldn't have to face him. Admitting he was right was something she wasn't ready to do. Ms. Ray had a way of getting under their skin and making them listen, whether they wanted to or not. It may have been tough love, but it always registered with them in some way.

"I have to pee." Monica excused herself.

As soon as she was out of sight, Jaz punched him in the arm.

"Ow!" he winced. "You hit like a man."

"I don't care! Why did you do that? If she comes back here crying, I'm going to beat your ass," Jaz promised him.

"I was being honest. I'm tired of everyone babying y'all."

"Y'all?" Jaz questioned. "I'm good." She ignored him as she sent a text to Shaun. They'd been in constant contact lately.

"Sure ya are. And while you're over there texting the delivery man, Kyree is delivering dick around the 757, trying to give Kylee a little brother or sister."

"Say wha?" Jaz cut her eyes at him.

He popped his tongue. "Bloop."

While Jaz and Ms. Ray were going at it, Monica was in the bathroom, sitting on the edge of the tub and contemplating everything that was just said to her. As soon as she saw Ms. Ray's finger pointed at her, her heart stopped. She knew he was about to tell her what no one else would, whether she wanted to hear it or not. And he couldn't have been more right. She missed Mario terribly. She'd unblocked his phone number a week ago in the hopes that he'd contact her, but he had yet to hit her line. The fear consumed her that he'd given up on her for real this time. Pride prevented her from making the first move, but she could no longer hold on to her pride. She wanted to be happy and she hadn't been happier than when she was in Mario's presence.

Taking a deep breath, she grabbed her phone and typed in his number. Deleting it did nothing. She knew the number by heart and thought about calling it every day. Too afraid to actually talk to him, she sent a text message.

>>>> **757-555-9876, 10:45PM: Hey, it's me. I don't want a break anymore. I'm sorry for the way I acted. It was immature and selfish of me to write you off based off the word of someone else. I know I can be hard to love sometimes, but I love how you love me despite all of that. I hope that you can forgive me, and I want us to work this out. I miss you!**

After reading the message twice to make sure her feelings came off exactly as she wanted them to, she took a deep breath and pressed send. Monica stood up and checked her face in the mirror. She cried as she typed the message and didn't want her friends to see her in that state. When she was satisfied, she reentered the room where Jaz and Ms. Ray were still going at it.

Monica didn't even bother breaking it up. She was too busy worrying about Mario's response to her message.

"You good, Mo?" Jaz asked with a hand on her shoulder.

"Yeah, I'm fine. I hate to admit it, but Ray was partially right. I texted Mario just a minute ago." She dropped her head in shame.

Ms. Ray kind of felt bad because he knew how brash he could be at times. "Well, what'd he say?"

"Nothing yet."

"He'd be a fool not to," Jaz assured her.

"See, and that's Jaz's problem."

"Here we go." She rolled her eyes.

"I got through to one of you tonight, but you might need a lot more convincing. Jaz, you're spoiled as shit." Her mouth dropped, appalled. She turned to look at Monica for backup, but Monica pretended to be looking elsewhere. She agreed with Ms. Ray, but she didn't want to be involved in the conversation. "Don't act so surprised. You want everything to go your way, and when it doesn't, you wipe your hands with it. You never want to work hard to make shit work."

Jaz turned her head and bit her bottom lip. Her leg bounced in agitation and her nostrils flared as Ms. Ray gave her the reality check she'd been avoiding for so long. "I know you hate me right now, but I love you, girl. And I hate to see you give up on something, that we all wish we had, whenever an obstacle comes to throw you off track."

"You done?" She stormed off before he could answer her and took to the steps two at a time to her bedroom.

Monica looked at him and shook her head. "Now you know you were wrong for that. We all know she's spoiled. Hell, even she knows it. But you know how much that shit fucked her up. You have to be more subtle."

Ms. Ray sighed heavily. Monica was right. Sometimes his lack of a filter could be harsh. He never meant to hurt anyone, especially not his two best friends. Even though what he said was right, his delivery was wrong. So he sucked it up and he and Monica went upstairs to check on Jaz.

When Jaz heard them coming, she quickly used her comforter to wipe the tears from her face. They knocked before entering.

"Jaz, can we come in? Ray wants to apologize."

"Fuck him!" she retorted.

Monica and Ms. Ray slightly snickered at her childish behavior. They entered the room anyway and Ms. Ray felt like shit as soon as he saw her red eyes and tearstained cheeks.

"Oh, I'm so sorry, boo." He ran over and tried to console her, but she pushed him away. He ignored her request and hugged her tightly. Eventually, Jaz couldn't resist the urge to laugh hysterically.

"I hate you." She laughed.

"I love you too."

"Ms. Ray, if I feel anything poke me through that damn night-gown, I swear I'm going to kill you," she threatened.

"Oh, please! Only rock hard steel makes this black snake moan."

"Ew, I think I'm going to be sick." Monica held her mouth.

"Me too. Get off me," Jaz giggled.

"Gladly. I don't know what kind of secretions are in this bed anyway." He released her and looked around, suspiciously.

"You may as well get over it. There isn't a room in this house that I haven't fucked in."

"Oh, Jaz, you nasty." Ms. Ray high-fived her. Monica could only shake her head as she took a seat on the edge of the bed. "You know I really am sorry and didn't mean the shit I said, right?"

"Oh, you's a lie, you meant every word!" Jaz said and they all laughed. "But it's okay. I needed to hear it. It's just that everyone wants me to forgive him, but I can never forget it."

Monica decided to speak up this time. "Jaz, you and Ky have been through worse shit than this."

"That's just it, y'all. I'm sick and tired of going through bad shit. Did I tell y'all Michael has been calling me lately?" They both turned up their noses.

"What the hell does he want now?" Monica wanted to know.

"I don't know. I haven't answered my phone. But his texts claim it's important information I need to know about Asia." She rolled her eyes and hugged her pillow. "This is the shit I'm talking about.

This type of shit doesn't happen to normal people. I just want to be happy without all of the hard work for once."

"Well, it's not supposed to be easy. And life is hard, but trust and believe, love is even harder." Ms. Ray shook his head and they all knew he was reminiscing on his own past experiences with love. His once open heart shut down five years ago after the man he loved decided that he wasn't ready for the world to know that he was gay. He cared more about what other people thought of him than his love for Ms. Ray. "Y'all have a chance to make shit work. Don't be so quick to give it up."

Ms. Ray's words resonated with Monica that whole week. She wanted her man back. He brought out a part of her that she never knew existed. Mario even brought out a crazy side of her that only someone you love can do. She was even reminded of his scent as she walked by the men's cologne counter at Macy's. Through all of the hundreds of fragrances flowing freely through the air, Mario's brand stuck out and when she smelled it, she got chills.

Wanting him back was one thing, but she also needed him back. Yet it had been a whole week and he hadn't responded to her text message. Her heart jumped every time her phone rang. She kept her phone face down and took a deep breath before turning it over, but it was never him. Her palms sweated with each notification alert. She dreamed about him every night, and when her alarm clock sounded, she jumped out of her sleep and quickly picked up her phone. He was taking over her every thought. She was pissed off that he'd yet to respond. She knew he'd received her message because his read receipts were on. At first she thought he was thinking of the right words to say, but it was a week later and still no response. The thought had crossed her mind several times that he was finally tired of her shit and was with someone who wasn't as complicated.

Monica tried desperately to forget about him, but when she

was by herself, it was harder than ever. Kayden was with his father for his last weekend before he left for Japan and her friends were going out. Monica really wasn't up for it so she decided to stay in for the night. She was in the kitchen making stir fry with chicken and shrimp when she thought she heard something. She paused and listened intently but didn't hear anything, so she continued what she was doing. Seconds later, she thought she heard something again. She picked up the stirring spoon from the pot and held it in front of her like a weapon. She was scared as hell as she approached her living room where she'd heard the noise. Peeping around the corner, she didn't see anything so she crept toward her front door.

"Ahhhhh!" she screamed as she hit the hooded intruder with the spoon.

"Yo, chill out, Mo!" Mario yelled as he tried to hold her wrists. It took a few seconds for Monica to finally come to her senses. When she did, she held her chest to stop her heart from beating out of her body.

"You scared the shit out of me!" she said, exasperated.

He chuckled and she hit him again with the spoon. She hadn't yet come to the realization that he was actually standing in front of her, but when she did, she was pissed. "Get out!" she fumed. He didn't budge; he just laughed at her. "Ugh!" She rolled her eyes and headed back to the kitchen.

Mario could see she was mad, but he couldn't stop laughing. "What the hell were you gonna do with that spoon, huh?" Monica ignored him and tended to her food. He walked in the kitchen and looked over her shoulder. "Fix me a plate. I'm 'bout ta go use the bathroom right quick."

Monica looked on in disbelief as he exited the kitchen. She couldn't believe he had the audacity to show up to her house like everything was cool. She missed him terribly, but she was starting to wish he wasn't there at that moment. His visit was unexpected and she didn't have time to prepare what she wanted to say. And on top of everything, he had the upper hand and he knew it. They hadn't spoken in weeks, he didn't responded to a text message that took everything inside of her to write, and he was acting like shit was all good.

After fixing her plate, she sat down at the table and waited for him to come out of the bathroom. She'd already decided that she was going to tell him to leave. No matter how much she wanted him to stay, she refused to let him play her. But as she watched him stroll down the hallway, she started to change her mind. Everything about him made her weak.

"Where's my plate?" he asked.

"You need to go," she stated firmly.

"Pish." He dismissed her and made his own plate.

"I'm serious, Mario."

"Yeah, so serious that you changed the locks, huh?" He smirked as he sat down in front of her.

Monica's mouth dropped as he ignored her to pray over his food. He had her there. She'd thought about changing the locks on several occasions, but she hoped every day that he'd decide to pop in. But he never showed, and she eventually lost hope that he ever would.

He sat there eating as she looked on in disbelief. She hadn't even touched her food yet. "This shit good, girl."

"Really?" she barked.

"What?"

She sucked on her bottom lip to keep herself from going completely crazy. "Mario, you're really going to sit down and act like shit's all good when we haven't spoken in almost three weeks?" He wiped his mouth with a napkin, rested his hands on his knees, and looked at her. "Oh, and don't act like you didn't get my fuckin' text message, nigga." She threw her napkin at him.

He waved her off and continued eating.

"So you're not even going to address why you read the message a week ago and you haven't responded?" He was aggravating her with his games.

"What you want me to say, Mo? You blocked me from contacting you. That shit messed me up. I realize I hurt you, but there was nothing for you to worry about. But you hurt me too."

Monica looked away. She never thought about how he might have been hurting.

"So no, I didn't respond right away. I needed you to know how it felt to be shut out."

Monica cut her eyes at him. He was still playing games. She was starting to think that she was taking this more serious than him. But if he wanted to play, then she could play too. "Mario, you should go. I have company coming over soon."

"Who, Jaz?" She shook her head no. "Ray?" He looked at her and she didn't answer. "Monica, I swear if you got some nigga coming over here, you better text him back and tell him to turn his ass back around before I fuck both of y'all up."

Monica snickered and the death glare he gave her made her straighten up quick. She quickly thought it best that she retract her statement. "Look, there's nobody coming. But can you leave, please? I'm not in the right mind state to deal with you right now. I wasn't expecting this."

"No. I will not leave. This has been the longest three weeks of my life. I don't want to miss another second with you, Mo." Monica blushed. He took three quick bites from his food and gulped down his drink. He stood up and held his hand out for her. "Come on."

"What?"

"Just ride with me. I have to show you something."

Monica was hesitant at first, but she took his hand and stood up. After throwing on a pair of sneakers, Monica was riding on the passenger side as Mario drove - to where, she didn't know. She was just happy to be in his presence again. The road he was taking her down was unfamiliar to her and they were suddenly in the bad part of town. Monica was no stranger to the hood, but she liked to be warned before she ventured that way.

"Mario, if you have me on an episode of Discovery ID's *The Ride She Took* or some shit, I swear I won't go down easy," she said.

Mario laughed as he watched her make sure her door was locked. "Don't nobody won't yo' ass but me."

Monica rolled her eyes as he pulled the car into a parking lot. "What is this place?" she asked.

"It's mine."

Monica dropped her mouth in complete awe as she admired the large garage. It was gray and white, on a standalone lot. It may have been hard for anyone else to see anything spectacular, but Monica saw so much potential. "I'm so proud of you!" She knew how important it was for him opening up his own service shop. She wrapped her arms tightly around his neck and he smiled in adoration. After realizing that she hadn't been this close to him in weeks, she cautiously released him. "Congratulations." She nodded. She still wasn't sure where they were in their relationship and the closeness made her feel uncomfortable.

Mario could sense her distance as he sighed heavily. He turned off the ignition and looked at her. "Look, Mo, when you said you wanted a break, it freaked me out. It made me realize that I had to do something with my life to secure a future with you in it. I felt like I had to do something more than tell you how I felt. I had to show you. You're the only one who was able to make me see Shannon for who she really was. You showed me how beneficial going into business for myself would be. I don't even go out as much as I used to. Mo, all I want to do is be with you. I'm getting my life right to make a permanent place for you, but I can't do that if you're not in it all the way."

Monica looked down as the guilt consumed her. She had a tendency to push away anyone who tried to get close and Mario had managed to get closer than anyone she'd ever been involved with. She used excuses and nitpicked at the smallest things in hopes that she wouldn't have to face her own reality.

"I'm just...scared," she admitted just above a whisper.

Mario raised her head with a finger under her chin. She faced him and could see the sincerity in his eyes. "I know you are. But you never have to be afraid as long as I'm around. And I'll be around for as long as you want me to be. You're not going to get rid of me that easy." He wiped a tear from her face. "You love me?"

She nodded her head. "Of course I do."

"Then let me love you back."

Monica wrapped her arms around his neck again and this time, she didn't let go. That night they drove home and spent the rest of the evening talking. They caught up on what they'd missed in each other's lives, discussed their relationship and where they had gone wrong, and made plans for the future. Monica promised to not let her fears get the best of her and Mario promised to not let anyone interfere with their relationship.

Shannon was no longer in his life, and he was in a better place because of it. Her last message to him said she was moving to Atlanta with her ex and that she really missed Mario. But he could care less. He hadn't even spoken to her since the night of the Percy's bachelor party. Shannon had ruined everything, and so had he by not speaking up before things got out of hand. Being at Percy's wedding without Monica by his side was an empty feeling he never wanted to experience again.

Mario didn't just want a relationship with Monica; he wanted a strong relationship with Kayden as well. So he even accepted Monica's offer to have him sit down and have a serious man-to-man over dinner with Latrell. She didn't want any bad blood between the two men in Kayden's life. Their talk was comforting to her and the future suddenly didn't seem so scary.

CHAPTER FIFTEEN

J az had been on a few dates with Shaun. It was always fun and he made her laugh. But it was still too soon after Kyree for her to fully commit herself. She felt selfish because Shaun was putting in a lot of effort, but she couldn't allow herself to do the same. The other day, Shaun had moved in to kiss her and she tensed up. He could feel that her heart wasn't in it, so he let up and didn't press the issue. He knew that she was still hung up on her ex, so he promised to take it slow. Jaz knew that she wasn't playing fair. Tonight she reasoned with herself that she would loosen up. They had a dinner date at eight o'clock.

Jackie was taking Kylee and Kayden to a birthday party so Jaz didn't have to worry about finding a sitter. Dressed to kill in a pair of light blue jeans, a white blouse rolled at the ends, and a pair of Nine West red pumps, Jaz was ready to go. She still hadn't let Shaun know where she lived so she was meeting him at Monica's house. Monica still wasn't happy about the two of them dating.

She did and said whatever she could to steer Jaz in another direction.

"How do I look?" Jaz asked Monica as she fixed her face in the mirror.

"You look great. You might want to do a nude lip with that 'fit."

"You're probably right. What do you have for me?"

Monica rolled her eyes. She hated that she had even mentioned it. She reached in her makeup box and picked out the perfect liner and lipstick to go with Jaz's outfit. "I want my shit back when you're done."

Jaz smirked. That lipstick was just as good as hers now.

"Soooo," Monica began. "You're still not comfortable with him coming to your house, huh? It's been three weeks. You don't find that a little odd?"

Jaz sighed heavily. She knew Monica was the campaign manager of the Get Back with Kyree election. Her girl meant well, but it still got on her nerves. "Mo, I just think it's best this way for now. If my crazy-ass baby daddy found out I had some nigga coming to the house where he still pays the mortgage, he would kill us both."

Monica gazed at the floor in disappointment. Jaz was well aware this was a losing battle for Monica, but she was just going to have to understand. "Look, until Kyree can understand that we can't be together, then I can move around as free as I please. But for now, it has to be like this. I don't know why he's even trippin'. I don't care if he goes out with other women."

Monica looked up at her. "Then I guess you won't mind that Ray's client, Melissa, asked him if it was okay to ask Kyree out now that you two aren't together."

Jaz's heart stopped instantly as she applied her lipstick. A lot of people didn't like Melissa because she was always running her mouth. Jaz thought she was funny and never really had a problem with her - until now, that is. Jaz wanted so badly to question Melissa's motives, but she didn't want Monica to see she cared.

"If it makes you feel any better, Ray told her he'd cut her from ear to ear if she went anywhere near him."

Jaz smirked. That did make her feel slightly better. "Like I said, Mo, Kyree is free to see whoever he wants."

"Uh huh." Monica nodded her head. She could see how much it got under Jaz's skin, but she wouldn't press the issue.

Mario walked by with Jaz's ringing phone in hand. "I think he's outside."

Jaz grabbed her phone and told Shaun she'd be right out. She did one last look in the mirror and slid Monica's lipstick in her purse.

"You need a jacket?" Mario asked. He was starting to act like a brother to her. He also didn't approve of Jaz dating anyone outside of Kyree. He really liked Kyree. Jaz waved him off. "I think I need to go meet this young man," Mario said as he started to walk toward the door.

Jaz quickly grabbed her bag and ran in front of him. "Please don't," she begged. "I promise I will introduce everyone in due time. But for now, I don't want y'all to run him off."

Mario looked at her and could see that she was serious. He reluctantly let her pass and Shaun knocked on the door. Jaz told them both goodbye and quickly shut the door behind her on her way out.

"Everything good?" Shaun asked. He could see the nervousness on her face.

"Of course." Jaz smiled and hugged him. He looked nice in a pair of slacks and a button-up.

Shaun took her to the Cinebistro, where they ate and saw the new Kevin Hart movie. Jaz had a great time. Shaun was such a nice guy. She wanted so badly not to like him, but he was so easy to be around. When their night ended, he pulled in front of Monica's house and they sat in the car and talked.

"You know, one of these days you're going to have to tell me where you live. Got me feeling like you saw me on a most wanted photo at the post office or some shit."

Jaz laughed. "You will. One day."

"I'd love to take you and your daughter out some time. My son will be in town next week, and I'd love for them to meet."

Jaz considered it for a moment. She'd thought on many occasions how she'd introduce her daughter to someone new. She didn't want to have just any and everyone around her, not unless things were getting serious.

"So, what do you say?" Shaun searched her face for confirmation.

Jaz looked up and reached across to put a hand behind his head. She brought him closer to her face and kissed him. She didn't hold back either and he welcomed the tongue she slipped in his mouth.

"Damn, girl," Shaun chuckled.

Jaz smiled and gave him one last peck before exiting to Monica's front door. She noticed when they pulled in that Monica and Mario weren't home, so she let herself in and sent Monica a text to let her know she didn't feel like driving home. Monica sent her one back to say that she was staying at Mario's that night. Jaz kicked her shoes off and headed to the guest bedroom. She grabbed a shirt and pajama pants from the drawer she kept in Monica's guestroom, showered, and turned on the TV. She plopped down on the bed and smiled at a text she received from Shaun letting her know that he was home. She was about to reply when the news caught her attention.

"I'm standing in front of Luxe nightclub, where shots were fired just hours ago. We have confirmed that two men are dead and three other club patrons are wounded. No word yet on any suspects. Police are currently waiting to inform the families before the victim's names are announced. If anyone knows anything, the police ask that you call – "

Jaz cut the TV off before the news anchor could finish speaking. That was one of the clubs that Kyree was in talks to purchase. He was supposed to be there tonight, trying to see if this was something he'd be interested in investing in. Jaz's heart raced as she immediately picked up her phone to dial Kyree's number. It was a little after midnight and she just hoped that he answered. With every ring, Jaz thought she was going to throw up.

"Hello?" Kyree groggily said into the phone.

Jaz took a huge sigh of relief upon hearing his voice. "I didn't want anything. I just..." she paused.

Kyree could hear her breathing and instantly assumed something was wrong. "What's up, Jazzy?" He sat up in bed, more alert than before.

"Really, it was nothing. I just heard Luxe was shot up, and I...I was just checking to make sure you weren't there."

Kyree smirked. "I didn't think you cared."

"Really, Kyree? Of course I care." She sucked her teeth, hurt that he'd ever think that. "You know what? Forget I called."

"Wait!" He called after her before she could hang up. It was good hearing her voice. He didn't want to let her go just yet.

"What?" she answered with agitation.

"I have a room at Towne Place Suites. I've been asleep all day, for real. I'm not fuckin' with Luxe anymore. I could've seen that shooting coming from a mile away. I didn't like how they did business. Shit was shady."

"Yeah, you've always been good at reading through people."

He smiled to himself and got up to head to the fridge in his suite for something to drink. "What're you doing up so late anyway?"

Jaz hesitated briefly. She wasn't sure how much she should say without making things awkward. "Oh, I just got in. I'm at Mo's house. She's staying the night at Mario's though."

Kyree swallowed hard. He knew what that meant. He sensed her hesitation immediately, and the last thing he wanted to do was wreck their conversation with the thoughts of her with another man, so he quickly changed the subject. He took a sip from the apple juice he got from the fridge.

"Ay, guess who I ran into?"

"Who?" she asked, getting up to raid Mo's pantry.

"Remember that woman your dad was dating that you hated? What was her name: Connie, Colette, Damn...I can't think of it, but I know it started with a C. Was it Claudine? Nah, it wasn't that. It was – "

"Claudette." Jaz cut him off and immediately rolled her eyes.

"Yep! That's it!" Kyree started to laugh. Jaz hated that woman. "She saw me at the store the other day and asked about you."

"Fuck her!" Jaz snarled. Kyree only laughed harder.

"Why did you hate that woman? All the young boys loved to watch her ass run up and down the block every morning. We thought yo' daddy was the man for that shit," he boasted.

"I hated her because she was a hoe. But my dad, like the rest of you niggas, couldn't see past her phat ass."

"Don't get mad because yo' daddy was gettin' some of that ass." He playfully laughed again.

"Oh, so we're bringing up family memories and shit?" Kyree was still laughing, but she had something for his ass. "Remember the time when we first started messing around? We were about two weeks in and hadn't told Mo yet."

Kyree stopped laughing. "A'ight, Jazzy." He got serious, and this time Jaz laughed.

"We were fooling around on my bed in the dorm room and we heard Mo coming, so you hid in the closet. And she walked in and started talking about the freak session she'd just had with Latrell."

"Jaz, chill!" he warned.

Jaz couldn't even finish the rest of the story, she was laughing so hard, but she didn't have to. Kyree had tried to erase that dreadful night from his memories. He was in the closet with nothing on but his underwear and his sister was talking some of the freakiest shit he'd ever heard. He wanted to throw up. After that, he made Jaz promise that they'd tell Monica about their relationship. He didn't want to have to ever hear shit like that again. It took Monica a few days to get over the disgust of their relationship, but she eventually gave in. Even back then she knew they loved each other.

Jaz continued to laugh. She couldn't remember the last time she'd laughed so hard with Kyree. Most of the time they ended up arguing, but she was glad they could play around and enjoy each other's company.

"You done laughing?"

"Hey, if you can't take the heat, you shouldn't have started it. You know how much I hated Hoedette." They both burst into laughter at the neighborhood name everyone called Claudette.

"So what're you eating?" He could hear her smacking on the phone.

"Mo's cookie dough ice cream."

"She's gonna kill your ass." They both laughed again.

They ended up talking for hours. They reminisced on old times, talked about Kylee, and caught up on what was going on in each other's lives. Jaz made sure to leave out her new friend, Shaun. Kyree could sense she was holding back, but he didn't press the issue. The less he knew, the better for everyone. Before either of them knew it, it was three hours later.

Jaz enjoyed their conversations. It made her realize how much she missed him. She hated the feeling of wanting him. But the fact that they could be so cordial with each other made her want to ask him a question she wouldn't have felt comfortable asking on a normal day.

"Hey, I have to ask you something, and please don't trip. If you say no, I'll completely understand."

Kyree could hear the worry in her voice. He had no idea what could be so important. "What's up, Jazzy? You can ask me anything."

She took a deep breath and tried to relax as best she could. "Well, I've been seeing someone." She could hear his breathing change its normal pattern, but she had to get this out before she lost the nerve. "He's a really great guy and his son is in town this weekend. He wants me to meet him and I was thinking, if it's okay with you of course, that I could introduce him to Kylee." There was a long pause, so Jaz thought she needed to explain further. "I wanted to ask you first. I know it's only been a few months, but I wanted to make sure you were comfortable with it before I said yes. If you're not, I completely understand."

Kyree paused for what seemed like forever to Jaz. In that brief moment he thought of how fucked up their lives had gotten. He couldn't believe that His Jazzy was seeing someone else and that she was serious enough about this person to want to introduce him to his daughter. This was his family. He wanted to ask so many questions. Had this man been in his house? Had he made love to his woman? Had he stolen the heart that once belonged to him?

Kyree wanted to find this dude and kill him. His trigger finger itched to body the man that was making moves on His Jazzy. But the worry in Jaz's voice told him that she wanted his approval. She wanted him to let her go. He could never do that. But her happiness was the only thing that ever mattered to him. He'd be willing to compromise if it meant keeping the peace in their relationship.

"Kyree," she spoke, breaking the silence, "if you're not cool with this, it won't even go down. I'll wait until you're comfortable."

"It's fine. But I need to meet dude first."

Jaz took a huge sigh of relief. She smiled on the inside. "Well, do you want to meet him Saturday?"

"Nah, I can't do it this weekend. I have to go out of town. Maybe next weekend."

"Oh." Jaz paused. "Well, I guess he can meet Kylee next weekend then." She smiled, trying to find the silver lining. At least he had agreed.

Kyree didn't have anywhere to be this weekend, but he'd stall on getting his family too close to someone new for as long as it took. He was confident that Jaz would never introduce them until he and the new guy had met.

She yawned. "Well, it's getting late. I know you have a busy day ahead of you."

"Yeah, I do, actually. And Jazzy?"

"Yes?"

"Thanks for checking up on my safety. I appreciate it."

She half smiled. "Kyree, I'll always care about you. Goodnight."

Kyree didn't want her to go, but he'd had enough Jaz-fix to last him one night. He wasn't sure how long he could go before he needed another dose. He was addicted and no other drug could compare. The three years of rehab he had by being in jail did little to cure his cravings. Every day he wanted more.

Monica saw her brother and best friend going through the motions every day. She tried her hardest to stay out of it, but it was next to impossible. They weren't the two lively people she loved when they weren't together. They made each other better. Kyree helped to level Jaz. She was always so wild and carefree, but Kyree gave her the perfect balance of calmness. And Jaz helped to bring out a more playful side to a mild-mannered Kyree. The two were perfect for each other. Monica had known it for years.

Monica could recall a time when they were all just teenagers. She'd listen and roll her eyes as Jaz went on and on about how much she despised Kyree, and when Jaz left, Kyree would do the same. They were always nitpicking with each other. But when Monica suggested that the two were secretly in love, they quickly nipped that idea in the bud, which was why when they finally got together, it was no surprise to her. She was, however, disgusted at first. It took some getting used to because Jaz was like a sister to her. They'd all grown up together, spent vacations together, and were more like family than friends. It was weird, at first, but now she couldn't see it any other way.

When Jaz started dating Michael, Monica was all for it. She was happy to see her moving on. But there was a spark about Jaz that no longer existed. It was hard to notice until Kyree came back into town and a piece of her friend that she hadn't seen in a long time resurfaced. It was then that she knew the two were better off together than apart.

When Monica expressed her disappointment to Kyree for his actions in sleeping with Kendall, he broke down. That night, she saw the strong, confident father figure she'd known her entire life shed a few tears. Kyree was like her Superman. She'd never seen him cry in her entire life. It was obvious to her that he'd had a moment of weakness and made a mistake, but she knew that Jaz wouldn't see it that way. So for both of their sakes, she had to make Jaz see the man that she'd seen that night.

CHAPTER SIXTEEN

Jaz pulled into the parking lot of the salon. She had no idea why Monica wanted to go over the books and do an inventory now. Monica was adamant that Jaz had to be at the salon tonight. Jaz figured she was meddling again and trying to mess up her plans with Shaun. But in her heart of hearts, Jaz knew it was too early since Kyree to be seeing someone else. Although Shaun did serve as a great distraction, the fact still remained that she wasn't ready. She thought that Kyree agreeing to meet Shaun would be all the confirmation she needed to move on, but it only scared her more. Instead of introducing them, Jaz slowly began to distance herself. She'd intentionally missed meeting Shaun's son last week because it was beginning to feel like it was getting too serious.

Jaz didn't feel the need to tell everyone. If people thought she was seeing someone, they were less likely to bring Kyree's name into every conversation. She hoped that her friends could one day get with the fact that she and Kyree were no more. It was like they wanted her relationship to work more than she did. Whether they were happy with her decision or not, Jaz was trying to move on.

Jaz walked into the salon, dressed comfortably in blue Nike sweats and a pair of white Air Max 95's, with her hair freshly blown out. She tossed her bag on her station. She didn't see anyone in the salon, but she knew someone was there because she saw Monica & Ms. Ray's cars in the parking lot.

"I'm here!" Jaz yelled out to anyone who could hear.

She grabbed a water bottle from the fridge just as Monica and Ms. Ray came strolling out from the back. Jaz looked at them suspiciously. "Are y'all the only ones here? I thought the meeting started at 9:00. It's 9:30."

"Yeah, so why are you late?" Monica reminded her.

Jaz squinted, feeling guilty. "That's beside the point."

"Uh huh." Monica shook her head.

"So, what's so important about this meeting that you just had to have during the season finale night of *Love and Hip Hop*?"

Ms. Ray threw his hand in the air. "Girl, I almost didn't come either. Mo be on that bullshit. She know better." He and Jaz cracked a smile and high-fived each other.

Monica rolled her eyes. "Whatever. But we didn't really call you here for a meeting."

Jaz's brow furrowed it. She had no idea what type of shit they were on tonight.

"I think maybe you should sit down, best friend." Ms. Ray grabbed her elbow and tried to usher her to a seat, but Jaz snatched her arm away.

Jaz folded her arms tightly under her breasts. "I'm good." She stood with all of her weight on one side.

Monica took a deep breath. She knew this wasn't going to fly over well. "Okay, well, with everything going on with you and Kyree, we felt it was only right that we offer our help."

Jaz sucked her teeth. "We don't need y'all's help. It's over between us," she stressed.

"Jaz, I've known you two all of my life. There's no one that makes either of you happier than the other, and I want y'all to be happy."

"But, Mo, I'm trying to be happy. I can only do that by moving on. Can't you see that?"

"I know, but can you just please hear me out? If this doesn't work, I promise we won't ever speak of this again."

Jaz looked between the two of them. She knew there was nothing they could say or do to convince her otherwise so, to get them off her back, she reluctantly agreed. "Okay. But after this, I swear, I don't want to EVER hear about this from either one of you. Ya got that?"

They both raised their hands in surrender.

"Okay, just follow us to the back so we can sit down and talk."

"Hell nah! Is this some kind of intervention?" Jaz interjected.

"Just come on, scary ass." Ms. Ray pushed her towards the back.

Jaz followed them to the back. She hated that they felt she couldn't be happy without Kyree. They didn't understand that she was trying her hardest to live without him and they gave her no hope that she ever would. It was disheartening that they lacked faith in her strength. There was nothing that could be said or done for her to change her mind - or so she thought.

"What the fuck is this?" Jaz barked.

Monica grabbed Jaz's shoulders. "We know it's a little unorthodox, but we were running out of options."

"Unorthodox? Monica, this shit is fuckin' crazy! You kidnapped someone!"

"Calm down, Jaz. She's not going to say anything?" Ms. Ray reasoned.

"Calm down?" Jaz looked at him like he was crazy. "Ray, untie her!" Jaz stomped her foot as she pointed to a tied-up Kendall.

"No, Jaz!" Monica yelled. "You need to understand why she did what she did and if it meant anything to Kyree. That way you can decide whether it's worth forgiving him or not."

"This is fuckin' nuts!" Jaz ran her hands through her hair and paced back and forth. She looked at a scared Kendall as she sat with her arms and legs tied to a styling chair. She tried to speak, but her mouth was also bound and gagged. Jaz thought for sure her friends had finally lost their damn minds. The serious looks on their faces had confirmed her suspicions that they really thought they were helping.

"Just remove the scarf from around her mouth and you can ask her whatever you want." Monica could see that she'd sparked something in Jaz, and she had.

As crazy as Jaz thought this was, she had to admit that there were a thousand questions she wanted to ask Kendall. She often wondered if the reason she couldn't see past everything was the fact that it was Kendall who he'd slept with. Not only was Kendall someone she knew, she was also Kyree's ex. It may have been years ago since their high school rivalry, but Jaz never liked her and as much as Kendall smiled in her face now, Jaz was sure she still didn't like her either.

Kyree had only been in two relationships his whole life. His first was Kendall, and his last was Jaz. Sure, there were plenty of insignificant women in between, but none had the lasting power that Jaz and Kendall had. If Kyree stated claims to anyone, it was serious. Seeing Kendall back in the picture brought out insecurities Jaz didn't even know existed. Kyree was her lifeline so if he said Kendall was just there for business, she was going to take his word for it. She didn't like it, but she trusted her man. That trust had been broken and Jaz felt like an idiot for believing him.

Jaz tried so hard to be the bigger person. She was too old to be fighting and carrying on like she wasn't almost thirty with a child at home. But there was a part of her that wanted to revert back to the old Jaz. She was tired of people fucking with her life. Every day she felt like she was losing control. Monica and Ms. Ray might have lost their minds completely, but Jaz was going to take advantage of the opportunity while it was right in front of her.

Jaz pursed her lips and nodded her head. She grabbed a nearby chair and pulled it up a few feet away from Kendall. With her legs crossed, she used a finger to direct Monica to untie her mouth. Monica quickly did as instructed.

Kendall stretched her jaw muscles and stared at the people before her. She was scared shitless. The situation was totally ridiculous and she couldn't believe she'd fallen for it. But Monica had finally responded to the message she'd sent her days ago asking her to do her hair. She had no idea when she showed up that this would be the predicament she'd fall victim to. Although Monica and Ms. Ray were the ones who lured her there under false pretenses and tied her up, Jaz frightened her more than any of them. The glare in her eyes was unmatched. She was calm as she sat - too calm for comfort. She was so unfazed that she'd even told Monica to untie her arms and legs. Kendall was relieved. She'd been tied up for two hours and she could finally stretch her legs. She didn't dare get up though. The look on Jaz's face said otherwise.

"I'm going against everything I believe in by allowing this to carry on, but my friends here seem to think there's something you can say to convince me that my man fuckin' another woman is okay." Jaz laughed to herself and shook her head. "So please...tell me."

Kendall nervously shrugged her shoulders. "Well, what do you want me to say? It just...happened."

"See, I'm done with this shit already!" Jaz hopped up from her chair but Monica pushed her back down. Jaz looked up at her, pissed. She tightly folded her arms and turned her head. She couldn't bear to look at any of them any longer.

"Kendall, don't play with us. Tell Jaz what you told Ray and me before she got here."

Kendall took a deep breath and weighed her options. She was outnumbered and couldn't fight or talk her way out of this one. When she spilled her soul out to Monica and Ms. Ray earlier, she thought they'd let her go. But when they didn't, she didn't see a reason she should tell Jaz. Her revelation would only make things worse.

"Okay. Well, as you know, I'm kinda in the spotlight in the media."

"Tuh ha," Jaz chuckled, not even bothering to look at her.

Kendall brushed Jaz off and continued. "Recently I've started not to have as many likes as I used to."

"What the fuck does this have to do with me?"

Ms. Ray put his hand to his head. "Chile, let her finish."

Jaz huffed, but Kendall ignored her. "Basically, I needed a story to get my name back out there. I was dating K.O., but people seemed to be getting tired of us so my homegirl came up with the idea to start a little drama."

She now had Jaz's attention and she turned to face Kendall.

"So I had her snap a picture of Kyree and me on the couch."

Jaz scrunched her face in confusion. "So what about y'all fuckin'? How did that happen?"

Ms. Ray was getting annoyed. He picked up a set of curlers and aimed them at Kendall's face. "Girl, if you don't tell her everything, I swear I will burn yo' ass with a set of 450's."

"Okay...okay." Kendall backed away from the curlers and he lowered them. "Well, Kyree wasn't really paying me much attention so when he sat down with me while I vented, I slipped an E pill in his drink."

"You did what?" Jaz shot up from her seat, causing it to fall to the floor.

Kendall started to cry, but Jaz really didn't care about her feelings at this point.

"I know it was fucked up. I didn't know he was going to react to it the way he did. But when the drug started to take effect, he got an erection and since I was already over top of him, shit just... happened. I don't think he wanted it to, but it did. He was so fucked up after it happened that he made me promise not to say anything."

"But you knew, and you didn't try to stop it?" Jaz was fuming, and all Kendall could do was shrug her shoulders. Jaz grasped her hands in the air, on the verge of choking her. But she clasped them together instead and paced the floor.

"What the fuck is wrong with you?" Jaz barked. "You don't fuck with people's lives like this! There's no way you fuckin' him just *happened*," Jaz used finger quotes. "You did this shit because you wanted to do it!"

"I'm sorry. I didn't mean for it to go this far."

"No, you're just sorry you got caught. Because after all of this shit happened, I went online and checked Kyree's call log. He missed twenty-five calls from you the first week. I thought it was odd, but I thought he'd just hit it and quit it. Now it all makes sense."

Jaz began to pace the floor again with her hands on her head.

"You okay, boo?" Ms. Ray asked, concern evident in his tone.

Jaz ignored him and helplessly plopped down in the chair. She covered her face with her hands and started to cry. "Ugh!" she groaned. Monica and Ms. Ray rushed to her side to rub her back. "What the fuck is wrong with me, y'all? Why does everyone hate me so much?" She desperately wanted to know what it was about her that made people do such deceitful things to interrupt her life. This wasn't the first time. It wasn't too long ago that Asia was trying to steal her fiancé and wreck her life. Jaz was nice to everyone she met. There wasn't a soul in the world she'd ever wronged.

Ms. Ray shook his head. "It's not you, boo. They hate what you have. You're beautiful, smart, and successful and you have a great man that adores the ground you walk on. Some women don't want to work for it."

Monica nodded in agreeance. "They'd rather take what someone else has, no matter who they hurt in the process."

Jaz quickly wiped her tears with the sleeve of her jacket and stood up.

"So what are you going to do?" Monica wanted to know.

Jaz shook her head. She had no idea what her next move was going to be, but she refused to take this lying down. Her mind was in overdrive and she just needed a moment to herself.

"But what about her?" Monica asked.

"What about her? Let her go. If Kendal knows what's best for her, she knows better than to tell anyone what happened here. Isn't that right?" Jaz glared at her and Kendall nodded her head profusely.

"I promise I won't say anything," she honestly replied. She knew better than to fuck with Kyree like that. If he found out, she'd be lucky to escape with her life.

Ms. Ray sucked his teeth. He and Monica were hoping for something a little more climactic. After hearing all of the conniving shit Kendall had been up to, they were sure Jaz was going to lose her shit, but she was actually being very mature about the situation.

Jaz held out Kendall's purse and Kendall hesitantly reached for it. Once her hands were wrapped around the straps, Jaz pulled the purse forward and hit her with a hard jab to the nose. She stumbled backwards and Jaz clipped her, causing her to fall on her ass.

"Ahhhh!" Kendall screamed.

Ms. Ray stood to his feet. "Bloop! And now we have a party!"

"That's my girl!" Monica high-fived Ms. Ray.

Jaz stood over Kendall and pulled her up by her shirt collar. "Bitch, I don't care how old we are, I will never be too old to tag your ass. And if you so much as think about me OR Kyree again, I'll know. This isn't high school anymore. I don't have time for your silly little games. Every time I see you, it's on sight." Jaz's words were venomous and she meant every word. She was tired of playing games with people. She was going to take back her control. "Now, get you shit, and get the fuck out of my salon!" Jaz dropped her collar and Kendall's head fell back. Monica and Ms. Ray laughed as she scrambled to get up and rushed out of the door.

"Girlllllll," Ms. Ray stressed. "I almost thought you were about to let her ass get out of here without tappin' that ass."

"You obviously had me fucked up." Jaz grabbed her purse and headed toward the door.

She had her hand on the doorknob ready to turn it, and then she hesitated. She quickly turned toward her girls, and simultaneously grabbed both of their necks in a warm embrace. "Thanks, y'all."

"We love you, girl. We'd do anything for you," Monica assured her.

Jaz left the salon with a heavy heart. She didn't know what she was going to do with the new information she'd been given. This changed everything. It wasn't completely Kyree's fault. He was just as much a victim to Kendall's petty games as she was.

Despite knowing that it wasn't entirely Kyree's fault, Jaz

couldn't get past the bad things that always seemed to happen to them. There was their hate for each other growing up, Kyree's jail sentence, the shooting that almost took his life, and then Kendall's crazy antics. No matter how hard they tried to make it work in the past, their happiness just never seemed to last. The giant cloud that followed them around wherever they went was unpredictable. Jaz could never tell when it was going to rain but when it did, it poured.

She tossed and turned that night, praying to God that the answer would come to her in the morning. But when she woke, she still had no idea what she was going to do. Jackie dropped Kylee off the next morning and her smiling face was the only thing that kept Jaz's focus off of her many worries. She and Kylee were playing on the floor in the den when there was a loud banging at the door. It scared Jaz and Kylee started to cry. Jaz picked her up and went to see who was knocking at the door like they'd lost their damn mind. She flung the door open and to her surprise, it was Kyree.

"Lee a'ight?" he frantically spoke. Jaz looked at him crazy as he took Kylee from her arms to examine her closely. "I came as soon as I got your message."

"Oh," Jaz uttered as it all started to come back to her. She'd forgotten all about the text message she sent him a few hours ago that read: **Come quick. It's Kylee!**

"What's wrong with her?"

Jaz smirked. "Nothing is wrong with her. I never said anything was wrong."

Kyree looked at her crazy. He wanted to hurt her for making him worry like that. He knew it was only payback for what he'd done to her while she was on her date. "Jaz, I'm gonna kill yo' ass."

She laughed. "Doesn't feel so good, huh?" He sucked his teeth.

"But she did do something pretty amazing." She grabbed Kylee from him. "Come look."

Kyree followed Jaz to the living room where she placed Kylee on the floor. Jaz stood on the other side of the room and beckoned.

"Come to Mommy, Kylee baby. Come on," she called out to her.

Kylee propped herself up on the couch and looked at Jaz. She smiled at her and her little legs started to move as she made her way closer. Kyree was in awe as he watched her travel wobbly across the room on her own. Jaz continued to call her over, but Kylee went right past Jaz and to her dad. Kyree fell out laughing as Jaz hung her head low in embarrassment. He picked Kylee off the floor and taunted Jaz. "See, she knows what's up. Ain't that right, Lee?" Jaz ignored them both. "Yo, when did she start doing that?"

"This morning. I was going to put it on Instagram, but I wanted you to be the first one to see it."

Kyree was more excited than Kylee. He put her on the floor and put different toys in front of her, trying to get her to walk toward different objects. Jaz decided to leave the two alone. She was making dinner and Kyree being there gave her the perfect opportunity to prepare her grilled chicken, brown rice, asparagus, and Hawaiian rolls. When she returned to the living room an hour later, Kyree and Kylee were fast asleep on the couch. Jaz admired them for a moment. They looked so calm. She didn't want to disturb them, but Kyree's eyes began to open. They locked eyes briefly and Kyree proceeded to pull himself up from the couch.

"I'll take her to her room," he said. Jaz nodded and he walked past her and up the stairs. Jaz took a long sigh. She wanted to tell him what she'd discovered in the last couple of days, but she knew it would just cause more drama. But as he bopped down the stairs with his usual stroll, Jaz suddenly wanted to tell him everything. There was something about him that was different. Kyree looked as though he hadn't shaved or slept in weeks. There was a melancholy glare in his eyes that spoke of his sullen mood. She'd never seen him like this and she wanted to ask him what was wrong, but she didn't know how.

"She's worn out." He chuckled.

"Yeah, her bad butt be tryna play me when you come around."

"Hey, my baby ain't bad. She just loves her daddy," he boasted and they both shared a laugh.

Jaz knew Kylee's attachment to Kyree was strong. She wished she could give them both what they wanted. She was also aware that if she wanted to, the ball was in her court.

"What you cookin'?"

"Oh, just some grilled chicken, rice, and vegetables."

"Word? Well shit, let's eat," Kyree joked. He knew she'd never agree to it.

"Well, why don't you stay?" Kyree eyed her skeptically. "For dinner," she quickly added.

Kyree coolly nodded his head, but inside, he was ecstatic. He couldn't remember the last time he'd had a home-cooked meal. He didn't want to make too much of it and get his hopes up, but he couldn't help it. Anytime he got to spend with her, he cherished.

"But first, you need to clean up before dinner."

Kyree turned toward the bathroom, but Jaz stopped him. "Nah, bruh. I mean that head. You look a hot-ass mess with this James Harden beard."

Kyree laughed as he ran his hands down his face. He had to admit that he had been looking a little ragged lately. But that was only because he'd stopped caring. Without Jaz, the part of him that wanted to get up and go was non-existent.

"What, you ain't gon' do it?" he dared her.

Jaz smirked and walked back to the closet she'd had converted into a small in-home salon. She often invited high-paying clients there for special appointments. Kyree followed behind her, watching the way her ass looked in the jean shorts she was wearing. There was no one more perfect in his eyes. She tapped the chair for him to have a seat and Kyree contemplated it for a moment, but it was clear that she wasn't taking no for an answer.

"Damn, I think I left my bag upstairs. Hold on." She left to retrieve her bag and Kyree sat and tried to get comfortable. Jaz hadn't done his hair in a long time and he needed to relax. He couldn't have her fucking up his head. But Jaz's ringing phone kept going off. He picked it up to silence the ring and he saw Shaun's name come across her screen. His jaw instantly grew tight, and he started to contemplate going back to jail for killing the nigga. He fought the urge to flip out on everybody, Jaz included. He had to remember that he was trying to get in her good graces. And starting trouble with her new "friend" would surely set them back a few weeks in their reunion. He placed the phone like he'd found it and tried to look as natural as possible before she returned.

"Found it." She smiled as she reentered the room. She put her bag down and rummaged through it for the clippers. Her cell phone started to ring again. When Jaz saw it was Shaun, she silenced it. This wasn't the time to talk to him. She didn't need anything to set Kyree off. She knew on most days he was just one pulsating vein in the side of his neck away from going back to jail. She decided it was probably best that she turn the phone off for now.

When Kyree saw her look at the phone, he waited for a reaction, but he didn't see one, so he decided to change the subject for his own worry. "Don't fuck up my line," he warned her.

"Boy, please. Don't forget, the same man that taught you, taught me first. I'm not new to this; I'm true to it." She laughed at her own corniness, and he joined her. She draped a cape around him and went to work.

With precision, Jaz worked the razor and clippers along Kyree's head and beard line. Her father had taught her at an early age how to cut hair. When he wasn't at his main job being a plumber, she'd watch him as he cut hair in the neighborhood and wanted to do exactly what he did. It wasn't until he caught her chopping off the hair on all of her Barbie's that he gave her a set of clippers and taught her how to use them. Jaz was a natural and by ten, she was helping her father when people would come over to get their heads cut. Men were skeptical about a young girl doing their hair at first, but Calvin stood by his belief in his daughter's abilities and if someone didn't like it, they could leave. But no one ever did. They all respected Calvin and soon came to recognize Jaz's skills as well. It wasn't until she was around twelve that she added more feminine styles to her resume, although she still dabbled when necessary.

Jaz and Kyree didn't speak much as she worked. They were each deep in their own thoughts. Kyree was contemplating how he could have fucked up his life so epically. Jaz was his everything. The sun didn't shine the same if he couldn't see her smile. She knew all of his strengths, his weaknesses, what made him laugh and what made him mad. But what she didn't know, what no one knew, was what made him scared, and losing her was right at the top of that list. Lately, he'd been more afraid than he'd ever been, and with the way her mood had been with him lately, he was also afraid of her being that close to his neck with the razor.

Jaz smirked. "Why are you so tense? I'm not going to cut you," she assured him. "If I was going to, I would've done it already. Just don't piss me off while I have this razor in my hand." She chuckled and he sucked his teeth. Jaz continued lining him up and when she was done, she cleaned off the extra hair around his neck. She tapped his shoulder and he got up from his chair to examine himself. Her work was perfect. She was so skilled in everything she did. Kyree tried his best to brush the extra hair off his white shirt, but it was no use.

"Damn, I'm supposed to meet with some clients in a few hours."

"Well, you still have a few shirts here. You can clean up before you leave." Kyree looked at her, uncertainty plastered on his face. "Don't look at me like that," she warned. "Now, go before I change my mind," she urged.

Kyree was still on edge about the whole thing, but he took her up on her offer. He didn't want to show up to his meeting looking like a bum. He just wasn't sure how to feel about Jaz being so nice all of a sudden. It was weird, and he was second-guessing the dinner she'd prepared. There had to be poison in it if she was offering it to him.

Kyree retreated to the hall bathroom and turned on the shower. He missed taking a shower in his home. The shower was large enough for two people with a double shower head, a sliding glass door, and a bench built into one of the corners. He stepped inside and let the steam consume him. He was pleased to see that Jaz still had his favorite soap. He lathered his face and neck with his eyes closed. He hadn't washed the soap off when he felt his torso being grabbed from behind. He quickly rinsed his face and turned to find Jaz in the shower with him. He'd never even heard her come in.

They stared at each other in silence, neither knowing what to say. She looked up at him with wanting eyes and Kyree wanted to give her everything she wanted, but he also knew it wouldn't end well and Jaz would later regret their encounter. He never wanted her to regret being with him.

Little did he know, but Jaz had contemplated what she was getting into when she heard the shower turn on. She fought with herself not to go any further past the sink, where she was putting a set of clean clothes for him, but upon entering the bathroom, she could see his silhouette through the steam-filled glass door. Kyree's body was perfect to her. His stomach was ripped with washboard abs and Ken doll slits that led to the perfect ten inches of meat hanging graciously down his legs. It was hard for her to resist the urge to be with him.

Kyree raised her chin while the other hand grazed her cheek. He gently kissed her lips. At that moment, Jaz didn't care if her hair got wet. She'd risk it all for this feeling. Kyree's kisses were like magic. She saw fireworks every time their lips touched. It was euphoric, and no one but Kyree could ignite those emotions inside of her.

Jaz could tell that Kyree wasn't sure about her advances so she wrapped her arms around him, pulling him in closer. Kyree didn't waste any time. He lifted her up onto the shower seat and massaged her breasts while he feverishly placed kisses down her neck. Jaz tossed her head back and relished the moment. He steadily traveled from her stomach down to the golden treasure she kept hidden between her legs. With each brush from his tongue, Jaz felt as though he were trying to suck the soul from her insides. She kept one hand on the wall to keep her balance while the other held onto his head.

"Ahhhhh," she whimpered.

Kyree didn't say anything. The only sounds coming from him were the sweet sounds of his tongue lapping up all of her juices.

"I can't...take it..." she breathlessly uttered. She bit down on her bottom lip and tightly closed her eyes. She felt so weak after cumming that all she could do was sit there and try to catch her breath. Kyree helped her up and held her body against the wall as he prepared to enter her from behind. He kissed her neck and slowly made his way into her opening. Jaz parted her lips and moaned sweetly. Jaz's warmth felt like heaven around his penis. He had a point to prove so he toyed with her by pulling in and out, only allowing her inches at a time. Jaz thought she was going to go crazy from the teasing.

"Fuuuuuuck," she moaned. "Kyree, baby...please stop playing with – " Her eyes shot open as she felt every inch of him penetrate her insides. "Shiiiiiit," she uttered. Kyree wasn't doing his normal shit talking as he tried to concentrate on not exploding from the nut he'd been holding in for weeks. But Jaz had to play too, so she contracted her walls and threw her ass back at him. Kyree grunted loudly and just waited for them each to catch their breaths before pulling out.

They both momentarily stared at each other. Kyree could no longer look at her so he turned and finished his shower while Jaz followed suit and used the shower head on the opposite side. As they stood in their own corners, they both felt more exposed than they'd ever been in their lives. Neither could believe what they'd just done. It wasn't supposed to be like this but somehow, it always seemed to go this way. If sex could fix everything, they'd be the perfect couple.

Kyree stepped out of the shower first and Jaz got out five minutes after. She walked into her room while drying her hair and noticed him getting dressed. She couldn't believe he was about to leave after what they'd just shared. It was awkward, sure, but they were more than that to each other. He had to respect her more than that. She couldn't allow him to leave without saying something.

"So you're just gonna leave?" She looked at him like he was crazy.

Kyree also looked at her like she was crazy. He didn't know what kind of games she was playing, but he wasn't in the mood for them right now. "Jazzy, I don't have time for your shit today. You're not about to let me get comfortable and then kick my ass out when your feelings start to kick in. I'm really not up for it, so you can kill that noise." He slipped on his shoes.

Jaz dropped her mouth, dumbfounded. She saw where he was coming from, but it still hurt. She felt cheap. She couldn't let him know he'd made her want to cry again.

"Well fine then, go!" She tried to storm past him and Kyree grabbed her arm before she could cross him. "Let me go!" She tried to pull her arm away.

"Yo, what the fuck is your problem?" he calmly asked her. Jaz rolled her eyes. She hated how calm he could be, even in a heated argument. But he didn't have to raise his voice with her. Jaz could tell his mood even if he said nothing, and right now, he was pissed.

"You're my fucking problem! Literally!" she growled through clenched teeth. She pulled away from him and walked over to her dresser. She grabbed an oversized T-shirt and pulled it over her head.

Kyree shook his head. He felt as though he were in the Twilight Zone. "Jazzy, do you hear yourself right now? You kicked me out of our home. Every time you look at me, all I can see is how much you hate me."

Kyree couldn't take it anymore. It was like he could do no right. When he tried to get closer, she pulled him away. When he tried to give her space, she tried pulling him back in. They were always left playing their usual game of tug of war. Kyree would play this game forever if it meant being close to her, but even he got tired and needed a break every now and then. It was clear to him that Jaz didn't know what she wanted.

Jaz wished she could just tell him about her encounter with Kendall, but that would just lead them back to the same place. Kyree would definitely have Kendall's head for fucking with his drink. Jaz was tired of the drama and just wanted to be done with it all. Niggas had lost their lives for less and she didn't want another Asia situation on her hands, no matter how much she hated Kendall.

Kyree looked at her before leaving, waiting for a response, but all he received was deafening silence as she turned her back to him. He smirked. It was typical of Jaz to throw tantrums and then go mute when she didn't get her way. He was done for now. His foot was almost out of the bedroom door when he thought he heard her mumble something under her breath.

"What?" he asked. She mumbled again, so he moved closer. "I can't hear you. Speak up!" he urged.

"I said I'm pregnant!" she yelled. She dropped her head and covered her eyes.

Kyree stood frozen for what felt like forever. "By wh – "

She cut her eyes at him. "And don't you dare let this be a repeat of last year!" Her nostrils flared with anger. "It's by your stupid ass, damn!"

Remembering when he'd questioned her when she told him she was pregnant with Kylee, Kyree thought it best he not say anything further. He helplessly put his hands in his pockets and leaned against the dresser. This should have been a joyous occasion, but Jaz was visibly upset. He couldn't blame her though. They were in a terrible place in their relationship and couldn't figure out how to get back right. Neither of them knew what to say. Kyree ran his hand down his freshly tapered beard. He was confused. He couldn't for the life of him figure out how this had happened. As far as he knew, Jaz was supposed to be on the five year birth control - or at least, that's what she'd told him.

"Help me to understand something though." She kept her head down, wishing she was somewhere else with another life because right now, this one wasn't working out for her. "When and how could this happen?"

Jaz finally looked up. She had to make sure he was serious

with such a stupid question. "Well, the when would have to have been last month after Mario's birthday party. And how? Nigga, really?" She stared at him blankly.

"I mean, I thought you were getting that new birth control you were raving about."

"I was supposed to, but with everything that was going on, I missed my appointment to get it done. So I was still taking my pills. And since we weren't together anymore, I stopped taking them."

Kyree sighed heavily. This was some serious news, but it was nothing they couldn't handle together.

Jaz tossed her hands in the air and stood up. She grabbed the water bottle off her nightstand and took a sip. She wished she could've had something stronger, but given her current situation, that was definitely a no-go.

"It doesn't really matter when or how this happened anyway. What matters is, it's still very early. I can't be more than four or five weeks so it's not too late to – "

"Not too late to what?" Kyree screwed his face. Jaz didn't say anything. She couldn't say it out loud without getting emotional so she simply shrugged. Kyree was pissed. He walked up on her and cornered her. He couldn't believe she what she was insinuating. "Jaz, you must take me for a fuckin' fool if you think I'd allow you to kill our child."

Jaz didn't like him being that close. Kyree was trying to intimidate her and it wasn't going to work this time. They'd been there and done that and, quite frankly, she wasn't in the mood for his scare tactics. She pushed him away from her and started pacing back and forth with her hands on her head. Life was scaring her more than Kyree ever could right now. Never in a million years did she think this would be where they would be in their relationship. An abortion should have been the furthest thing from her mind.

She and Kyree were supposed to grow old together. He wanted at least five kids, and although Jaz wasn't going to go for it, she would've given him at least three. She had a plan. Their next child would be thought out after sitting together and discussing things. Kylee was supposed to be in school by the time they even considered having another child. Hell, she'd just started walking a few hours ago. And most importantly, she and Kyree would have been married and stronger than ever.

"Man, fuck!" Kyree yelled and punched the wall, causing Jaz to jump and the baby to start crying.

Jaz diverted her attention to the baby monitor and could see Kylee awake on the screen, so she rushed to her room. It took about five minutes, but Kylee eventually went back to sleep. When she returned to her bedroom, Kyree was sitting on the floor with his knees up and his hands, one now covered with a towel, covering his face. She stepped over him to grab her moisturizer, but then she thought she heard him sniffle. She turned toward him and her heart dropped when she saw the red in his eyes. He'd tried to hide it, but he'd obviously allowed a few tears to fall while she was tending to Kylee. Upon seeing the weary look in his eyes, she instantly ran to comfort him.

Jaz knelt down beside him and brought his head onto her chest. He wasn't crying at the moment, but just knowing that she'd made him cry broke her heart. His head rested on her chest and they both remained silent, wrapped up in their own thoughts. Kyree knew how bad things were, but never did he think it would go this far. They were constantly hurting each other.

"Jaz, I know I fucked up. I shouldn't have been there, baby. I shouldn't have allowed myself to be so weak," he pleaded with her. He knew he'd pleaded with her a thousand times, but hell, he'd plead and beg her 1001 times if he had to. "I lied to you, and I know you'll probably never forgive me. But, please, don't take away the life of our child." His voice was cracking and his jaw tightened, but he refused to allow himself to cry in front of her.

Seeing how remorseful he was and knowing what she knew about Kendall made Jaz want to ease some of the burden he felt. It was tearing her apart seeing him like this. She'd only seen him cry twice in her life: the day her mother died and she went running into his arms, and the day she told him she'd lost their first child. It was only last year when she told him about the child she never got to take to term when he was locked up. He was crushed. And honestly, Jaz didn't know what she wanted to do about the new life growing inside of her. She barely had time to really think about it. But she also didn't want to rush into things. So far, it was just a thought lingering in her mind. No matter what, Jaz couldn't hurt Kyree like that. When he hurt, she hurt. She'd do anything to ease the pain in his heart.

"Kyree, I have something else to tell you." She sniffled and lifted his head so that he was staring at her. "I saw Kendall the other day." His brow furrowed. He wondered why she would even think about meeting Kendall's conniving ass. "She told me that it wasn't completely your fault. She said that she, too, played a major role in what happened. You were both drunk and not in your right state of mind. She also admitted that she provoked you." Kyree started scratching his head. Jaz looked like she was holding some-thing back, but he didn't pressure her; he just impatiently waited for her to finish. "Kyree, listen to me," she urged. "I forgive you!" she cried. It was hard for her to say, and it was even harder for her to actually accept, but she did forgive him.

Hearing her say those words made Kyree want to jump for joy. He started to speak, but Jaz held up her hand to stop him.

"Let me finish." She took a deep breath. "I think what fucked me up so bad was because it was her." Jaz licked her lips and paused. She couldn't say her name out loud without getting an ill taste in her mouth. "I've never really liked her, and to know that y'all had history and you've kept in contact with her for so long, it really made me feel insecure. I know it's juvenile, but that's how I felt. So when I had my conversation with her, it all made sense because I know her, and I know you even better. I know that you'd never do anything to intentionally hurt me. And I care about you, I do, but I just...I don't know. Why does bad shit always have to happen to us?" She dropped her head and cried.

Kyree raised her head. "Listen to me. I love you, Jazzy. Shit doesn't make sense without you. We've gotten past a lot over the years. I need you to give me a second chance to be the man you fell in love with all of those years ago. I need you to love me again."

"Again?" She looked at him crazy. "Kyree, I can't stop loving you!" She raised her voice. "That's my problem. And I can't move on with my life, because it doesn't move without you in it. I can mess with a million men to pass the time, but the only man that will forever be on my mind is you."

Kyree used his thumb to wipe the tears from her face. He placed her head on his chest and wrapped her in his arms. His warm embrace calmed her sobs and made her feel at ease.

"Kyree, getting married and growing our family is something I want to give you in a heartbeat, but I just don't think it's what we need right now. I know you're having a hard time understanding where I'm coming from but, baby, I don't want us to have to work this out because we have kids. I don't want that to be the reason. I want us to work this out for us."

Kyree took a long sigh. He didn't agree with this at all. He knew he couldn't make her keep the child, but he was going to do everything in his power to change her mind. Yet he still understood her reasoning for wanting to. They needed to work on rebuilding their relationship and commitment to each other.

"Jaz, I don't like it and I'm not going to let this shit go, but I understand what you're saying. I just know we can overcome this to become stronger than we were before."

She randomly fiddled with a loose string on his sweat pants as her head rested perfectly on his chest. "Where do we start?"

"I don't know," he replied honestly.

"Well, you can move back in."

Kyree looked down at her to make sure she was serious. She smirked at him and he gave her a sly grin.

"You're sleeping in the guest room though."

He sucked his teeth and dropped his head. Jaz could only giggle. She knew that was going to piss him off. She had no intention, at the beginning of their conversation, on letting him back in the house. But it was also a start to them getting back on track. She wanted to ease their way back into things. This wasn't a rash decision for her. It was just the only one that made sense. The thought crossed her mind to tell him about Kendall drugging him, but she knew it would only lead to more chaos. After talking it over with Monica the other night, they both agreed that all of the details that happened in the salon that night needed to end there. Right now, Jaz only wanted to focus on the future.

CHAPTER SEVENTEEN

The next morning Jaz awoke with a newer outlook than she'd had weeks ago. She almost felt complete. But she knew there was still something she needed to do before everything in her life could fall rightfully in place. Being without Kyree was like trying to fit a corner piece of a puzzle in the middle. It just didn't work, and her puzzle would never be complete without all of the correct pieces in line.

Jaz brushed her teeth and prepared herself for the rest of the day. Her first appointment wasn't until noon, but she wanted to get a head start on the day. She fed, bathed, and dressed Kylee, and then she was out like a light again. She usually fell asleep right after her morning feedings. She placed her into her bassinet and rolled it into the room with Kyree. She was serious about him sleeping in the guest room for a while. She shook his shoulder to wake him, and he turned over. He blinked his eyes to adjust them to the sunlight peeking through the blinds. He stretched his arms to the sky. He couldn't remember the last time he'd slept so well. Something about being in his own home calmed him. Even if they weren't in the same bed, he could still feel Jaz's presence a few feet away.

"Wassup?"

"Hey, Lee just went down for her morning nap. I have to get out of here a little early today. Can you take her to the sitter?"

"No problem. I might not take her though. We might just chill here for today."

Jaz nodded her head. "Okay, that works too. Just call Ms. Johnson if you decide not to take her."

Kyree agreed and watched as she bent down to give Kylee a goodbye kiss. "Do I get one too?" He smirked.

"Nah, bruh, you need to go gargle first." She held her nose and he sucked his teeth. "I'm kidding," she laughed. She leaned over to kiss him, and he didn't hold back. Jaz embraced his tongue. She'd missed his touch. He playfully pulled her down on the bed with him and wrapped her in a strong bear hug from behind. He started to tickle her and she giggled and squirmed.

"Kyree, stop!" she laughed. "You're going to wake the baby."

"I can't help it. You made me sleep in this damn room instead of letting me sleep in our bed and get some ass."

"I had to. Kyree, we ain't fuckin' for a while so get over it."

"Oh, word?" he questioned her.

"Yes, word. I'm serious, Kyr - " she paused because his mouth was now right on her spot, the one behind her ear, the one that only he could find with ease, the one that made her tingle between her legs and her eyes roll. "Ahhhhh, shit!" she moaned. She finally managed to squirm her way out of his arms and stand to her feet. "See, why you playin'?" Kyree laughed and she tossed a pillow at him.

"I'm messin' with you, girl. Calm down."

She folded her arms under her breasts. She hated that he made her so weak. Kyree sat up and pulled her closer to him. He wrapped his arms around her waist and rested his head on her stomach. Jaz swallowed hard as she looked down at him. This conversation was definitely headed down a path that Jaz didn't want to visit. Last night they'd spent hours on the subject of the baby. Her mind was already made up and she didn't need Kyree trying to convince her otherwise.

"Alright, I have to get going."

He nodded in understanding and then saw her to the door. Jaz took a deep breath once in the safety of her car. It wasn't an easy decision to not have this child, and she never expected it to be, but it was the only option that made any sense. She started up her car and asked for God's forgiveness with her choice. By the time she arrived at her destination, the calming sounds of Algebra Blessett coming from her car's stereo had soothed her and put her mind at ease. She needed all of the energy and strength she could muster to do what she was about to do. She stepped outside of the car dressed in white ass-hugging jeans, a blue sleeveless top that hung off her shoulders, nude sling back heels, and a white bag. No matter what she was doing, she always remained on her A-game.

It was Tuesday, so The Egg Bistro wasn't as packed as when she usually went there on the weekends. She was able to walk right up to the hostess, who escorted her to her awaiting party. The inviting scent of bacon and pancakes made her stomach growl. She hadn't eaten this morning in anticipation of this meeting. Jaz thanked the hostess and Shaun stood and greeted her with a hug and a huge smile. He was so excited when she finally returned his call and agreed to meet him for breakfast. He thought he felt her pulling away from him, but her phone call gave him hope.

"Damn, girl. You look good." He licked his lips as he admired her shape in her outfit.

"Thanks," she hesitantly said.

"I was so happy when you returned my call. A nigga was getting kinda worried," he chuckled.

"Well, that's kind of why I wanted to meet you here today." Shaun's eyebrow raised. "I feel like you're a great guy, but I really don't think I'm ready to see anyone new right now."

"I know you have your reservations after dealing with dude, but I'm willing to wait on you to come around," he assured her.

"That's just it, Shaun. I don't think I'm over him just yet. I kind of want to see where it goes with him. Our daughter is still so young, and I want to give her a chance at having a real family."

"Wowwwww," Shaun chuckled and shook his head, almost like he knew this was coming. He ran his hand down his face. "Damn, Jaz. You could've told me this shit over the phone."

"I'm sorry, Shaun. I felt like you deserved more than just a text message or a phone call. I really did care about you. And as corny as it sounds, it's not you, it's me." Shaun didn't say anything. Jaz looked in his eyes, and he stared blankly at her. It was almost like he'd stepped outside of himself. It almost scared Jaz how not there he was. "Shaun...Shaun...Shaun?" she said, tapping him.

"Yeah, man." He snapped back into reality. "It's cool, Jaz. I hope everything works out for you." He rose to his feet.

"Please don't take this personally. I really hope you find someone who recognizes what a great guy you are."

"A'ight." He dropped a twenty dollar bill on the table. A few people started to stare, and it made Jaz uncomfortable. He abruptly left without even looking at her. Jaz took a defeated breath and sat for a moment contemplating what happened. Kyree was who she wanted, so there was no question in her mind whether or not she'd made the right decision. It still hurt to know that she'd hurt Shaun in any way. He didn't deserve that. But she couldn't continue to lead him on, knowing Kyree was who her soul longed for. It wasn't right to anyone.

Jaz was about to leave too, but then the waitress approached her table. "Did you decide on your order?"

"Um, I think I will order something. Let me get the seafood omelet with bacon, sausage links, and an order of the cinnamon bun French toast. And can you make that to go, please?"

"Alright, I'll have that out to you in about fifteen minutes."

"Thank you," Jaz smiled at her.

Jaz felt like shit. Food was the only thing that could fix her mood - until she saw a text message from Kyree, causing her to smile from the depths of her soul.

>>>> **9:15AM Kyree: I love you!**

<<<< **9:15AM Me: I love you more!**

>>>> **9:17AM Kyree: So when you tryna change your last name?**

<<<< **9:19AM Me: Just say when. I'm there.**

>>>> **9:22AM Kyree: Bet. Next month.**

<<<< **9:23AM Me: It's a date then.**

>>>> **9:25AM Kyree: AND PUT YOUR DAMN RING BACK ON!**

Jaz literally laughed out loud reading his message. Her food arrived and she gave the waitress $20, plus the $20 Shaun had left for his drink, and headed out the door. On her way to her car, she replied back to Kyree.

<<<< **9:29AM Me: Yes, sir.**

Kyree smirked at the message as Kylee started to cry. He got up to tend to her and she perked right up. "See, you gotta stop all of that fussin'. Just like yo' mama." He laughed and Kylee smiled. They spent the whole day together watching cartoons, eating ice cream – Jaz would flip if she knew - and he even took her to the baby gym. Around 4:00, Kylee was beat. He smirked as he placed her down in her crib. He couldn't wait to rub it in Jaz's face how good she was for him, so he called her. When she didn't answer the phone, he sent her a quick text message.

Kyree couldn't wait for Jaz to get home. The surprise he had awaiting her was most certainly going to get him some ass tonight. He'd spent the entire time during their breakup, staying in contact with the wedding planner. After Jaz stopped answering her phone, the wedding planner, Whitney, called him to get an update on what was going on. Kyree told her the truth about them breaking up, but he assured her that everything should proceed as normal. Whitney was skeptical at first, but Kyree gave her a little extra toward her normal commission to seal the deal. Jaz had done most of the grunt work already, like picking colors and venue, but Kyree single-handedly arranged the seating chart, picked out the invitations, found a reasonable florist, and found a pastor to marry them. He held onto their love for each other to get him through everything. He was confident that their love would prevail and it had. Sure, they still had their issues, but it was nothing they couldn't figure out together.

Now all Jaz had to do was pick out her dress and the clothes for the rest of the wedding party. Kyree didn't dare try to plan that. He waited impatiently for her to get home, and when she didn't show around 7:00, he called her. Her phone went straight to voicemail again. That's when he realized that she hadn't responded to the text message he'd sent that afternoon, so he decided to call the salon.

"Thanks for calling Mo' Jaz Salon, how can I help you?" Monica answered, balancing the phone on her shoulder while finishing a client's hair.

"What you doin', Big Head?" Kyree asked.

"Just finishing up with my last client. What's up?"

"I was looking for Jaz. Has she left yet?"

"Left? She never showed up. I figured you two were still trying to work things out. I've been calling her all day though, because Ray and I have been taking her clients."

Kyree took a deep breath and ran his hand down his beard.

Monica could hear the worry in his silence. "Ky, you mean to tell me you haven't heard from her?" Monica put the curlers down, she needed to hear this.

"Nah, Mo. Let me call you back."

"Wait, this isn't like her, Ky. Something's not right."

"I know, Mo, and I swear I'll call you back as soon as I find out something."

Kyree quickly ended the call before Monica got too emotional. He hated to cut her short, but he had to get answers quick. He tried Jaz again and was met with her voicemail. Kyree massaged his temples, trying to think of his next course of action. And then it hit him. He picked up his phone and dialed his friend, Casper.

"Kyree, my man, what can I do for ya?"

"Yo, Cas, you think you can track something for me?"

"Can't nothing get past me. They don't call me the friendly ghost for nothing," he chuckled. "What can I do ya for, man?"

"I need you to track my girl's car, cell phone, every and anything you can."

"Oh, I don't do domestics." He laughed.

"Nah, it's nothing like that. No one has heard from her since this morning, and I'm getting kind of worried."

"Alright, I think I can do that. Give me a couple of hours."

"Yo, if you can put a rush on this, I'll double your normal rate."

"Bet! I'll have that info for you in about three hours. Just text me her phone number, any info you have on her vehicle, and the last time you've heard from her. Don't worry, I'm on it."

Kyree ended the call and tried to calm his nerves. Casper was a beast as a hacker. They called him Casper the Ghost because the Feds had been looking for him for years, but had yet to find him.

Also, he was the friendliest white guy anyone had ever met. Kyree trusted that he could get the job done. In the past, Kyree had used Casper on many occasions to find people who didn't want to be found, like Asia.

He didn't want to fear the worst, but Jaz was such a creature of habit that it just didn't sit well with him. He couldn't sit still, so he picked up Kylee and put her in the car seat. He dropped her off at his mother's house, who had heard everything from Monica and was now just as worried. Calvin was also blowing his phone up. Kyree answered his call and told him to trust that he had things under control. Calvin said he'd drive around to look for her while Kyree did his own investigating. Kyree ignored all of the other calls and headed over to Monica's house.

As soon as she saw him, she hugged him tight. "Did you find out anything?"

Kyree shook his head no and walked inside. He plopped down on the couch and put his head back. His phone was ringing off the hook. He refused to answer unless it was Casper.

Monica's lips quivered. She was worried sick and wanted answers. "I'm going to call the police." She picked up her phone and Kyree leaped up to stop her.

"No, Monica. All they're going to say is that we have to wait at least forty-eight hours before we can report her missing. I don't want them involved just yet. Trust me."

Monica sighed heavily, but nodded in agreement.

Kyree's phone rang again, and this time, it was Casper.

"Yo, what you find?"

"Well, her car was last pinged at a place in Suffolk. I'll text you the address. I'm still working on getting her cell phone records. Give me another hour and I'll have it for you, man."

"Good looking out."

Kyree ended the call and turned to look at Monica. She wanted answers, and he only wished he had better news to give her.

"I think I might know where she is. It's probably nothing, Mo. Jaz has a lot on her mind, and she probably just needed some time to herself to digest everything. It's all going to be okay," he assured her. "I'll call you as soon as I find out more information." He turned to leave, and Monica was right on his tail.

"I'm coming with you."

"Mo, chill. I'll call you. I promise."

"Kyree, I can't just sit around here waiting for you to call. So either I'm riding in the car with you, or I'm going to follow you."

Kyree shook his head. He didn't have time to argue with her, so he let her ride with him. When they arrived at the address Casper texted them, they saw that it was one of Jaz's favorite breakfast restaurants. The restaurant closed at 3:00, so it was no wonder the parking lot was so empty. The only standalone car was Jaz's black QX80. Monica was nervous as they approached the car. She didn't know what to expect. She gripped Kyree's forearm and he placed a hand on top of hers to calm her. He approached Jaz's car and took a sigh of relief when he saw that it was empty. He shook his head at Monica, who was waiting impatiently in the car, and she, too, sighed heavily.

Kyree reached for his spare key in his pocket. When he climbed inside, he saw neatly packed to-go boxes sitting in her passenger's seat. He opened the bags, only to see that none of the food had been touched. It reeked from the heat and he knew that it had been sitting there all day.

Bam! He hit the dashboard. "Fuck!" he yelled. Kyree didn't want to show it, but he was now worried. Shit wasn't sitting too well with him. Something had happened to Jaz and he didn't know what. It was killing him. Jaz would never not call to check on Kylee, no matter how mad she was with the world. He looked around the car, but didn't see anything else that could be helpful. When he got back in his car, Monica was bawling her eyes out. Kyree brought her in for a hug.

"Ky, do you think she's okay?"

"Yeah, Mo. She's going to turn up."

Kyree held Monica until she calmed down, and then he headed home to wait on more info from Casper. He was going to drop Monica off at her house, but he thought it best that she not be alone, since Mario was out of town on business.

They retreated to separate rooms in the house, each to sulk alone. Kyree's phone rang and he quickly answered it.

"What you got?"

"Well, I was able to hack into her cell phone records and get the numbers to the last couple of people she contacted, along with her text messages. I was also able to get the security camera from the parking lot of the restaurant where I found her car. And, um, I don't know if you want to see this, man." Casper gulped.

"Send it to me. I don't care what's on it. Send it now!" Kyree ordered, and then hung up the phone.

It was the longest thirty seconds of his life waiting on the video to come through. When he finally opened it and watched it, tears started to form in his eyes. His jaw clenched and his nostrils flared. He'd never felt so helpless in his life as he watched his Jazzy being pulled form her car and forced into the back of another.

Once he pulled himself together, he called Casper back to see if he had any more information for him. Once he got what he needed, he called Fat Boy to tell him he was on his way to pick him up, and retreated to his closet and into his safe. Monica came into his room just in time to see him retrieve twin Glocks.

"Kyree, what're you doing?" Her voice quivered.

"I'm going to handle business. I swear, if this doesn't work, I'll let you call the police. But trust, your brother has this under control," he assured her as he placed a gun in his back waist and another on a strap at his leg.

Monica knew she couldn't stop her brother. The look in his eyes said that he was ready to body a nigga. She knew that look. It'd been a while since she'd seen it, but she knew it. Many people didn't know this side of him, and he liked to keep it that way. Kyree's past wasn't that far behind him. It could resurface when he wanted it to. The businessman he'd been trying to be since getting out of jail would have to take a seat while the street nigga in him went to handle business that couldn't be sorted out with paperwork and compromise.

Monica didn't know what was going on and she knew better than to ask questions she was sure she didn't want to know the answers to. But there was something she was wondering. She twiddled her fingers as she watched him lace up his black Timberlands. "Kyree, does this have anything to do with Kendall?"

He squinted his forehead. He knew there was something Jaz was leaving out about her encounter with Kendall, but right now he didn't have time to worry with that. "Nah, it's not Kendall. I think it's that fuckboy she was messing with."

"Shaun?"

Kyree nodded. He now had his confirmation that was exactly who was responsible for all of this. Shaun was the same name Casper gave him that was tied to the phone number Jaz was last in contact with.

Monica followed him down the stairs. "Just promise me you'll be safe."

"Always. Yo' big brother ain't going nowhere. And Jaz is fine. Everything is going to be fine, MoMo."

"How can you be so sure that she's okay?" Monica sniffed and wiped the tears from her face.

"Because my heart is still beating. If I lost her, I'd feel it."

Monica gave a weak smile and he brought her in for a hug and kissed her on the forehead. "And I don't want you here by yourself so I'll follow you to Ma's house, and Mr. Calvin is supposed to come over there to sit with y'all."

Monica nodded. In the car, she said a silent prayer to God to watch over her family.

CHAPTER EIGHTEEN

Across town, Jaz sat in a cold and dark building, afraid for her life. Her captor had taken her over twelve hours ago and she'd been alone since waking up from the chloroform used to knock her out. She was tied to a chair and the only sound she heard was that of water dripping somewhere off in the distance. She could barely see, besides the dim light from the street that shone through a small window. Every now and then she'd regain consciousness, take a look at her surroundings, get scared, and then go back into unconsciousness. But now the medicine was starting to wear off and she was a little bit more alert. She wanted to scream, but that hadn't done much for her earlier.

Her hands and ankles were tied tightly around the chair and she had no wiggle room. After thirty minutes of trying to use her legs, she grew restless. All she could do was sob uncontrollably. She just knew this was the end of her life. There was still so much she wanted to do. Her salon was just starting to take off, her friends and family were still growing, she and Kyree were trying to get back on the right track, and more important than anything,

Kylee would never get to know her mother. Jaz knew that horrible feeling, and suddenly she had a new will to not give up - not only for Kylee, but also for the life growing inside of her. She had to think, and she had to think fast. She maneuvered her hands, trying to get out of the tape. She bit her bottom lip as she strategically tried to wiggle her hands free.

"Shit!" she cried out. She was starting to lose faith and her hands were cramping up. Just when she thought she had a little bit of traction, she heard the door open and someone come down the stairs. Her heart instantly stopped as she watched the sick bastard walk down the stairs. The sadistic look in his eyes made her hair stand on end.

There was once a time that she really liked Shaun. He was such a great guy. He made her laugh, forget about her problems, and just enjoy life again. But the moment she decided she no longer wanted to be with him, he turned on her. This wasn't the sweet guy she'd met at the club. The person coming down the stairs was unrecognizable.

"Sorry it took me so long. I still had to punch in at work. Can't have people thinking anything was out of whack." He chuckled.

"Please let me go," Jaz begged. "I promise I won't say anything."

He smirked. "I bet that's how my baby sister cried when y'all took her too, huh?"

Jaz squinted in confusion. "What are you talking about?"

"See, Tori said you might say some slick shit like that."

"Tori? What does she have to do with – " Jaz gasped as it finally hit her. She hadn't been able to put two and two together before, but now it was all starting to make sense. The familiar look that Jaz always noticed in Shaun's eyes was none other than that of her former employee and worst enemy, Asia. It was like deja vu - only this time, no one knew where she was to save her. Jaz watched as he walked over to a set of tools and she instantly started to cry.

Shaun was obviously crazier than his sister. She watched as he walked to a table filled with an assortment of gadgets. She could see a gun in the back of his waist, but the tools on that table frightened her even more.

"Please, don't hurt me. I'm pregnant," she whimpered, hoping he'd show some compassion. She may not have wanted to keep the child at first, but that was still her decision to make. Now that their lives were in danger, she wanted to save them both.

Shaun didn't even flinch at the mention of her being pregnant. He just picked up one of his tools and slowly started to approach Jaz. She squinted trying to see what it was. Shaun smirked and sparked it so that she could see the electricity and hear the buzz from the small stun gun. Jaz jumped in fear and he started to laugh. Now she knew what Michael meant about her life still being in danger. She wished she'd answered his messages to get more details, but that was then, and shoulda coulda's didn't help her case now.

"So are you going to tell me what happened to my sister?" He gave her a death glare.

Jaz knew she couldn't tell him that Asia was dead and probably buried somewhere no one would ever find her. That would only make him even more upset and it gave her no leverage to stay alive. In Jaz's mind, as long as he had hope of finding Asia, he had no reason to kill her.

She shook her head as she cried. "I don't know. I haven't seen Asia in months."

"Wrong answer."

Click click bzzzzz

"Ahhhh!" she screamed.

The stun gun on Jaz's shoulder caused her to grit her teeth, her muscles to tighten, and her body to shake uncontrollably for five seconds. The pain was unbearable and she briefly passed out for two minutes. When she came to, her ears were ringing and she had a massive headache. Her heart beat rapidly and she couldn't stop the flow of tears as she looked down at the mess she'd made by peeing in her pants.

Shaun sat backwards in a chair, staring her down. "So can you answer my questions now, or do I have to sting you again?" Jaz rapidly shook her head no. "Good. Because right now, I just want answers. I've spent weeks courting your ass, listening to you whine and complain about the same nigga and then go right back to him." Shaun laughed and shook his head. "But that's all beside the point. Tori told me that y'all might have had something to do with my sister's disappearance. She's the only fuckin' family I have. So tell me, where the fuck she is?" he seethed, spittle flying from his mouth and onto Jaz.

Jaz remembered Tori asking her questions about Asia. Jaz pretty much told her the last time that she never wanted to hear Asia's name again. Now Asia's name would be the last name she ever heard. Jaz was terrified as Shaun paced the floor, going on and on about the whereabouts of his sister while freely waving his gun around. All she could do was cry. Her usual quick tongue couldn't get her out of this one. This was going to be her end. The fear that kept her up sleepless nights wondering and fearing for her life was now here. She was in the eye of the storm, and it was too late for her to do anything about it.

So while Shaun went on and on about both his parents being dead and him and Asia being in and out of foster homes, Jaz said a silent prayer to God to forgive all her sins and to watch over her family.

"Amen," she said aloud.

Boom!

"Ahhhhh!" Jaz screamed with her eyes squeezed tightly. Her heart beat with fear as she slowly opened her eyes to see where she'd been hit. Her body was covered in blood. But as she took a closer look, she noticed that it wasn't hers. She looked on the ground and could see Shaun lying down in a pool of his own blood. She then heard someone trying to break down the door.

Boom!

Another shot rang out, and Jaz continued to scream as heavy footsteps descended the stairs.

"Jaz, baby! It's me!"

Jaz couldn't hear anything over her own screams. But as he got closer and she saw his face, all she could do was gasp. Kyree ran over to her and quickly untied her hands and feet as Jaz continued to cry.

"Are you hurt, baby?" He frantically checked her for wounds even though she shook her head no. Specks of blood were on her face and a lot more was on her clothes, but that was only from the shot Kyree took to Shaun's head as he sat perched on the only window in the abandoned warehouse. Kyree wanted to kill his ass as soon as he saw him, but he wanted the shot to count. He waited until he had the right opportunity and fired a clean shot to his skull.

Kyree took the sleeve of his shirt and wiped Jaz's face. She couldn't even look at him, she was so shaken up. "Jazzy, baby, look at me." He held her face in both of his hands. "I'm here now. You're okay. I'll never let anything happen to you. You hear me, baby?" Jaz slowly nodded her head and he hugged her tightly. She cried in his arms for five minutes, until she heard Fat Boy come down the stairs with two of Kyree's former goons.

It hurt Kyree's heart to see how scared she was. He wanted to break down with her, but he knew he had to be strong. She was shaking like a leaf in the wind, so he picked her up in his arms and cradled her. She buried her face in his chest because she didn't want to see Shaun's dead body.

Kyree instructed Fat Boy to handle things from there. He put Jaz in the backseat of his SUV and pulled off from the scene. On his way home, he made a few calls, first to his family to let them know that Jaz was fine, then to Fat Boy to remind him to leave the place spotless, and the last call was to Casper to make sure the world thought Shaun had disappeared. When Casper was done with him, the world would think he'd moved out of state and a paper trail would back it up. Kyree wasn't afraid that anyone would come looking but just in case, he wanted to have all of his ducks aligned.

When he pulled up to their home, he picked Jaz up from the backseat. She hadn't said a word the whole ride. Kyree wanted to know if Shaun had touched her or harmed her in any other way. Dead or not, Kyree would go back and shoot the nigga six more times just on principal if he had to. But Jaz's clothes appeared to all be intact, except from the wet stain running down her thigh and leg.

He carried her up the stairs and straight to the bathroom, where he ran a hot shower for her. He undressed her, stripped down to his briefs, and climbed in with her. He sat her down on the shower seat and grabbed the detachable shower head. Kyree washed her whole body while Jaz continued to cry, and he assured her that everything was going to be okay.

Jaz felt safe in his presence. There was never any question about that. She was just still shaken from the whole incident.

After her shower, Kyree dried her off and put her in a T-shirt and her favorite pajama pants. He walked with her to their bed and tucked her in under the covers. It pained him to see the faraway look in her eyes. He exhaled slowly and then turned to head to the bathroom to wash himself too.

"Wait," she spoke for the first time since he'd seen her. He quickly turned around. "Don't leave me," she weakly replied. She couldn't even face him. She just reached out her hands for him from behind. Kyree was still wet from being in the shower with his briefs on, but he couldn't deny her request. He removed them, threw on a pair of shorts, and climbed in the bed beside her. He wrapped her in a warm tight hug from behind and rocked her. Jaz finally felt at ease in his embrace.

Kyree started to wonder if they'd ever have a moment of peace. He was beginning to think Jaz was right, that maybe they were doomed to fail. But as he held her in his arms and watched her drift off to sleep, he decided that he didn't care. He'd go to the ends of the world for Jaz, and he'd do everything in his power to keep his family safe - even if that meant leaving so that they could live peacefully. He'd do whatever it took. Forever wasn't meant to actually last forever.

EPILOGUE

Through all of the ups and downs, the highs and lows, no one would ever believe that Kyree and Jaz would've lasted as long as they had. A string of bad luck seemed to follow them wherever they went. It was exhausting trying to stay together at times, and they'd finally come to realize their fate, a mutual understanding and decision that would affect both their lives forever. As hard as it was for Kyree to accept, Jaz made the decision for both of them. Jaz told him she'd wait for him forever if she had to. Kyree was totally against it, at first, but as he waited for his Jazzy, late as usual, he couldn't be happier.

Kyree walked his mother to her seat right in front as Jesse Powell's "You" played in the background. He donned an ivory jacket with a black tie, white shirt, and black pants. He kissed her on the cheek and took his place on the platform of the elegant hall. The song switched to Gerald Levert's "Made to Love You" and he watched his groomsmen guide Jaz's bridesmaids down the aisle one by one. The bridesmaids were dressed in sequined pink mermaid style dresses with their hair in French fishtail braids with loose curls. His groomsmen looked just as good in all-black tuxes with white shirts and black bowties. Even Ms. Ray wore a tux tonight, adding his own flare by not wearing any socks and cuffing his pants at the ankle.

The last to walk down from the bunch was his best man and Jaz's maid of honor, Fat Boy and Monica. She winked at him and he winked back. Monica nearly cried when she watched Kayden come down the aisle holding the ring in his little black tux. Kyree and Kayden did a quick dab as he took his place in front of the groomsmen. A huge smile graced his face as he watched Kylee walk down the aisle, escorted by Tameka's five-year-old daughter, Shay. Both of them wore ivory-colored frilly dress. Shay patiently walked with Kylee down the aisle, through all of the aw's from the guests, and helped her to drop the flowers on the ground. Shay walked Kylee to Jackie and then took her place in front of the bridesmaids. The music stopped and they all focused their attention to the double doors of the venue.

Everyone stood and the music dropped for Dave Hollister's "Forever". The doors opened simultaneously and Jaz stood on the other end holding a beautiful bouquet mixed with white, ivory, pink, and gold. She wore an ivory lace trumpet bridal gown with a beaded back necklace and an eight foot chapel train. Her face was beat to the gods and her hair hung freely down the middle of her back in loose curls. Not a strand was out of place. She grabbed her father's arm and they slowly walked hand in hand down the aisle. Jaz was nervous, but she walked with style and grace, smiling at a few familiar faces every now and then.

Jaz was fine until she reached the middle of the aisle. She'd rehearsed with the coordinator exactly where she'd stop for photos and she never thought that would be the hardest thing she'd have to do. She and Kyree instantly locked eyes and she could see his jaw tighten as he tried to keep it together. He placed his hand over his mouth and turned his head as he felt his emotions get the best of him. Fat Boy placed a hand on his shoulder, forcing him to keep it together. Jaz swore she wouldn't ruin her makeup, but when she saw his reaction, a single tear fell down her face. She continued walking, and it felt like she would never get to the end. Her father gave her away, and dapped Kyree up in the process. No words needed to be said between the two men. They had an understanding. Calvin knew his daughter would forever be safe and well taken care of with Kyree.

When they were finally face to face, Jaz playfully stuck out her tongue at him to break the tension from their emotions. He slightly laughed and shook his head. Pastor Donaldson instructed everyone to have a seat and then he began to mention how the two had written their own vows.

Jaz went first. "Kyree, I can't believe we're finally here. I think anyone in attendance today can attest to the fact that they didn't think it would last as long as it has. But, baby, like I told you all of those years ago, back in my heyday when I had to get a little out of character..." Jaz paused as everyone laughed. "This right here is forever, baby. Being without you feels like I'm missing the part of me that makes me complete. You know me better than anyone. Sometimes you know what I'm going to say before I even know. Our love is the kind of tale that people write stories about and no one can ever wait for the sequel. We've weathered storms bigger than natural disasters and we always pick back up to rebuild our world stronger and better than before. I know sometimes I can be a brat." She paused for the laughter again. "But I want to thank you for setting boundaries while still providing me with the world. I love you, baby."

Kyree wiped a tear from her cheek with his thumb. He pulled his cell phone from his pocket. "A'ight, I'll be honest with y'all. I just wrote this last night, even though Jaz has been gettin' on me about doing it for weeks." The whole crowd laughed, but Jaz only squinted. "Y'all see that scowl she's giving me now?" Everyone laughed at the visible discontent on her face and she quickly forced a smile. "Let me get this over with before she kills me before the reception." Everyone laughed again and Kyree cleared his throat.

"Jazzy, you make me want to be a better man. Everything I do, it's all for Jazzy. When I got my life on the right track, it was all for Jazzy. Seeing you happy is the only thing that gives me the initiative to get up and go. It's always been about my Jazzy, whether she knew it or not. Even as a kid playing football trying to show off so that she'd see me, it was all for Jazzy." Jaz smiled as tears fell freely from her eyes. "You've given me the family I never knew I wanted. And as much as I used to think it was all for Jazzy, I realize now that it was all for me too, because I wouldn't be the better man that I am today if it wasn't for you pushing me along the way. You make me want to be better than I was the day before. So, Jazzy, I want to thank you for helping me to grow, giving me a reason to smile, and for loving me despite me writing this a few hours ago." Everyone chuckled at his foolishness. "I want to spend the rest of my life becoming better for us. I love you, Jazzy."

Jaz pursed her lips together, trying not to get too choked up. When it was time to put on the rings, her dutiful maid of honor handed her the ring and dabbed her tears with a tissue. Jaz thanked her with an air kiss. When it was time to kiss his bride, Kyree happily brought her in for a strong, classy kiss while managing to slip a little tongue in. The two held their hands in the air and all of the guests applauded.

After taking dozens of pictures with their wedding party, everyone made an entrance into the beautiful reception hall. The DJ introduced the wedding party as they danced to their assigned seats to Beyoncé's "Crazy in Love". The DJ then introduced Kyree and Jaz as Mr. and Mrs. Wright for the first time. Jaz was beaming from ear to ear. Kyree played it cool but he, too, was overjoyed.

At the sound of Leela James's "Fall for You", Kyree led Jaz to the middle of the floor for their first dance. Jaz felt like she was floating as a cloud of fog covered her feet. She looked up at Kyree and smiled at him.

"What?" he asked her.

"I'm just so happy. This is all so beautiful." She looked in awe at how wonderful everything turned out. It was perfect. A beautiful chandelier hung above their heads. Hues of ivory, gold, and pink surrounded the tables. And before her stood the only man she'd ever dreamed about.

"I'm happy you're happy, bae." He kissed her forehead as they swayed to the music. He kissed her neck and secretly flicked her spot with his tongue. She quickly moved her neck, hoping no one saw her knees almost give out.

"Kyree, come on now," she giggled.

"I can't help it. You look fuckin' amazing. And you haven't let me have no ass in damn near a month," he whispered in her ear.

Jaz laughed. She didn't think she could hold out for as long as she did, but it would all be worth it tonight when they were in their hotel room.

Kyree hung his head in defeat. He wrapped one had around her stomach as they danced back to chest. Jaz closed her eyes and relished the moment. She whispered, "You think they can tell?" Kyree smirked and shook his head. There was no question after surviving being kidnapped, whether or not she'd keep the baby. Jaz was only seven weeks pregnant, but she didn't want to wait nine months to get married. Monica, Ms. Ray, and Fat Boy were the only other ones who knew and they assured her that the lace she wore made it damn near impossible to see the very tiny pudge she had.

"Well, this is the last time I'll be carrying anymore of your water-head kids."

"Ha ha, but you promised me five."

She snaked her head to look at him. "You're crazy, because we said three. So this right here is it," she promised him.

He chuckled. "Okay, okay. But that just means we have one more."

"No, baby. This is it." She smiled gleefully.

He looked at her skeptically. "We're having twins?"

"Shhh!" she calmed him down, hoping no one heard. They could tell by the clueless looks on everyone's faces that they had no idea what they were saying. Jaz looked at him and smiled. "I wanted to surprise you."

Kyree was ecstatic. He lifted her off the floor and spun her around. To everyone else, they seemed to be two very happy newlyweds. Kyree placed her down and kissed her lips.

"I have a few surprises for you too," he smirked.

Jaz didn't even have time to ask him what he had up his sleeve when the music stopped and they were escorted to their seats for dinner. The food was divine. Jaz gave Kyree his praise on doing such a great job with everything in her absence. He'd really stepped up to the plate and surprised her with how well every-thing turned out.

After Monica and Jaz both boo-hooed during Monica's speech, Mario escorted Monica to the dance floor. They danced to Ed Sheeran's "Tenerife Sea". Mario kissed her on the lips. She looked gorgeous. Since having Monica in his life, Mario couldn't see his life without her. Everyone in his family loved her, her voice bright-ened his day, she was always encouraging him, and her love was unfaltering. He'd obviously done something right in his life to deserve someone so great.

Monica stopped dancing momentarily, noticing Kayden

running around like he'd lost his mind. "Why the hell is my child running around here like I won't beat his little butt? Kayden!" she yelled.

Kayden ignored her as he screamed, "The bride is coming! The bride is coming!"

Jaz laughed from her seat at the dinner table. "Kyree, go get Kayden. Tell him the wedding is over, baby."

"Nah, let him do his thing," Kyree confidently said. He took a sip of his champagne and placed an arm behind Jaz's chair. Jaz looked at him like he was crazy. "Just chill out and enjoy the ceremony."

"Kayden!" Monica was about to go chase after him, but Mario grabbed her arm to stop her. "Hold on, baby," she said, but Mario continued to hold her arm. She huffed and turned to him. The stare he gave her made her nervous. It was bad enough everyone was staring at her because she couldn't control her son.

Mario locked eyes with her and slowly dropped down to one knee.

"Oh my God," Monica covered her face with her hands. Her heart beat rapidly and Kayden approached them and handed Mario a small red box. Mario smirked and he dapped Kayden up.

"Monica, you made my life better the moment I saw you smile and I wanted to keep that smile there forever. You made me want to step my game up. With you, I'm more successful, happier, and stronger. I can't lose that feeling of completeness." He opened the ring box and Monica couldn't stop crying. "Monica Wright, will you marry me?"

Monica vigorously nodded her head. "Yes...yes!" she yelled. He placed the ring on her finger and everyone applauded as he stood to kiss her.

Kyree stood up to applaud and with tear-filled eyes, Jaz joined him.

Jaz nudged Kyree. "Oh, so you knew?" He simply smirked. When Mario approached him about having his sister's hand in marriage, Kyree happily obliged. It was Kyree's suggestion that the proposal be at the wedding. He knew Jaz wouldn't mind. And she didn't, she was happy for her friend. "I'm going to get you for not telling me."

"You would've told, with ya big mouth."

She sucked her teeth. "Whatever. This better be the last of your surprises."

He laughed. That was hardly the end of what he had in store for her. He gave a cue to the DJ and then guided Jaz to the dance floor again. This time there were chairs for her and her brides-maids. They each took their seats, with Jaz sitting right in the middle. Kyree and his groomsmen got into a line with Kyree leading the pack. The DJ dropped LL Cool J's "I Need Love" and Kyree spun around as soon as the lyrics dropped and he started to lip sync.

Jaz nearly fell out of her chair, she was laughing so hard. His groomsmen backed him up with a simple two-step. After the second verse, the song switched to New Edition's "Candy Girl". Kyree and Fat Boy did the Kid N' Play kick-step, and Fat Boy ended it with a full 360 spin. Jaz was having a good time rocking with them. She couldn't remember the last time she'd laughed so hard. The song then changed to Mark Ronson featuring Bruno Mars's "Uptown Funk" and Jaz was ready to throw in the towel. Kyree was sliding all across the floor. His groomsmen were following suit too. They each picked a bridesmaid and danced for them. Monica couldn't breathe because she was laughing so hard at Mario, who had decided to do a Michael Jackson spin kick and a split for her.

When the music stopped, all of the groomsmen were sweating and there wasn't a dry eye in the house from all the laughter. Jaz was in awe. Kyree would've never done anything like this. He hated dancing. He was always too cool to do anything besides post up at a party. But there was one thing Kyree knew about his Jazzy: she loved to dance. So he enlisted Ms. Ray's help to choreograph something for the whole group. He'd do anything to make her happy.

"Oh my God, baby!" Jaz helped him to wipe the sweat from his forehead. "That was the shit."

"Did ya man surprise you, or what?" Kyree huffed, out of breath.

"Nah, baby, my *husband* surprised me," she corrected him. He smirked and she kissed him, inserting her tongue into his mouth.

Jaz stayed on the dance floor with him for the slow song, John Legend's "You and I". She rested her head on his chest and he held her close.

No one knew the obstacles they faced on a daily just to be together. No one would ever understand the strength of their bond. They'd found each other early in life and it had taken some growing up for them to realize that there was no one else for them. Neither one could dream of someone more perfect.

Jaz looked up at him. "I love you."

"Forever?" He winked at her.

Jaz smirked. "Forever isn't even enough."

They both smiled and swayed to the music. This moment was perfect. They were one, and no one else in the world existed. Most importantly, they were happy.

THE END

www.ingramcontent.com/pod-product-compliance
Lightning Source LLC
Chambersburg PA
CBHW071105250626
47159CB00002B/604